Penguin Books
The Spoilt City

D0609901

Olivia Manning was born in Portsmouth, Hampshire,
spent much of her youth in Ireland and, as she puts it,
'has the usual Anglo-Irish sense of belonging nowhere'.
She married just before the war and went abroad with
her husband, R. D. Smith, a British Council lecturer in
Bucharest. Her experiences there formed the basis of the
work which makes up *The Balkan Trilogy*. As the
Germans approached Athens, she and her husband
evacuated to Egypt and ended up in Jerusalem where
her husband was put in charge of the Palestine
Broadcasting Station. They returned to London in 1946
and have lived there ever since.

Olivia Manning's publications include *Growing Up*
(short stories, 1948), *School for Love* (1951), *A Different
Face* (1953), *The Balkan Trilogy* (1960–65) of which
The Spoilt City is the second volume, published
simultaneously in Penguins with *The Great Fortune* and
Friends and Heroes, and *The Play Room* (1969). She has
spent a year on the film script of *The Play Room* and is
at present engaged on another novel.

Olivia Manning

The Spoilt City

Volume Two of
The Balkan Trilogy

Penguin Books

Penguin Books Ltd, Harmondsworth,
Middlesex, England
Penguin Books Australia Ltd, Ringwood,
Victoria, Australia
Penguin Books Canada Ltd, 41 Steelcase
Road West, Markham, Ontario, Canada

First published by William Heinemann Ltd, 1962
Published in Penguin Books 1974
Copyright © Olivia Manning, 1962

Made and printed in Great Britain by
Hunt Barnard Printing Ltd,
Aylesbury, Bucks
Set in Monotype Times

To Ivy Compton-Burnett

Contents

PART ONE

The Earthquake

1

THE MAP OF FRANCE had gone from the window of the German Propaganda Bureau and a map of the British Isles had taken its place. People relaxed. There was regret that the next victim was to be their old ally, but it might, after all, have been Rumania herself.

The end of June brought a dry and dusty heat to Bucharest. The grass withered in the public parks. Up the Chaussée, the lime and chestnut leaves, fanned by a breeze like a furnace breath, curled, brown and papery, and started falling as though autumn had come. Each day began with a fierce, white light splintering in between blinds and shutters. When people ate breakfast on the balconies, there was a smell of heat in the air. By noonday, the ingot of the sun dissolved in the sky as in a vat of molten silver. The roads, oozing tarmac, shimmered with mirages. The dazzle hurt the eyes.

During the afternoon, the hot air concentrated between the cliff-faces of buildings, seemed visible and tangible in the ochre dust-fog. Deadened by it, people slept. When the offices closed for the midday meal, the tramway cars were hung with clerks fighting their way home to darkened bedrooms. At five, when the atmosphere was like felt, the offices reopened, but the rich and the workless remained inactive until evening.

It was evening when rumours of the ultimatum spread. The streets were full of people strolling in the light of early sunset.

Passers-by, keeping an eye on the map in the German Propaganda Bureau window, were speculating on how long the British could hold out, when they learnt of the Russian demand and Britain was forgotten.

The demand had not, of course, been officially announced. The evening papers did not mention it. As usual with any cause for alarm, the authorities were trying to keep it secret, but in Bucharest nothing could be kept secret for long. The Soviet Minister had scarcely delivered the ultimatum when details of it were brought to the foreign journalists in the Athénée Palace Hotel. Russia required the return of Bessarabia and, with it, a segment of the Bukovina on which she had no real claim. The ultimatum was due to expire at midnight on the following day.

Within minutes of its reception in the hotel, the news reached the crowded streets and passed to restaurants and cafés. Apprehensions quickened at once into ferment, for panic was an incipient condition in the capital. People became possessed by an hysteria of alarm.

That evening Guy Pringle, a lecturer in English at the University, was sitting in Mavrodaphne's with his wife, Harriet. Someone, entering at one end of the large, brilliant café, shouted across the room and at once disorder spread through it like a tidal wave. People leapt to their feet and, shrill with grievance, bawled right and left, stranger protesting to stranger. The Pringles could hear them blaming the Jews, the Communists, the defeated allies, Madame Lupescu, the King and the King's hated chamberlain, Urdureanu – but blaming them for what?

Harriet, a dark, thin girl who had grown thinner during their months in this disintegrating society, was set on edge now by any unnatural stir. She said: "It must be the Germans. We shall be trapped," for there were always rumours of a German invasion.

Guy attempted to make an inquiry at a neighbouring table. At once, the man to whom he spoke, recognising an Englishman, accused him in English: "It is Sir Stafford Cripps who has done this thing."

"What thing?"

The man said: "He has made the Russians take our Bessarabia."

"And," added his female companion, "steal our Bukovina with its beautiful beech forests."

Guy, a large young man whose mild and guileless air was enhanced by spectacles, answered with his usual good humour, pointing out that Cripps, having arrived in Moscow only that morning, had scarcely had time to make anyone do anything; but the other turned impatiently from him.

Harriet said: "You might suppose that no one had ever thought the Russians a danger before," whereas, in fact, the Communists with their ungodly Marxist creed, were more dreaded here than the Nazis.

Hearing English spoken, an elderly man leapt up from a nearby table and reminded everyone that Britain had guaranteed Rumania. Now that Rumania was menaced, what were the British going to do? "Nothing, nothing," he screamed in rage. "They are finished," and he made a lunge towards the Pringles with his tussore parasol.

Harriet looked uneasily about her. When, ten months before, she had first arrived in Bucharest, the British here had been respected: now, on the losing side, they were respected no longer. She half feared actual attack – but no attack came. A certain sentiment, even affection, persisted for the once great, protecting power which was believed to be doomed.

Unwilling to show fear by taking themselves off, the Pringles sat still amid a hubbub which suddenly changed its tenor. A man had risen and, attracting attention by the reasonable quiet of his speech, asked if their fears might not be premature. It was true that the British could do nothing for Rumania, but what of Hitler? Hadn't the King recently changed his allegiance? He could now call on German aid. When the Führer heard of this ultimatum, he would force Stalin to withdraw it.

Ah! The shouting died down. People, taking up this reassurance, nodded to one another. Those who had been most fearful, became in a moment cheerful and hopeful. Those who had complained loudest were now loud with confidence. Nothing was lost yet. Hitler would protect them. For once the King was in favour. His cunning, from which the country had so long suffered, was now applauded. He had declared for the Axis at just the right moment. There was no doubt about it, he was going to prove himself the saviour of his country.

This sudden euphoria spread as rapidly as the earlier panic. The Pringles walked home through streets in which people were congratulating each other as though upon a victory. But next morning the refugee cars began to arrive from the north. Grey with dust and strapped over with baggage, they looked much as the Polish cars had looked when they drove into Bucharest ten months before.

They brought the German land-owners of Bessarabia who, warned by the German Legation, had fled, not in fear of the Russians but of the peasants who hated them. Their appearance brought a new wave of anxiety, for if anyone had been told of Hitler's intentions, they must have been told.

The Pringles' flat overlooked the main square. During the

morning, people began to fill the square, standing silently and gazing towards the palace.

Prince Yakimov, an Englishman of Russian origin, whom Harriet unwillingly tolerated as a guest in the flat, came back from his haunt, the English Bar, and said: "Everyone's very optimistic, dear girl. I'm sure a solution will be found," and when he had eaten he retired to untroubled sleep.

Guy was supervising end-of-term examinations and did not come home to luncheon. During the afternoon, Harriet went out to the balcony and saw the crowds still standing beneath the torrid sun. The siesta was the traditional time for making love, but no one had heart now for sleep or love. There was still no official confirmation of the ultimatum, but it was known that the King had summoned the Crown Council. The ministers were unmistakable in their white uniforms. Everyone saw them arrive.

Immediately below Harriet's balcony was a small Byzantine church with golden domes and crosses looped with beads. Its door creaked continually as people entered to pray for help in this time of crisis.

The church was surrounded by buildings left partly demolished when the war brought the King's "improvements" to an end. Beyond these ruins was the sun-scorched square with the waiting crowds and the palace where state officials came and went. Cars were crowded within the palace railings. New arrivals had to park outside.

Harriet could smell her hair toasted by the sun. The heat was a burden on her head. Yet she stood for a while watching a peasant crossing the cobbles below her. He was a vendor of chickens. A cage of live birds hung on either side of him from a yoke across his shoulders. Every few minutes he lifted his head and squawked like a fowl. A servant shouted to him from one of the lower balconies, then appeared down in the street. Together vendor and buyer examined the chickens, stretching out their wings and poking at their breasts. In the end, one chosen, the peasant, amid a cackling and flurry of feathers, wrung its neck.

Harriet went back to the room. When she came out again, the peasant was sitting on the church step, the chicken plucked, the feathers about his feet. Before he went on his way again he pulled a piece of sacking over each cage to protect his birds from the sun.

At five o'clock there was a movement among the crowd as office workers started back to offices. A little later, when the newsboys began crying a special edition, the whole square came to life. Harriet hurried down to discover the news. People were pressing against the boys, snatching the papers and leafing frantically through them. One man, coming to the last page, shook his paper in the air, then throwing it to the ground, stamped wildly upon it.

Harriet feared this meant that Bessarabia was lost, but when she bought a paper, the headlines stated that the Prince had passed his baccalaureate with 98.9 marks out of a possible hundred. The King, though pale and apparently anxious, had left the Council Chamber to congratulate his son. Everywhere about her she could hear the words "*bacalaureat*", "*printul*", "*regeul*" being spoken with derisive anger, but there was no news of Bessarabia.

As the sunset threw its reds and purples across the sky, the waiting crowds grew restless. Time was passing. Those in the square had been mostly men of the working classes. With evening, women appeared, their light clothes glimmering in the twilight. The first breath of cool air brought the prosperous Rumanians out for the promenade. Though they walked from habit into the Calea Victoriei and the Boulevard Carol, they were drawn back again and again to the square, the centre of tension.

When Guy returned from the University, Harriet said they must eat quickly, then go out and discover what was happening.

In the street, meeting people they knew, they learnt that the King had appealed to Hitler, who had promised to send a personal message before the ultimatum should expire. Everyone was suddenly hopeful again. Inside the palace, the King and his ministers were awaiting the message. The King was reported to have said: "We must look to the Führer. He will not fail us in our hour of need."

Darkness was falling. A bugle sounded in the palace yard. As though it were a call to arms, a man in the square started to sing the national anthem. Others took it up, but the voices were sparse, choked by uncertainty, and soon died away. Inside the palace the chandeliers sprang alight. Someone shouted for the King. The cry was taken up, but the King did not appear.

The moon rose, bland and big, and floated above the city. All the time there was a slamming of car doors as people came and went at the palace. One of the arrivals was a woman. Immediately the story went round that an attempt had been made on the life of Madame Lupescu, who had fled from her villa in Alea Vulpache and had come to the King for protection.

There was a new stir at the arrival of Antonescu, a proud man, out of favour since he had supported the Iron Guard leader. It was said that, recognising the situation as desperate, the General had begged an audience with the King. The press in the square grew. Something would happen now. But nothing happened and soon the General drove away again.

The next time they approached the Athénée Palace Guy said: "Let's go in and have a drink." If there were any real news it would immediately be brought there.

The area outside the hotel was packed with the Bessarabian cars, many of them still loaded with trunks and suitcases, rolled carpets and small, valuable pieces of furniture. Within the hall, beneath the brilliant lights, were heaped more trunks, cases, carpets and rich possessions. As the Pringles picked their way through them, they came face to face with Baron Steinfeld, one of the Bessarabians, more often in Bucharest than on his estate. The Pringles, who had met him only once, were surprised when he accosted them. They had thought him a charming man, but he was charming no longer. His square, russet-red face was distorted, his large teeth bared; he spoke with such anguished rage, his words seemed to be shaken from him: "I have lost everything. But everything! My estate, my house, my apple orchard, my silver, my Meissen ornaments, my Aubusson rugs. You cannot imagine, so much have I lost. You see here these things – they were all brought by the lucky ones. But I – I was in Bucharest, so I lose all. You English, what are you doing that you fight against the Germans? It is the Bolsheviks you must fight. You must join with the Germans, who are good men, and together you must fight these Russian swine who steal my everythings."

Shocked by the change that had come over the baron, Guy did not know what to say. Harriet began: "Bessarabia isn't lost yet . . ." but paused, confused, as the baron broke down, saying through tears: "I have even lost my little dog."

"I am sorry," said Harriet, but the baron raised a hand, rejecting pity. What he wanted was action: "It is necessary to fight. Together we must destroy the Russians. Do not be fools. Join with us before it is too late." On this dramatic note, he pushed out through the swing door and left the Pringles alone.

Hall and vestibule were deserted. Even the booking-clerk had gone out to watch events in the square, but a sound of English voices came from the next room.

Guy said: "The journalists are back in the bar."

The bar – the famous English Bar—had been, until a month before, the preserve of the British and their associates. The enemy had been kept out. Then, on the day Calais fell, a vast crowd of German businessmen, journalists and legation officials had entered in a body and taken possession. The only Englishmen present – Galpin, and his friend Screwby – had retreated before this triumphant, buffeting mob and taken themselves to the hotel garden. Now they were back again.

Galpin was one of the few journalists permanently resident in Bucharest. An agency man, living at the Athénée Palace and seldom leaving it, he employed a Rumanian to scout for news, which was brought to him at the hotel. The other journalists in the bar had flown in from neighbouring capitals to cover the Bessarabian crisis.

As the Pringles entered, Galpin seized on them and began at once to describe how he had marched into the bar at the head of the new arrivals and called to the barman: "Vodka, *tovarish*."

Whether this was true or not, he was now drinking whisky. He let Guy refill his glass, then, glancing towards the dispirited Germans who had been pushed into a corner, he toasted the ultimatum: "A slap in the eye for the bloody Boche," apparently seeing the Russian move as a British triumph.

Surely, Harriet thought, it was rather the Allies who were being flouted. They had condoned the Rumanian seizure of the Russian province in 1918 and now in 1940 it was their weakness that prompted the Russians to demand it back again.

When she started to say this, old Mortimer Tufton, staring aloofly over her head, cut her short with: "The Paris Peace Conference never recognised the annexation of Bessarabia."

Tufton, after whom a street in Zagreb had been named, was a noted figure in the Balkans. He was said to be able to scent the coming of events and was always on the spot before they occurred. Informed, dry, consciously intimidating, he had the manner of a man accustomed to receiving deference, but Harriet would not let herself be put down. "You mean that Bessarabia was never really part of Greater Rumania?"

She gave a false impression of confidence and Tufton, snubbing her for her sex and impudence, answered casually: "One could say that," and turned away from her.

Disbelieving, but lacking knowledge with which to contend against him, she looked for support to Guy who said: "The

Soviets never recognised Bessarabia as Rumanian. They're perfectly justified in taking it," and, elated by the sudden, unusual
popularity of the country which interpreted his faith, he added:
"You wait and see. Russia will win this war for us yet."

Tufton gave a laugh. "She may win the war," he said, "but not
for us."

This was too much for the journalists, who ridiculed the idea of
Russia winning any war, let alone this one. A man who had been
in Helsinki spoke at length of "the Finnish fiasco". Galpin then
said the reputed power of Soviet armour was one huge bluff and
described how during the war in Spain a friend of his had run
into a Soviet tank which had buckled up like cardboard.

Guy said: "That's nonsense, an old story. Every hack journalist
with nothing better to write up was putting it around." Now that
his ideals were attacked, he was on the defensive, no longer mild
but ready to argue with anyone. Harriet, though the ideals were
too political and disinterested to appeal to her, was prepared to
take his side; but Galpin shrugged, giving the impression he
thought the whole thing unimportant.

Before Guy could speak again, Mortimer Tufton, who had no
patience with the conjectures of inexperienced youth, broke in
with a history of Russian-Rumanian relations, proving that only
Allied influences had prevented Russia from devouring the Balkans long ago. Rumania, he said, had been invaded by Russia on
eight separate occasions and had suffered a number of "friendly
occupations", none of which had ever been forgotten or forgiven.
"The fact is," he concluded, "the friendship of Russia has been
more disastrous to Rumania than the enmity of the rest of the
world."

"That was Czarist Russia," said Guy. 'The Soviets are a
different proposition."

"But not a different race – witness this latest piece of oppor-
tunism."

Catching his small, vain, self-regarding eye fixed severely upon
her, Harriet, deciding to win him, smiled and asked: "To whom
would *you* award Bessarabia?"

"Hmmm!" said Tufton. He looked away, appearing to swallow
something astringent in his throat, but, mollified by her appeal, he
gave the question thought. "Russia, Turkey and Rumania have
been squabbling over that particular province for five hundred
years," he said. "The Russians finally got it in 1812 and held on to

it until 1918. I imagine they kept it rather longer than anyone else managed to do, so, on reflection . . ." he paused, hemmed again, then impressively announced: "I'd be inclined to let them have it."

Harriet smiled at Guy, passing the award on to him, and Galpin nodded, confirming it.

Galpin's dark, narrow face hung in folds above his rag of a collar. Elbow on bar, sourly elated by his return to his old position, he kept staring about him for an audience, his moving eyeballs as yellow as the whisky in his hand. As he drank, his yellow wrist, the wrist-bone like half an egg, stuck out rawly from his wrinkled, shrunken, ash-dusty dark suit. A wet cigarette stub clung, forgotten, to the bulging, purple softness of his lower lip and trembled when he spoke.

"The Russkies are sticking their necks out demanding this territory just when Carol's declared for the Axis."

Guy said: "I imagine the declaration prompted them to do it. They're staking their claim before the Germans get too strong here."

"Could be." Galpin looked vague. He preferred to be the one to theorise, "Still, they're sticking their necks out." He looked for Tufton's agreement and when he got it grunted, agreeing with himself, then added: "If the Germans ever attacked them, I wouldn't give the Russkies ten days."

As they were discussing the Russian war potential, in which Guy alone had faith, a small man in dilapidated grey cotton, an old trilby pressed against his chest, sidled in and nudged Galpin. This was Galpin's scout, a shadow who lived by nosing out news, takin one version of it to the German journalists at the Minerva, and another to the English in the Athénée Palace.

When Galpin bent down, the scout whispered in his ear. Galpin listened with intent interest. Everyone waited to hear what had been said, but he was in no hurry to tell them. With a sardonic, bemused expression, he took out a bundle of dirty paper money and handed over the equivalent of sixpence, which reward was received with reverent gratitude. Then he paused, smiling around the company.

"The eagerly awaited message has arrived," he said at last.

"Well, what is it?" Tufton impatiently asked.

"The Führer has asked Carol to cede Bessarabia without conflict."

"Hah!" Tufton gave a laugh which said he had expected as much.

Galpin's close companion, Screwby, asked: "This is a directive?"
"Directive, nothing," said Galpin. "It's a command."

"So it's settled," said Screwby bleakly. "No chance of a scrap?"

Tufton scoffed at him: "Rumania take on Russia single-handed? Not a chance. Their one hope was Axis backing if they stood firm. But Hitler doesn't intend going to war with Russia – anyway, not over Bessarabia."

The journalists finished their drinks before making for the telephones in the hall. No one showed any inclination to hurry. The news was negative. Rumania would submit without a fight.

When they left the hotel, the Pringles were surprised at the quiet outside. The Führer's command must be known to everyone now, but there was no hint of revolt. If there had been a show of anger, it was over now. The atmosphere was subdued. A few people stood outside the palace as though there might still be hope, but the majority were dispersing in silence, having recognised that there was nothing more to be done.

After the tense hours of uncertainty, acceptance of the ultimatum had probably brought as much relief as disappointment. Whatever else it might mean, it meant that life in Bucharest would go on much as before. No one would be called upon to die in a desperate cause.

Next day the papers were making the best of things. Rumania, they said, had agreed to cede Bessarabia and the northern Bukovina, but Germany had promised that after the war these provinces would be returned to her. Meanwhile, in obeying the Führer's will, she was sacrificing herself to preserve the peace of Eastern Europe. It was a moral victory and the officers withdrawing their men from the ceded territory might do so with breasts expanded and heads held high.

Flags were at half-mast. The cinemas were ordered to shut for three days of public mourning. And the rumour went round that the Rumanian officers, now pelting down south, had abandoned their units, their military equipment and even their own families, in panic flight before the advancing Russians. By the end of June, Bessarabia and the northern Bukovina had become part of the Soviet Union.

When the Pringles next visited the English Bar, Galpin said: "Do you realise the Russian frontier is less than a hundred and twenty miles from here? The bastards could be on top of us before we'd even known they'd started."

2

HARRIET HAD IMAGINED that when the term ended they would be free to go where they pleased. She longed to escape, if only for a few weeks, not only from the disquiet of the capital, but from their uncertain situation. She thought they might leave Rumania altogether. A boat went from Constanza to Istanbul, and thence to Greece. Excited by the prospect of such a journey, she appealed to Guy, who said: "I'm afraid I can't go just now. Inchcape's asked me to organise a summer school. In any case, he feels none of us should leave the country at the moment. It would create a bad impression."

"But no one spends the summer in Bucharest."

"They will this year. People are afraid to leave in case something happens and they can't get back. As a matter of fact, I've already enrolled two hundred students."

"Rumanians?"

"A few. The Jews are crowding in. They're very loyal."

"I should say it's not just loyalty. They want to get away to English-speaking countries."

"You can't blame them for that."

"I don't blame them," said Harriet but, disappointed, she was inclined to blame someone. Probably Guy himself.

Now she was coming to know Guy, she was beginning to judge him. When they had married ten months before, she had accepted him, uncritically, as a composite of virtues. She did not demur when Clarence described him as "a saint". She still might not demur, but she knew now that one aspect of his saintliness was composed of human weaknesses.

She said: "I don't believe Inchcape thought of this school. He's lost interest in the English Department. I believe it's all your idea."

"I discussed it with Inchcape. He agreed that one can't spend the summer lazing around while other men are fighting a war."

"And what is Inchcape going to do? I mean, apart from sitting in the Bureau reading Henry James."

"He's an old man," said Guy, deflecting criticism as much from

himself as from his superior. Since Inchcape, who was the professor, had become Director of Propaganda, Guy had run the
English Department with the help only of three elderly ex-
governesses and Dubedat, an elementary school-teacher, ma-
rooned in the Balkans by war. With uncomplaining enthusiasm,
Guy did much more than was expected of him; but he was not
imposed upon. He did what he wanted to do and did it, Harriet
believed, to keep reality at bay.

During the days of the fall of France, he had thrown himself
into a production of *Troilus and Cressida*. Now, when their Rumanian friends were beginning to avoid them, he was giving himself up to this summer school. He would not only be too busy to
notice their isolation, but too busy to care about it. She wanted to
accuse him of running away – but how accuse someone who was,
to all appearances, steadfast on the site of danger, a candidate for
martyrdom? It was she, it seemed, who wanted to run away.

She asked: "When does the school start?"

"Next week." He laughed at her tone of resignation, and, putting an arm round her, said: "Don't look so glum. We'll get
away before the summer ends. We'll go to Predeal."

She smiled and said: "All right," but as soon as she was alone
she went to the telephone, looking for comfort, and rang up the
only Englishwoman she knew here who was of her generation.
This was Bella Niculescu, who had very little to do and was
usually only too ready to talk. That morning, however, she cut
Harriet off abruptly, saying she was dressing to go out to
luncheon. She suggested that Harriet come to tea that afternoon.

Harriet waited until nearly five o'clock before venturing into
the outdoor heat. At that time a little shade was stretching from
the buildings, but in the Boulevard Breteanu, where Bella lived,
the buildings had been demolished to make way for blocks of
flats, only two or three of which had been built when war brought
work to a stop. The pavements were shadeless between the white
baked earth of vacant lots.

In summer this area was a dormitory for beggars and unem-
ployed peasants, and the dust-filled air carried a curious odour,
sweetish, unclean yet volatile, distilled by the sun from earth
saturated with urine and ordure.

Bella's block rose sheer from the ground like a prow from
water. Against its side-wall a peasant had pitched a hut for the
sale of vegetables and cigarettes. Several beggars sleeping in the

shade of the hut made an attempt to rouse themselves at Harriet's step and whined in a half-hearted way. One of them was well known to her. She had seen him first on her first day in Bucharest: a demanding, bad-tempered fellow who, recognising a foreigner, had thrust his ulcerated leg at her like a threat and refused to be satisfied with what she gave him. At that time she had been horrified by the beggars, especially this beggar. Having just journeyed three days to the eastern edge of Europe, she had seen him as a portent of life in the strange, half-Oriental capital to which marriage had brought her.

Guy had said she must become used to the beggars; and, in a way, she had done so. She had even become reconciled to this man, and he to her. Now she handed him the same small coins a Rumanian would have given and he accepted them, sullenly, but without protest.

The smells of the boulevard did not enter the block of flats, which was air-conditioned. In its temperate, scentless atmosphere, Harriet's head cleared, and, stimulated and cheerful, she thought of Bella to whom she could look for companionship during the empty summer ahead. She contemplated their meeting with pleasure, but as she entered the drawing-room she realised something was wrong. She felt so little welcome that she came to a stop inside the door.

"Well, take a pew," Bella said crossly, as though Harriet were at fault in awaiting the invitation.

Sitting on the edge of the large blue sofa, Harriet said: "It's beautifully cool in here. It seems hotter than ever outside."

"What do you expect? It's July." Bella pulled a bell-cord, then stared impatiently at the door as though she, who chattered so easily, were now at a loss how to entertain her guest.

Two servants entered, one with the tea, the other with cakes. Bella watched, frowning in a displeased fashion, as the trays were put down. Harriet, discomfited, also found herself at a loss for conversation and looked at an early edition of the evening paper which lay beside her on the sofa. When the girls went, she made a comment on the headline: "I see Drucker is to be tried at last."

Bella inclined her head, saying: "Personally, I'd let him rot. He made out he was pro-British, but his rate of exchange was all in favour of Germany. Lots of people say his bank was ruining the country." She spoke tartly, but in a refined tone reminding Harriet of their first tea-party when Bella, fearing that her guest might have pretensions to family or wealth, had overwhelmed her with gentility. Eventually set at ease, Bella had revealed a hearty appetite for gossip and a ribaldry which Harriet, in need of a friend, had come to enjoy. Now here was Bella, a great classical statue of a woman in an unnatural pose, again barricaded behind her best electro-plated tea-service. For some reason they were back where they had started from.

Harriet said: "I met Drucker once. His son was one of Guy's students. He was a warm-hearted man; very good-looking."

"Humph!" said Bella. "Seven months in prison won't have improved his looks." Unable to repress superior knowledge, she took a more comfortable pose and nodded knowingly. "He was a womaniser, like most good-looking men. And, in a way, that's what did for him. If Madame hadn't thought he was fair game, she'd never have tried to get him to part with his oil holdings. When he refused her, she took it as a personal affront. She was furious. Any woman would be. So she went to Carol, who saw a chance to get his hands on some cash and trumped up this charge of dealing in foreign currency. Drucker was arrested and his family skedaddled."

Pleased by her own summary of the circumstances leading to Drucker's fall, Bella could not help smiling. Harriet, feeling the atmosphere between them relaxing, asked: "What do you think they will do to him?"

"Oh, he'll be found guilty – that goes without saying. He'll have to forfeit his oil holdings, of course; but there's this fortune he's got salted away in Switzerland. Carol can't take that, so if Drucker makes it over he might get off lightly. Rumanians are quite humane, you know."

Harriet said: "But Drucker can't make it over. The money's in his son's name."

"Who told you that?" Bella spoke sharply and Harriet, unable to disclose the source of it, wished she had kept her knowledge to herself.

"I heard it some time ago. Guy was fond of Sasha. He's been trying to find out what became of him."

"Surely the boy bolted with the rest of the family?"

"No. He was taken away when they arrested his father, but apparently he's not in prison. No one knows where he is. He's just disappeared."

"Indeed!" Used to being the authority on things Rumanian,

Bella was looking bored by Harriet's talk of the Druckers, so Harriet changed to a subject which was always of interest. "How is Nikko?" she asked.

Conscripted like the majority of Rumanian males, Bella's husband was usually on leave. It was Bella's money that bought his freedom.

"He's been recalled," she said bleakly. "They're all in a funk, of course, over Bessarabia."

In the past Harriet would have heard this news on arrival and it would have kept Bella in complaints for an hour or more.

"Where is his regiment at the moment?" Harriet encouraged her.

"The Hungarian front. That damned Carol Line, not that there's anything anyone could call a line. A fat lot of good it would be if the Huns did march in."

"I expect you'll be able to get him back?"

"Oh, yes. I'll have to cough up again."

Bella had nothing more to say and Harriet, attempting to keep some sort of conversation going, spoke of the changing attitude of the Rumanians towards the English, saying: "They treat us like an enemy – a defeated enemy: guilty but pitiable."

"I can't say I've noticed it," said Bella, her tone aloof: "But, of course, it's different for me."

There was a long silence. Harriet, exhausted by her attempts to break down Bella's restraint, put down her teacup, saying she had shopping to do. She imagined Bella would be relieved by her departure, but, instead, Bella gave her a troubled look as though there was still something to be resolved between them.

They went together into the hall where Harriet, making a last approach, suggested they might, as they often did, meet for coffee at Mavrodaphne's. "What about tomorrow morning?" she said.

Bella put her large, white hands to her pearls and stared down at the chequered marble floor. "I don't know," she said vaguely as she placed her white shoe exactly in the centre of a black square. "It's difficult."

Knowing that Bella had almost nothing to do, Harriet asked impatiently: "How, difficult? Whatever is the matter, Bella?"

"Well . . ." Bella paused, watching the toe of her shoe, which she turned from side to side. "Me being an Englishwoman married to a Rumanian, I have to go carefully. I mean, I have to think of Nikko."

"But, of course."

"Well, I think we'd better not be seen together at Mavro-daphne's. And about ringing each other up: I think we should stop while things are as they are. My phone's probably tapped."

"Surely not. The telephone company is British."

"But it employs Rumanians. You don't know this country lke I do. Any excuse and they'd arrest Nikko just to get a bribe to release him. It's always being done."

"I don't honestly see . . ." Harriet began, then paused as Bela gave her a miserable glance. She said: "But you'll come and see me sometimes?"

"Yes, I will." Bella nodded. "I promise. But I'll have to be careful. I must say, I wish I'd never appeared in *Troilus*. It was a sort of declaration."

"Of what? The fact you are English? Everyone knows that."

"I'm not so sure." Bella drew back her foot. "My Rumanian's practically perfect. Everyone says so." She jerked her face up, pink with the effort of saying what she had said, and her look was defiant.

Six, even three, months ago, Harriet would have despised Bella's fears; now she felt compassion for them. The time might soon come when the English would have to go and Bella would be left here without a compatriot. She had to protect herself against that time. Harriet touched her arm: "I understand how you feel. Don't worry. You can trust me."

Bella's face softened. With a nervous titter, she took a hand from her pearls and put it over Harriet's hand. "But I *will* drop in," she said; "I don't expect anyone will notice me. And, after all, they can't deprive me of my friends."

3

THAT EVENING, on their way to the Cişmigiu Park, the Pringles met Clarence Lawson.

Clarence was not one of the organisation men. He had been seconded to the English Department by the British Council and at the outbreak of war had gone with Inchcape into the Propaganda Bureau. Bored by the work, or lack of work, there, he had taken on the administration of Polish relief and organised the escape of interned Polish soldiers.

Guy said to him: "We're going to have a drink in the park. Why not come with us?"

Clarence, as tall as Guy but much leaner, drooped sadly as he considered this proposal and, rubbing a doubtful hand over his lean face, said: "I don't know that I can."

As he edged away a little, apparently feeling the pull of urgent business elsewhere, Harriet said: "Come on, Clarence. A walk will do you good."

Clarence gave her an oblique, suspicious glance and mumbled something about work. Harriet laughed. Aware of his eagerness to be with her, she took his arm and led him up the Calea Victoriei. As he went, he grumbled: "Oh, all right, but I can't stay long."

They walked through crowds that, having accepted the loss of Bessarabia, were as lively as they had ever been. Harriet was used to the rapid recovery of these people who had outworn more than a dozen conquerors and survived eight hundred years of oppression, but now she thought they looked almost complacent. She said: "They seem to be congratulating themselves on something."

"They probably are," said Clarence. "The new Cabinet has repudiated the Anglo-French guarantee. The new Foreign Minister was a leader in the Iron Guard. So now they know exactly where they are. They're really committed to Hitler and he must protect them. They think the worst is over, and – " he pointed to the placard of the *Bukarester Tageblatt* which read: FRIEDEN IM HERBST – "they think the war is over, too."

At the park gate, he paused, murmuring: "Well, now, I really think I . . ." but as the Pringles went on, ignoring his vagaries, he followed them.

Passing from the fashionable street into the unfashionable park, they moved from hubbub into tranquillity. Here, as the noise of the street faded, there was nothing to be heard but the hiss of sprinklers. The air was sweet with the scent of wet earth. Only a few peasants stood about, admiring the spectacle of the *tapis vert*. The only flowers that thrived in the heat were the canna lilies, now reflecting in their reds and yellows and flame colours the flamboyance of the sunset sky.

Down by the lakeside, the vendors of sesame cake and Turkish delight stood, as they had stood all day, silent and humble beneath the chestnut trees. Beyond the trees, a little gangway led to a café which was chiefly used by shop assistants and minor clerks. It was here that Guy had arranged to meet his friend David Boyd.

As they crossed the flexing boards of the artificial island, Harriet could see David sitting by the café rail in the company of a Jewish economist called Klein.

Guy and David had met first in 1938 when they were both new-comers to Bucharest. David, a student of Balkan history and languages, had been visiting Rumania. He reappeared the follow-ing winter, having been appointed to the British Legation as an authority on Rumanian affairs. The two men, of an age and physically similar, resembled each other in outlook, both believ-ing that a Marxist economy was the only remedy for the feudal mismanagement of Eastern Europe.

At the sight of the new arrivals Klein leapt to his feet and ad-vanced on them with arms wide in welcome. The Pringles had met him only twice before, but at once Guy, like a fervent bear, caught hold of the stout, little, pink-cheeked man, and the two patted each other lovingly on the back. David snuffled his amuse-ment as he watched this embrace.

When released, Klein swung round excitedly to greet Harriet, the flush rising from his cheeks to his bald head. "*And* Doamna Preen-gal!" he cried. "But this is nice!" He wanted to include Clarence in his rapture, but Clarence hung back with an uneasy grin.

"So nice, but so *nice*!" Klein repeated as he offered Harriet his seat by the rail.

The evening was very warm. Guy had been walking with his

cotton jacket over his arm and his shirt-sleeves rolled up, a state of undress which the Rumanians regarded as indecent. The café patrons, though shabby, sweaty, and only a generation or two away from the peasantry, were all tightly buttoned up in the dark suits that indicated their respectability. They looked askance at Guy, but Klein took off his jacket, revealing braces and the steel bracelets that held up the sleeves of his striped shirt. He also removed his tie from under his hard collar, laughing at himself as he said: "In this country they do not dress for taking off the coat, but here, I ask you, what does it matter?"

Meanwhile David, who had raised himself slightly in greeting, now slumped back into his chair to indicate it was time for these pleasantries to cease and serious talk to begin again. Chairs were found. Everybody was seated at last.

David, his bulk enhanced by a linen suit that had shrunk in the wash, his large square dark face glistening with sweat, pushed his glasses up his moist nose and said to Klein: "You were saying . . . ?"

Called to order, Klein surveyed the company and said: "First you must know, Antonescu has been flung into jail."

"For speaking the truth again?" David asked.

Klein grinned and nodded.

Harriet did not know what David's occupation was at the Legation, and if Guy knew he kept his knowledge to himself. David was often away from Bucharest. He said that he went to watch the bird life of the Danube delta.

Inchcape claimed that once, in Brașov, he had recognised David under the disguise of a Greek Orthodox priest. He had said: "Hello, what the devil are you up to?" and as the other swept by had received the reply: "*Procul, o procul este, profani.*" Whether this story, and all it implied, was true or not, David, whose subject was Balkan history, was noted for his inside knowledge of Rumanian affairs, some of which was obtained from associates like Klein.

"It is such a story!" Klein said, and ordered another bottle of wine. While the glasses were filled, he paused, but kept his brilliant glance moving from one to the other of his companions. When the waiter was gone, he asked: "What am I? An illegal immigrant, let out of prison to advise the Cabinet. What do I know? Why should they heed me? 'Klein,' they say, 'you are a silly Jew.'"

Rather impatiently, David interrupted to ask: 'But what was the cause of Antonescu's arrest?"

"Ah, the arrest! Well – you know he went to the palace on the night of the ultimatum. He asked to see the King and was prevented. Urdureanu prevented him. The two men came to blows. You heard that, of course? Yes, to blows, inside the palace. A great scandal."

"Was he arrested for that?"

"Not for that, no. Yesterday he received a summons from the King himself. Being fearful that from emotion he could not speak, he wrote a letter. He wrote: 'Majesty, our country crumbles about us.' Now, did I not say that the country would crumble? You remember, I described Rumania as a person who has inherited a great fortune. From folly, he loses it all."

"What else did Antonescu say?' Clarence asked, his slow, deep voice causing Klein to glance round in surprise.

Delighted at hearing Clarence speak, Klein went on: "Antonescu said: 'Majesty, I cry to you to save our nation,' and begged the King to rid himself of the false friends about his throne. When he read the letter, the King instantly ordered his arrest. It is for Urdureanu a great victory.'

Klein sounded regretful and Guy asked: "Does it matter? Urdureanu is a crook, but Antonescu is a fascist.'

Klein stuck out his lower lip and rocked his head from side to side. "It is true," he said. "Antonescu supported the Iron Guard, but, in his way, he is a patriot. He wishes to end corruption. How he would act in power one cannot tell."

"He would just be another dictator," Guy said.

The talk turned to criticism of the King's dictatorship, out of which Clarence suddenly said: "The King has his faults, but he's not insensitive. When he knew Bessarabia was lost, he burst into tears."

"Crying over the oysters he's eaten – or, rather, got to cough up," David said, sniffling and snuffling with amusement at his own wit.

"Anyone can cry," said Harriet. "In this country it doesn't mean much."

Clarence gave her a pained look and, tilting his chair back from this unsympathetic company, drawled: "I'm not so sure of that." After a pause in which no one spoke, he added: "He's our only friend. When he goes, we'll go – if we're lucky enough to get away."

"That's true," David agreed; "and we can thank ourselves for it. If we'd protected the country against the King instead of the King against the country, the situation here would have been very different."

Klein stretched out his short, plump, shirt-sleeved arms and beamed about him. "Did I not tell you if you stayed it would be interesting? You have not seen a half. Already this new Cabinet arranged to ration meat and petrol." As the others looked at him in astonishment, he threw back his head and laughed. "This new Cabinet! Never have I laughed so much. First they repudiate the Anglo-French guarantee. That is easy, everyone feels big work is done – but then, what to do? One has an idea. 'Let us,' he says, 'order for each of us a big desk, a swivel chair, a fine carpet!' 'Good, good!' they all agree. Then rises the new Foreign Minister. Once he was a nobody, now he is the great man. He calls to me to approach. He says, 'Klein, give me a list of our poets.' I bow. 'You will have them in what order?' I ask. 'Sometimes such a list is put in order of literary merit. How naïve! How arbitrary! Why not in order of height, of weight, of income, or the year they did their military service?' 'So,' says the Foreign Minister, 'so we will have it: the year they did their military service. I propose now that these poets write poems to the great Iron Guard leader Codreanu, who is dead but in spirit still lives among us. Domnul Prime Minister, what opinion have you of this proposition?' 'Hm, hm,' mumbles the Prime Minister. What can he say? Was not Codreanu the enemy of the King? 'The opinion I have . . . the opinion I have . . . oh!' He sees me and looks very stern. 'Klein,' he says, 'what opinion have I of the proposition!' 'You think it is good, Domnul Prime Minister,' I tell him."

Klein's stories went on. The others were content to let him talk.

The sunset was fading. Electric light bulbs of different colours sprang up along the café rail. A last tea-rose flush coloured the western sky, giving a glint to the olive darkness of the water. Harriet watched the trees on the other side of the lake as they drew together in the twilight, sombre and weighty as the trees in an old tapestry.

"The other day," said Klein, "in marched His Majesty. 'I have decided,' he said, 'to sell to my country my summer palace in the Dobrudja. It will be like a gift to the nation, for I am asking only a million million *lei*.' 'But,' cried the Prime Minister, 'when Bulgaria takes the Dobrudja, they will take the palace as well.' 'What!' cried the King. 'Are you a traitor? Never will Bulgaria take our Dobrudja. First will we fight till every Rumanian is dead. I will lead them myself on my white horse.' And everyone leaps up and cheers, and they sing the national anthem; but when it is all over, they find they must buy the palace for a million million."

Harriet, laughing with the rest, kept her face turned towards the lake from which came a creak of oars and the lap of passing boats. She looked down on a creamy scum of water on which there floated sprays of elder flower, flat-faced and lacy, plucked by the boatmen and thrown away. A scent of stocks came from somewhere, materialising out of nothing, then passing and not returning. The wireless was playing "The Swan of Tuonela," bringing to her mind some green northern country with lakes reflecting a silver sky. About them, she thought, were the constituents of peace and yet, sitting here talking and laughing, they were, all of them, on edge with the nervous city's tension.

She began to think of England and their last sight of the looped white cliffs, the washed white and blue of the sky, the sea glittering and chopped by the wind. They should have been stirred by the sight, full of regrets, but they had turned their backs on it, excited by change and their coming life together. Guy had said they would return home for Christmas. Asked how they took life, they would have said: "Any way it comes." Chance and uncertainty were part of it. The last thing she would have wanted for them was a settled life lived peaceably in one town. Now her attitude had changed. She had begun to long for safety.

". . . and then the new Prime Minister makes a great speech." Klein raised his hand and gazed solemnly about him. "He says: 'Now is the time for broad issues. We do not worry about trifles . . .' then, suddenly, he stops. He points to the things on his table. His eyes flash fire. 'Cigarettes,' he cries, 'pastilles, mineral water, indigestion tablets, asprin. Auguste,' he calls, 'come here at once. How many times I say to you what must be on my table? Tell me, Auguste, where is the aspirin? Ah, so! Now I speak again. This, I say, is the time for broad issues . . .' "

A gipsy flower-seller, trailing around her an old evening dress of reseda chiffon, came to the table and placed some tight little bunches of cornflowers at David's elbow. She said nothing, but held out her hand. He pushed them aside and told her go away.

She remained where she was, silent like a tired horse glad to stand rather than move, and kept her hand out. If they ignored her, she might stand there all night. "Oh, for God's sake," said David in sudden, acute irritation, and he gave her a few *lei*. Shyly, with an ironical grin, he slid the flowers over to Harriet.

The park was now in darkness. During the early summer it had been illuminated, but the lights had been switched off when Paris fell and never switched on again. The café floating, an island of brilliance on the water, drew the boats towards it. Though poor, it had its pretensions. It did not admit peasants in peasant dress, but these were allowed to hire the cheap and shabby boats. Now, stopping just beyond the water's luminous verge, the boatmen gazed with envious respect at the patrons in their city suits.

Klein was saying: ". . . then the Prime Minister says: 'Here is the report. Domnul Secretary, never must this report be shown to Herr Dorf. You understand?' The secretary writes across the report: 'Never to be shown to Herr Dorf.' One minute later the door opens and in comes Herr Dorf. The secretary holds the report to his chest. Never will he show it; first will he die. But what does the Prime Minister say? 'No,' he says, 'Herr Dorf shall see the report. Always I play with my cards on the table.'"

At Guy's shout of laughter, the nearest boatload realised that here were foreigners. The opportunity was too good to miss. Their oars touched the water: they drifted into the light. The man in the middle seat began to do some simple acrobatics, then managed, clumsily, to stand on his hands. While this was going on, his companions stared expectantly towards the English. The acrobatics over, they began singing together a sad little song, after which they made diffident attempts to beg. Harriet, the only one who had been aware of the performance, threw some coins. They lingered awhile, hoping for more but lacking the courage to ask, then at last took themselves off.

The talk had now moved to the Drucker trial. It was Klein who had obtained for Guy the little information he had about Sasha Drucker's disappearance. He grimaced now as the others questioned him about the trial, saying he was not much interested in this Drucker "who had lived well and now was not so well".

"Will the Germans protect him?" Guy asked.

Klein shook his head.

"As his business was with Germany," said Clarence, "the trial could be interpreted as an anti-German gesture?"

Klein laughed. "A gesture perhaps, but not anti-German. They try to show him Rumania is still a free country. She is not afraid before the world to bring this rich banker to justice. And the trial diverts people. It keeps their minds off Bessarabia. But the Germans, what do they care? Drucker is no use now. Ah, Doamna Preen-gal" – as Klein leant towards Harriet a pink light coloured his cheek – "was I not right? I said if you stayed here it would be interesting. More and more is it necessary to buy off the Germans with food. Believe me, the day will come when this" – he touched the saucers of sheep-cheese and olives that came with the wine – "this will be a feast. You are watching a history, Doamna Preengal. Stay, and you will see a country die."

"Will you stay, too?" she asked him.

He laughed again – perhaps because laughter was the only answer to life as he saw it: but it occurred to her, for the first time, that his was the laughter of a man not completely sane.

Speaking seriously, David asked him: "Can you stay? Are you safe here?"

Klein shrugged. "I doubt. The old ministers would say to me: 'Klein, you are a Jew and a rogue. Make the budget balance,' and they would joke with me. But the new men do not joke. When I am no longer of use, what will they do to me?"

"Are you ever afraid?" Harriet asked.

"But I am always afraid," Klein laughed, and taking Harriet's hand, stared at her. "Perhaps," he said, "Doamna Preen-gal should not stay too long."

An hour or so later, Clarence was still with them, though he had had nothing to say since his remark about the Drucker trial. When they left, he let Guy go ahead with David and Klein, and loitered behind, hoping Harriet would join him. She had seen very little of him, since at the party given for Guy's production of *Troilus and Cressida* she had been unable to take seriously the suggestion she should return to England with him. Now their friendship was, as she supposed, at an end, she found herself regretting it. Usually silent under the pressure of competitive talk, she did not enjoy the audience Guy liked to have around him. With a single companion, however, she talked readily enough and, herself the child of divorced parents, neither of whom had found it convenient to give her a home, she had felt a rather unwilling sympathy for Clarence, whose childhood had been wretched. She did not want to share his distrust of the world. She had rallied him, scoffed at him, but the sympathy had been there nevertheless. Now, as she walked with him, she felt his distrust turned against her. He had accused her of encouraging him and rejecting him – and perhaps she had. They passed in silence under the chestnut trees, avoiding the peasants who had settled down to spend the night there, and turned into a side lane, overhung by aromatic trees, where the air, damp and cool, was occasionally scented by unseen flowers.

To start him talking she asked if he were busy, though she knew he was not. He answered, rather sullenly: "No," and added after a long pause: "I don't know what I'm doing here at all."

"Since Dunkirk the Bureau's been at a standstill. That doesn't worry Inchcape, of course. He never did do much. What have we ever had to propaganda, apart from the evacuation of the Channel Islands and the loss of Europe?" He laughed bitterly.

"What about the Poles?"

"They're practically all gone. I've worked myself out of work."

"Why not come back to the English Department? Guy needs help."

"Oh!" Clarence sighed. She could visualise his face drawn down with guilty dejection as he said: "I loathe teaching. And the students bore me to tears."

"Then what are you going to do?"

"I don't know. I might get some decoding at the Legation."

"I thought you despised the Legation and everyone in it."

"One has to do something."

Clarence, keeping his distance as they walked on the narrow path, was putting up a show of detachment from her; an unconvincing show. From sheer need for distraction she was tempted to make a gesture to regain him, but she did nothing. A romantic, he was never likely to be content with the prosaic companionship which was all she had to offer.

They were approaching the park gate and could hear the traffic of the main road. Clarence slowed his pace, unwilling, now that he had started talking, to leave the park's encouraging cover for the interruptions and buffetings of the street.

Sighing again and saying reflectively: "I don't know!" he let his thoughts wander into the metaphysical byways that skirted his self-pity and self-contempt. "How much easier life must be when one has that little bit of extra something that tips one to the manic rather than the depressive side."

"You think it's just a matter of chemistry?"

"Well, isn't it? What are we but a component of chemicals?"

"Surely something more."

Not wanting to leave the particular for the general, he said: "The truth is, I've been frustrated all my life. I'll die of it. But I'm dying already. The beginning of death is ceasing to desire to live."

"Oh, we're all dying," Harriet answered him impatiently.

"Some of us are alive – anyway, for the moment. Look at Guy!"

They both looked ahead at Guy whose white shirt could be seen glimmering through the darkness. His voice came to them. He was on to his favourite subject – the sufferings of the peasants, the sufferings of the world. Sufferings, Harriet thought, that would remain long after Guy had talked himself into his grave. Catching the word "Russia," she smiled.

Clarence had caught it, too. On a high, complaining note of inquiry, as though the question had never occurred to him before, he asked: "What *is* the basis of his love affair with Russia?"

She said: "I think it's the need to put his faith into something. His father was an old-fashioned radical. Guy was brought up as a free thinker, but he has a religious temperament. So he believes in Russia. That's another home for little children above the bright blue sky."

"In fact," said Clarence, "he's simply what the psychologists call 'a rebel son of a rebel father'."

This idea was new to Harriet. She might consider it later but was not prepared to let Clarence dismiss Guy so easily. She said: "There's more to it than that," and there probably was more to it. When Guy was growing up the mills and mines were idle. The majority of the men he knew, his own father among them, had been on the dole. He had watched his father, a skilled man, highly intelligent, decline and become, through despair and the illness brought by despair, unemployable. He had resented this waste of human energy and became absorbed in the politics of the waste-land and the welfare of the wasted.

Mildly scornful, Clarence went on: "And David's another one. They both imagine that life can be perfected by dialectical materialism."

She said: "David is more realistic, and probably more rigid."

"And Guy?"

"I don't know." It was true, she did not know. She had discovered, but still could not elucidate, the resolute impracticability of Guy's way of life. She said: "I told him once that when I married him, I thought I was marrying the rock of ages. I pretty soon found he was capable of absolute lunacy. For instance, he once thought of marrying Sophie just to give her a British passport."

Harriet's tone of criticism at once caused Clarence to change his attitude. He said reprovingly: "Still Guy is not like most of these left-wing idealists. He doesn't just talk, he does things. For instance, he visited the political prisoners in the Vacaresti jail. Quite a risky business in a country like this."

"When did he do that?" Harriet asked, alarmed.

"Before the war. He took them books and food."

"I hope he doesn't do it now?"

"I don't know. He doesn't tell me."

He did not tell Harriet either. She realised he resented her intervention in his activities and could be secretive. She felt resentful, too, thinking that when he was out of the flat – which he often was – he might be up to anything.

"He's an idealist, of course," Clarence said.

"I'm afraid he is."

"You're becoming critical of him."

"It's not that I'm no longer grateful for his virtues, but they extend too far beyond me. He's too generous, too forbearing, too easily called upon. People feel they can call on him for anything, but he's always somewhere else when I need him."

"Yet what better could you find?"

She did not attempt to answer this question. Her feeling was that she had been taken in, and too easily: perhaps because he was so unlike herself. In early adolescence she had been skinny and charmless. Feeling unwanted, she had been both aggressive and withdrawn, so her aunt had nagged at her: "Why can't you make yourself pleasant to people? Don't you want them to like you?" Whether she wanted it or not, she soon learnt not to expect it. When she did make an effort to please, it seemed to her she aroused not liking but suspicion. Being unsuccessful in the world herself, she had to find someone who would be successful for her. And who better than Guy Pringle, that large, comfortable, generous, embraceable figure? But she should have recognised warning signs. There was, for instance, the fact that he had so few possessions. She had put this down to poverty, but quickly discovered that when he was given anything he promptly lost it. She began to suspect that he saw possessions as a tie. They revealed too much. They defined their owner and so limited him. Guy was not to be defined or limited or held in fee.

There was, she admitted, an emotional shyness about him, but his elusiveness came from a deeper cause than that. And yet, as Clarence had asked, what better could she find? She envisaged a creature similar, but dependent; someone she could compass; her own possession; a child, she supposed. That might be permitted one day, but Guy insisted that at the moment their circumstances were too insecure for children. Was that a reason or an excuse? After all, children were possessions. They, too, defined and limited their possessors.

Meanwhile, Clarence was saying: "I believe in Guy. I think you're lucky to have found him. He has integrity, but I suppose that's the trouble. You're trying to destroy it."

"What do you mean?"

"You're filling him with middle-class ideas. You make him bath every day and get his hair cut."

"He has to grow up," Harriet said. "If he hadn't married me, he'd probably have wasted his life as a sort of eternal student, living out of a rucksack. I think he was probably thankful for an excuse to compromise."

"That's just the point. One is corrupted by compromise. And respectability is compromise. Look at me. I went to an expensive school where I was flogged like a beast. I wanted to revolt and I dared not. I wanted to fight in Spain and I dared not. I could have entered any profession I chose: I chose nothing. That was my revolt against my own respectability – and it led to nothing. I compromised with respectability and was corrupted."

"I expect it would have been the same whatever happened. You offer yourself to be corrupted."

He considered this in silence for some moments, then concluded: "Anyway, I'm lost. I let everyone down. I'd even let Guy down."

"I doubt it."

"Why are you so sure?"

"You don't mean enough to him."

"Hah!" said Clarence in sombre satisfaction that she should diminish him in this way.

The others had come to a stop at the gate. Seeing Harriet and Clarence appear, they were about to pass through when someone darted out of the shadows and accosted them. David and Klein went on, but Guy remained talking to the newcomer.

Clarence distastefully asked: "What lame duck has Guy picked up now? Is it a beggar?"

"It doesn't look like a beggar," Harriet said. Despite their dissension, she and Clarence were at once united in disapproval of Guy's readiness to encourage everyone and anyone.

As soon as they were within earshot, Guy called excitedly to Harriet: "Who do you think this is?"

Harriet did not know and she could see no reason for excitement. The man, about whom nothing was familiar, wore the decayed and dirty uniform of a conscript. When she had seen him moving in the distance, she had thought he was young. Now, in the uncertain light from the main road, he had an appearance of decrepitude found in poverty-stricken old age.

He was tall, skeletal, narrow-shouldered and stooped like a consumptive. His head, that had been shaved, was beginning to show a greyish stubble. The face, grey-white, with cheeks clapped in on either side of a prominent nose, would have seemed the face of a corpse had not the close-set, dark eyes been fixed on her, alive in their apprehensive anguish of need.

She was repelled by such misery. She wanted to go out of sight of it. She shook her head.

"But, darling, it's Sasha Drucker."

She did not know what to say. Sasha, when she saw him nine months before, had been the well fed, well dressed son of a wealthy man. Now he smelt of the grave.

"What has happened to him? Where has he been?"

"In Bessarabia. When his father was arrested, he was taken to do his military service. He was sent to the frontier. When the Russians marched in, the Rumanian officers just took to their heels. There was disorder and Sasha got away. He's been on the run ever since. He's starving. Darling, he must come back with us."

"Yes, of course."

Too shocked to say anything else, she moved out of the aura of Sasha's desperation and walked ahead with Clarence, wondering. When Sasha was fed, where was he going?

As they crossed the square towards the Pringles' block, Harriet, feeling the need of some other presence to share the burden of Sasha's condition, asked Clarence to come in.

"No fear," he said, rejecting responsibility.

"What on earth are we going to do with this boy?" she asked on a note of appeal, but she could expect neither help nor sympathy from Clarence that evening. He laughed. "Put him in with Yakimov," he said as he made off.

There was nothing to eat in the kitchen except bread and eggs. In this heat, in a country where refrigerators were almost unknown, fresh food had to be bought each day. While she made an omelette, Harriet could hear from the cupboard-sized room next door the snores of Despina, the maid, and Despina's husband.

As Sasha ate the omelette with apologetic eagerness, a little colour came into his face. He looked, Harriet thought, like a sapling devastated by storm. She had remembered Sasha Drucker as a dark, gentle, protected youth, the darling of a large family, who had the gentle and unsuspecting air of a domestic animal. Now when he glanced at her, he did so with the wary look of the hunted.

Opposite him, watching him, Guy's face was constricted with concern for the boy. He was deeply hurt by Sasha's condition. He turned to Harriet and said in the persuasive tone she had come to suspect: "We can put him up somewhere, can't we? He can stay?"

She said: "I don't know," exasperated that Guy spoke openly in this way. She felt the realities of the situation should be privately discussed before any decision could be taken. Where, for instance, was Sasha to be put?

Sasha himself sat silent. Ordinarily, he would surely have shown some reluctance to be forced on her hospitality like this, but now she was his only hope. When he had eaten, he looked at her and smiled with an agonised emptiness.

Guy offered him the arm-chair. "Make yourself comfortable."

Sasha shifted diffidently, not rising. "I would prefer this wooden chair. You see . . . I have lice."

"Would you like a bath?" said Harriet.

"Yes, please."

When she had given him towels and shown him the bathroom, she returned to the room free to confront Guy. "We can't possibly have him here," she said. "Our position is insecure enough. What would happen if we were caught harbouring a deserter – especially Drucker's son?"

Guy stared at her and asked with a suffering expression: "How can we refuse? He has nowhere else to go."

"Has he no other friends?"

"No one who would dare take him in. He's at the end of his tether. We can't put him out on the street. We must let him sleep here, anyway for tonight."

"Well, where?"

"On the sofa."

"What about Yakimov?"

Guy looked disconcerted. Blustering a little, he said: "Oh, Yaki's all right," but he knew Yakimov was not all right. They dare not trust him.

Seeing the consternation on Guy's face, Harriet pitied him, but the impasse was of his own making. He had persuaded her to take in Yakimov much against her will; and she could not help feeling some satisfaction as she waited for him to offer a solution. He had none to offer.

He asked unhappily: "Can you think of anyone who would give him a bed?"

"Can you?" There was a long pause while Guy's face grew more troubled, then she said: "You could tell Yakimov to go."

"Where could he go? He hasn't a penny."

During the silence that followed, Harriet reflected on their diversity. Guy, typically, wanted Sasha in the flat without giving any thought to the problem of having him there. She, perhaps, was over-conscious of difficulty. If it rested with Guy alone, there might be no difficulties. He would have trusted Yakimov and Yakimov might have proved trustworthy. She was annoyed at the same time, seeing his willingness to have Sasha here as a symptom of spiritual flight – the flight from the undramatic responsibility to one person which marriage was.

Guy gave her a pleading look as though she could, if she would, reveal a solution. And there was a solution. Pitying him at last, she said: "There's a room of some sort on the roof: a second servant's bedroom."

"That belongs to us?"

"It belongs to the flat. We couldn't use it without telling Despina. She keeps some of her things there."

"Darling!" In his relief, his face glowed with delight in her. He sprang up and threw his arms round her shoulders. "What a wife! You're wonderful!"

Which, she told herself, was all very well: "He can only stay one night. You must find somewhere else for him. I'm not sure we can trust Despina."

"Of course we can trust Despina."

"What makes you think so?"

"She's a decent soul."

"Well, if you think it's all right, you must go and wake her up. She knows where this room is. I don't."

Guy, about to go happily off to tell Sasha that all was well, paused, blankly surprised at being given the onerous task of waking Despina.

"You wake her," he cajoled her, but she shook her head.

"No, you must wake her."

As he moved reluctantly towards the kitchen, she almost said: "All right, I'll do it," but checked herself and for the first time in their married life stood firm.

4

Yakimov had played Pandarus in Guy's production of *Troilus and Cressida*. The play over, his triumph forgotten, he was suffering from a sense of anti-climax and of grievance. Guy, who had cosseted him through it all, had now abandoned him. And what, he asked himself, had come of the hours spent at rehearsals? Nothing, nothing at all.

Walking in the Calea Victoriei, in the increasing heat of midday, his sad camel face a-run with sweat, he wore a panama hat, a suit of corded silk, a pink silk shirt and a tie that was once the colour of Parma violets. His clothes were very dirty. The hat was brim-broken and yellow with age. His jacket was tattered, brown beneath the armpits, and so shrunken that it held him as in a brace.

During the winter he had felt the ridges of frozen snow through the holes in his shoes: now he felt, just as painfully, the flagstones' white candescence. Steadily edged out to the kerb by the vigour of those about him, he caught the hot draught of cars passing at his elbow. He was agitated by the clangour of trams, by the flash of windscreens, blaring of horns and shrieking of brakes – all at a time when he would ordinarily have been safe in the refuge of sleep.

He had been wakened that morning by the relentless ringing of the telephone. Though from the lie of the light he could guess it was no more than ten o'clock, apparently even Harriet was out. Damp and inert beneath a single sheet, he lay without energy to stir and waited for the ringing to stop. It did not stop. At last, tortured to full consciousness, he dragged himself up and found the call was for him. The caller was his old friend Dobbie Dobson of the Legation.

"Lovely to hear your voice," Yakimov said. He settled down in anticipation of a pleasurable talk about their days together in *Troilus*, but Dobson, like everyone else, had put the play behind him.

"Look here, Yaki," he said, "about those transit visas . . ."

"What transit visas, dear boy?"

"You know what I'm talking about." Dobson spoke with the edge of a good-natured man harassed beyond endurance. "Every British subject was ordered to keep in his passport valid transit visas against the possibility of sudden evacuation. The consul's been checking up and he finds you haven't obtained any."

"Surely, dear boy, that wasn't a serious order? There's no cause for alarm."

"An order is an order," said Dobson, "I've made excuses for you, but the fact is if you don't get those visas today you'll be sent to Egypt under open arrest."

"*Dear boy!* But I haven't a bean."

"Charge them to me. I'll deduct the cost when your next remittance arrives."

Before he left the flat that morning, it had occurred to Yakimov to see if he could find anything useful in it. Guy was careless with money. Yakimov had more than once picked up and kept notes which his host had pulled out with his handkerchief. He had never before actually searched for money, but now, in his condition of grievance, he felt that Guy owed him anything he could find. In the Pringles' bedroom he went through spare trousers and handbags, but came upon nothing. In the sitting-room he pulled out the drawers of sideboard and writing-desk and spent some time looking through the stubs of Guy's old cheque-books which recorded payments made into London banks on behalf of local Jews. In view of the fact Drucker was awaiting trial on a technical charge of black-market dealing, he considered the possibility of blackmail. But the possibility was not great. Use of the black market was so general that, even now, the Jews would laugh at him.

In the small central drawer of the writing-desk he came on a sealed envelope marked "Top Secret." This immediately excited him. He was not the only one inclined to suspect that Guy's occupation in Bucharest was not as innocent as it seemed. Affable, sympathetic, easy to know, Guy would, in Yakimov's opinion, make an ideal agent.

The flap of the envelope, imperfectly sealed, opened as he touched it. Inside was a diagram of a section through – what? A pipe or a well. Having heard so much talk of sabotage in the English Bar, he guessed that it was an oil well. A blockage in the pipe was marked "detonator". Here was a simple exposition of how and where the amateur saboteur should place his gelignite.

This was a find! He resealed and replaced the empty envelope, but the plan he put into his pocket. He did not know what eventual use he might make of it, but he would have some fun showing it around the English Bar as proof of the dangerous duties being exacted from him by King and country. He felt a few moments of exhilaration. Then as he trudged off to visit the consulates the plan was forgotten, the exhilaration was no more.

The consulates, taking advantage of the times, were charging high prices. Yakimov, disgusted by the thought of money wasted on such things, obtained visas for Hungary, Bulgaria and Turkey. That left only Yugoslavia, the country that nine months before had thrown him out and impounded his car for debt. He entered the consulate with aversion, handed over his passport and was – he'd expected nothing better – kept waiting half an hour.

When the clerk returned the passport, he made a movement as though drawing a shutter between them. "*Zabranjeno*," he said.

Yakimov had been refused a visa.

It had always been at the back of his mind that when he could borrow enough to remit the debt, he would reclaim his Hispano-Suiza. Now, he saw, they would prevent him doing so.

As he wandered down the Calea Victoriei, indignation grew in him like a nervous disturbance of the stomach. He began to brood on his car – the last gift of his dear old friend Dollie; the last souvenir – apart from his disintegrating wardrobe – of their wonderful life together. Suddenly, its loss became grief. He decided to see Dobson. But first he must console himself with a drink.

During rehearsals, to keep a hold on him, Guy had bought Yakimov drinks at the Doi Trandifiri, but Guy was a simple soul. He drank beer and *ţuică* and saw no reason why Yakimov should not do the same. Yakimov had longed for the more dashing company of the English Bar. As soon as the play was over, he returned to the bar in expectation of honour and applause. What he found there bewildered him. It was not only that his entry was ignored, but it was ignored by strangers. The place was more crowded than he had ever known it. Even the air had changed, smelling not of cigarettes, but cigars.

As he pushed his way in, he had heard German spoken on all sides. Bless my soul, German in the English Bar! He stretched his neck, trying to see Galpin or Screwby, and it came to him that he was the only Englishman in the room.

Attempting to reach the counter, he found himself elbowed back with deliberate hostility. As he breathed at a large man

"Steady, dear boy!" the other, all chest and shoulders, threw him angrily aside with "*Verfluchter Lümmel*!"

Yakimov was unnerved. He lifted a hand, trying to attract the attention of Albu, who, because of his uncompromising remoteness of manner, was reputed to be the model of an English barman. Albu had no eyes for him.

Realising he was alone in enemy-occupied territory, Yakimov was about to take himself off when he noticed Prince Hadjimoscos at the farther end of the bar.

The Rumanian, who looked with his waxen face, his thin, fine black hair and black eyes, like a little mongoloid doll, was standing tiptoe in his soft kid shoes and lisping in German to a companion. Relieved and delighted to see a familiar face, Yakimov ran forward and seized him by the arm. "Dear boy," he called out, "who *are* all these people?"

Hadjimoscos slowly turned his head, looking surprised at Yakimov's intrusion. He coldly asked: "Is it not evident to you, *mon prince*, that I am occupied?" He turned away, only to find his German companion had taken the opportunity to desert him. He gave Yakimov an angry glance.

To placate him, Yakimov attempted humour, saying with a nervous giggle: "So many Germans in the bar! They'll soon be demanding a plebiscite."

"They have as much right here as you. More, in fact, for they have not betrayed us. Personally, I find them charming."

"Oh, so do I, dear boy," Yakimov assured him. "Had a lot of friends in Berlin in '32," then changing to a more interesting topic: "Did you happen to see the play?"

"The play? You mean that charity production at the National Theatre? I'm told you looked quite ludicrous."

"Forced into it, dear boy," Yakimov apologised, knowing himself despised for infringing the prescripts of the idle. "War on, you know. Had to do m'bit."

Hadjimoscos turned down his lips. Without further comment, he moved away to find more profitable companionship. He attached himself to a German group and was invited to take a drink. Watching enviously, Yakimov wondered if, son of a Russian father and an Irish mother, he could hint that his sympathies were with the Reich. He put the thought from his mind. The British Legation had lost its power here, but not, alas, over him.

The English Bar was itself again. The English journalists had re-established themselves and the Germans, bored with the skirmish, were drifting back to the Minerva. The few that remained were losing their audacity.

Hadjimoscos was again willing to accept Yakimov's company, but cautiously. He would not join him in an English group – that would have been too defined an attachment in a changing world – but if Yakimov had money he would stand with him in a no-man's land and help him to spend it.

Yakimov, though not resentful by nature, did occasionally feel a little sore at this behaviour. Practised scrounger though he was, he was not as practised as Hadjimoscos. When he had money, he spent it. Hadjimoscos, whether he had it or not, never spent it. With his softly insidious and clinging manner, his presence affected men like the presence of a woman. They expected nothing from him. By standing long enough, first on one foot then on the other, he remained so patiently, so insistently *there*, that those to whom he attached himself bought him drinks in order to be free to ignore him.

Yakimov, entering the bar that morning, saw Hadjimoscos with his friend Horvatz and Cici Palu, all holding empty glasses and watching out for someone to refill them.

He bought his own drink before approaching them. Seeing them eye the whisky in his hand, he began, in self-defence, to complain of the high cost of the visas he had been forced to buy. Hadjimoscos, smiling maliciously, slid forward a step and put a hand on Yakimov's arm. "*Cher prince*,' he said, "what does it matter what you spend your money on, so long as you spend it on yourself!"

Palu gave a snigger. Horvatz remained blank. Yakimov knew, had always known, they did not want his company. They did not even want each other. They stood in a group, bored by their own aimlessness, because no one else wanted them. To Yakimov there came the thought that he was one of them – he who had once been the centre of entertainment in a vivacious set. He attempted to be entertaining now: "Did you hear? When the French minister, poor old boy, was recalled to Vichy France, Princess Teodorescu said to him: '*Dire adieu, c'est mourir un peu.*' "

"Is it likely that the Princess of all people would be so lacking in tact?" Hadjimoscos turned his back, attempting to exclude Yakimov from the conversation as he said: "Things are coming to a pretty pass! What do I learn at the *cordonnier* this morning? Three weeks to wait and five thousand to pay for a pair of hand-made shoes!"

"At the *tailleur*," said Palu, "it is the same. The price of English stuff is a scandal. And now they declare meatless days. What, I ask, is a fellow to eat?" He looked at Yakimov, for all the world as though it were the British and not the Germans who were plundering the country.

Yakimov attempted to join in. "A little fish," he meekly suggested, "a little game, in season. Myself, I never say no to a slice of turkey."

Hadjimoscos cut him short with contempt: "Those are *entrées* only. How, without meat, can a man retain his virility?"

Discomfited, casting about in his mind for some way of gaining the attention he loved, Yakimov remembered the plan he had found that morning. He took it out. Sighing, he studied it. The conversation faltered. Aware of their interest, he lowered the paper so it was visible to all. "What will they want me to do next!" he asked the world.

Hadjimoscos averted his glance. "I advise you, *mon prince*," he said, "if you have anything to hide, now is the time to hide it."

Knowing he could do nothing to please that morning, Yakimov put the plan away and let his attention wander. He became aware that a nearby stranger had been attempting to intercept it. The stranger smiled. His shabby, tousled appearance did not give much cause for hope, but Yakimov, always amiable, went forward and held out his hand. "Dear boy," he said, "where have we met before?"

The young man took his pipe out from under his big, fluffy moustache and spluttering like a syphon in which the soda level was too low, he managed to say at last: "The name's Lush. Toby Lush. I met you once with Guy Pringle."

"So you did," agreed Yakimov, who had no memory of it.

"Let me get you a drink. What is it?"

"Why, whisky, dear boy. Can't stomach the native rot-gut."

Neighing wildly at Yakimov's humour, Lush went to the bar. Yakimov, having decided his new acquaintance was "a bit of an ass," was surprised when he was led purposefully over to one of the tables by the wall. He did not receive his glass until he had sat down and he realised something would be demanded in return for it.

After a few moments of nervous pipe-sucking, Lush said: "I'm here for keeps this time."

"Are you indeed? That's splendid news."

With his elbows close to his side, his knees clenched, Lush sat as though compressed inside his baggy sports-jacket and flannels. He sucked and gasped, gasped and spluttered, then said: "When the Russkies took over Bessarabia, I told myself: 'Toby, old soul, now's the time to shift your bones.' There's always the danger of staying too long in a place."

"Where do you come from?"

"Cluj. Transylvania. I never felt safe there. I'm not sure I'm safe here."

It occurred to Yakimov that he had heard the name Toby Lush before. Didn't the fellow turn up for a few days in the spring, bolted from Cluj because of some rumour of a Russian advance? Yakimov, always sympathetic towards fear, said reassuringly:

"Oh, you're all right here. Nice little backwater. The Germans are getting all they want. They won't bother us."

"I hope you're right." Lush's pale, bulging eyes surveyed the bar. "Quite a few of them about though. I don't feel they like us being here."

"It's the old story," said Yakimov, "infiltrate, then complain about the natives. Still, it was worse last week. I said to Albu: 'Dry Martini' and he gave me three martinis."

Squeezing his knees together, Lush swayed about, gulping with laughter. "You're a joker," he said. "Have another?"

When he returned with the second whisky, Lush had sobered up, intending to speak what was on his mind: "You're a friend of Guy Pringle, aren't you?"

Yakimov agreed. "Very old and dear friend. You know I played Pandarus in his show?"

"Your fame reached Cluj. And you lodge with the Pringles?"

"We share a flat. Nice little place. You must come and have a meal with us."

Lush nodded, but he wanted more than that. "I'm looking for a job," he said. "Pringle runs the English Department, doesn't he? I'm going to see him, of course, but I thought perhaps you'd put in a word for me. Just say: 'I met Toby Lush today. Nice bloke,' something like that." Toby gazed earnestly at Yakimov, who assured him at once: "If I say the word, you'll get the job tomorrow."

"If there's a job to be got."

"These things can always be arranged." Yakimov emptied his glass and put it down. Lush rose, but said with unexpected firmness: "One more, then I have to drive round to the Legation. Must make my number."

"You have a car? Wonder if you'd give me a lift?"

"With pleasure."

Lush's car was an old mud-coloured Humber, high-standing and hooded like a palanquin.

"Nice little bus," said Yakimov. Placing himself in an upright seat from which the wadding protruded, he thought of the beauties of his own Hispano-Suiza.

The Legation, a brick-built villa in a side street, was hedged around with cars. On the dry and patchy front lawn a crowd of men – large, practical-looking men in suits of khaki drill – were standing about, each with an identical air of despondent waiting. They watched the arrival of the Humber as though it might bring them something. As he passed among them, Yakimov noted with surprise that they were speaking English. He could identify none of them.

Lush was admitted to the chancellery. Yakimov, as had happened before, was intercepted by a secretary.

"Oh, Prince Yakimov, can I help you?" she said, extruding an elderly charm, "Mr. Dobson is so busy. All the young gentlemen are busy these days, poor young things. At their age life in the service should be all parties and balls, but with this horrid war on they have to work like everyone else. I suppose it's to do with your *permis de sejour*?"

"It's a personal matter. *Ra*-ther important. I'm afraid I must see Mr. Dobson."

She clicked her tongue, but he was admitted to Dobson's presence.

Dobson, whom he had not seen since the night of the play, raised his head from his work in weary inquiry: "Hello, how are you?"

"Rather the worse for war," said Yakimov. Dobson gave a token smile, but his plump face, usually bland, was jaded, his eyes rimmed with pink; his whole attitude discouraging. "We've had an exhausting week with the crisis. And now, on top of everything, the engineers have been dismissed from the oil-fields."

"Those fellows outside?"

"Yes. They've been given eight hours to get out of the country.

A special train is to take them to Constanza. Poor devils, they're hanging around in hope we can do something!"

"So sorry, dear boy."

At the genuine sympathy in Yakimov's tone, Dobson let his pen drop and rubbed his hands over his head. "H.E.'s been ringing around for the last two hours, but it's no good. The Rumanians are doing this to please the Germans. Some of these engineers have been here twenty years. They've all got homes, cars, dogs, cats, horses . . . I don't know what. It'll make a lot of extra work for us."

"Dear me, yes." Yakimov slid down to a chair and waited until he could introduce his own troubles. When Dobson paused, he ventured: "Don't like to worry you at a time like this, but . . ."

"Money, I suppose?"

'Not altogether. You remember m'Hispano-Suiza. The Jugs are trying to prig it." He told his story. "Dear boy," he pleaded, "you can't let them do it. The Hispano's worth a packet. Why, the chassis alone cost two thousand five hundred quid. Body by Fernandez – heaven knows what Dollie paid for it. Magnificent piece of work. All I've got in the world. Get me a visa, dear boy. Lend me a few thou. I'll get the car and flog it. We'll have a bean-feast, a royal night at Cina's – champers and the lot. What d'you say?"

Dobson, listening with sombre patience, said: "I suppose you know the Rumanians are requisitioning cars."

"Surely not British cars?"

"No." Dobson had to admit that the tradition of British privilege prevailed in spite of all. "Mostly Jewish cars. The Jews are always unfortunate, but they *do* own the biggest cars. What I mean is, this isn't a good time to sell. People are unwilling to buy an expensive car that might be requisitioned."

"But I don't really want to sell, dear boy. I love the old bus. . . . She'd be useful if there were an evacuation."

Dobson drew down his cheek and plucked at his round pink mouth. "I'll tell you what! One of us is going to Belgrade in a week or so – probably Foxy Leverett. You've got the receipt and car key and so on? Then I'll get him to collect it and drive it back. I suppose it's in order?"

"She was in first-class order when I left her."

"Well, we'll see what we can do," Dobson rose, dismissing him. Outside the Legation, the oil-men were still standing about, but

4

the Humber had gone. As Yakimov set out to walk back through the sultry noonday, he told himself: "No more tramping on m'poor old feet. And," he added on reflection, "she's worth money. I'd make a packet if I sold her."

5

A WEEK AFTER THE VISIT to the park café, Harriet, drawn out to the balcony by a sound of rough singing, saw a double row of marching men rounding the church immediately below her. They crossed the main square.

Processions were not uncommon in Bucharest. They were organised for all sorts of public occasions, descending in scale from grand affairs in which even the cabinet ministers were obliged to take part, to straggles of school-children in the uniform of the Prince's youth movement.

The procession she saw now was different from any of the others. There was no grandeur about it, but there was a harsh air of purpose. Its leaders wore green shirts. The song was unknown to her, but she caught one word of it which was repeated again and again on a rising note:

"*Capitanul, Capitanul.* . . ."

The Captain. Who the captain was she did not know.

She watched the column take a sharp turn into the Calea Victoriei, then, two by two, the marchers disappeared from sight. When they were all gone, she remained on the balcony with a sense of nothing to do but stand there.

The flat behind her was silent. Despina had gone to market. Yakimov was in bed. (She sometimes wished she could seal herself off, as he did, in sleep.) Sasha – for he was still with them despite her decree of "one night only" – was somewhere up on the roof. (Like Yakimov, he had nowhere else to go.) Guy, of course, was busy at the University.

The "of course" expressed a growing resignation. She had looked forward to the end of the play and the end of the term, imagining she would have his companionship and support against their growing insecurity. Instead, she saw no more of him than before. The summer school, planned as a part-time occupation, had attracted so many Jews awaiting visas to the States, he had had to organise extra classes. Now he taught and lectured even during the siesta time.

On the day the oil engineers were expelled from Ploesti, the Pringles, like other British subjects, received their first notice to quit the country. Guy was just leaving the flat when a buff slip was handed him by a *prefectura* messenger. He passed it over to Harriet. "Take it to Dobson," he said. "He'll deal with it."

He spoke casually, but Harriet was disturbed by this order to pack and go. She said: "But supposing we have to leave in eight hours?"

"We won't have to."

His unconcern had made the matter seem worse to her, yet he had been proved right. Dobson had had their order rescinded, and that of the other British subjects in Bucharest, but the oil engineers had had to go.

At different times during the day, Harriet had seen their wives and children sitting about in cafés and restaurants. The children, becoming peevish and troublesome, had been frowned on by the Rumanians, who did not take children to cafés. The women, uprooted, looked stunned yet trustful, imagining perhaps that, in the end, it would all prove a mistake and they would return to their homes. Instead, they had had to take the train to Constanza and the boat to Istanbul.

Despite the Rumanian excuse that the expulsion had been carried out on German orders, the German Minister was reported to have said: "Now we know how Carol would treat us if we were the losers."

Well, the engineers, however unwillingly they may have gone, had gone to safety. Harriet could almost wish Guy and she had been forced to go with them.

While she stood on the balcony with these reflections in mind, the city shook. For an instant, it seemed to her that the balcony shelved down. She saw, or thought she saw, the cobbles before the church. In terror she put out her hand to hold to something, but it was as though the world had become detached in space. Everything moved with her and there was nothing on which to hold. An instant – then the tremor passed.

She hurried into the room and took up her bag and gloves. She could not bear to be up here on the ninth floor. She had to feel the earth beneath her feet. When she reached the pavement, that burnt like the Sahara sand, her impulse was to touch it.

Gradually, as she crossed the square and saw the buildings intact and motionless, the familiar crowds showing no unusual alarm, she lost her sense of the tremor's supernatural strangeness. Perhaps here, in this inland town with its empty sky ablaze and the sense of the land-mass of Europe lying to the west, earthquakes were common enough. But when, in the Calea Victoriei, she came on Bella Niculescu, she cried out, forgetting the check on their relationship: "Bella, did you feel the earthquake?"

"Didn't I just?" Bella responded as she used to respond: "It scared me stiff. Everyone's talking about it. Someone's just said it wasn't an earthquake at all, but an explosion at Ploesti. It's started a rumour that British agents are blowing up the oil-wells. Let's hope not. Things are tricky enough for us without that."

The first excitement of their meeting over, Bella looked disconcerted and glanced about her to see who might have witnessed it. Harriet felt she had done wrong in accosting her friend. Neither knowing what to say, they were about to make excuses and separate when they were distracted by a lusty sound of singing from the distance. Harriet recognised the refrain of "*Capitanul.*" The men in green shirts were returning.

"Who are they?" Harriet asked.

"The Iron Guard, of course. Our local fascists."

"But I thought they'd been wiped out."

"*That's* what we were told."

As the leaders advanced, lifting their boots and swinging their arms, Harriet saw they were the same young men she had observed in the spring, exiles returned from training in the German concentration camps. Then, shabby and ostracised, they had hung unoccupied about the street corners. Now they were marching on the crown of the road, forcing the traffic into the kerb, filling the air with their anthem, giving an impression of aggressive confidence.

Like everyone else, the two women silenced by the uproar of "*Capitanul,*" stood and watched the column pass. It was longer than it had been that morning. The leaders, well dressed and drilled, gained an awed attention, but this did not last. The middle ranks, without uniforms, were finding it difficult to keep in step, while the rear was brought up by a collection of out-of-works, no doubt converted to Guardism that very morning. Some were in rags. Shuffling, stumbling, they gave nervous side-glances and grins at the bystanders and their only contribution to the song was an occasional shout of "*Capitanul.*" This was too much for the Rumanian sense of humour. People began to comment and snigger, then to laugh outright.

"Did you ever see the like!" said Bella.

Harriet asked: "Who is this '*capitanul*'? "

"Why the Guardist leader – Codreanu: the one who was 'shot trying to escape,' on Carol's orders, needless to say. A lot of his chums were shot with him. Some got away to Germany, but the whole movement was broken up. Who would have thought they'd have the nerve to reappear like this? Carol must be losing his grip."

From the remarks about them, it was clear that other onlookers were thinking the same. The procession passed, the traffic crawled after, and people went on their way. From the distance the refrain of "*Capitanul*" came in spasms, then died out.

Bella was saying: "They tried to make a hero of the Codreanu. It would take some doing. I saw him once. He looked disgusting with his dirty, greasy hair hanging round his ears. *And* he needed a shave. Oh, by the way,' she suddenly added, "you were talking about that Drucker boy. Funny you should mention him. A day or two after, I got a letter from Nikko and he'd been hearing about him too. Apparently they only took him off to do his military service. (I bet old Drucker had been buying his exemption. Trust *them*!) Anyway, the boy's deserted and the military are on the look-out. They've had orders to find him at all costs. I suppose it's this business of the fortune being in his name. They'll make him sign the money over."

"Supposing he refuses?"

"He wouldn't dare. Nikko says he could be shot as a deserter."

"Rumania's not at war."

"No, but it's a time of national emergency. The country's conscripted. Anyway, they're determined to get him. And I bet, when they do, he'll disappear for good. Oh, well!" Bella dismissed Sasha with a gesture. "I'm thinking of going to Sinai. I'm sick of stewing in this heat waiting for something to happen. My opinion is, nothing will happen. You should get Guy to take you to the mountains."

"We can't get away. He's started a summer school."

"Will he get any students at this time of the year?"

"He has quite a number."

"Jews, I bet?"

"Yes, they are mostly Jews."

Bella pulled down her mouth and raised her brows. "I wouldn't encourage that, my dear. If we're going to have the Iron Guard on the rampage again, there's no knowing what will happen. They beat up the Jewish students last time. But they're not only anti-Semitic, they're anti-British." She gave a grim, significant nod then, when she was satisfied that she had made an impression, her face cleared. "Must be off," she cheerfully said. "I've an appointment with the hairdresser." She lifted a hand, working her fingers in farewell, and disappeared in the direction of the square.

Harriet could not move. With the crowd pushing about her, she stood chilled and confused by perils. There was the peril of Sasha under the same roof as Yakimov, a potential informer – she did not know what the punishment might be for harbouring a deserter, but she pictured Guy in one of the notorious prisons Klein had described; and there was the more immediate threat from the marching Guardists.

Her instinct was to hurry at once to Guy and urge him to close down the summer school, but she knew she must not do that. Guy would not welcome her interference. He had put her out of his production on the grounds that no man could "do a proper job with his wife around". She wandered on as a preliminary to action, not knowing what action to take.

When she reached the British Propaganda Bureau, she came to a stop, thinking of Inchcape, who could, if he wished, put an end to the summer school. Why should she not appeal to him?

She stood for some minutes looking at the photographs of battleships and a model of the Dunkirk beaches, all of which had been in the window a month and were likely to remain, there being nothing with which to replace them.

She paused, not from fear of Inchcape but of Guy. Once before by speaking to Inchcape she had put a stop to one of Guy's activities and by doing so had brought about their first disagreement. Was she willing to bring about another?

Surely, she told herself, the important point was that her interference in the past had extricated Guy from a dangerous situation. It might do so again.

She entered the Bureau. Inchcape's secretary, knitting behind her typewriter, put up a show of uncertainty. Domnul Director might be too busy to see anyone.

"I won't keep him a moment," Harriet said, running upstairs before the woman could ring through. She found Inchcape stretched on a sofa with the volumes of *A la Recherche du Temps Perdu* open around him. He was wearing a shirt and trousers. Seeing her, he roused himself reluctantly and put on the jacket that hung on the back of the chair.

"Hello, Mrs. P.," he said with a smile that did not hide his irritation at being disturbed.

Harriet had not been in the office since the day they had come here to view Calinescu's funeral. Then the rooms had been dilapidated and the workmen had been fitting shelves. Now everything was painted white, the shelves were filled with books and the floor close-carpeted in a delicate shade of grey blue. On the Biedermeier desk, among other open books, lay some Reuter's sheets.

"What brings you here?" Inchcape asked.

"The Iron Guard."

He eyed her with his irritated humour: "You mean that collection of neurotics and nonentities who trailed past the window just now? Don't tell me they frightened you?"

Harriet said: "The Nazis began as a collection of neurotics and nonentities."

"So they did!" said Inchcape, smiling as though she must be joking. "But in Rumania fascism is just a sort of game."

"It wasn't a game in 1937 when Jewish students were thrown out of the University windows. I'm worried about Guy. He's alone there except for the three old ladies who assist him."

"There's Dubedat."

"What good would Dubedat be if the Guardists broke in?"

"Except when Clarence puts in an appearance, which isn't often. I'm alone here. I don't let it worry me."

She was about to say: "No one notices the Propaganda Bureau," but stopped in time and said: "The summer school is a provocation. All the students are Jews."

Although Inchcape retained his appearance of urbane unconcern, the lines round his mouth had tightened. He shot out his cuffs and studied his garnet cuff-links. "I imagine Guy can look after himself," he said.

His neat, Napoleonic face had taken on a remote expression intended to conceal annoyance. Harriet was silenced. She had come here convinced that the idea of the summer school had originated with Guy – now she saw her mistake. Inchcape was a powerful member of the organisation in which Guy hoped to make a career. Though she did not dislike him – they had come to terms early on – she still felt him an unknown quantity. Now she had challenged his vanity. There was no knowing what he might not say about Guy in the reports which he sent home.

When in the past, she had been critical of Inchcape, saying: "He's so oddly mean: he economises on food and drink, yet spends a fortune on china or furniture in order to impress his guests," Guy had explained that Inchcape's possessions were a shield that hid the emotional emptiness of his life. Whatever they were, they were a form of self-aggrandisement. She realised the summer school was, too.

Knowing he could not be persuaded to close it, she decided to placate him. "I suppose it *is* important," she said.

He glanced up, pleased, and at once his tone changed: "It certainly is. It's a sign that we're not defeated here. Our morale is high. And we'll do better yet. I have great plans for the future . . ."

"You think we have a future?"

"Of course we have a future. No one's going to interfere with us. Rumanian policy has always been to keep a foot in both camps. As for the Germans, what do they care so long as they're getting what they want? I'm confident that we'll keep going here. Indeed, I'm so confident that I'm arranging for an old friend, Professor Lord Pinkrose, to be flown out. He's agreed to give the Cantecuzene Lecture."

Meeting Harriet's astonished gaze, Inchcape gave a grin of satisfaction. "This is a time to show the flag," he said. "The lecture usually deals with some aspect of English literature. It will remind the Rumanians that we have one of the finest literatures in the world. And it is a great social occasion. The last time, we had eight princesses in the front row." He started to lead her towards the door. "Of course, it calls for a lot of organisation. I've got to find a hall and I'll have to book Pinkrose into an hotel. I'm not sure yet whether he'll come alone."

"He may bring his wife?"

"Good heavens, he has no wife." Inchcape spoke as though marriage were some ridiculous custom of primitive tribes. "But he's not so young as he was. He may want to bring a companion."

Inchcape opened the door and said in parting: "My dear child, we must maintain our equilibrium. Not so easy, I know, in this weather, when one's body seems to be melting inside one's clothes. Well, goodbye."

He shut the door on her, and she descended to the street with a sense of nothing achieved.

Shortly before the Guardists passed the University, Sophie Oresanu had come to see Guy in his office. The office had once been Inchcape's study, and the desk at which Guy sat still held Inchcape's papers. The shelves around were full of his books.

Sophie Oresanu, perched opposite Guy on the arm of a leather chair, had joined the summer school with enthusiasm. She now said: "I cannot work in such heat," leaning back with an insouciance that displayed her chief beauty, her figure. She pouted her heavily darkened mouth, then sighed and pushed a forefinger into one of her full, pasty cheeks. "At this time the city is terrible," she said.

Guy, viewing Sophie's languishings with indifference, remembered a conversation he had overheard between two male students:

"*La* Oresanu is not nice, she is *le* 'cock-tease'."

"*Ah, j'adore le* 'cock-tease'."

He smiled as she wriggled about on the chair-arm, flirting her rump at him. Poor girl! An orphan without a dowry, possessed of a freedom that devalued her in Rumanian eyes, she had to get herself a husband somehow. Remembering her grief when he had returned to Bucharest with a wife, he said the more indulgently: "The other students seem to be bearing up."

She shrugged off the other students. "My skin is delicate. I cannot tolerate much sun."

"Still, you're safer in the city this summer."

"No. They say the Russians are satisfied there will be no more troubles. Besides" – she made a disconsolate little gesture – "I am not happy at the summer school. All the students are Jews. They are not nice to me."

"Oh, come!" Guy laughed at her. "You used to complain that because you are half-Jewish, it was the Rumanians who were 'not nice' to you."

"It is true," she agreed: "No one is nice to me. I don't belong anywhere. I don't like Rumanian men. They live off women and despise them. They are so conceited. And the women here are such fools! They want to be despised. If the young man gives them *un coup de pied*, they do like this." She wriggled and threw up her eyes in a parody of sensual ecstasy. "Me, I wish to be respected. I am advanced, so I prefer Englishmen."

Guy nodded, sympathising with this preference. He had avoided marrying her himself, but he would have been delighted could he have married her off to a friend with a British passport. He had attempted to interest Clarence in her unfortunate situation, but Clarence had dismissed her, saying: "She's an affected bore," while of Clarence she said: "How terrible to be a man so unattractive to women!"

"Besides," she went on, "it is expensive, Bucharest. Every quarter my allowance goes, pouf! Other summers, for an economy, I let my flat and go to a little mountain hotel. Already I would have taken myself there, but my allowance is spent."

She paused, looking at him with a pathetic tilt of the head, expecting his usual query: "How much do you need?"

Instead, he said: "You'll get your allowance next month. Wait until then."

"My doctor says my health will suffer. Would you have me die?"

He smiled his embarrassment. Harriet had forced him to recognise Sophie's wiles and now he wondered how he had ever been taken in by them. Before his marriage, he had lent Sophie what he could not afford, seeing these loans, which were never repaid, as the price of friendship. With a wife as well as parents dependent on him, he had been forced to refuse her. His refusal had kept her at bay for the last few months and he was acutely discomforted at the prospect of having to refuse her again.

Leaning forward with one of the persuasive gestures she had effectively used in *Troilus*, she said: "I worked hard for the play. It was nice to have such a success, but I am not strong. It exhausted me. I have lost a kilo from my weight. Perhaps you like girls that are thin, but here they say it is not pretty."

So that was it! She wanted a return for services rendered. He looked down at his desk, having no idea, in the face of this, how to reject her claim. He could only think of Harriet, not certain whether the thought came as a protection or a threat. Anyway, he could use her as an excuse. Sophie knew she could get nothing out of Harriet.

He was beginning to recognise that Harriet was, in some ways, stronger than himself. And yet perhaps not stronger. He had a complete faith in his own morality and he would not let her override it. But she could be obdurate where he could not, and though he stood up to her, knowing if he did not he would be lost, he was influenced by her clarity of vision; unwillingly. It was probably significant that he was physically short-sighted. He could not recognise people until almost upon them. Their faces were like so many buns. Good-natured buns, he would have said, but Harriet did not agree. She saw them in detail and did not like them any the better for it.

He was troubled by her criticism of their acquaintances. He preferred to like people, knowing this fact was the basis of his influence over them. The sense of his will to like them gave them confidence: so they liked in return. He could see that Harriet's influence, given sway, could undermine his own successful formula for living and he felt bound to resist it. Yet there were occasions when he let her be obdurate for him.

While these thoughts were in his mind Sophie's chatter had come to a stop. Looking up, he found her watching him, puzzled and hurt that he let her talk on without the expected interruption.

As she concluded in a small, dispirited voice: "And I need only perhaps fifty thousand, not any more," she dropped all her little artifices and he saw the naïveté behind the whole performance. He had often, in the past, thought Sophie unfairly treated by circumstances. She had been forced, much too young, to face life alone with nothing but the weapons her sex provided. He thought: "The truth is, she's not much more than a scared kid," thankful nevertheless that he did not have fifty thousand to lend her.

He said as lightly as he could: "Harriet looks after the family finances now. She's better at it than I am. If anyone asks me for a loan, I have to refer them to her."

Sophie's expression changed abruptly. She sat upright, affronted that he should bring Harriet in between them. She rose, about to take herself off in indignation when a sound of marching and singing distracted her. They heard the repeated refrain "*Capitanul*".

"But that is a forbidden song," she said.

They reached the open window in time to see the leading green shirts pass the University. Sophie caught her breath. Guy, having talked with David's informants, was less surprised than she by this resurgence of the Iron Guards. He expected an appalled outcry from her, but she said nothing until the last stragglers had passed, then merely: "So! We shall have troubles again!"

He said: "You must have been at the University during the pogroms of 1938?"

She nodded. "It was terrible, of course, but I was all right. I have a good Rumanian name."

Remembering her annoyance with him, she turned suddenly and went without another word. She apparently had not been much disturbed by the spectacle of the marching Guardists, but Guy, when he returned to his desk, sat there for some time abstracted. He had seen a threat manifest and knew exactly what he faced.

When they had discussed the organisation of the summer school, Guy had said to Inchcape: "There's only one thing against it. It will give rise to a concentration of Jewish students. With the new anti-Semitic policy, they might be in a dangerous position."

Inchcape had scoffed at this. "Rumanian policy has always been anti-Semitic and all that happens is the Jews get richer and richer."

Guy felt he could not argue further without an appearance of personal fear. Inchcape, who had retained control of the English Department, wanted a summer school. His organisation must do something to justify its presence here. More than that, there was his need to rival the Legation. Speaking of the British Minister, he would say: "The old charmer's not afraid to stay, so why should I be?" If anyone pointed out that the Minister, unlike Inchcape and his men, had diplomatic protection, Inchcape would say: "While the Legation's here, we'll be protected too."

Guy knew that Inchcape liked him and, because of that, he liked Inchcape. He also admired him. With no great belief in his own courage, he esteemed audacious people like Inchcape and Harriet. Yet he tended to pity them. Inchcape he saw as a lonely bachelor who had nothing in life but the authority which his position gave. If a summer school made Inchcape happy, then Guy would back it to the end.

Harriet, he felt, must be protected from the distrust that had grown out of an unloved childhood. He would say to himself: "O, stand between her and her fighting soul," touched by the small, thin body that contained her spirit. And he saw her unfortunate because life, which he took easily, was to her so unnecessarily difficult.

He picked up a photograph which was propped against the ink-stand on his desk. It had been taken in the Calea Victoriei: one of those small prints that had to be provided when one applied for a *permis de sejour*. In it Harriet's face – remarkable chiefly for its oval shape and the width of her eyes – was fixed in an expression of contemplative sadness. She looked ten years older than her age. Here was something so different from her usual vivacity that he said when he first saw it: "Are you really so unhappy?" She had denied being unhappy at all.

Yet, he thought, the photograph betrayed some inner discontent of the confused and the undedicated. He replaced the photograph with a sense of regret. He could help her if she would let him; but would she let him?

He remembered that when he had set about her political education, she had rebuffed him with: "I cannot endure organised thought," and, having taken up that position, refused to be moved from it.

Before she married, she had worked in an art gallery and been the friend of artists, mostly poor and unrecognised. He had pointed out to her that were they working in the Soviet Union they would be honoured and rewarded. She said: "Only if they conformed." He had argued that in every country everyone had to conform in some way or other. She said: "But artists must remain a privileged community if they're to produce anything important. They can't just echo what they're told. They have to think for themselves. That's why totalitarian countries can't afford them."

He had to admit that she, too, thought for herself. She would not be influenced. Feminine and intolerant though she might be in particular, she could take a wide general view of things. Coming from the narrowest, most prejudiced class, she had nevertheless declassed herself. The more the pity, then, that she had rejected the faith which gave his own life purpose. He saw her muddled and lost in anarchy and a childish mysticism.

What did she want? The question was for him the more difficult because he was content. He wanted nothing for himself. Possessions he found an embarrassment, a disloyalty to his family that had to survive on so little. While he was taking his degree, he had worked as a part-time teacher. His mother had also worked. Between them they had paid the rent and kept the family together.

He had envied no one except the men without responsibilities who had been free to go and fight in Spain. These men of the

International Brigade had been his heroes. He would still recite their poetry to himself, with emotion:

> "From small beginnings mighty ends:
> From calling rebel generals friends,
> From being taught at public schools
> To think the common people fools,
> Spain bleeds, and Britain wildly gambles
> To bribe the butcher in the shambles."*

The marching Guardists that morning had brought to his mind the Blackshirts and their "Monster Rally" in his home town. That was when his friend Simon had been beaten up and he had recognised the fact that one day he, too, would have to pay for his political faith.

Simon had arrived late and sat by himself. When the rest of them, sitting in a body, attempted to break up the meeting they were frogmarched into the street. Simon, left alone, had with a fanatical, almost hysterical courage, carried on the interruptions unsupported. The thugs had had him to themselves. They had dragged him out through a back door to a garage behind the hall. There he was eventually found unconscious.

At that time the stories of fascist savagery were only half believed. It was a new thing in the civilised world. The sight of Simon's injured and blackened face had appalled Guy. He told himself he knew now what lay ahead – and from that time had never doubted that his turn would come.

While he sat now at his desk, confronting his own physical fear, his door opened. It opened with ominous slowness. He stared at it. A tousled head appeared.

With playful solemnity, Toby Lush said: "Hello, old soul! I'm back again, you see!"

Harriet, walking home with all her fears intact, allayed them with the determination to act somehow. If she could not surmount one danger, she must tackle another. There was the situation at home – at least she need not tolerate that.

She must make it clear to Guy that they could not keep both Yakimov and Sasha. He had brought them into the flat. Now it

* Acknowledgements are due to Mr. Edgell Rickworth for kind permission to print his lines.

was for him to decide which of the two should remain, and to dismiss the other.

When, however, she entered the sitting-room and found Yakimov there, awaiting his luncheon, she decided for herself. Sasha was the one who needed their help and protection. As for Yakimov, only sheer indolence kept him from fending for himself. And she was sick of the sight of him. Her mind was made up. He must go. She would tell him so straightaway.

Yakimov, sprawled in the arm-chair, was drinking from a bottle of *ţuică* which Despina had brought in that morning. He moved uneasily at the sight of her and, putting a hand to the bottle, excused himself: "Took the liberty of opening it, dear girl. Came in dropping on m'poor old feet. The heat's killing me. Why not have a snifter yourself?"

She refused, but sat down near him. Used to being ignored by her, he became flustered and his hand was unsteady as he refilled his glass.

Her idea had been to order him, there and then, to pack and go, but she did not know how to begin.

His legs were crossed and one of his narrow shoes dangled towards her. His foot shook. Through a gap between sole and upper, she could see the tips of his toes and the rags of his violet silk socks. His dilapidation reproached her. He lay back, pretending nonchalance, but his large, flat-looking, green eyes flickered apprehensively, looking at her and away from her, so she could not speak.

He tried to make conversation, asking: "What's on the menu today?"

She said: "It is a meatless day. Despina bought some sort of river fish."

He sighed. "This morning," he said, "I was thinking about *blinis*. We used to get them at Korniloff's. They'd give you a heap of pancakes. You'd spread the bottom one with caviare, the next with sour cream, the next with caviare, and so on. Then you'd cut right through the lot. Ouch!" He made a noise in his throat as at a memory so delicious it was scarcely to be endured. "I don't know why we don't get them here. Plenty of caviare. The fresh grey sort's the best, of course." He gave her an expectant look. When she made no offer to prepare the dish, he glanced away as though excusing her inhospitality with: "I admit there's nothing to compare with the Russian Beluga. Or Osetrova, for that matter."

He sighed again and on a note of yearning, asked: "Do you remember ortolans? Delicious, weren't they?"

"I don't know. Anyway, I don't believe in killing small birds."

He looked puzzled. "But you eat chickens! All birds are birds. What does the size matter? Surely the important thing is the taste?"

Finding this reasoning unanswerable, she glanced at the clock, causing him to say: "The dear boy's late. Where *does* he get to these days?" His tone told Harriet that, having been dropped from Guy's scheme of things, he was feeling neglected.

She said: "He's started a summer school at the University. I expect you miss the fun of rehearsals?"

"They were fun, of course, but the dear boy did keep us at it. And, in the end, what came of it all?"

"What could come of it? I mean, so far from home and with a war on, you could not hope to make a career of acting?"

"A career! Never thought of such a thing."

His surprise was such, she realised he had probably looked for no greater reward than a lifetime of free food and drink. The fact was, he had never grown up. She had thought once that Yakimov was a nebula which, under Guy's influence, had started to evolve. But Guy, having set him in motion, had abandoned him to nothingness, and now, like a child displaced by a newcomer, he scarcely knew what had happened to him.

He said: "Was happy to help the dear boy."

"You'd never acted before, had you?"

"Never, dear girl, never."

"What did you do before the war? Had you a job of any sort?"

He looked slightly affronted by the question and protested: "I had m'remittance, you know."

She supposed he lived off a show of wealth: which was as good a confidence trick as any.

Conscious of her disapproval, he tried to improve things: "I did do a little work now and then. I mean, when I was a bit short of the ready."

"What sort of work?"

He shifted about under this enquiry. His foot began to shake again. "Sold cars for a bit," he said. "Only the best cars, of course: Rolls-Royces, Bentleys . . . M'own old girl's an Hispano-Suiza. Finest cars in the world. Must get her back. Give you a run in her."

"What else did you do?"

"Sold pictures, bric-à-brac . . ."

"Really?" Harriet was interested. "Do you know about pictures?"

"Can't say I do, dear girl. Don't claim to be a professional. Helped a chap out now and then. Had a little flat in Clarges Street. Would hang up a picture, put out a bit of bric-à-brac, pick up some well-heeled gudgeon, indicate willingness to sell. 'Your poor old Yaki's got to part with family treasure.' You know the sort of thing. Not work, really. Just a little side-line." He spoke as though describing a respected way of life, then, as his shifting eye caught hers, his whole manner suddenly disintegrated. He struggled upright in his seat and, with head hanging, gazing down into his empty glass he mumbled: "Expecting m'remittance any day now. Don't worry. Going to pay back every penny I owe . . ."

They were both relieved to hear Guy letting himself into the flat. He entered the room, smiling broadly as though he were bringing Harriet some delightful surprise. "You remember Toby Lush?" he said.

"It's wonderful to see you again! Wonderful!" Toby said, gazing at Harriet, his eyes bulging with excited admiration, giving the impression that theirs was some eagerly awaited reunion.

She had met him once before and barely remembered him. She did her best to respond but had never been much impressed by him. He was in the middle twenties, heavy-boned and clumsy in movement. His features were pronounced, his skin coarse, yet his face seemed to be made of something too soft and pliable for its purpose.

Sucking at his pipe, he turned to Guy and jerked out convulsively: "You know what she always makes me think of? Those lines of Tennyson: 'She walks in beauty like the night of starless climes and something skies.' "

"Byron," said Guy.

"Oh, crumbs!" Toby clapped a hand over his eyes in exaggerated shame. "I'm always doing it. It's not that I don't know: I don't remember." He suddenly noticed Yakimov and crying: "Hello, hello, hello," he rushed forward with outstretched hand.

Harriet went into the kitchen to tell Despina there would be a guest for luncheon. When she returned, Toby, with many irrelevant guffaws, was describing the situation in the Transylvanian capital from which he had evacuated himself.

Although Cluj had been under Rumanian rule for twenty years, it was still a Hungarian city. The citizens only waited for the despised regime to end.

"It's not that they're pro-German," he said, "they just want the Hunks back. They shut their eyes to the fact that when the Hunks come the Huns'll follow. If you point it out, they make excuses. A woman I know, a Jewess, said: 'We don't want it for ourselves, we want it for our children.' They think it'll happen any day now."

Toby was standing by the open French window, the dazzle of out-of-doors limning his ragged outline. "I can tell you," he said, "the only Englishman among that lot, I had to keep my wits about me. And what do you think happened before I left? The Germans installed a Gauleiter – a Count Frederich von Flügel. 'Get out while the going's good,' I told myself."

"Freddi von Flügel!" Yakimov broke in in delighted surprise. "Why, he's an old friend of mine. A dear old friend," He looked happily about him. "When I get the Hispano, we might all drive to Cluj and see Freddi. I'm sure he'd do us proud."

Toby gazed open-mouthed at Yakimov, then his shoulders shook as though giving some farcical imitation of laughter. "You're a joker," he said and Yakimov, though surprised, seemed gratified to be thought one.

While they were eating, Harriet asked Toby: "Will you remain in Bucharest?"

"If I can get some teaching," he said. "I'm a free-lancer, no organisation behind me. Came out on my own, drove the old bus all the way. Bit of an adventure. The fact is, if I don't work, I don't eat. Simple as that." He gazed at Guy, supplicant and inquiring. "Hearing you were short-staffed, I turned up on the doorstep."

The question of his employment had obviously been raised already, for Guy merely nodded and said: "I must see what Inchcape says before taking anyone on."

Harriet looked again at Toby, considering him not so much as a teacher as a possible help in time of trouble. She had noticed his heavy brogues. He was wearing grey flannel trousers bagged at the knees and a sagging tweed jacket, much patched with leather. It was the uniform of most young English civilians and yet on him it looked like a disguise. 'The man's man!' The last time he had arrived in Bucharest, during one of the usual invasion scares, he had fled from Cluj in a panic: but she was less inclined to condemn panic since she had experienced it herself. How would he react to a sudden Guardist attack? All this pipe-sucking masculinity, this casual costume, would surely require him, when the time came, to prove himself 'a good man in a tight corner'. She looked at Guy, who was saying: "If Inchcape agrees, I might be able to give you twenty hours a week. That should keep you going."

Toby ducked his head gratefully, then asked: "What about lectures?"

"I would only need you to teach."

"I used to lecture at Cluj – Mod. Eng. Lit. I must say, I enjoy giving the odd lecture." Toby, from behind his hair and moustache gazed at Guy like an old sheepdog confident he would be put to use. Harriet felt sorry for him. He probably imagined, as others had done before him, that Guy was easily persuadable. The truth was, that in authority Guy could be inflexible. Even if he needed a lecturer, he would not choose one who mistook Byron for Tennyson.

"The other day," Yakimov suddenly spoke, slowly and sadly, out of his absorption in his food, "I was thinking, strange as it must seem, I haven't seen a banana for about a year." He sighed at the thought.

The Pringles had grown too used to him to react to his chance observations, but Toby rocked about, laughing as though Yakimov's speech had been one of hilarious impropriety.

Yakimov modestly explained: "Used to be very fond of bananas."

When luncheon was over and Yakimov had retired to his room Harriet looked for Toby's departure, but when he eventually made a move Guy detained him saying: "Stay to tea. On my way back to the University, I'll take you to the Bureau to meet Inchcape."

Harriet went into the bedroom. Determined to incite him to act while the power to incite was in her, she called Guy in, shut the door of the sitting-room and said: "You must speak to Yakimov. You must tell him to go."

Mystified by the urgency of her manner and unwilling to obey, he said: "All right, but not now."

"Yes, *now*." She stood between him and the door. "Go in and see him. It's too risky having him here with Sasha around. He must go."

"Well, if you say so." Guy's agreement was tentative, a playing for time. He paused, then said: "It would be better if you spoke to him."

"You brought him here, you must get rid of him."

"It's a difficult situation. I was glad to have him here while he was rehearsing. He worked hard and helped to make the show a success. In a way, I owe him something. I can't just tell him to go now the show's over, but it's different for you. You can be firm with him."

"What you mean is, if there's anything unpleasant to be done, you prefer that I should do it?"

Cornered, he reacted with rare exasperation: "Look here, darling, I have other things to worry about. Sasha is up on the roof. Yakimov's not likely to see him and probably wouldn't be interested if he did see him. So why worry? Now I must go back and talk to Toby."

She let him go, knowing nothing more would be gained by talk. And she realised it would always be the same. If action had to be taken, she would have to be the one to take it. That was the price to be paid for a relationship that gave her more freedom than she had bargained for. Freedom, after all, was not a basic concept of marriage. As for Guy, he did not want a private life: he chose to live publicly. She said to herself: "He's crassly selfish" – an accusation that would have astounded his admirers.

She went over to the window and leant out. Looking down the drop of nine floors to the cobbles below, she thought of the kitten that had fallen from the balcony five months before. The scene dissolved into a marbling of blue and gold as her eyes filled with tears, and she suffered again the outrageous grief with which she had learnt of the kitten's death. It had been her kitten. It had acknowledged her. It did not bite her. She was the only one who had no fear of it. Possessed by memory of the little red-golden flame of a cat that for a few weeks had hurtled itself, a ball of fur and claws, about the flat, she wept: "My kitten. My poor kitten," feeling she had loved it as she could never love anything or anybody. Guy, after all, did not permit himself to be loved in this way.

She did not return to the room until she heard Despina taking in the tea things. Toby was saying: "But someone's certain to march in here sooner or later. I suppose the Legation'll give us proper warning?"

Guy did not know and did not seem much to care. He said:

"The important thing is not to panic. We must keep the school going."

Toby ducked his head in vehement agreement. "Still," he said, "one must keep the old weather eye open."

Yakimov had appeared for tea in his tattered brocade dressing-gown and when Guy and Toby went off to see Inchcape there he still was, his apprehensions forgotten, comfortably eating his way through the cakes and sandwiches that were left. Well, here was her opportunity to say: "You have been living on top of us since Easter. I've had enough of you. Please pack your bags and go." At which Yakimov, with his most pitiful expression, would ask: "But where can poor Yaki go?" There had been no answer to that question four months before, and there was no answer now. He had exhausted his credit in Bucharest. No one would take him in. If she wanted to get rid of him, she would have to pack his bags herself and lock him out. And if she did that, he would probably sit on the doorstep until Guy brought him back in again.

When he had emptied the plates he stretched and sighed: "Think I'll take a bath." He went, and she had still said nothing. Knowing herself no more capable than Guy of throwing Yakimov out, she had thought of a different move. She would go and see Sasha. The boy probably imagined that they, like the diplomats, were outside Rumanian law. She could explain to him that by shelter-ing him Guy ran the same risk as anyone else. Then what would Sasha do?

The problem of their responsibility lay between desperation and desperation. The only loophole was the possibility that Sasha could think of a friend who might shelter him, perhaps a Jewish school-friend. Or there was his stepmother, who was claiming maintenance from the Drucker fortune. Somebody surely would take him in.

She went out to the kitchen. Despina was on the fire-escape, bawling down to other servants who had a free hour or so before it was time to prepare dinner. Feeling anomalous in these regions, Harriet slipped past her and started to ascend the iron ladder, but Despina missed nothing. "That's right," she called out. "Visit the poor boy. He's lonely up there."

Despina had adopted Sasha. Although Despina had been told that he must not come into the flat, Harriet had several times heard them laughing together in the kitchen. Despina scoffed at her fears, saying she could pass the boy off to anyone as her relative. Sasha was settling into a routine of life here and would soon, if undisturbed, become, like Yakimov, an unmovable part of the household.

The roof, high above its neighbours, was in the full light of the lowering sun. The sun was still very warm. Heat not only poured down on to the concrete but rose from it.

A row of wooden huts, like bathing-boxes, stood against the northern parapet, numbered one for each flat. Harriet, as she reached the roof-level, could see Sasha sitting outside his hut, holding a piece of stick which he had been throwing for a dog. The dog, a rough, white mongrel, apparently lived up here.

As soon as he saw her, Sasha got to his feet while the dog remained expectant, swaying a tail like a dirty feather.

She explained her visit by saying: "How are you managing up here? Is Despina looking after you?"

"Oh, yes." He was eagerly reassuring, adding thanks for all that was done for him. The fact of his presence being a danger to them seemed not to have occurred to him.

While he talked she looked beyond him through the open door of the hut where he was living. The hut had no window and was ventilated by a hole in the door. On the floor was a straw pallet that Despina must have borrowed for him, a blanket, some books Guy had brought up and a stub of candle.

Before she left England she would have believed it impossible for a human being to survive through the freezing winter, the torrid summer, in a cell like this. She had discovered in Rumania that there were millions to whom such shelter would be luxury. She took a step towards it but, repelled by the interior smell and heat, came to a stop saying: "It's very small."

Sasha smiled as though it were his place to apologise. He had been here only a few days but he was already putting on weight. When she had seen him on the night of his reappearance, she had been repelled by his abject squalor. Now, clean, wearing a shirt and trousers Guy had given him, the edge of fear gone from his face, his hair beginning to show like a shadow over his head, he was already the boy she had first met in the Drucker flat.

He was rather an ugly boy with his long nose, close-set eyes and long drooping body, but there was an appeal about his extreme gentleness of manner, which on their first meeting had made her think of some nervous animal grown meek in captivity. Because of this, he seemed completely familiar to her.

Feeling no restraint with him, she put out her hand and said: "Let us sit on the wall," and jumping up, she settled herself on the low parapet that surrounded the roof. From here she could see almost the whole extent of the city, the roofs gleaming through a heat-mist that was beginning to grow dense and golden with evening. Sasha came and leant against the wall beside her. She asked him what he passed for among the servants who slept in the other huts.

He said: "Despina says I come from her village."

He looked nothing like a peasant, but he might be the son of some Jewish tallyman. Anyway, no one, it seemed, took much notice of him. Despina said the kitchen quarters of Bucharest harboured thousands of deserters.

"How long had you been in Bucharest when we met you?" she asked.

"Two nights." He told her that he had separated from his company in Czernowitz and stowed away in a freight train that brought him to the capital. On the night of his arrival, he had slept under a market stall near the station, but had been turned out soon after midnight by some beggars whose usual sleeping place it was. The next night he had tried to sleep in the park, but there had been one of the usual spy scares on. The police, in their zeal, had tramped about all night, forcing him repeatedly to move his position.

He had not known what had happened to his family. When in Bessarabia, he had written to his aunts but received no reply. When he reached Bucharest, he had looked up at the windows of the family flat and seeing the curtains changed, realised the Druckers were not there. In the streets he had caught sight of people he knew, but in his fear of re-arrest dared approach no one until he saw Guy.

While he talked, he glanced shyly aside at her, smiling, all the misery gone from his gaze.

She said: "You know that your family have left Rumania?"

"Guy told me." If he knew they had taken flight immediately, without a backward glance for him or his father, he did not seem much concerned.

She decided the time had come to mention the possibility of his finding another shelter. She said: "Your stepmother is still here, of course. Don't you think she could help you? She might be willing to let you live with her."

He whispered: "Oh, no," startled and horrified by the suggestion.

"She wouldn't hurt you, would she? She wouldn't give you away?"

"Please don't tell her anything about me."

His tone was a complete rejection of his stepmother. So much for her. Then what about the possible friends? She said "You must have known a lot of people in Bucharest. Isn't there anyone who would give you a better hiding-place than this?"

He explained that, having been at an English public school, he had no friends of long standing here. She asked, what about his University acquaintances? He simply shook his head. He had known people, but not well. There seemed to be no one on whom he could impose himself now. Jews did not make friends easily. They were suspicious and cautious in this anti-Semitic society, and Sasha had been enclosed by a large family. The Druckers formed their own community, one which depended on Drucker's power for its safety. His arrest had been the signal for flight. If they had hesitated, they might all have suffered.

Watching him, wondering what they were to do with him, Harriet caught Sasha's glance and saw her questions had disturbed him. He had again the fearful, wary look of the hunted, and she knew she was no better than Guy at displacing the homeless. Indeed, she was worse for, unlike Guy, she had been resolved and had failed. When it came to a battle of human needs, her resolution did not count for much.

Glancing away from her, Sasha saw the dog, stick in mouth, patiently awaiting his attention. He put out his hand to it.

The extreme gentleness of his gesture moved her. She suddenly felt his claim on her and knew it was the claim of her lost red kitten, and of all the animals to whom she had given her love in childhood because there had been no one else who wanted it. She wondered why Yakimov had not moved her in this way. Was it because he lacked the quality of innocence?

She said to Sasha: "There's someone living with us in the flat, a Prince Yakimov. We have to keep him for the moment, he has nowhere else to go, but I don't trust him. You must be careful. Don't let him see you." She slid down from the wall, saying as she left him: "This is a wretched hut. It's the best we can do for the moment. If Yakimov leaves – and I hope he will – you can have his room."

Sasha smiled after her, his fears forgotten, content like a stray animal that, having found a resting-place, has no complaint to make.

Next morning only *Timpul* mentioned the "trickle of riffraff in green shirts that provoked laughter in the Calea Victoriei". By evening this attitude had changed. Every paper reported the march with shocked disapproval, for the King had announced that were it repeated the military would be called out to fire on the marchers.

The Guardists went under cover again, but this, people said, was the result not of the king's threat but an address made to the Guardists by their chief, Horia Sima, who was newly returned from exile in Germany. He advised them to leave off their green shirts and sing *"Capitanul"* only in their hearts. The time for action was not yet come.

Their leading spirits again hung unoccupied about the streets, sombre, shabby, malevolent, awaiting the call. These men, whom it seemed only Harriet had noticed in the spring, suddenly became visible and significant to everyone, giving rise to fresh excitements and apprehensions, and renewed terror among the Jews.

PART TWO

The Captain

6

THE NEXT TIME HARRIET WENT UP to see Sasha she took with her a bowl of apricots and a copy of *L'Indépendence Romaine*. The paper contained the date on which Drucker's trial would begin, an announcement overshadowed by the news that the Hungarian premier and his foreign minister had been granted an audience with the Führer. What were the Hungarians after?

Harriet, eating her supper alone, made her way through the leading article on Transylvania: "*le berceau de la Nation, le coeur de la Patrie*". No mention was made of Hungary's old claim to this territory, but at the end of the article asked: Had the Rumanian people not suffered enough in their efforts to preserve Balkan peace? Was yet another sacrifice to be demanded of them? And answered: No, yet again no. If rumours of such a sacrifice were circulating they must be instantly suppressed.

The Pringles had been invited to dine that evening with a Jewish couple who, granted a visa to the United States, wanted to know how to conduct themselves in the English-speaking world. Invitations of this sort were frequent. Though Guy knew no more about the States than he had learnt from American films, he was always happy to give advice, but Harriet was becoming bored with listening to it. She said: "You go. They don't really want me," for at the back of her mind was the intention to see Sasha again.

As she climbed up the iron ladder to roof-level, she was startled by the grandeur of the sky from which plumes of puce and crimson had been pulled downwards by the setting sun. The concrete glowed like marble, but for all the richness of the light the air was heavy, almost thunderous, though thunder was rare here.

Sasha was sitting on the parapet, an intent and solitary figure, scribbling on something. As she stepped up on to the roof, she saw him lift his head and stare towards the cathedral which, built on high ground, overlooked the city. Its golden domes were afire now and the whole building stood like an embossed enamel against the luminous darkness of the lower sky.

At the sound of her step, he jerked his head round and his face brightened at the sight of company, so she ceased to feel any need to account for her visit.

She asked where the dog was.

He said: "It didn't live here. Despina was keeping it for someone. Now it has gone home."

"Do any of the servants sleep on the roof?"

"No, there's no one but me."

As she had thought, these advertised 'second servant rooms' were merely an attempt to smarten the jerry-built, ill-planned block. No one needed or could afford the extra staff.

She felt sorry for the boy alone up here. She put the apricots on the parapet and said: "Those are for you," then she looked at his sketch of the cathedral done on the concrete with a lump of rough charcoal Despina had found for him somewhere. She said: "It's quite good."

"Is it?" he asked eagerly. "You really like it?" so surprised and trusting of her judgement that she felt ashamed of her unthinking praise, and looked at it again. It was boldly done, the rough surface of the parapet giving the lines a comic distortion.

"Yes, it is good," she confirmed her own judgement and he smiled in naïve pleasure.

"If you like this," he said, "you'd like some things I saw in Bessarabia. They were super."

As she hoisted herself on to the wall, she asked: "Where were you in Bessarabia?"

He had been on the frontier, in a fortress that was as bare, cold and ill-lit as it would have been in the Middle Ages. There was nothing at all in the district but a village that comprised two rows of desolate huts with a pitted mud track running between. The whole area had been raided so often, it was like the environs of a volcano: only the most desperate would make a home there. In winter it had been swept by gales and blizzards and in spring, when the snow melted, it became a quagmire.

"The village was jolly queer," he said. "All the people living there were Jews."

"Why did they live there, of all places?"

"I don't know. Perhaps they'd been driven out of everywhere else."

She had imagined she would have difficulty in persuading him to talk about his experiences, but it seemed he had already put them at a distance. He had adopted Guy and Harriet in place of his family so, feeling protected again, he could chat away as though nothing had ever happened in his life to check his confidence. While he talked, she wondered at the simplicity of a nature able so rapidly to regain itself.

"And what about these things you saw? Were they drawings?"

"No. Paintings. They were shop-signs."

He described the Jews of the villages – the men gaunt wraiths in their tattered caftans, the women wearing black woollen wigs over heads shaven because they suffered from some skin disease which had died out elsewhere. They were sly and obsequious, and Sasha, who had always known Jews who were the richest members of the community, had been amazed to find any as debased as these.

"They couldn't even read," he said. "They were terribly poor – but they could do these paintings."

"What were they like?"

"Oh – sort of fantastic. People, animals, and things in the most super colours. I'd always go and look at them when I could."

He spoke as though the shop signs had been his only entertainment and she asked: "Did you have any friends in the army?"

"I knew a boy in the village. His father kept the place where the soldiers went to drink ţuică. It was just a room, very dirty, but all the soldiers said the man was an awful crook and making lots of money."

Sasha described the boy, thin, white-faced, in a black skull-cap, knickerbockers that fastened below the knee and black stockings and boots. Tufts of red down were appearing on his glazed white cheeks, and red ritual curls hung before his ears. "You never saw anyone look so funny," Sasha said.

"But all the Orthodox Jews look like that," Harriet said. "Surely you've seen them down the Dâmboviţa?"

Sasha shook his head. He had never been near the ghetto area. His aunts would not allow him to go there.

"Did you speak to the boy?" Harriet asked.

"I tried, but it wasn't much good. He only spoke Yiddish and Ukrainian, and he was very shy. Sometimes he'd run away when he saw me in the street."

"But hadn't you friends among the soldiers?"

"Well . . ." Sasha sat silent for some moments, staring down and rubbing the palm of his hand on the rough edge of the wall. "Yes, I did have a friend." He spoke as though making an admission painful to him. "He was a Jew, too. He was called Marcovitch."

"Did he run away with you?"

Sasha shook his head, then after a moment said: "He died."

"How did he die?"

Sasha said nothing for some minutes, and she saw there was an area of experience, unnaturally imposed upon his natural innocence, to which he would not willingly revert. She said persuasively: "Tell me what happened."

"Well . . ." He spoke casually, like one old in knowledge. "You know what it is like here. If anything happens, they say: 'It's the Jews.' In the army it was the same. They blamed the Jews for Bessarabia. They said we called in the Russians because of the new laws against us. As though we could!" He looked at her and laughed. "Just silly, of course." His self-conscious attempt at sophistication made her realise how young he was.

"Did they ill-treat you?" she asked.

"Not very much. Some of them were quite decent, really. It was beastly for everyone, being conscripted. The barracks were full of bugs. When I first went there I was bitten so much, I looked as though I had measles. And every day maize or beans, but not much. There was money for food, but the officers kept it."

"Is that why you ran away?"

"No." He picked up his charcoal and began darkening the lines of his drawing that had started to disappear with the light. "It was because of Marcovitch."

"Who died? When did he die?"

"After we were ordered out of Bessarabia. We were on the train and he went down the corridor and he didn't come back. I asked everyone, but they said they hadn't seen him. While we were waiting at Czernowitz – we stayed on the platform three days because there were no trains – they were saying a body had been found on the railway-line half-eaten by wolves. Then one of the men said to me: 'You heard what happened to your friend, Marcovitch? That was his body. You be careful, you're a Jew, too.' And I knew they'd thrown him out of the train. I was afraid. It could happen to me. So in the night, when they were all asleep, I ran down the line and hid in a goods train. It took me to Bucharest."

While they were talking, the sound of the last post came thin and clear from the palace yard. The sunset clouds had stretched and narrowed and faded in the sky, leaving a zenith of clear turquoise in which a few stars were appearing. The square below was lit not only by its lamps but by a reflection from the sky that was like a sheen on water.

She thought she had made Sasha talk enough and Guy might soon be back. She slid down from the wall and said: "I must go, but I'll come again." Before she left, she handed Sasha the paper. "It says your father's trial starts on August 14th. The sooner it is over, the better. After all, he may be acquitted."

Sasha took the paper, which could not be read in this light, and said: "Yes," but his agreement was simply politeness. He knew as well as she did that the law required Drucker's conviction before his oil holdings could be forfeit to the Crown. What hope then of an acquittal?

As she set out across the roof area, Sasha went to his hut. When she turned to descend, she could see he had already lit his candle and, kneeling, was bent over the paper that was spread on the ground before him.

7

YAKIMOV SAW THE GREAT YELLOW CAR outside the Legation as soon as he turned into the road. The hood was down, hidden beneath a panel, so there was nothing to break the long, fine line from nose to tail. His eyes filled with tears. "The old girl herself," he said. As he added: "I love her," he scarcely knew whether he referred to the Hispano-Suiza or to Dollie, who had given it to him.

The car was now seven years old, but he had taken care of it as he had never taken care of himself. He opened the bonnet and examined the engine. When he closed it, he patted the stork that flew down-drooping wings from the radiator cap. He walked round the car, noting that the body was dusty but no worse, and the pigskin leather of the seats was in "good shape". "Bless the old Jugs," he thought. "They haven't treated her so badly."

He spent so long rejoicing over the car that Foxy Leverett noticed him from a window and came out to give him the keys.

"She's a beaut," said Foxy.

Even during the days of triumph in *Troilus*, Yakimov had not received much attention from Foxy, who accorded the same off-hand goodwill to everyone. Now, acknowledging a compeer in the owner of a Hispano-Suiza, he became voluble: "Went like a bird. The worst road in Europe, but she did a steady sixty. If I hadn't got the Dion-Bouton, I'd make you an offer."

"Wouldn't sell her for a king's ransom, dear boy," Yakimov said, adding with a hint of hauteur: "In this part of the world I'd never get what she's worth. The chassis alone cost two and a half thou, sterling. Body by Fernandez. Wonderful work. Had one before this. Lovely job. Body built all of tulip wood. You should have seen it. Had m'man then, of course. He kept it like a piece of Chippendale."

Yakimov talked for some time, too elated to feel the sweltering sunlight. Foxy, his hair and moustache the colour of marigolds, his eyes as blue as the eyes of a china doll, turned peony-pink under the heat. When Yakimov paused he cut short his reminiscences by saying: "I put two hundred litres in the tank at Predea. There's plenty left."

"I'm in your debt, dear boy." Yakimov became more subdued. "Don't know what I owe, but it'll all be settled when m'remittance shows up."

"That's all right," said Foxy.

His nonchalance prompted Yakimov to try his luck: "Like to get her cleaned, dear boy. Wonder if you could spare a thou?"

Foxy's moustache twitched, but, trapped and making the best of it, he pulled out some notes and handed one over.

"*Dear boy!*" Yakimov took it gratefully. "Y'know," he said, "if you'd get me a C.D. plate, there's no end to the stuff we could run in and out. And not only currency, mind you. There's a demand here for rhino horn – aphrodisiac, y'know. You can get it in Turkey. And hashish . . ."

With a guffaw of derisive laughter, Foxy turned on his heel and shot back into the chancellery.

Yakimov climbed into the car and started it up – the Hispano was an extravagance: despite its size and power it was designed to seat only two persons – and as he gazed along the six-foot bonnet, he saw his status restored and his old glory returned to him. He had not driven for eleven months. He took himself to the Chaussée for a trial run. Discomposed at first by the delirium howl of passing cars, he steadily regained his old confidence and felt the impulse to outstrip them. He rounded the fountain at the extreme end of the Chaussée, then, returning, pressed down on the accelerator and saw with satisfaction that he was touching ninety. Unperturbed by the klaxons that bayed about him like a hungry pack, he swung into the square, circled round it and stopped outside the Pringles' block. Having had no tea, he was, he realised, a trifle peckish.

After tea he dressed in such items of decent clothing as remained to him. In the Athénée Palace that morning, he had noticed the main rooms were being decorated for a reception.

The Rumanians these days were in a buoyant mood, for the Hungarian ministers had left Munich apparently having achieved nothing. When this was reported, Hadjimoscos soberly told his circle: "The Führer said to them: 'Do not forget, I am Rumania's father, too.' Such a sentiment is very gratifying, don't you think? Baron Steinfeld tells me it is thanks to the fine fellows in the Iron Guard that we stand so high in German favour."

To Yakimov the Guardists were merely the murderers of Calinescu. He had been amused by the fact they claimed still to be led by a young man two years in his grave. He seized upon this mention of them to make a joke: "I take it, dear boy, you refer to the non-existent members of the totally extinguished party which is led by a ghost?"

Hadjimoscos stared coldly at Yakimov a moment before he said: "Such quips are not *de rigueur* in these times," and paused impressively before adding: "They are not even safe."

Yakimov was used to Hadjimoscos' changes of mood and had to accept them. That morning he had listened in silence while the reception was discussed with a respect he found bewildering in view of the fact no one present had been invited. It was to be an Iron Guard reception, held in defiance of the King, to promulgate the growing power of the party.

"Under the circumstances," Hadjimoscos said, with knowing complacency, "it is not surprising that people like us, members of the old aristocracy, have received no *official* invitation, but I am confident it will be indicated to us that our presence is desired."

Yakimov was surprised that any sort of gathering could be given in defiance of the King, but told himself: "Hadji is pretty cute. Hadji knows which way the wind blows," and that evening, although he had not been invited, he prepared to attend the reception himself.

The hotel was only a hundred yards away, but when he set out he took the Hispano as an earnest of past opulence, a visa to better times. As he drew up outside the hotel, Baron Steinfeld was arriving with Princess Teodorescu, both in full evening dress, and he was a trifle disconcerted, not having realised the occasion merited such a rig, but was gratified to see the Baron eyeing the Hispano with interest.

The Princess had not recognised Yakimov since last September, when Hadjimoscos had brought him to her party; but now she lifted the tail of one of her silver-fox furs and waggled it playfully as she called to him: "Ah, *cher prince*, you have been a long time out of sight." Yakimov sped towards her and kissed her hand in its rose-coloured glove. The Princess was noted for the directness of her approach and now, without preamble, she said: "*Cher prince*, I want so much tickets for the Drucker trial."

In the failing light, the runnels of her handsome, haggard face seemed filled with ink. Her eyes, within their heavily darkened lids, were fixed avidly on Yakimov as she explained: "I received, of course, my two-three tickets, but always my friends are asking me: 'Please get for me a ticket.' What can I do? Now you, *mon prince*, are *journalist*. You have many tickets, isn't that so? Do for me a little favour. Give me two-three tickets!"

The tickets for the trial had been allotted to persons of importance, who now were selling them for enormous sums to persons of less importance. Yakimov, needless to say, had none, but he smiled happily. "Dear girl, of course, I'll do what I can. 'Fraid I've given mine away, but I'll get more. There are ways and means. Leave it to your Yaki."

"But how kind!" said the Princess and as a mark of favour she off-loaded her foxes into Yakimov's arms. Delighted by this hot and heavy burden, he said: "We must get a lead for these, dear girl," and the Princess smiled.

As they strolled to the hotel, the Baron said: "It is remarkable, don't you think, that the Germans have not yet made their invasion of the British Isles?" His tone suggested that it was not only remarkable but unfortunate. When Yakimov said nothing, the Baron went on: "Still, there are grave newses from England. They say that racing under Jockey Club rules has been given up. Clearly all is not well there." He turned appealingly to Yakimov. "Surely it is time to end this foolish disagreement between our great countries. You are a prince of old Russia: cannot you induce your English friends to turn their armours against the Soviets?"

Yakimov looked as though he could, but did not feel he should. "Don't want to start any more trouble, do we?" he said. They had reached the red carpet and then he was able to change the subject. "Bit of a do on, I see."

"A reception given by the Iron Guard leaders," said Steinfeld. "An important occasion. Horia Sima is to be present."

The vestibule was banked with carnations, tuberoses and ferns. A notice informed the public that only ticket holders would be admitted to the main salon, which could be seen through the glass doors already very crowded. Hoping to identify himself with the occasion, Yakimov said: "I hear that my dear old friend Freddie von Flügel has been appointed Gauleiter in Cluj. He has asked me up to stay with him."

"Gauleiter? Indeed! A position of power," said Steinfeld, but the Princess was less impressed: "Surely," she said, "you are an Englishman? Is it correct, in time of war, to visit the enemy?"

The Baron brushed this query aside: "People in our position can dispense with such *convenances*," he said, and Yakimov agreed with enthusiasm.

They were approaching the salon entrance where some young men stood on guard. Yakimov, keeping close to his companions, still had hope of entering under their auspices, but the Princess was having none of that. He had been rewarded enough. She stopped, took her furs out of his arms, and said: "Well, toot-el-ee-ooh, as you English say. Do not forget my two-three tickets," and she handed the furs to Steinfeld. Yakimov knew himself dismissed.

He watched as the couple reached the salon entrance. There they were stopped and made to produce their invitations. There was no sign of a buffet inside and the guests were drinking wine. Deciding the "do" looked a pretty poor one, Yakimov went into the English Bar.

At this moment the Pringles, crossing the square, heard behind them the furious and persistent hooting of an old-fashioned motor-horn. They moved to the pavement. The hooting persisted. Supposing it was some sort of anti-British demonstration, they did not look round. Britain was rumoured to be trying to sell her oil shares to Russia and the Rumanian Cabinet had declared it would take steps to prevent any such perfidy. Anti-British feeling was growing stronger.

The hooting, drawing nearer, demanded attention, and the Pringles turned to see an old, mud-coloured car being driven at them by Toby Lush. Toby grinned. Inchcape had approved his appointment and he had started work at the University. He stopped the car. Confident of welcome, he thrust out his disordered, straw-coloured head and shouted "Hello, there!"

"Why, hello," said Guy.

Beside Toby sat Dubedat. Between the two assistant teachers there had sprung up one of those close, immediate friendships that puzzle everyone but the pair concerned. Harriet had not only been puzzled by it, but rather annoyed. Seeing Toby as a comrade in danger, she had been prepared to accept him into her circle, but she was not prepared to accept Dubedat.

Sitting now in the sunken car seat, Dubedat did not greet the Pringles but stared straight ahead, his profile, with its thin hooked nose and receding chin, taut and disapproving as ever.

They had stopped in the centre of the square, beside the statue of the old king who rode a horse too big for him. Cars were parked round the pediment. Toby said: "I'll leave the jalopy here and stretch my legs."

The Pringles had been invited by David to the English Bar and it was evident the two assistant teachers were coming with them. Harriet looked at Guy and as he avoided her eye she knew he had invited Toby to join them. If she had asked him "Why?" he would probably have replied. "Why not?" Surely anyone would agree that it was better to drink with several people than with just one or two?

Guy, delighted to have more company, walked ahead with Toby while she, left, to follow with Dubedat, found herself wondering, not for the first time, whether life with Guy was not more often an irritant than a pleasure.

She glanced at Dubedat, noticing a smile lingering round his lips – "like the grime left by bath-water," she told herself – and felt sure he was aware of her irritation. That irritated her more. He had nothing to say. She did not attempt to break the silence.

Dubedat, an elementary school-teacher from Liverpool, had been "thumbing" his way through Galicia when war broke out and been given a lift in one of the refugee cars that streamed down to Bucharest when Poland collapsed. Describing himself as a "simple-lifer", he had gone about Bucharest in shorts and open-neck shirt until the winter wind forced him into a sheepskin jacket.

His appearance had improved since those early days. He had been teaching at the University for nearly a year now and as a result of prosperity had given up the "simple-life" outfit, and was wearing a suit of khaki twill. It looked very grimy. He no longer lived in the Dâmboviţa area, but had rented a modern flat in the centre of the city. Toby had moved in with him. Guy used to excuse Dubedat, saying that his old lodging did not give him opportunity to wash, but it seemed to Harriet that his personal aroma was much as it used to be. Or was it merely an emanation of her own dislike of him?

Ahead, Toby, moving with exaggerated strides, was giving crows of nervous laughter. Despite the heat, he still wore his tweed jacket with its patches of leather. As he walked, he scuffed his brogues in the dust, one shoulder drawn up, his fists bagging out his pockets. She heard him say: "Don't want to be a bottle-washer all my life."

"Even in these times," Guy replied, "we must expect a lecturer to have a degree."

Dubedat, beside Harriet, snorted his private disgust at this statement.

They had reached the hotel, where the striped awning was out, the carpet down and a gigantic Rumanian flag hung the length of the façade. People had gathered round to watch events. A lorry arrived and from it jumped a dozen young men in dark suits, who at once began pushing back the docile onlookers and forming a cordon of six on either side of the pavement. Before anyone could inquire into this behaviour, a Mercedes drew up and a man alighted – a small, lean man of unusual appearance. The cordon at once flung up arms in a fascist salute, sharp, businesslike and un-Rumanian, and the new arrival responded, holding the salute dramatically for some moments, his head thrown back so all might see his hollow, bone-pale face and lank, black hair.

Guy whispered: "I believe that's Horia Sima."

Whoever he was, he was clearly an intellectual and a fanatic, someone totally different from the lenient, self-indulgent Rumanian males now strolling in the Calea Victoriei. He dropped his arm, then strode to the swing door. He gave it a push, treating it as an unimportant impediment, but the door was not to be coerced. It creaked round slowly and he was forced, in spite of himself, to shuffle in at its pace. The young men, following after, did no better.

Harriet, as she watched, could hear Toby gasping nervously at his pipe. "Never seen the like," he said, The English party, much sobered, entered the hotel hall as the Guardists went striding into the main salon.

David was in the hall. Guy asked him: "Was that Horia Sima?"

David nodded. "He's joining the Cabinet. That's the excuse for the reception, of course, but it's really a gesture of defiance. I wonder how His Majesty's going to take it." David gave Dubedat an unenthusiastic "Hello," then looked blankly at Toby whom he had never seen before.

Guy introduced them, saying: "Toby comes from Cluj. I thought you might be interested to hear what's going on there."

"Oh!" said David, and he said nothing more.

They went into the bar, where Guy bought a round of drinks.

Toby had evidently heard of David, for he kept close to him, and with eyes bulging excitedly asked: "Is it true they're starting concentration camps in the Carpathians?"

"I've never seen them myself," David said, keeping his gaze on his glass.

Toby continued to ask questions about the country's situation and its dangers, receiving answers that were brief and discouraging, while Dubedat stood on one side, obviously annoyed by Toby's eagerness and David's lack of it.

As soon as Guy entered the conversation, Dubedat took the opportunity to pluck at his friend's arm, at which Toby turned with a jerk and, seeing Dubedat's frown, asked in a fluster: "What is it, old soul? What's the matter?" Hissing through his teeth so he looked like an angry rat, Dubedat made a movement of the head that directed Toby to step aside with him. Puffing and spluttering in apprehension, Toby let himself be led off.

"Where did you pick up that impossible ass?" David asked Guy.

Guy looked surprised. "He's working for me. He's not a bad chap."

David lowered his voice. "I've something to tell you. Klein has gone."

"He's left the country?"

"No one knows. He might have been arrested, but I don't think so. I think he's crossed the frontier into Bessarabia. There's a secret route over the Pruth: thousands are going, I'm told. Anyway, I doubt whether we'll ever see him again."

Guy nodded in a sad approval of this escape and Harriet thought of how Klein had several times advised her to wait and see the break-up of a country – "revolution, ruin, occupation by the enemy – all so interesting"; but he had not waited himself. She felt disconsolate at this flight, as though an ally had abandoned them.

While the others talked, she glanced around the bar, seeing, but avoiding seeing, Yakimov, who was with his Rumanian friends. Clarence was sitting alone at one of the tables. She had heard nothing from him since their evening in the park and now when she looked at him he avoided meeting her eye.

Something in the odd turn of his head made her think of those boys described by Klein who, violently raped during their first days in prison, had acquired a taste for the indignity and afterwards offered themselves to all comers. Clarence, too, had been raped. His spirit had been broken by physical violence. As Harriet made a move towards him his eyes slid sideways, his expression became furtively defensive as though at a threat of chastisement both feared and desired.

Galpin entered briskly, his girl-friend Wanda at his heels. He wore an air of waggish self-congratulation that meant news. Harriet returned to hear what he had to say.

The heat of the day hung clotted in the bar. Although Rumanian convention did not permit men to appear in any sort of undress, they might, in mid-summer, wear their jackets cape-fashion. In Hadjimoscos' group, only Yakimov was lax enough to do this. His tussore coat, hanging limp and frayed from his shoulder-bones, permitted his neighbours to note that the silk of his shirt had rotted away under the armpits. The shirt was a deep Indian yellow, and he wore with it not a tie but a neckcloth of maroon velvet. The neckcloth seemed to Hadjimoscos excessively daring and he had been brought to tolerate it only by the assurance that it came from the most expensive outfitters in Monte Carlo.

Hadjimoscos merely changed for the summer from a suit of dark wool to one of dark alpaca. He said he had never before spent a summer in Bucharest and he frequently described the heat as *incroyable*. That evening he was in low spirits, as were Palu and Horvatz. No one had indicated to them that their presence was desired at the reception. Yakimov had spent most of his thousand *lei* on drinks for his companions, but their gloom persisted. "It looked a pretty dull party to me," he said.

Ignoring Yakimov, Hadjimoscos moaned to Palu and Horvatz: "We may take it that we members of the old aristocracy are not in favour."

"Oh, I wouldn't say that," said Yakimov, "The Princess was invited."

For some reason this remark, intended to console, merely angered Hadjimoscos who turned on Yakimov, saying: "The Princess, I can assure you, was invited merely as the companion of Baron Steinfeld. Since his losses in Bessarabia the Baron has thrown himself heart and soul into the Nazi cause, with the result that, unlike us members of the old aristocracy, he is *très bien vu* with the Guard."

"Really, dear boy," Yakimov protested out of his bewilderment: "I don't know what you're all so worried about. Apparently these Guardists were put down by the King – a lot of them were shot or something. How could they suddenly become so impor-

tant? What do you care whether they invite you to their junket-
ings or not?"

"Believe me," Hadjimoscos said, "the day is fast coming when
those they do not recognise may as well be dead."

Impressed by the solemnity of Hadjimoscos' statement, Yakimov began for the first time to think seriously about the Iron
Guard. He remembered how, during his brief period as a journalist, he had, on Galpin's advice, written dispatches condemning in
violent language the murderers of Calinescu. The chief villain had
been someone called Horia Sima. The despatches had not been
allowed to leave the country. What had become of them? A chill
pang struck the pit of his stomach, and as he stood like the others
with an empty glass in his hand he began to feel as gloomy as they
did.

"Well, well," Galpin said throwing his thumb back over his
shoulder, "if that lot knew what I know, there'd be no reception
tonight."

Everyone looked expectantly at him.

David asked, smiling: "What's happened now?"

"The Rumanian ministers have been summoned to Salzburg –
the Hunks and Bulgars, too. Herr Hitler is ordering them to settle
their frontier problems."

"Is that all?" said Harriet.

"It's enough," said Galpin sharply: "What are Rumania's
frontier problems? Simply other people's demands. All she wants
is to hang on to what she's got. Now, you wait and see! There's
going to be trouble here."

David's smile had changed to a look of startled interest. "When
did you hear this?" he asked.

"A moment ago. The Cabinet's been summoned. I met my
scout in the square. He's got a contact in the palace. It's hot news,
but I needn't try to send it. The authorities are trying to keep it
secret. Look at them," he said, and they all looked through the
open door of the bar at the guests passing on their way to the
main salon. "The poor bastards! They think they've got on to the
band-wagon. They're calling it the New Dawn. And here's their
Führer once again demanding a sacrifice in the interests of Balkan
peace."

David sniggered into his glass. "Perhaps the Führer is not
finding world dictatorship so easy after all. I imagine, if he could

he'd shelve all these problems until the war was over, then settle them his own way. But Hungary and Bulgaria are not having that. They are demanding immediate payment for their support."

"What about Rumania?" Harriet asked.

"She's not in a position to demand anything."

Clarence had joined them to ask what the excitement was all about. When she told him that the Rumanians had been summoned to a conference at Salzburg, he shrugged slightly, having expected worse. She, too, felt that in a world so full of dangers those that did not immediately affect them could be put on one side.

He remained on the fringe of the group and Harriet, realising he was more dispirited than usual, said: "What's the matter?"

He looked up, responding at once to her sympathy: "Steffaneski left this morning. He's going to try to join Weygand. That's the last of my Poles."

"We'll all have to go sooner or later."

"He was my friend." Clarence hung his head, repudiating consolation.

Harriet said: "You have other friends." He did not reply but after a moment, nodding at Guy and David, he said: "They'll go on talking all night. Why don't you come and have supper with me?"

She recognised this as a peace offering and refused it regretfully: "David has invited us out, so I'm afraid . . ."

"Oh, don't apologise." Clarence turned his face away. "If you don't want to come, someone else will."

Harriet laughed. "Who for instance?" she asked.

Clarence sniffed and smirked, so she realised, not without a touch of pique, that he really had some substitute up his sleeve. She could see he was waiting for her to ask who it was. Instead she moved away from him, giving her attention elsewhere, and found herself listening to Dubedat, who had by now had several drinks handed to him.

Taciturn when sober, garrulous when drunk, he was keeping Toby away from the others with a stream of talk. His subject at the moment was poverty, his own poverty, a condition which he had once flaunted as a virtue.

Before the war he had climbed arduously into a scholarship worth £150 a year. He had become an elementary school-teacher. Remembering his description of the Dâmboviţa Jews as "the poorest of the poor and the only decent folk in this dirty, depraved, God-forsaken capital", Harriet realised that his attitude, like his dress, was changing. Now he was saying: "God, how I hate poverty. It's not only an evil, it's a disease and if you don't get rid of it, it becomes an incurable disease. It rots your guts. You become gutless. You crawl. You don't give a damn for yourself. Any way of escaping it is excusable. When you're poor you can only afford to mix with people as poor as yourself. If they're stupid, they bore you. If they're intelligent, they're discontented and depress you. So you never escape. Your nose is kept firmly down in the dirty water of reality. It's the greatest destructive force in the world, poverty. Half the world's intellect has been blunted or destroyed by it. None of us escape from it whole. Even the elephant hides are marked by it."

All this was spoken rapidly, in a hectoring tone that Harriet recognised as the tone in which he had played Thersites in Guy's production of *Troilus*. He had excelled in the part, and something of it seemed to have entered into him. Here, she thought, was a transformed Dubedat, a Dubedat who had found eloquence.

The main salon must have overflowed, for the guests could now be seen standing about in the hall. Soon the hall was also crowded. Suddenly the occupants of the bar were startled to hear a chorus of singing from both salon and hall. Community singing at an Athénée Palace reception!

People looked at one another as they recognised the song which the members of the Iron Guard had been advised to sing "only in their hearts".

"*Capitan-ul, Capitan-ul,*" came from the resplendent guests outside.

Before any of the English could say anything the man whom Galpin called his scout appeared struggling in through the press at the bar door. Once through, he paused to straighten out his wrinkled cotton jacket, then sidled over to Galpin. Galpin bent down to receive the news, his eyes roving about with intent attentiveness.

"Well," he said when all had been told, "this is really something! Didn't I tell you there'd be trouble? A voice has been raised, a solitary but significant voice – and it has called on the King to abdicate."

His listeners gazed at him, too startled to comment. He went on to explain that, seeing the Cabinet ministers arriving, people had collected outside the palace. "Then the news began leaking out. People realised the next question was going to be Transylvania – and suddenly someone bawled out '*Abdicati*'."

David said: "Good God!"

"What happened then?" Guy asked.

"Nothing – that's the extraordinary thing. Everyone bolted, of course. They probably expected the guards to shoot, but they did nothing. There wasn't a murmur from the palace . . ."

Wanda broke in anxiously: "But the King would not abdicate? No?" She spoke so seldom that everyone stared at her and she turned her eyes from one to the other with an expression of dramatic agony.

Accredited to an English Sunday paper that did not inquire too closely into the truth of what it printed, she had recently lost her job because the news she was sending bore no relation of any kind to the news being sent by other journalists. The result was that she had turned to Galpin for help and their relationship, once broken, had been renewed.

She was wearing a black Schiaparelli suit like a man's dinner suit, lightened by a tie of very bright pink. The heels of her shoes were also pink, and so overrun that her feet slipped sideways. She had tilted a miniature top-hat over one eye and from under it her hair streamed to her waist like pitch. She was as grimy as ever and dramatically beautiful, and as she looked at Clarence he looked back with bleak and lustful gloom murmuring: "I don't know,' which meant, Harriet knew: "How is it other men can get women and I can't?"

When she looked at David, he sniggered and answered her: "Who knows? I hear he keeps a plane ready in the back-yard just in case. You can't really blame these Balkan kings if they're a bit light-fingered. They never know from one day to the next what's going to happen."

Wanda gave a gasp of disgust at David's levity and turned her tragic inquiring gaze on Galpin, who said: "No need to worry about Carol. He and his girl-friend have got vast sums salted away abroad. Anyway the Germans will keep him here. It takes a crook to hold this country together."

David's mouth dipped in contempt of Galpin's predictions and he contradicted them authoritatively: "The Germans will not keep him here. They're not taken in by his conversion to totalitarianism. They know it's mere expediency. The new men in

Germany are, in their way, idealists. They're not like the old-fashioned diplomats who don't care how dishonest a man is so long as he's playing their game. They're dedicated men who'd hand Carol over to the firing-squad without a blink."

"But this is terrible," Wanda moaned: "He is such a splendid king with his helmet and his white cloak and his beautiful white horse."

"It may be terrible," David indulgently agreed, "but he's brought it on himself. He tried to play off the powers one against the other – and he didn't succeed. As for us, we haven't done much better. We could have bought up the Iron Guard any time we liked. Had we given a hint of recognition to the Peasant Party, they would have been with us. It's not too late. Maniu could still start a pro-British rising in Transylvania. But, even now, all the Legation is worrying about is how to keep in with the bloody sovereign."

Wanda sparked with exalted indignation. "You are an Englishman," she accused him. "You have a great empire and a fine king, and yet you want your Legation here to rouse a rabble of peasants! Is it possible?" Excited into unusual volubility, she gazed again from one to the other of the circle, and cried: "The last words I write to my paper were: 'At the word of command, every man in Rumania will rise to defend the throne.' "

Snuffling happily to himself, David murmured to Guy: "Just what you'd expect from the Poles. They still sing 'Poland has not perished yet'!"

Whether or not the news of the Salzburg conference had reached the reception, the singing went on. Harriet saw the view from the bar door was blocked by the backs of men standing in a row, shoulder to shoulder, across the doorway.

There was a pause ouside, then the voices of the Guardists rose in the *Horst Wessel*. Someone gave a command, and gradually this song was also taken up by the guests.

From the other side of the bar Hadjimoscos' voice rose in admiring awe: "Such a demonstration of loyalty I have never before heard."

"I think we ought to go," said Harriet.

David agreed: "It is a bit sinister."

They took their leave of Galpin and moved towards the door. Guy, glancing round to include all his faction, noticed that Clarence was lingering uncertainly behind. "Coming with us?" he asked.

"I don't know. I . . ." Clarence looked at Harriet, but when she did not wait to listen, he followed after her.

They reached the row of bodies wedged across the door. Beyond could be glimpsed the glitter of the women guests, the white shirt-fronts of the men. Here was Bucharest's wealthiest and most frivolous society standing, grave-faced, almost at attention, singing the Nazi anthem.

David bent to the ear of the central figure blocking the doorway and said: "*Scuză, domnuli.*" The figure remained rigid. David repeated his request and, when it was ignored, put his hand on the man's shoulder and shook it.

Angrily the man half turned his face to say: "*Hier ist nur eine private Gesellschaft. Der Eintritt ist nicht gestattet.*"

Amused and reasonable, David replied: "*Wir wollen einfach heraus.*"

The man jerked his face away with the word "*Verboten*".

David looked round. "We are – how many?" Noting Clarence, Dubedat and Toby in the rear, he made a grimace of humorous resignation and said: "The more the merrier, I suppose. Well, come along. Put your shoulders against these fellows and when I say 'Shove', let's all shove."

"Wait," said Harriet, "I know a better way." She unclasped a large brooch of Indian silver and held the pin at the ready. Before anyone could intervene – Clarence breathed "*Harry!*" in horror – she thrust the pin into the central backside. Its owner skipped forward with a yelp, leaving a space through which she led her party.

As the Rumanians observed this incident the *Horst Wessel* faltered, but nobody smiled.

Having reached the vestibule, the men wanted to get away quickly, but Harriet felt a desire to linger on the scene of triumph.

The occason, she felt, called for some sort of demonstration. She moved towards the table where the newspapers lay.

Guy said warningly: "Harriet!" but she went on.

At one time the table had displayed copies of every English journal published; now among the German and Rumanian newspapers there still remained the last copy of *The Times* to reach Bucharest. It bore the date June 12th 1940. Harriet picked it up and began to read a report of the French retreat across the Marne, but the paper was too limp and ragged to remain upright. As its pages sagged, she saw she was being watched by a woman whose face was familiar to her.

Guy caught her elbow. "Come along," he said, "you're being silly."

The woman, plainly dressed in black, was holding a glass as though unaware she held it. Her flat, faded, colourless face seemed to have on it the imprint of a heel. About her was an atmosphere of such unhappiness, it affected the air like a miasma.

Harriet said: "Yes, I am being silly . . ." As she let Guy lead her away, she remembered who the woman was: Doamna Ionescu, the wife of the ex-Minister of Information who had been pro-British but was pro-British no longer.

The singing had gathered strength again, but everyone watched the English party as it went.

"Well," said Clarence out in the square, "this may be Ruritania, but it's no longer a joke."

Guy looked about for Dubedat and Toby. The pair had not waited to support Harriet; they had fled. Half-way across the square Dubedat could be seen strutting at an indecorous speed while Toby, shoulders up, head down, hands in pockets, pinching himself with his own elbows, was scurrying like a man under fire.

8

OCCASIONALLY WHEN YAKIMOV OVERSLEPT in the afternoon, he would awake to find the Pringles had gone out and Despina – to spite him – had cleared away the tea things. When this happened on one of the molten days of late July, he suddenly felt to the full the deterioration of his life and could have wept for it. There had been a time when the world had given him everything: comfort, food, entertainment, love. He had been a noted wit, the centre of attention. Now he did not even get his tea.

He threw himself into the arm-chair in a state of revolt. No one had loved him since Dollie died. Perhaps no one would ever love him again – but why should he have to suffer as he did suffer in this wretched flat, in this exhausting heat? He wanted to get away.

A bugle call, coming from the palace yard, said: "Officers' wives have puddings and pies, soldiers' wives have skilly," and he thought: "Precious few puddings and pies we get these days." He did not entirely blame Harriet for that. Food was abominable everywhere in Bucharest these days.

Pushing his chair back as the lengthening fingers of sunlight burnt his shins, he asked himself: why did he live – why did any-one live – here, on this exposed plain, where one was fried in summer and frozen in winter? And now starved! Nothing to eat but fruit.

Apricots! He was sick of the sight of apricots.

That morning he had seen a barrow laden with raspberries – a great mountainous mush of raspberries – the peasant asleep beneath it. The man had probably walked all night to bring his produce to town, but the market was glutted. The raspberries were rotting in the heat and the man's shirt was crimson with the drip-ping juice.

In his youth, in a reasonable country, Yakimov had said he could live on raspberries. Now he dreamt of meat. If one got any here, it was the flesh of an old ewe or of a calf so young it was nothing but gristle. What he wanted was steak or roast beef or pork! – and he thought he knew where he could get it.

When he told the Baron that Freddi von Flügel had invited him to stay, it had been just "a little joke". He had heard nothing from Freddi, but that was no reason why Yakimov should not visit him. Freddi had received a great deal of Dollie's hospitality. Why should he not return it now that he was in "a position of power" and poor old Yaki was on his uppers?

Yakimov had practically made up his mind to set out – the only thing that detained him was the need for money. He had studied maps of Transylvania and realised the journey from Bucharest to Cluj was a long one. He would have to spend the night on the road. He would have to eat. In short, he would have to wait until his remittance turned up.

When he had mentioned to Hadjimoscos that he planned to drive to Cluj, Hadjimoscos had been discouraging. Apparently, as a result of some wretched conference being held in Salzburg, Cluj was now in disputed territory and liable to change hands any day. After hearing that, Yakimov had begun to inquire of Galpin and Screwby about the progress of the conference, and soon came to the conclusion that nothing was happening at all. And he had been right. Even Hadjimoscos now agreed with him that the Conference would probably drag on until the war put a stop to the whole business.

Meanwhile, he had to remain here in a comfortless flat where he was not wanted by the hostess, and the host, having made use of him, had scarcely time to throw him a word. His acute sense of hardship was suddenly aggravated by a sound of laughter coming from the kitchen: and his curiosity was aroused.

The laughter had not been the usual sniggering of servants. He had heard Despina laugh, he had heard her husband. This was unfamiliar laughter. Who had she got in there? It occurred to him to put his head into the kitchen and make some jocular reference to tea.

The kitchen door had a glass panel. He approached quietly and looked in. Himself hidden by the lace curtain, he could see Despina and a young man sitting at the table preparing vegetables for the evening meal. A young man, eh! Despina was married to a taxi-driver who was more often out than in. Well, well! The two at the table were chattering in Rumanian. The fellow started laughing again.

Yakimov opened the door. At the sight of him, the young man's laughter stopped abruptly. Yakimov had the odd sensation that the youth knew who he was and was afraid of him. Surprised at this, he essayed in English – his Rumanian was poor – a leading inquiry: "Believe we've met before, dear boy?"

The young man stammered out: "I don't think so." Looking ghastly, he managed to get to his feet and stood there trembling as though stupefied by fear. He was as long and lean as Yakimov himself, and unmistakably Jewish.

"Are you staying with the Pringles?" Yakimov asked.

"No," the young man said, then added: "I mean, yes." After a moment, encouraged by Yakimov's courtesy of manner, he added more easily: "I'm on a visit."

Yakimov was puzzled, not because the boy spoke English – English was widely spoken among Bucharest Jews – but because he spoke it with the accent of an English public school. Where had he come from? What was he doing here? But before Yakimov could make further inquiries, Despina broke in in the high, abusive tone she always adopted with Yakimov. He gathered she was claiming the young man as her nephew.

An educated Jew Despina's nephew! A likely story. It roused Yakimov's suspicions. He looked at the boy, who nodded, his colour returning, as though relieved at hearing this explanation of his presence.

Yakimov said: "You speak English extremely well."

"I learnt at school."

"Indeed!" With no excuse for lingering longer, Yakimov made his request for tea and retreated. Despina shouted after him: "*Prea târziu pentru ceai*," and before he reached the sitting room door he heard her hooting with laughter. She thought she had fooled him. His suspicion deepened.

He went into the bathroom and filled the bath. Lying in the water, he reflected on the presence of the young man in the kitchen. He could only suppose the fellow was some fugitive of the troubled times whom Guy was keeping under cover. He felt a vague jealousy, then, remembering the plan of the oil-well he had found in Guy's desk, it came to him that the young man in the kitchen might be a British spy. His jealousy changed to disapproval and concern.

He often himself hinted that he was engaged in espionage, but everyone knew that was just a little joke. This was a serious matter. He thought: "If Guy gets caught, it'll be a bad look-out for him," then he realised, with indignant alarm, that it would be a bad look-out for all of them. He, poor old Yaki, innocently involved in this fishy business, would have to suffer with the rest.

Spies were shot. Even if he were not actually shot, he would be ordered out of the country. And where could he go? Bad as things were here, Bucharest was the last outpost of European cooking.

Levantine dishes upset his stomach. He could not bear the luke-warm food of Greece.

Worse than that, he would never reach Cluj and dear old Freddi. He would not even have the harbour of this flat but, ageing and penniless, would have to face the unfriendly world again.

He sat up, all pleasure gone from the bath, and considered the possibility of safeguarding himself by acting as informer. That would never do, of course. "Lucky for the dear boy," he told himself, "that Yaki's not one to give the game away."

The Salzburg Conference did not outlast the war, but petered out in failure by all parties to agree. Yakimov, like almost everyone else in Bucharest, decided that that was the end of the matter.

"What did I tell you, dear boy?" he said to the few persons willing to listen. "I've been a journalist, y'know. I've a nose for how these things will shape," and he was happy that nothing stood between him and his visit to Freddi but the need for a little cash.

The Transylvanian question forgotten, interest in the Drucker trial returned. *L'Indépendence Romaine* predicted that the trial would be "*l'évenement social le plus important de l'été*".

In every café and restaurant that Harriet visited, she heard talk of Drucker. People discussed his origins and the origins of his fortune and his love of women. She heard women envying his young second wife who, having reverted to her maiden name and started an affair with the German military attaché, was claiming, and would probably receive, fifty per cent of her husband's estate.

Galpin had a story of how Drucker, when first placed in the common prison cell, had been held down and raped by old lags. There were a great many similar stories. Harriet realised that among all this talk Drucker's own identity was lost. No one doubted the innocence of this friendless man, but that factor did not bear discussion. No one could help him. He was a victim of the times.

As for the war, it was at a standstill. Events, it seemed, were becalmed in the oppressive, dusty, windless heat of midsummer.

People believed the worst was over. A euphoria, one of the periodic intermissions in its chronic disease of dread, possessed the city. Gaiety returned.

Then, in a moment, the mood changed. The Pringles, out walking after supper, heard among the crowds the shrill ejaculations of panic. The newsboys came shrieking through the streets with a special edition. Those who did not already know learnt that the Führer had called another conference. The Hungarian and Rumanian ministers, ordered to Rome, were required to reach speedy agreement.

The sense of outrage was the more violent because only that morning the new Foreign Minister had broadcast a speech of the highest optimism. He had pointed out that in 1918 the Germans had been as weak as the Rumanians, and today, by their energy and determination, they ruled the world. The implication had been that Rumanians might do likewise – yet here they were ordered to reach agreement with an enemy whose sole intention was to eat them up.

Gabbling in their rage, people shouted to one another that they had been betrayed. Rumania was to be divided among Russia, Hungary and Bulgaria. The whole of Moldavia would be handed to the Soviets as the price of Russia's neutrality. The Dobrudja, of course, would go to Bulgaria. Even now the Hungarians were marching into Transylvania.

Word went round that the Cabinet was sitting, then that the King had summoned his generals. Suddenly people were convinced that Rumania would fight for her territory and they began shouting for war. As they swarmed towards the square to demonstrate the defiance of the moment, Guy and Harriet made their way to the English Bar, where Galpin was in a state of excitement. His scout had brought the news that Maniu, the leader of the Transylvanian peasants, was making a speech calling on the King to defy Hitler and defend what was left of Greater Rumania. "This means war," said Galpin, "this means war."

On the way home, Harriet said: "Do you think they will fight?"

"I doubt it," said Guy, but the violence of feeling about them seemed to be such that they went to bed in a half-expectation that they would awake to find the country in arms.

Next morning all was quiet and when Guy telephoned David he learnt that Maniu had indeed made an impassioned speech demanding that they hold Transylvania by force, but he had been ridiculed. The new Guardist ministers had pointed out that while the Rumanian army was defending the western front Russia would march down from the north. It was their belief that only by implicit obedience to Hitler could they hope for protection from the arch-enemy, Russia. At this an old statesman had burst into tears and scandalised everyone by crying out: "Better to be united under the Soviets than dismembered by the Axis."

But the Rumanians, harried themselves, decided to harry someone. Next morning, as Guy was leaving for the University, a messenger handed him a second order to quit the country within eight hours.

He gave it to Harriet, saying: "I haven't time to deal with this. Go and see Dobson."

"But supposing we have to go?" she protested.

He said, as he had said last time: "We won't have to go," but Harriet did not find Dobson so reassuring.

When she entered his office with the paper, he sighed and said: "We're getting a lot of this bumf at the moment." He rubbed a hand over his baby-soft tufts of hair and gave a laugh that deprecated his own weariness. "I wonder," he said, as though the matter were not of much importance one way or the other, "do you really *want* to stay? The situation is tricky, you know. There's a pretty steady German infiltration here. Whether you realise it or not, they're taking this country over. I very much doubt whether the English Department will be permitted to reopen when the autumn term begins."

Harriet said: "We're not supposed to leave without orders from London."

"That's theoretical, of course. But if Guy's work here is finished . . ."

"He doesn't see it as finished. At the moment he's running the summer school and he's extremely busy."

"Oh, well!" Dobson gave his head a final rub and said: "I'll see what I can do. But don't be too hopeful."

She returned to the flat to await a call from him, not hopeful, indeed prepared for the possibility that they would be given no choice but to go. Whether she liked it or not, their going would cut through a tangle of anxieties.

Wandering round the room, examining their possessions, wondering what to take and what to leave, she looked into the writing-desk drawers and came upon the envelope marked "Top

Secret". As she took it up, the flap fell open and she saw there was nothing inside. Some moments passed before she could remember what it had contained.

The previous winter a certain Commander Sheppy – described by David as "a cloak and dagger man" – had come to Bucharest to organise the young men of the British colony into a sabotage group. His intention had ended abruptly with his arrest and deportation. All that had remained of "Sheppy's Striking Force" was a plan, handed out to the men, a copy of which had been inside this envelope; a section through an oil well, intended to show the inexperienced saboteur where to place a detonator. Both Guy and Harriet had forgotten its existence. Now, here was the envelope unsealed and empty. The plan had disappeared.

This fact bewildered her, then it began to work on her imagination and she was chilled.

As soon as Guy came in to luncheon, she said: "Someone has stolen the oil-well plan Sheppy gave you."

She remembered as she spoke that she was supposed not to know what had been inside the envelope, but Guy had forgotten that. He said merely: "But who would take it?"

"Perhaps Yakimov."

"That's unlikely."

"Who then? Surely not Despina or Sasha. It means someone has been in while we were out. The landlord perhaps. Despina says he's a member of the Iron Guard. And probably has a key." The realisation brought down on her a painful sense of doom and Guy, seeing her distraught, changed his attitude and said: "It *could* have been Yakimov . . ."

"Then you had better speak to him."

"Oh, no, that would give the whole thing false importance. Better say nothing, but you could try and be nicer to him. Let him see we trust him."

She said, exasperated in anxiety: "You think that will make a difference? If Yakimov isn't grateful now, he never will be. In fact, he's resentful because you take no notice of him. Why didn't you leave him to fend for himself? You interfere in people's lives. You give them a false idea of themselves, an illusion of achievement. If you make someone drunk, he's likely to blame you when he wakes up with a hangover. Why do you do it?"

Buffeted by this attack, he remonstrated: "For goodness' sake! The plan might have been taken months ago. We can't tell who took it – but whoever it was, if he'd wanted to make trouble we'd have heard by now."

She thought this equivocal comfort.

After Guy had gone to the University, she threw herself on to the bed, oppressed by the sense of events becoming too much for her. A few days earlier Despina, treating the matter as a joke, had described Yakimov's discovery of Sasha in the kitchen. "But I was ready for him," she said. She had told him the boy was her nephew and he had believed it. "The imbecile!" she cried, tears of laughter in her eyes, but Harriet could not believe that Yakimov had been so easily deceived. She had hoped he would mention the incident himself, so she could tell him that Sasha was one of Guy's students; but he did not mention it, and his silence disturbed her more than any questioning could have done.

Suddenly, with the thought of Sasha in her mind, she sat upright, shocked by the realisation that when they went they would have to leave him behind. What would become of him? Where could he go?

Thinking of Sasha's trust in them, his dependent innocence and need, she was stricken by her own affection for the boy. She could no more abandon him than she could abandon a child or a kitten. But he was not a child or a kitten to be carried to safety: he was a grown man who could not leave the country without a passport, exit visa and transit visas, and he was a man for whom every frontier official would be on the watch.

It had been in her mind that their going, if they had to go, would cut through a tangle of anxieties. Now all these anxieties were forgotten in her concern for Sasha.

She put her feet to the ground in an impulse to rush up to him, to insist that he think of someone, anyone, whom they could approach on his behalf, but stopped herself. They had had this out. There was no one, so what point in alarming the poor boy?

She was still sitting on the bed edge, brooding on this problem, when the telephone rang. Dobson said: "It's all right. I've been through to the *prefectura* and told them H.E. requires Guy's presence here. The order's rescinded."

"Thank goodness for that," she said with a fervour that must have surprised him.

"By the way," he said before he rang off, "you're wanted at the Consulate. Just a formality. No particular hurry. Drop in when you get a chance."

The next afternoon, Guy having no classes, they went to the Consulate.

The Vice-consul, Tavares, shouted: "Come in, come in, come in." Elaborately casual and cheerful, he said: "It's like this . . ." He opened a drawer and pulled out some roneoed sheets, which he threw down in front of Guy and Harriet. "Every British subject required to fill one in. Never know these days, do you? So, just for the records, we want a few details: religion, next-of-kin, whom to notify in the event of death (as it were!), where to send kit, etcetera, etcetera. *You* understand!"

"Yes," said Harriet.

When the forms were filled, Tavares noticed that Guy had failed to disclose his religion. Guy said he had no religion. Tavares laughed off this revelation: "What were you baptised?" he asked.

"I wasn't baptised."

Tavares flicked a finger to show that nothing could surprise him. "Must put something," he said. "Y'wouldn't want to be planted without ceremony. Why not put 'Baptist'? Baptists don't get baptised."

In the end, Guy put in "Congregational", having been told that old soldiers who claimed this denomination were able to avoid church parades.

Walking home, Harriet said: "Why didn't you tell me you'd never been baptised?"

"I didn't think of it. But you knew I was a rationalist."

"But no one's *born* a rationalist."

"In a way, I was. My father would not let me be baptised."

"This means when we die we'll be in different places. You'll be in limbo."

Laughing, Guy said: "I don't think so. We'll be in the same place, don't worry. A hundred years from now we shall be exactly where we were a hundred years ago – which is nowhere at all."

But Harriet was not satisfied. She brooded over their post-obitum separation all during tea, then suddenly, when Yakimov had gone off to have a bath, she lifted the teapot and poured cold tea over Guy's head. While he sat stolidly acceptant of her follies, she said: "I baptise thee, Guy, in the name of the Father and of the Son and of the Holy Ghost," which was all she knew of the baptismal service.

9

HARRIET HAD NEVER HEARD the word "*abdică*" before the night of the Guardist reception, now she heard it everywhere. The King had been deposed for his misdeeds once before. The concept of deposition was not new, yet people seized upon it as though it were a prodigious solution of their problems. During the apprehensive days of the Rome Conference they talked of nothing else.

The King had always had his enemies – if he ever emerged from the palace, it was in a bullet-proof car – but to most people he was only one knave of many, and a shrewd, diverting knave, the hero of half the jokes that went around. This attitude changed overnight. Suddenly, he diverted no one. He was the bane of the country. True he had been clever: he had declared for the Axis – but too late. *Too late*. He had been too clever. He had played a double game and lost. Anyway, Hitler loathed and distrusted him. The country was paying for his sins. He must be abjured, for with such a man on the throne there could be nothing ahead but disaster.

These opinions were so widespread that they penetrated even to the King's apartments.

He was induced to broadcast, a thing he did seldom and never very well. The radio vans were already outside the palace when the Pringles were having breakfast. Another van, with a loudspeaker on its roof, stood beside the statue of Carol the First. It had been announced that the King would speak at ten o'clock; he came to the microphone shortly before noon.

During the morning a few dozen idlers hung round the loudspeaker van, and when the speech began it gathered in a few more. The listeners showed no enthusiasm, appearing to have nothing to do but listen, and Harriet, watching them from the balcony, switched on her radio set for the same reason. She had heard a broadcast by the King a year before (when he had promised that Rumania would never suffer defeat) and had little hope of understanding his halting Rumanian, but when he started to speak she realised he had been very thoroughly coached for this occasion.

He pronounced each word with an earnest deliberation, in a charged voice, so she imagined him shocked into a painful sobriety.

While he was talking, she watched a file of young men who came out of the Calea Victoriei and crossed the square, carrying banners and distributing leaflets. Whatever their message was, it aroused more interest than the King, who was, she gathered, promising his people that whatever sacrifices they might be called upon to make, he would be beside them, whatever their sufferings, he would be there to suffer with them. Dramatically, his voice breaking with emotion (much as he had made the promise that Rumania would never suffer defeat), he promised that he would never abdicate.

As he spoke the words "*Nu voi abdică niciodată*", the young men reached the palace railing, where they came to a stop and stood with banners held in view of the palace windows.

Harriet had no doubt who these young men were. They were members of the Iron Guard. The Guardists did not wear uniform or march in formation or sing "*Capitanul*", but they had started to possess the streets, Having noted the first insecure few who had come from Germany after the spring amnesty, she marvelled at the numbers who were crowding back with all the confidence in the world and gathering adherents – the indigent and the afflicted. Once lost in the back streets, these men now swaggered through the Calea Victoriei while timorous passers-by stood aside to let them pass.

The speech over, Harriet decided to take a closer look at the Guardist banners. The sun stood overhead. The square was clearing under the onslaught of midday heat, but the young men remained steadfast. Harriet, long-sighted, stopped near the statue and saw that one banner called on the King to abdicate. Another demanded the arrest of Lupescu, Urdureanu, the Chief of Police, and other despoilers of the country. The third promised that once the King and his followers were cast out, the Axis would return Bessarabia to the Rumanian people.

Harriet was not the only one who chose to read these demands from a safe distance. People about her were murmuring in amazement and trepidation. And she, too, was amazed that this demonstration could proceed in full view of the palace without a movement from the guards.

Inside the palace someone was pulling down the cream-coloured blinds, masking the windows one after another – perhaps against the sun, perhaps against the sight below. Nothing else happened.

Before returning, Harriet walked past the young men to receive a pamphlet – a manifesto headed "*Corneliu Zelea Codreanu*" – which she hurried home to read while awaiting Guy's return. She settled down to it with a dictionary.

The truth (said the manifesto) could now be told. Codreanu had not been shot while trying to escape. He had been assassinated by order of the King. His death had come about in this way.

The Iron Guard, also called the Legion of the Archangel Michael, had gained sixty-six seats at the election of 1937. The King, insanely jealous of Codreanu's power, had at once dissolved all parties and declared himself dictator. At this, Hitler had said: "For me there exists only one dictator of Rumania and this is Codreanu." Codreanu had won the love and confidence which the King, corrupt instigator of a corrupt regime, had lost. Young, noble, saintly, tall, of divine beauty, Codreanu had been directly inspired by the archangel Michael to redeem his country by forming the Iron Guard. He possessed a mysterious power which was felt by all who approached him. When he appeared, dressed in white, on his white horse, the peasants at once recognised him as the archangel's envoy on earth. His purpose was to unite all Rumanians in brotherhood, not only the living but the souls of the unborn and the dead . . .

Harriet hastened on to the tragic end. Skipping the suppression of the Iron Guard, the evidence of the forged letter and the farcical trial in which Codreanu was found guilty of high treason, for which he was imprisoned, she reached the cold November night on which Codreanu and his thirteen comrades were taken in trucks, bound and gagged, to the forest of Ploesti, where each in turn was strangled with a leather strap. At Port Jilava, acid was poured over the bodies; they were burnt, and what remained was buried in a grave which was sealed with a massive slab of concrete.

Yet all these precautions had been in vain. Codreanu was an immortal. Even now his spirit was moving through the land, regathering forces . . . inspiring . . . exhorting . . . leading . . . and so on.

Harriet had read enough. Her imagination excited by this romance of a young leader murdered by a jealous King, she thought of the men who had handed it to her in the square. Bare-headed and dark-skinned, wearing singlets or cheap shirts without collars, they may have been artisans. They were scarcely more than peasants. Guy, seeing the Guardist groups pushing through the streets, had said: "How rapidly they are gathering in their kind: the hopeless, the inadequate, the brute." And yet, she thought, they were the only people in this spoilt city whose ideals rose above money, food and sex. Why should the brute not be infused with ideals, the hopeless given hope, the inadequate strength?

She was stimulated, too, by the revelation of a mystical strain in this pleasure-loving people. It was easy to see how a visionary like Codreanu could excite half-starved and superstitious peasants, but one supposed that the townspeople would find the King, with his mistresses, his chicanery and his love of money, a more likely projection of themselves. Or were all people at variance with themselves? Anyway, it had been here in Bucharest, during the funeral of Guardists killed in Spain, that people had given Codreanu so frenzied a welcome that the King determined to kill his rival and stamp out the whole Guardist movement.

When Guy came in, Harriet was impatient to talk about Codreanu, but he showed no interest. He had heard all the stories before.

"You must admit," she said, "that the Iron Guard concepts are not so very different from your own."

Guy glanced up sharply and, with a gesture, indicated that here and now, in the absurdity of this statement, he could pin down the root trouble of the world. "Codreanu," he said, "was a murderer, a Jew-baiter and a thug. He had a following of nonentities who wanted only one thing – power at any price."

"But if, having power, they could remake the country ..."

"Do you imagine they could? The incompetence of Carol's set would be as nothing compared with the incompetence of Codreanu's bunch of thugs."

"Well, one could give them a chance."

"Before the war there were quite a lot of sentimentalists like you. They did not realise that while they were being mesmerised and misled by the romantic aspects of fascism, they were being made to sell their souls ..."

Having used this phrase inadvertently, he paused, and Harriet, feeling ignorant and something of a fool, leapt in with: "If the fascists make you sell your soul, the communists make you deny it."

Guy grunted and picked up a newspaper. She knew he had no use for religion, seeing it as part of the conspiracy to keep the rich powerful and the poor docile. He was prepared to discuss very little that did not contribute towards a practical improvement in mankind's condition. Harriet's own theories, of course, were too simple-minded to matter.

At the moment he held up the paper to screen him from any more of her nonsense. She said to provoke him: "Clarence says you're merely the rebel son of a rebel father."

"Clarence is an ass," Guy said, but he put the paper down. "In fact I could say I reacted against my father. The poor old chap was a bit of a romantic. He imagined the moneyed classes were the repository of culture. He used to say: 'That's their function, isn't it? If they don't safeguard the arts, what the hell do they do?' When I began to meet rich people I was shocked by their ignorance and vulgarity."

"Where did you meet these rich people?"

"At the University – the sons of local manufacturers. They weren't aristocrats, it's true, but they were rich. And not first-generation rich, either. They were the country-house-owning class of the Midlands. They were always talking about 'parvenus', but even the most intelligent of them preferred the fashionable to the good."

She laughed. "They're much like everyone else. How many people do love the highest when they see it? They just about tolerate it if they're told often enough that it's the right thing."

He agreed and was about to go back to his paper when she said: "But did you know these people well? Did you go to their houses?"

"Yes. I suppose I was taken up by them – in a way. At first they wouldn't believe I was a genuine member of the proletariat. I was too big and untidy. According to them I should have been a bony little man in a dark suit, permanently soul-sick. When they found I was quite genuine, they adopted me as their favourite member of the working class."

"And you didn't mind? You liked them? You liked the Druckers?"

He had to admit it was true. He could not help liking people who liked him. They became, and remained, his friends.

"But," he said, "I know that humanity's superiority depends on a few persons of intellectual and moral structure: people like my father, for instance, who almost never have money or power, and have no sense at all of their own importance."

With that, Guy went back to his students; and Harriet, as soon as the heat began to relax, took herself up to the roof to talk to Sasha.

Guy had said once that, although she was nearly twenty-three, she still had the mentality of an adolescent. Perhaps her relationship with Sasha was a relationship of adolescents.

Guy's all-knowingness, his lack of time for any sort of fantasy, was frustrating her. She felt gagged. Sasha, on the other hand, had unlimited time. He did not say much himself, but he listened to her with the intent interest of someone new in the world. He was delighted to be entertained, watching her with warm, attentive eyes that made her feel whatever she said was pertinent and exciting. He believed – or rather, his silent extrusion of sympathy led her to believe he believed – that he, as she did, related life to eternity rather than to time.

Now when Guy was out she had somewhere to go. During the day, she had occupation enough. It was in the evening, the time of relaxation, when the changing light, giving a new spaciousness to the city, induced a sense of solitude, that she thought of Sasha who was lonely, too.

That evening, when she went to see him after tea, she spoke of Codreanu, saying: "He loved the peasants. He gave them this idea of a nation united in brotherhood. Surely the important thing was that people believed in him?"

Sasha listened uneasily. "But he did terrible things," he said. "He started the pogroms. My cousin at the University was thrown out of a window. His spine was broken."

That was the reality, of course. "But why did the reality have to be that?" she said. The ideals had been fine enough. They had been formulated to combat a corrupt régime in which the idle, self-seeking and dishonest thrived. Why then, she wanted to know must they degenerate into a reality of blackmail, persecution and murder? Were human beings so fallible and self-seeking that degeneration was inevitable?

Guy, who had dismissed pretty sharply any suggestion of a flirtation with the Legion of the Archangel Michael, knew the answer to human fallibility: it was a world united under left-wing socialism. Sasha did not know the answer.

To please her, he was trying to consider the problem with

detachment, but as he looked at her his soft, vulnerable, loving gaze was troubled.

She remembered the moment at the Drucker table when one of his aunts had asked: "Why do they hate us?" Drucker had sent the little girls out of the room, but he did not send Sasha. Sasha had to be prepared for reality. However much his wealth might protect him, he could not be protected from prejudice. But, of course, he had not been prepared. Enclosed and loved as he had been, he could not relate their stories of persecution to himself.

He said: "The peasants are very simple people. It wouldn't be difficult to make them believe in Codreanu. They'd believe in anything," and he gazed appealingly at her as though to say: "Let that explain away the mysterious influence of Guardism and all that came of it." In short: "Let us talk of something else." He probably wanted to talk about the peasants who had shown him, at times, a rough kindness. They had respected him because he spoke English, though they could scarcely believe he had actually been to England. England they held to be a sort of paradise, the abode of titans.

He described how they stood, as patient as their own beasts, all day on guard in the midsummer heat, clad in winter clothing. Money was allotted for the purchase of cotton uniforms but it was misspent somewhere. Who were they to complain?

"What did they guard?" Harriet asked.

"Oh, a bridge or a railway-station or a viaduct. It was silly. When the Russians came, the officers just piled into cars and drove away. We didn't know what to do . . ."

She saw his face change as this mention of the army's flight recalled Marcovitch. By now she had heard other stories – of the Orthodox Jew whose skull had been kicked in "like a broken crock"; and the distinguished folklorist who, having been beaten by his sergeant, had appeared next day wearing a medal. "So you have decorated yourself!" said the sergeant. "No," replied the scholar, "the King decorated me," for which piece of impertinence he had been struck violently across the face.

Nothing very terrible had happened to Sasha himself, but, unprepared as he was, he had been appalled at this treatment of his scapegoat race. He had run away.

He said: "I can remember some of the songs the peasants sang. The folklorist used to collect them."

As he talked, she looked over the parapet and saw Guy crossing the square on his way home. In the early days of their marriage, she would have sped down the stairs; now she leant still and watched him, thinking of Sasha's theory that Guardism had grown not from the power of its founder but the credulity of his followers. She felt that the argument had, as arguments often did, come full circle. Wonders were born of ignorance and superstition. Do away with ignorance and superstition and there would be no more wonders, only a universe of unresponsive matter in which Guy was at home, though she was not. Even if she could not accept this diminution of her horizon, she had to feel a bleak appreciation of Guy, who was often proved right.

She broke in on Sasha to say: "I'm afraid I must go now."

He smiled, as uncomplaining and unquestioning as the peasants, but as she went he said forlornly: "I wish I had my gramophone here."

"You should be studying," she said, for at her suggestion Guy had set him some tasks: an essay to write, books to read. The books lay scattered over the ground. He had opened them, but she doubted whether he had done much more. "Why not do some work?"

"All right," he said, but as she turned to descend the ladder she saw he had picked up his charcoal and was scribbling idly on the wall.

10

ONE MORNING, while the city quivered like a mirage in the August heat, Harriet came face to face with Bella in the Calea Victoriei. Bella gave a smile and hurried into a shop. So she had not gone to Sinai after all, but had remained here, like everyone else, the prisoner of uncertainty and fear.

The Rome Conference had broken down. This time no one imagined that that was the end of the matter. There would be another conference. When it was announced, there was no stir and no more talk of defiance. The new Cabinet had announced complete fealty to the Führer and the Führer required a peaceful settlement. A settlement of any kind could only mean Rumania's loss. Around the cafés and bars this fact was beginning to be accepted with a half-humorous resignation. What else was there to do? Yakimov, inspired by the tenor of conversation about him, had thought up a little joke. "*Quel débâcle!*" he said whenever opportunity arose: "As you walk cracks appear on the pavement," and even Hadjimoscos had not the heart to snub him.

The young men still stood with their banners on the palace pavement, supported now by an admiring crowd. As for the King, having made his speech, his declaration of constancy, he had retired into silence, and a song was being sung which David did his best to put into English verse:

"They can have Bessarabia. We don't like corn.
The best wheaten bread's the stuff in our New Dawn.

Let them have the Dobrudja. Ma's palace, anyway,
Has been sold to the nation for a million million *lei*.

Who wants Transylvania? Give it 'em on a plate.
Let them take what they damn well like. I'll not abdicate."

The last phrase "*Eu nu abdic*" was the slogan of the moment. Jokes were told and the point was "*Eu nu abdic*". Riddles were asked and the answer was always "*Eu nu abdic*". However recondite, it was the smartest retort to any request or inquiry. It always raised a laugh.

In the face of the threat to Transylvania, no one gave much thought to the southern Dobrudja, but the story went round that the old minister who had wept over Bessarabia, had wept – probably from habit – when the Bulgarian demand was received. He reminded the Cabinet that Queen Marie's heart was buried in the palace at Balcic and the queen had believed her subjects would safeguard it with their lives. He stood up crying: "To arms, to arms," but no one, not even the old man himself, could take this call seriously. The queen, though barely two years dead, symbolised an age of chivalry as outmoded as honour, as obsolete as truth.

The transfer of the southern Dobrudja was announced for September 7th.

That, Harriet thought, was one frontier problem peaceably settled, but when she made some comment of this sort to Galpin, he eyed her with the icy irony of one who has good cause to know better.

They had met on the pavement outside the Athénée Palace and Galpin was carrying a suitcase. "For my part," he said, "I'm keeping a bag ready packed and my petrol-tank full."

"Oh?"

He crossed to his car and put the case into the boot, then remarked in a milder tone: "I thought it darn odd they were willing to settle for that mouldy bit in the south when they could grab the whole coast."

"Do you mean they *are* grabbing the whole coast?"

"They and one other. I expect it was arranged months ago. When the Bulgars take the south, the old Russkies will occupy the north. *Between* them they'll hold the whole coastal plain. It's a Slav plot."

When Harriet did not look as alarmed as he felt she should be, he said on a peevish note: "Don't you see what it means? Rumania will be cut off from the sea. The Legation plan is to evacuate British subjects from Constanza. You'll be one of the ones to suffer. There'll be no escape route."

"We can go to Belgrade."

"My dear child, when the Germans march this way, they'll take Yugoslavia *en route*."

"Well, we can go by air."

"What, the whole blessed British colony? I'd like to see it. And anyway, when there's trouble the air service is the first thing to pack up. I've seen it time and again. Well, I'm taking no risk. When I get wind of the invasion, I'm into the flivver and off."

"Ah, well,' said Harriet, attempting to lighten the situation, "perhaps you'll take us with you?"

Galpin's eyes bulged. "I don't know about that. I've got baggage. I've got Wanda. The Austin's old. The road over the Balkans is bad. If we broke a spring, we'd be done for." Looking as though she had attempted to take an unfair advantage, he got into the car, slammed the door and drove away.

When she reached the flat, the telephone was ringing. Inchcape was looking for Guy. "Tell him I'll be in after luncheon," he shouted and she felt the jolt of his receiver violently replaced.

He arrived while the Pringles and Yakimov were still at table. Guy had scoffed at Galpin's story of a Slav plot, saying the Russians would not seize territory on which they had no claim. Even if they did occupy the northern Dobrudja, that would not prevent British subjects leaving from Constanza.

Yakimov brought out his "*Quel débâcle!*" joke and showed an inclination to sit and talk but Inchcape walked about the room with such a show of impatience that it eventually came to Yakimov that he was not wanted. When he went, Inchcape swung a chair round, sat astride it and said: "They're trying to get us out. They want us to go."

"Who wants us to go?" Guy asked. "The *prefectura* or the Legation?"

"The Legation. They're trying to thin out the British colony. They want to get rid of what they call the 'culture boys'."

"Because of this Dobrudja business?" Harriet asked.

"That among other things. Dobson had the cheek to suggest we've outlived our usefulness here. He said: 'You must realise that having you around means extra work for us.' That's all they're worrying about."

"Do you mean it's a definite order?"

"An attempt at one." Inchcape lit a cigarette and stamped angrily on the match. "But they can't expel us without good reason. Their first move is to get us to close down the English Department. Once they do that, they can say: 'What is the point of your being here?' I'm determined to stay open."

Guy nodded his support and Harriet wondered if any mention

had been made of the Propaganda Bureau, which, inactive in its heyday, was now moribund. Before she could ask, Inchcape stubbed out his cigarette, two-thirds unsmoked, into a saucer, and said: "When I was summoned to the Legation this morning, I insisted on seeing Sir Montagu."

"What happened then?" Guy asked.

Inchcape, his hand shaking, lit another cigarette. The war between nations was forgotten. He was waging his old war against the Legation. "I was called in, ostensibly about these notices to quit which we keep getting. Dobson said: 'We think it would be better if the summer school closed down.' I refused to discuss it with him. I demanded to see one of the top brass. They tried to fob me off with Wheeler. In the end, believe it or not, I got in to the old charmer himself. And what do you think he said? 'Summer school?' he said. 'What summer school?' I told him that before we could stop work we'd have to get a direct order from our London office. That's not likely to come in a hurry. No one at home has any real idea of what's going on here."

"And – ?"

"The old boy blustered a bit. I stood firm. So he said: 'If you stay, you do so at your own risk. I don't guarantee to get one of your fellows out of here alive.' "

"What about Woolley and the other businessmen?"

"He said they could look after themselves. They've got cars. When the time comes, they can drive into Bulgaria. He said: 'You chaps without cars won't find it so easy. The trains will be taking troops to the frontier. The civilian aircraft will be commandeered by the army. There won't even be a boat if Constanza's in Russian hands.' I said it was a risk we were prepared to take." Inchcape looked for confirmation to Guy.

Guy said: "Of course."

"Why?" asked Harriet.

"Because we have a job to do," Guy said: "While we're of any use here, we must stay."

"Exactly," said Inchcape. He sat down again, calmed by Guy's support. "Besides," he said, "there's the Cantecuzeno Lecture in the offing. Pinkrose is being flown out. He's getting a priority flight to Cairo. That's not granted to everyone. I shall certainly be here to welcome him."

"What else did Sir Montagu say?"

"He tried persuasion. 'You can only speak for yourself,' he

said. 'The other men should be consulted.' I said: 'I know my men. I can speak for them.' 'Nevertheless,' he said, 'they should get together and discuss the situation. Let Dobson have a word with them!' I could see the wily old bastard thought I'd keep you in the dark, so I said: 'Very well. I'll call a meeting this very evening. Anyone can attend. I know my men, I know what they'll say.' " Inchcape gazed intently at Guy, who again nodded his support, Inchcape stood up, satisfied: "The staff-room at six, then."

"Can I come?" Harriet asked.

Inchcape looked round, surprised that she should feel concerned in this. "If you like," he said, then he turned to Guy again "Alert the others. Dubedat, Lush and the old ladies. I think you'll find they're all behind us. No one wants to lose his job."

By six o'clock the haze was lifeless and yellowish, like a thin smoke over the inert streets. The heat was stale and without fervour. The shops, though open, seemed asleep.

In the Calea Victoriei one pavement baked in the honey-yellow sun, the other was Prussian blue. Harriet walked in the shade until she reached the German Propaganda Bureau and there, before crossing the road, she paused. The map of France had appeared and disappeared in less than a month, but the map of the British Isles had remained so long, people were losing interest in it. Harriet was the only one looking in the window. She said to herself: "They'll never get there," and saw that among the towns ringed with flames was the one where she had been born – a town she hated. Her eyes filled with tears.

On the other side of the road the gipsies, rousing themselves from behind their great baskets, were squirting their flowers with water from old enema bulbs. The sweet and heavy scent of tuberoses hung about the University steps. "Doamna, doamna," screeched the gipsies as Harriet made her way up.

When she passed into the building's gothic gloom, she could hear Guy's voice. He was still in the lecture-room. She went back to sit on the balustrade and watch the street waking up. When the students came out she was surprised that they dispersed so quickly. She waited, expecting more to come, but instead Guy came out to look for her.

She said: "Why are there so few students?"

"Numbers have dropped off," he admitted. "It's quite usual. Some of them get bored. Come along. The meeting has begun."

He hurried ahead of her down the long main passage that was too narrow for its height, and opened the common-room door. Inchcape was saying: ". . . a ridiculous state of affairs. The fact is, the Legation's trying to close down the summer school. I've called you all here to discuss it. After all, it's your bread and butter."

Elegant in a grey silk suit, he was sitting on the common-room table with one foot latched into a chair-rung. He smiled as he mentioned the malapert Legation. Apparently his rancour had gone, but his hands were gripping the back of the chair and he watched intently as the Pringles took their seats.

Clarence, stretched in the arm-chair from Guy's office, slid an oblique glance at Harriet as she sat down beside him. Frowning, he slid lower in the chair and began biting the side of his right forefinger. Toby caught her eye and grinned as though a particular understanding existed between them. The three women teachers watched Guy warmly. Dubedat kept his gaze fixed on Inchcape who, as soon as the room was settled again, said: "I happen to have good news up my sleeve. It came in just before I left the Bureau." As everyone fixed him expectantly, he smiled, holding the situation a moment before he said: "When our friend Dobson arrives, we may find the Legation has changed its tone."

Harriet wondered, was it possible that the war had ended? Miraculously and yet, of course, unsatisfactorily. No, the war couldn't end with the enemy unbeaten.

"I've just heard," Inchcape went on, "that last night the R.A.F. bombed Berlin."

"Why, that's splendid!" Guy said. Everyone murmured agreement, but they had clearly expected more.

"It *is* splendid. It means we're hitting back," said Inchcape. "This is the first time the German civilian has tasted this war. It is only a question of time before we're keeping them busy in the west, an eastern front will be out of the question."

Mrs. Ramsden gave an "ah!" of appreciation.

"A lot of things can happen before that day comes," Dubedat sombrely said.

"I'm not so sure," Inchcape pushed the chair from him and folded his arms. His smile suggested that he could, if he wished, justify his confidence. The others waited, but he said no more.

Feeling the silence begin to drag, Guy stood up. The women teachers turned to him as though he were about to solve something. He said: "The important thing is for us to stay. I mean, we should not run away. There are too many people here who need our support."

"I agree," Clarence's voice came rich, resonant and magnanimous from the depths of his chair.

The door fell open. "I do apologise," Dobson said as he hurried through it, his linen suit rumpled, a large patch of damp between his shoulder-blades. "They keep us at it day and night." He did not look at anyone but opened his eyes in amusement at things as they were and searched for a handkerchief. His face and head were pink. Beads of moisture stood among the downy hairs that patched his skull.

Inchcape stretched out his legs and jerked himself upright. "The floor is yours," he said.

Finding his handkerchief, Dobson patted all over his head. "Well now!" He smiled round with an appearance of easy faith in the good sense of those about him. "There isn't much to be said. I'm speaking for H.E., needless to say." At this, he stopped smiling and became serious. "Things are becoming unstuck here. You can see it for yourselves. Even His Majesty isn't feeling too secure on his throne. No one can be certain what will happen next. Our guess is that the Germans are planning to overrun the place. There's a pretty consistent pattern of events these days. A fifth column – in this case it would be the Iron Guard – creates trouble, giving Axis troops an excuse to march in and keep order. If this happens here, you may be given a chance to get out; then again, you may not. If you did get a warning, you might still fail to get transport. In any case, you'd probably have to abandon all your stuff. It could happen any time – next week, tomorrow, even tonight . . ." He looked round gravely and, meeting despondent eyes, smiled in spite of himself. "I don't want to scare you" – he swallowed his smile – "but there's not much point in waiting till it's too late. The English Department has done its bit. *Troilus and Cressida* was a simply splendid effort. The production boosted morale just when a boost was needed. I might say" – he gave a giggle – "you stuck to your posts like Trojans. Still" – he straightened his face again – "your work here is over. You must see that. H.E. thinks the department should close down and the staff pack up and get away in good order."

Having spoken, he glanced at Inchcape, restoring him to the centre of the attention. Inchcape did not move. Staring down at his white buckskin shoes, his hands clasped before him, he conveyed a modest intent to influence no one. After a long pause, he glanced up and from side to side, inviting independent opinion. Mrs. Ramsden's vast hat, trimmed with pheasant feathers, swung about as she looked for the next speaker, and her taffeta creaked. When no one else spoke, Miss Turner, the eldest of the three, said in her plaintive little voice: "We do know that things are bad here, but surely now that our aeroplanes have raided Berlin . . . I mean, surely that makes a difference?"

Dobson, leaning courteously towards her, explained as to a child: "We are all delighted about the raid. It's enormously good for our prestige, of course, but the situation here has deteriorated much too far to be affected by it. The truth is – we have to face it! – Rumania is, to all intents and purposes, in enemy hands."

Miss Turner looked sorrowfully at Inchcape, hoping for more favourable comment, but Inchcape had nothing to say. Guy again rose to his feet: "We've all known for some time that our situation here is precarious. In spite of that, we've chosen to stay. Probably we are a trouble to the Legation, but the point is . . ."

"My dear fellow," Dobson expostulated, "we're concerned for your safety."

"I am just twenty-four," Guy said. "Clarence, Dubedat and Lush are all of military age. Our contemporaries are in uniform. I do not think we're in any more danger here than we would be in the Western Desert."

Having decided what he would say, Guy said it with firm directness, but Harriet, watching him, realised he was under strain. He pressed the lower edge of his right palm against his brow and held it there as though for support. Coming from a provincial University and a background of poverty, he did not find it easy to withstand the majesty of the British Minister and his Legation.

He paused, then said quickly, almost aggressively: "I think we should remain in Bucharest while there is a job to be done."

"Here, here!" said Mrs. Ramsden.

"But *is* there a job to be done?" Clarence's tone had changed now to languid indecision. "What can we do – or the Legation, either, for that matter – remnants of a discredited force in what is virtually an enemy-occupied country?"

Guy said: "It's true, the British have failed here; but if we can stay to the end, we may give someone something to believe in during the time ahead. There are many people here in much greater danger than we are. For them we represent all that is left of Western culture and democratic ideals. We cannot desert them."

"Be reasonable, Pringle!" Dobson spoke amiably enough: "What have you got here now? A handful of Jewish students."

Guy answered: "While the Jewish students are loyal to us, we must remain loyal to them."

Dubedat, his face expressionless, was picking at an eye-tooth with one of his long dirty fingernails. Toby, pipe-sucking just behind him, leant forward and whispered something. Dubedat frowned him into silence.

Inchcape, bland now and smiling, sauntered forward, saying: "We must also remember the Cantecuzeno Lecture. Professor Lord Pinkrose is being flown out."

"Who the hell is Professor Lord Pinkrose?" Clarence asked. Lying there, supine, vacillating between truculence and sentiment, he was, Harriet realised, more drunk than sober.

Still smiling, Inchcape looked about him. "Does anyone need me to answer that?" he asked.

"The students are the first consideration," said Guy, dogged now in combating Legation indifference to his cause.

Harriet felt a stab of pride in him, yet felt, at the same time, some resentment that his first consideration was not their own safety. She knew, were it not for Sasha she would be concerned for nothing but getting Guy away before it was too late. Trapped here by her sense of responsibility for him, she was near to resenting Sasha too. And, she thought, it was Guy's easy, almost feckless willingness to adopt the world that had brought the boy into their home.

She did not really imagine that the Legation could persuade them to go 'in good order'. She had faith in Inchcape's determination to remain while there was any excuse for remaining, but she saw now that the problem of Sasha must be settled somehow. They must, when the time came, be free to go without a qualm.

Inchcape had taken the centre of the room again and was saying: "Pinkrose is out of the top drawer. That sort of thing goes down well with the Rumanians."

Apparently it also went down well with Dobson. He was already retreating. He had not been impressed by Guy's appeal for loyalty to the students, but here he was nodding in reverent approval as Inchcape enlarged on the social importance of the lecture and the lecturer. She was surprised that Dobson did not comment on the fact that the London office knew no better than to fly out this professor. Inchcape, of course, had kept them in ignorance of the true situation here – not wantonly, but from sheer unwillingness to face it. She smiled a little bleakly as it occurred to her that, thanks to Inchcape's vanity, Lord Pinkrose might end like the rest of them, in a German concentration camp.

"The lecture's a consideration, I agree." Dobson said, "though I'm sure H.E. would advise you to warn Lord Pinkrose what to expect here. If he knew the risks, he might think twice about coming . . ."

"I doubt that, I doubt that," Inchcape broke in affably.

"Well," Dobson concluded, "I suppose if your men are set on staying we'll have to let them stay, anyway for a while, But" – he turned to Mrs. Ramsden, Miss Turner and Miss Truslove – "the ladies are another matter. H.E. says he cannot accept liability for unmarried English ladies. That is, ladies without menfolk to look after them."

A moan passed among the three women. The feathers on Mrs. Ramsden's hat quivered as though set on wires. They looked at Dobson, who was beaming so pleasantly upon them, then turned to Inchcape for succour, but Inchcape, in high spirits at his victory, was willing to concede the women teachers. "On this point," he said, "I agree with His Excellency. I am sure you ladies would not wish to feel you were in the way here. Apart from that, your work is coming to an end. How many students enrolled for the summer school? Some two hundred. Now we've got – how many?" He cocked an inquiring eye at Guy, who answered reluctantly:

"About sixty. But the school is in five grades."

"It can be reorganised. The fact is," Inchcape looked at the women teachers, "your jobs will soon be folding up. You'd be better off elsewhere."

"We don't want to go," said Mrs. Ramsden.

"It's up to you, of course," Dobson said agreeably, "but when you next receive an order to quit I shall not be able to claim that your presence here is essential. It would be better for you to go in your own good time."

"But look here!" Mrs. Ramsden spoke with vigour, "We had all this when the war began. Mr. Woolley gave his general order for the ladies to leave Rumania. He sent his wife home. Dozens of others went at the same time and most of them never came back. We three went to Istanbul. We had to stay in a *pension* – a hole of a place, filthy dirty *and* expensive. We were miserable. We just sat about with nowhere to go and nothing to do. We spent all our savings – and for nothing, as it turned out. In the end we came back again. This is where we belong. Our homes are here. We're only old girls. The Germans wouldn't touch us."

"And I have my little income here," said Miss Turner, whose complexion had the bluish pallor of skimmed milk. "The Prince lets me have it, you know. I looked after his children for twenty years. I can't take this money out of the country. They won't let me. If I leave here, I'll be penniless."

"We'd rather stay and risk it," said Mrs. Ramsden.

"Dear lady," Dobson patiently explained, "if the Germans come in, they won't let you stay in your homes. You'll be sent to prison camps, somewhere like Dachau, a terrible place. You might be there for years. You'd never survive it."

Miss Truslove was dabbing at her eyes with a cotton glove. She spoke with an effort: "If I have to go away again, it'll kill me . . . kill me." Her speech ebbed and became a sob.

Inchcape patted her shoulder, but he was not to be moved. "In war-time," he said cheerfully, "we must all do things we don't like."

Miss Turner plucked at his sleeve: "But surely you said . . . this raid on Berlin . . ."

"Alas, that doesn't mean the end of the war," and he made a little gesture dismissing the whole subject.

Miss Truslove, near weeping, began struggling with her gloves. She moaned: "I can't get them on. I can't get them on."

Watching the old ladies, seeing them pitiable, Harriet knew nevertheless that Dobson was right. Mrs. Ramsden might eke out a few years in a prison camp, but Miss Turner and Miss Truslove, frail and nervous creatures, would be doomed. They were not looking so far ahead. Catching her eye, Mrs. Ramsden said: "I'm sure Mr. Pringle doesn't want us to go. I'd like to speak to him but" – she looked wistfully at Guy, who was talking to Dobson – "I suppose I shouldn't worry him now."

Harriet said: "Professor Inchcape is still in charge of the department. I'm afraid he has the last word."

As they moved off, they glanced back at Guy, hoping he would see them and somehow save them. But what could he do? He kept his back to them, probably in painful consciousness of their plight, and, with no excuse for lingering, they went.

Behind Harriet, Toby was talking about Cluj – the dangers he had foreseen there and his own wisdom in getting away before the present crisis developed. He claimed that the professor had attempted to 'bully-rag' him with all sorts of threats into keeping his contract, but Toby knew that as a foreigner he could plead *force majeure*. It was typical of Toby's stories. He led one to believe he had always been involved in such a morass of University politics, only a very wily fellow could have survived. It occurred to her, as she glanced round at his soft, fleshy face, his soft chin slipping back from under his moustache, hearing him say in self-congratulation: "A chap's got to survive," that he might well survive where the rest of them would not.

Suddenly Dubedat stepped briskly over to Dobson and broke into his talk with Guy. "About this Slav plot," he said as though he had no time to waste: "is there any basis for believing we'll be cut off from Constanza?"

Dobson, abashed for only a moment, answered lightly: "So far as we know, none at all," then turning from this intrusion, continued his conversation with Guy: "Hitler cares nothing for Balkan politics. He is interested only in Balkan economics. He has ordered the Rumanians to settle these frontier problems simply to keep them busy until his troops are free to march in. That could be any day now."

Dubedat glanced at Toby and made a movement with his head. He left the room. Toby followed him without a word.

The porter came to ask if he could lock up. Inchcape led Dobson, Clarence and the Pringles from the building. On the terrace, they paused in the greenish glow of evening. As the swaddling bands of heat loosened and the air moved and cooled, people were crowding out of doors. This was the pleasantest hour of daylight. Dobson offered a lift to whomsoever should want it, but the others preferred to walk. "I must be off then," he said, and with his front line curving out before him he ran trippingly down the steps.

Waiting till he was out of earshot, Inchcape laughed. "The day is ours," he said.

Guy was not responsive. His face was creased with concern for the victims of their victory. He said: "Perhaps we could give Mrs. Ramsden and the others introductions to our representative in Ankara? They're good teachers. He could use them."

"Why not? Why not?" said Inchcape, adding at once: "Now

how are we to entertain Pinkrose? I'm afraid he's a bit of a stick."

Harriet leant on the balustrade, gazing down into the flower-baskets. As she had expected, Clarence made his way over to her, though slowly and, she felt, unwillingly. When he reached her, she said: "Will we ever get away?"

Clarence was not in a sympathetic mood. "You're free to go any time," he said. "You haven't even a job to keep you here."

"I have a husband. Even if I were willing to go without him, he couldn't afford to keep two homes going."

"You could get work of some sort."

"That's not so easy in a foreign country. Anyway, I'm staying while Guy stays."

The gipsies, excited by the growing crowds, were darting about in their chiffon flounces, accosting people with shrieks of "Domnuli . . . domnuli . . . domnuli."

Harriet noticed Sophie standing among the flowers in a yellow dress cut to enhance her large bosom and small waist. Whom was she waiting for? She looked up and, noting Clarence above her, began moving from basket to basket with the peculiar precision of someone conscious of the limelight. She smiled admiration all about her, then paused at a basket packed with rosebuds. She picked one out, sniffed at it ecstatically, then held it at arm's length. Harriet half-expected her to stand on the point of one foot and pirouette. Instead, she approached the vendor.

The summer before, Harriet had watched Sophie bargaining for violets. Then she had bargained sharply; now she was all art-less sweetness. When the gipsy named a price, she made a little movement of hurt protest but, helpless in a world where even beauty had a price, she paid without argument.

Harriet looked at Clarence. Clarence was watching Sophie with a peculiar smile. "Is she waiting for you?" Harriet asked.

"I suppose so." Clarence smirked, knowing he had surprised her: "Sophie seems to have become attached to me for some reason. She said the other day that when I'm drunk I have a dangerous look."

"Oh, really!" Harriet laughed with more irritation than amusement: "I've seen you drunk often enough, but I've never seen you dangerous."

Clarence grunted, saying after a pause: "Sophie says you have no heart. I'm sure she isn't right."

"Do you want a woman with a heart?"

"No. I want someone as tough as old boots. In fact I want you. I knew you were my sort of woman the first time I set eyes on you. You could save me."

"You'd do better with Sophie."

Guy called to Harriet and he and Inchcape descended the steps. She followed with Clarence. Sophie, down on the pavement, showed surprise at seeing Clarence, but it was all spoilt by Clarence's reluctance to see her. She had to catch his arm. "I have had," she said, "a little chat with Mr. Dubedat and Mr. Lush. Ah, how nice is Mr. Lush! So straightforward, so honest, so simple and so kind of heart. A true representative of England, I would say." Her glance at Guy and Inchcape suggested they might well take a lesson from Mr. Lush, then she smiled at Clarence. Mumbling, shamefaced, he asked where they were going.

"I like so much Capa's," said Sophie. "The garden there is so nice."

Clarence looked at Inchcape and the Pringles, but there was no escape. As they went in one direction, he was led off in the other.

11

DRUCKER'S TRIAL HAD BEEN TWICE POSTPONED, then suddenly, at the end of August, it was announced for the following day.

There was consternation among ticket-holders given less than twenty-four hours in which to arrange the luncheon and cocktail parties attendant upon such an occasion. Princess Teodorescu, with so many friends to be transported to the court-house, was forced to appear herself in the Athénée Palace foyer and commandeer every car-owner with whom she could claim acquaintance. Among them was Yakimov. Delighted to be drawn into the fun, if only in the capacity of chauffeur, he spent his last hundred *lei* getting the Hispano cleaned.

These were the dog days of summer when, at noon, the sky was like an open furnace, but Yakimov was not much discomposed by the heat. He walked nowhere. He would drive the distance between the Pringles' flat and the hotel, even though the Hispano accelerated so rapidly, he was scarcely started before he must stop again. He enjoyed what he called "the cut and thrust" of Bucharest traffic. He had regained all his old skill as a driver. Foxy Leverett, seeing him pull up outside the Athénée Palace, said: "You ride that car, old boy, as though you're part of it." Although he had to admit that drink and misfortune had bedevilled his nerves, he could, when he chose, keep 'the old girl' going at a steady hundred.

On the first morning of the trial he rose early and, bathed and dressed in his best, reported at the hotel lobby.

Galpin was there, watching preparations. "Going to the trial?" he asked.

"Why, yes, dear boy," smiled Yakimov.

The English journalists were the only ones not invited and Galpin said glumly: "A waste of time, the whole slapstick. His Majesty won't get a penny out of it."

"You mean he can't confiscate the oil holdings?"

"I mean he'll be out on his ear."

Before Yakimov had time to be perturbed by this prediction, he was seized on by Baron Steinfeld, who ordered him to escort Princess Mimi and Princess Lulie. The two girls were clearly displeased at being relegated to Yakimov, who could only hope that the sight of the Hispano, newly polished, its chrome asparkle, would console them. Mimi, indeed, gave him a cold smile, but Lulie kept her narrow, sallow face averted and her eyes fixed on the distance. Even when crushed with him in the seat, the girls maintained an aloof silence. He pressed the starter. The engine whirred and died. He pressed it again. Again the engine whirred and died, whirred and died.

The girls gazed blankly through the windscreen.

The indicator marked "*Essence*", broken some years before, stood permanently at "*demi*", but the tank was empty. He had been driving on Foxy's two hundred litres and had completely forgotten the need to replenish them.

Lulie, dropping her eyelids, murmured: "*Quel ennui!*"

"We'll have to take a taxi," Mimi said and looked at Yakimov, but Yakimov had no money for a taxi. He jumped from the car, promising to be back "in a brace of shakes", and hurried to the bar, where he set about trying to borrow money. Galpin did not lend money. No one else had any money to lend. By this time the lobby had cleared. The other cars had started off. When Yakimov emerged again, still penniless, the princesses had disappeared.

He stood for a long time beside the car, mourning over it and begging help of everyone known to him who entered or left the hotel – but there was no one in Bucharest these days who was willing to lend him anything.

In the end he had to leave the car where it stood, immediately outside the hotel entrance, and after two days the manager ordered him to move it.

He had begged Dobson to make him an advance on his remittance and had been reminded that the whole sum had gone on his visas and the cost of retrieving the Hispano from the Yugoslavs. Yakimov's heart sank. However would he get to Freddi?

"Couldn't you lend your Yaki a thou or two?"

"No," said Dobson. Guy also said: "No." This was the end. The days of his refulgence were over for ever. He was not only penniless, he was nearly in rags. He had only two things left in the world – his car and the sable-lined greatcoat which the Czar had given his father.

He would have to sell the car. Having made that decision, he was suddenly gleeful. He would be in the money again. He would "make a packet". With this thought in mind, he set out to visit car salesrooms, which confirmed what Dobson had said. Only a few persons could afford to run a car like the Hispano, and those few were all Jews. As Jewish cars were being requisitioned by the army, it was unlikely anyone would buy it at all.

At last a salesman, whose window was at the junction of the Calea Victoriei and the Boulevard Breteanu, lent Yakimov a can of petrol with which to bring the car to the shop. "*C'est beau,*" he admitted when he saw it, but he would not buy. He agreed to display the car and would try to sell it for Yakimov. So it was driven into the large triangular window and left there.

Yakimov received no sympathy in the bar for the loss of the Hispano. When it had first appeared in Bucharest, Hadjimoscos had refused to go out and look at it, implying with a gesture that his life had been littered with such cars. Now he said: "Even were there no requisitions, only a fool would buy an Hispano. It eats up the *essence* and is without accommodation. No doubt, too, there will be many such cars for sale. The English, having failed to protect us, now run away to protect themselves."

Yakimov, quite bewildered, said: "It's true, dear boy, that a few old ladies have gone – Mrs. Ramsden and that lot – but . . ."

"I do not refer to old ladies," Hadjimoscos, agleam with malice, spoke very distinctly. "I refer to Mr. Dubedat and Mr. Lush."

"Lush and Dubedat? I'm sure you're mistaken, dear boy."

"I think not. They were seen leaving the town with very much luggage. People say they are no longer at the University."

Knowing nothing of this, Yakimov could only shake his head. When he returned to luncheon, he said to Guy: "There's a *canard* going round that Lush and Dubedat have packed their traps and hopped it. Not true, I'm sure."

Guy said nothing.

"They're still here, aren't they?" Harriet asked.

Guy shook his head. "I'm afraid they *have* gone."

"You said nothing about it. When did they go?"

"I've been expecting them to turn up. They told me they were going away for the week-end. I took their classes on Monday, then, when they weren't back on Wednesday, I sent a porter round to their flat. There was no one there, but the hall-porter there told him they'd paid off their servant and taken all their stuff away.

This morning they heard at the Consulate that Toby's old car has been found abandoned on the quayside at Constanza."

"They've bolted! They've gone to Instanbul."

After a pause, Guy said: "I suppose one can't blame them."

"Why can't one blame them?"

"They don't belong to the organisation. It's chance employment for them. Why should we expect them to take such a risk?"

"And now you have no help at all? You're alone at the University!"

"I'll manage somehow," said Guy.

That was all that was said in front of Yakimov. When he had retired, Harriet said: "With all these things happening, I have a feeling we won't be here much longer."

"Oh, I don't know. Things could settle down."

"I'm getting worried about Sasha."

Guy, preoccupied, said: "He's all right up there, isn't he?"

"Yes, he's all right. But what is going to happen to him if we go."

"We'll have to think about that. Would Bella take him in?"

"Bella? You're crazy."

"You said she was a decent sort."

She laughed at the fact Guy had simply taken her word for it, and said: "So she is, in a way, but one couldn't expect her to take in a Jewish deserter whom she has never met. Anyway, left alone here, she'll have her own problems. What about your students? Isn't there one who would hide him?"

"Several would, I'm sure," he said, then on reflection, he added: "But would it be fair to ask them? Besides, they're all hoping to get away. He would merely exchange one temporary refuge for another."

"Then what do you suggest?"

"Nothing at the moment." Mildly exasperated by her persistence, he added: "Now that Lush and Dubedat have gone, I have to rearrange all the classes. We can discuss this problem of Sasha when we have more time."

"All right," she said, wondering as she did so whether he had ever given any thought to it. How much feeling had he for Sasha? He had been fond of the boy when they were master and pupil. He had been grateful to the Druckers for extending their friendship to him while he was alone here. But how involved was he now? She felt the trouble was that Guy was fond of too many people.

Allegiance was a narrow business. She had almost ceased to expect it from him. It would be as difficult, she thought, to tie him down on Sasha's behalf as on her own.

Her long silence caused him to say: "Don't worry. We're not leaving tomorrow. We'll think of something." When she still did not speak, he went round the table, took her hands and pulled her up. "You don't trust me enough," he said.

She slid her arms round his waist and felt reassured by the nearness of his warm, muscular body. "Of course I trust you," she said and, their dissensions forgotten, they went into their room. But Guy could not forget the time for long. With all the work of the summer school on his hands, he would not even wait for tea.

As he was dressing, she said: "Couldn't I take some of the classes for you?"

He shook his head doubtfully: "You've no experience of teaching, you're quite unqualified and it's more difficult than you think."

12

WHEN GUY LEFT, Harriet, fretted by the peculiar insipidity of life at that hour, went out to the balcony and looked over the empty square. The air was furred with heat. On the pavement the Guardist youths with their banners and pamphlets, were still trying to rouse revolt. Although a sense of revolt agitated the nerves like an electric storm that would not break, the city was lethargic, the palace dormant, its white blinds drawn down against the tedium of the afternoon.

A third conference had broken down and now the Transylvanian question was being discussed in Vienna. People had begun again to believe it would be solved by proving insoluble. Yakimov, repeating the opinion of the bar, had said: "Dear girl, it'll all trickle out in talk, talk, talk."

It was barely five o'clock, but already the light had an autumnal richness. The height of summer was past. The dahlias were ablaze in the Cismigiu. Up the Chaussée, the trees were parched, their few leaves dangling like burnt paper, as they had been the first time she saw them. The brilliant months had gone down in fear and expectation of departure.

She had been married a year. It was, as Guy liked to point out, a pre-war marriage. With a sadness that seemed an emanation of the deepening, dusty colour of the air, she thought perhaps it might not, after all, prove to be what it had seemed at first, an eternal marriage. She could imagine the loosening of the bond. Guy had said to her: "You can't trust me enough," yet he had not had cause to say that when, after three week's acquaintance, she had crossed Europe with him. If she did not trust him now, if, left on her own, she sought companionship elsewhere, he had himself to blame.

At that moment, she remembered that Sasha had asked her to do something for him. He had asked her to try and see his father.

Drucker was, for the moment, the most talked-of man in Bucharest; the *u* sound of his name seemed constantly in the air. Despina's husband had brought in the information that at different

times of the day the accused man could be seen entering and leaving the back entrance of the court-house. Despina, always eager
to impart news, had run at once to tell Sasha. The next time
Harriet had gone up on the roof, she had found him awaiting her
in great excitement. He began eagerly to beg to be allowed to go,
that very evening, to see his father leave the court, and perhaps
even accost him.

Harriet had been appalled at the suggestion. "It's out of the
question," she said. "The military police are looking for you.
They might be waiting there for you, and there's the danger
someone might recognise you, expecially if you spoke to him . . ."

He had interrupted eagerly: "I could stand where no one would
see me. I could just look at him."

"Wherever you stood, someone might see you. The risk is too
great."

Used to his gentle compliance, she was surprised when he persisted, his face becoming vivid with his eagerness to go. She
reasoned with him as with a child that must be protected against
its own rashness.

After a few minutes, his fervour suddenly collapsed. He looked
so desolate that she felt guilty and wondered how much of her
own opposition came of a will to control him. In a way Guy had
eluded her, but Sasha was not only her pet and dependent, he
was her prisoner. Nevertheless, she could not permit him to walk
into a trap.

Watching her, he said: "If you won't let me go, will you go
yourself? If you saw him, you might be able to speak to him."

Startled by this suggestion, Harriet said: "If I went, what could
I say."

"Tell him I'm with you. Say: 'Don't worry about Sasha. We
are looking after him.' "

That had been yesterday morning. Although she had not agreed
to go, she had not actually refused. She discovered that Drucker
left the court-house at midday, returned at three o'clock and left
again at six o'clock, but she made no attempt to see him at any of
those times. If she did go, she knew she would not speak to him.
For one thing, his warders would probably not permit such a
thing. For another, the English were conspicuous here. She must
not give the outside world cause to connect her with the Druckers.
Apart from all that, she had no wish to seem to gape at a man who
had suffered the rigours of nine months in a Rumanian prison.

She decided she could not go. Yesterday evening, when Sasha was expecting her to bring him news of his father, she had failed to visit him. As she wondered how she could excuse her dereliction, she suddenly felt that he had not asked so much of her. Turning to her image of Guy, she protested: "If you give your devotion to others, why shouldn't I?"

She started out immediately after tea. As she crossed the square she noticed the blinds were being raised in the palace and cars were entering through the palace gates. She could see from their white uniforms that the new arrivals were Crown councillors. The square, too, was coming to life. People were strolling in from the side-streets and gathering on the pavement outside the palace rail. Their pace suggested not so much an event as hope of one.

By the time she had reached the main road, the newsboys were out. She bought *L'Indépendence Romaine* and read two lines in the stop press. Agreement had been reached in Vienna. Terms would be announced.

No time was given for the announcement, but people were coming out into the streets, all, for some reason, lively, as though expectant of good news.

The trial was again of secondary importance. On previous days, crowds of spectators had gathered to view the ticket-holders and the famous forty-nine witnesses called against the accused. This evening there were scarcely a dozen round the front entrance. At the back, in an area of small warehouses and workrooms still at work, there were some six or eight. They were discussing the news of the Transylvanian settlement and took no notice of Harriet.

A smell of salt fish hung in the air and the narrow, cobbled pavements were gritty with sand. A windowless van was at the kerb, its doors open to receive Drucker, who was due to appear at any minute. Harriet stood behind a group of clerks and gathered from their conversation that the prevailing optimism was based on the fact that Rumania had been acknowledged as a partner of the Axis. The Führer would see that she received fair treatment. One clerk said they might have to cede a province or two, but no more. In his opinion the German minorities in Transylvania favoured the Rumanian cause because the Rumanians, as a people, were more amenable than the arrogant, independent Hungarians.

The court door was thrown open and two warders emerged.

Harriet, who had seen Drucker only once, ten months before,

remembered him as a man in fresh middle age, tall, weighty, elegant, handsome, who had welcomed her with a warm gaze of admiration.

What appeared was an elderly stooping skeleton, a cripple who descended the steps by dropping the same foot each time and dragging the other after. The murmurs of "Drucker" told her that, whether she could believe it or not, this was he. Then she recognised the suit of English tweed he had been wearing when he had entertained the Pringles to luncheon. The suit was scarcely a suit at all now. As he approached, she noticed his trousers were so worn at the knees that she could see, as it bent against the cloth, the white bone of his knee-cap, but the broad herringbone pattern showed through the grime.

From the bottom step he half-smiled, as though in apology, at his audience, then, seeing Harriet, the only woman present, he looked puzzled. He paused and one of the warders gave him a kick that sent him sprawling over the narrow pavement. As he picked himself up, there came from him a stench like the stench of a carrion bird. The warder kicked at him again and he fell forward, clutching at the van steps and murmuring "*Da, da*," in zealous obedience.

As soon as the van doors closed on him, Harriet, unconscious now of the ferment of the pavements, hurried back to the Calea Victoriei. By the time she reached the end of it, she had decided she could safely deceive Sasha. He was never likely to see his father again.

There was now a considerable crowd in the square. Approaching her block of flats, she glanced up at the roof and saw Sasha on the parapet, staring down towards her. When she reached him, she was able to say convincingly: "Your father looked very well."

"You really saw him?" He had jumped down at the sight of her and brushed his cheeks with the back of his hand, but she could see he had been crying. He asked eagerly: "And were you able to speak to him? Did you tell him I was living here."

"Yes of course."

"I am sure he was pleased."

"Very pleased. I can't stay, I'm afraid. Guy is bringing a friend in to supper," and she went to avoid answering further questions.

The friend was David Boyd whom Harriet had not seen since their last meeting in the English Bar. He had then gone for a "bird-watching week-end", which had become so protracted that Guy had at last telephoned the Legation to ask for news of him. Foxy Leverett's secretary would say nothing but "The Legation is not alarmed by Mr Boyd's absence."

When David telephoned that morning Harriet had felt relief at his safe return, realising he had become important to her as one of their small and dwindling community. His sound nerves were comforting. And he was Guy's friend. Whoever might desert them, David, she was sure, would stay to the end.

While awaiting the men, she heard a sound of agitation in the square and was about to send Despina to discover the cause of it, when Guy and David came in through the front door. David was talking loudly: "It's exactly what Klein predicted. You remember his image of the great fortune? Well, this is the last of it down the drain. The country is falling to pieces."

As they entered the room the two men, both large, their dissimilarities masked by sunburn, looked remarkably alike. They differed only in the colour of their hair. Guy had become bleached by the sun, David had remained very dark. His black curls glistened with moisture, and moisture lay along the ridge of his large dark chin. Both were carrying their jackets caught under their elbows. They had been walking and their shirts were soaking. A smell of sweat entered with them.

Guy said: "The terms of the settlement are out. Rumania has to cede the whole of Northern Transylvania: the richest part of it."

"Quite a nice bit of territory," David said, snuffling in delight: "Area about seventeen thousand square miles, population two and a half millions. But it means more than that. The Rumanians are emotional about Transylvania, 'the cradle of the race'. This means trouble – as I imagine His Majesty will soon discover."

Harriet asked: "What's happening outside now?"

"People are weeping in the streets."

Harriet, shocked, felt like weeping herself. If asked, she would have said she expected nothing different and yet she had, she realised, ingested the baseless, febrile hopes that had lately possessed the Rumanians.

While they ate supper the sun slipped down behind the sunset clouds, heaped, livid, in the west, their gloom hung over the square. The crowds seemed muted now as by catastrophe. Even the traffic had stopped. Harriet, with little appetite for food, felt, as she had felt after the earthquake, a desire to be in the open and touch the ground.

She said: "But are the Rumanians bound to accept this?"

"What else can they do?" David asked. "The terms were dictated by Ribbentrop and Ciano. The Rumanian ministers were told that if they did not accept, their country would immediately be occupied by German, Hungarian and Russian troops."

"The Rumanians might fight," said Harriet.

Eating heartily, exhilarated by events, David said in tolerant amusement at her folly: "A war between Rumania and Germany would be like the life of primitive man: nasty, brutish and short."

"Why are the Rumanians being treated in this way?"

"They must be asking that themselves. I suppose they're being made to pay for their old friendship with Britain. There's also a story going round that Carol, while pretending to play ball with Hitler, was in fact trying to form a military alliance with Stalin."

"Do you think that's true?" Guy asked.

"Whether true or not, it will be believed. Carol is a clever man whose behaviour from beginning to end has been that of a fool. The worst thing is that this division is not going to solve any of the Transylvanian problems. Hitler is simply cutting the baby in half. But what does he care? He's keeping the Hunks quiet; and if he ever wants their help, he'll probably get it."

They took their coffee out on to the balcony where the twilight had almost turned to dark. The chandeliers were alight inside the main rooms of the palace. A great crowd filled the square. The stunned silence was breaking now and a sense of perturbation came up upon the air. The shadows below were moving; someone was addressing them, then a single tenor voice was lifted in the national anthem that began "*Treasca Regili*" – Hail the King!

The first words were scarcely out when the singing was lost in a hubbub of angry shouting. The word "*abdică*" rose above the uproar and was taken up and repeated in different parts of the square, gathering volume until it seemed all the country's protest was resolved into the single demand that the King be king no longer.

13

THE WEEK THAT FOLLOWED was a trying one for Yakimov. Whenever, on his way to and from the bar, he tried to cross the square, he was harangued and buffeted by people demonstrating for or against the King – usually against. Leaflets were pushed into his hand in which Carol was condemned as a traitor. The Guardists declared they had proof of his attempt to form an alliance with Russia. This shocking act of treachery, they said, had alienated their German friends. In view of this the Axis decision on Transylvania had been a just one. The country had paid for the sins of its ruler.

The Guardists, however, were the only ones who had a good word for the Axis these days. So this, people said, was how the Führer treated his children! This was their reward for sending their beasts, crops and oil to Germany! The truth was, Hitler had failed in his attempts to invade Britain, and had turned, in spite, against Rumania! Yakimov had actually seen a swastika torn from a car and trodden underfoot, but the sight had merely increased his trepidation at these disturbances. "*Quel débâcle!*" he said, "*quel débâcle!*" and it was no longer a little joke.

Hadjimoscos especially upset him by describing the frightful consequences should the King be dethroned. Ignored by the Guardists and having nothing to hope for from them, Hadjimoscos had become a fervent royalist. The departure of the King, he declared, would bring "absolute anarchy". "We of the old aristocracy," he said to Yakimov, "would be the first to suffer. You, as a member of the English ruling class, would face immediate arrest. The Guardists are frantically anti-British. I would not put it past those fellows to erect the guillotine. It will be *la Terreur* all over again, I assure you. We are in this together, *mon prince*," and he gave Yakimov's arm a squeeze, for the Rumanians, in their bitterness against Germany, were remembering their attachment to their old ally.

Britain had declared against the division of Transylvania and suddenly everyone was saying that, in spite of everything,

Britain would win the war and restore all Rumania's possessions. And perhaps she would! But not in time to save poor Yaki.

Sunday afternoon being a time when everyone was free, the commotion in the square was much greater than usual. Someone, bawling in the midst of the crowd, was rousing so much anger that Yakimov was prompted to make a detour, but he felt too tired. Bemused from his siesta and the dense heat, he slipped into the crowd and moved vaguely towards the hotel. The going was easy for a dozen yards, then he began to strike impassable knots of people. He changed direction again and again, each time finding the press growing thicker about him. When he glimpsed the speaker – a young man flinging himself wildly about on a platform – he realised he was going in the wrong direction. He attempted retreat, but the ranks had closed in behind him. Here people were not only compacted but, in full hearing of the frenzied oratory, were in a state of furious excitement. Tense, inflamed, straining and shouting, they had no awareness of Yakimov, who, murmuring apologies, began trying to edge out through any crack he could find.

Suddenly, it seemed to him, his neighbours went mad. They not only shouted, they threw up their arms, shook fists, stamped feet, and he, inadvertently struck and jolted, could only cower and plead: "Steady, dear boy, steady!" As the turbulence grew about him, there was a violent surge forward and Yakimov was carried with it, so tightly held that he could not raise his arms. He felt stifled, not only by the pressure on his frail chest and belly, but by the heat of the crowd and its reek of sweat and garlic. Feeling that his lungs had collapsed, so he could not even call for help. In terror, knowing that if he lost consciousness he would be dragged down and trampled underfoot, he reached out and clung to the man in front of him. This was a large black-bearded priest whose veiled headgear had been dodging about before Yakimov's eyes like a ship's funnel in a gale. The priest was howling with the rest of them – something to do with Transylvania, of course – while Yakimov, certain the killing was about to begin, hung round his shoulders, pleading in a whisper: "For God's sake, save me, Let me out."

He was thinking: "This is the end for Yaki," when he felt a slackening of the frenzy about him. Warning shouts were coming from the edge of the crowd. In a moment, the speaker had dropped from his platform and disappeared into anonymity. People began straining round, and as calls of *"Politeul"* passed among them the struggle turned outwards. Caught in this new movement, Yakimov, almost dead of compression and fear, held like a drowning man to the priest, who stood still, anchored by sheer weight in the current.

Through the thinning crowd Yakimov could see the reason for the dispersal. The police were preparing to turn hoses on the demonstrators. As the jets of water were raised, he tried to run with the rest, but now the priest to whom he had clung, clung to him, seizing and gripping his hand to hold him upright as men pelted past them, bouncing against them like boulders in an avalanche. Yakimov, thrown in every direction by these blows, felt as though his arm was being wrenched from its socket. He cried to be released, but the priest held to him, all the while grinning reassuringly at him with gigantic, grey-brown teeth.

The square cleared. No one remained by Yakimov and the protector from whom he was still struggling to escape. Both of them were soaked. At last the priest thought it safe to let go his hold. Smiling the smile of a benefactor, he brushed Yakimov down, patted him on the back and sent him on his way.

Yakimov made straight for cover. Stumbling, trembling, dripping with water, he fell into the English Bar, which at that time of day was packed with journalists. Galpin and Screwby were there together with old Mortimer Tufton and the visitors from neighbouring capitals who always turned up when trouble was in the air.

Yakimov did not wait to see if anyone would offer him a drink. He went to the bar and bought one for himself. He longed to talk of his experience, but those around were too busy discussing what had occurred to notice someone who had been in the midst of it. He swallowed his *ţuică*, then, trembling and sweating and seeking comfort, he stood as near as he dared to Galpin.

When Galpin bought a round of drinks, a glass came accidentally to Yakimov, who gulped it down before anyone could take it from him. Short of a drink, Galpin looked round to account for it and, noticing Yakimov, shot out an arm and seized him. "I've been looking for you," he said.

Terror following on terror, Yakimov cried: "I didn't mean to. I thought it was meant for me."

"Pipe down. I'm not going to eat you." Still holding to him,

Galpin led him out of the bar into the lobby. "I want you to do a little job for me."

"A *job*, dear boy?"

"You did a job for McCann once, remember? Well, I want you to give me a hand. I suppose you've heard that the Hungarians march into Transylvania on the fifth. I ought to get to Cluj to see the take-over, but I've got to stay here in case the balloon goes up. So I want you to go to Cluj for me."

Yakimov's immediate thought was of Freddi, but all the spirit had been shaken out of him. "I don't know, dear boy," he said, hesitant. "It's a long journey, and with the country in revolt . . ."

"You'd be a lot safer there than here," Galpin assured him. "*This* is where the trouble will be. It's all centred round the palace. Cluj is unaffected. Good food, charming place, nice people. Restful journey. All expenses paid. Could you ask for more?"

"What would I have to do?"

"Oh, just keep your eyes and ears open. Get the atmosphere of the place. Look around, tell me what's going on." When Yakimov still showed no enthusiasm, Galpin added: "I helped you when you needed help. You want to help me, don't you?"

"Naturally, dear boy."

"Well, then . . . You'd only be away a couple of nights. I must have the news hot."

Yakimov, recovering as the attraction of the trip took hold of him, said: "Delighted to go, of course. Delighted to help. And, I may say, you've come to the right man. I've a friend there in a very important post. Count Freddi von Flügel."

"Good God! The bloody Gauleiter?" Galpin's yellow eyeballs started out at Yakimov. "You can't go and see *him*." Then as Yakimov's face fell, he added quickly: "It's up to you, of course. After all, he's a friend of yours. That makes a difference. Go and see him if you want to, but leave me out of it." Galpin drew out a note-case. "I'll advance you five thousand for expenses. If that doesn't cover things, we'll settle up when you get back."

Yakimov held out a hand, but Galpin, on reflection, put the case back again. "I'll give it to you when you leave. That'll be Wednesday. Give them time to get steamed up. You'd better take the midday train. I'll call for you eleven-thirty, take you to the station myself. Come along." He gripped Yakimov as though intending to keep him in custody until he went: "I'll buy you another drink."

14

AWAKENED BY EXCITEMENT on Wednesday morning, Yakimov was up and dressed before ten o'clock. The idea of Cluj now possessed him. His one thought was to get to safety, Freddi and good food; his one fear that transport might stop before he could set out.

The disturbances during the last days had been an agony to him. There had been constant uproar in the square. Shots had been fired at the palace. Rumours of every sort had gone round. Antonescu had been summoned to the palace and ordered to form a government. He had said he would not serve under a non-constitutional monarchy. At this, he had been sent back to prison again.

Yakimov had scarcely hoped to reach Wednesday alive. And now at last it was Wednesday. The square was quiet. The King was still in his palace and so far as Yakimov was concerned, all was right with the world.

Harriet was still at the breakfast table when he made his early appearance. She had just heard on the radio that the Drucker trial had ended late the previous evening. Drucker had been found guilty and sentenced to three terms of imprisonment for different currency offences: seven years, fifteen years and twenty-five years to run consecutively. She added these up on the margin of a newspaper and discovered that the banker was to be imprisoned for forty-seven years. And nobody cared, nobody was interested. The court had been almost empty when sentence was pronounced. The trial which was to be "the major social occasion of the summer", had become a hurried, paltry affair, precipitated by crisis and fear of invasion.

Harriet was astonished when Yakimov told her he was leaving for Cluj. It had never entered her head that he might take himself off, even for a couple of nights.

She said: "Do you think it's a good idea leaving Bucharest at a time like this?"

"Yaki will be all right. Going on important business, as a matter of fact. Could call it a mission."

"What sort of mission?"

" 'Fraid I can't divulge, dear girl. Hush-hush, you understand? But between you and me and the gate-post, I've been told to keep m'eyes and ears open."

"Well, I hope you don't end up in Bistrita."

He gave a nervous laugh. "Don't frighten your poor old Yaki."

When he had finished breakfast – one of those wretched skin-flint meals that made him impatient for Freddi's hospitality – he went back to his room to pack. Most of his clothing was now beyond repair. He picked out the best of it and filled his crocodile case. When he took his passport from a drawer, he found, folded inside it, the plan of the oil-well which he had taken from Guy's desk. Not knowing what else to do with it, he put it into his pocket. He was forced, for fear of rousing Galpin's suspicions, to leave behind his sable-lined greatcoat; but, if need be, his old friend Dobbie could send it on to him through the diplomatic bag.

Yakimov travelled in the dining-car. Even had he wished to sit anywhere else, there would have been no room for him. He had arrived to find every carriage of the midday train crowded and the corridors made impassable by peasants packed together, their feet entangled in their gear. The dining-car was locked. At either entrance affluent-looking men, carrying brief-cases, stood await-ing admission. A few minutes before twelve the doors were unlocked. The men elbowed one another in and Yakimov went in with them. "There you are," said Galpin, "You'll do the trip in style." Yakimov found a seat and was well satisfied.

Luncheon was served at once; a wretched luncheon. A Hun-garian complained and the head waiter shouted at him: "You'll get nothing at all when your German friends follow you into Transylvania."

Some deplorable coffee followed: there was no sugar. Now that beet was being exported to Germany, sugar was becoming scarce in Rumania. When the meal ended, the stifling heat of the car became weighted by cigarette smoke. It was past three o'clock. The train still stood in Bucharest station. There was no explana-tion of the delay and no one seemed perturbed by it. It was enough for the passengers that they were on a train that must move some time, while outside there were vast and agitated numbers of those who were not on any train at all.

The meal was paid for, the tables cleared. Conversation failed in the oppressive heat and one by one the men – Yakimov among them – folded their arms on the wine-stained, rumpled cloths, dropped down their heads and slept among the crumbs. Most of them did not know when the train started.

Somehow or other it crawled up into the mountain. Yakimov was awakened when the waiters brought round coffee and cakes. Anyone refusing these refreshments was told he must give up his seat.

Munching the dry, soya-flour cakes and sipping the grey coffee, Yakimov gazed out at the crags and pines of the Transylvanian Alps. The train stopped at every small station. People on the platform were wearing heavy clothing, but the air, unchanged inside the carriage, remained warm, flat and clouded like stale beer. Depressed by the magnificence of the scenery, Yakimov hid his face in the dusty rep window curtain and went to sleep again.

The afternoon faded slowly into evening. Every half an hour or so, coffee was served, each cup weaker than the last. Yakimov began to worry as his money dwindled. He knew he should leave the car but, seeing at either end of the carriage the doorways packed with men only too ready to displace him, he stayed where he was.

At Braşov a seat became vacant and the first of those waiting hurried into it. He slapped down a brief-case and a large weighty bag, took off his silver-coloured Homburg and sat down, an important-looking Jew. Despite his importance, he could not refrain from nervously opening and shutting the brief-case, taking out papers, glancing at them, putting them back and so bringing Yakimov to full wakefulness. Yakimov sat up, yawning and blinking, and the Jew, looking critically at him, said: "*Sie fahren die ganze Strecke, ja?*"

When he discovered that Yakimov was English, his manner changed, becoming confiding though overweening. He took out a Rumanian passport and waved it at Yakimov. "You see that?" he said. "It is mine since two years. For it I pay a million *lei*. Now" – he struck it contemptuously with the back of his fingers – "what is it now? A ticket to a concentration camp."

"Surely not as bad as that?" Yakimov said.

The Jew sniffed his contempt. "You English are so simple. You cannot believe the things that happen to others. Have you not seen those madmen of the Iron Guard? In 1937 what did they do? They took the Jews to the slaughter-house and hung them on meat-hooks."

"But you're going to Cluj," said Yakimov. "When the Hungarians come in, you can get a Hungarian passport."

"What!" The Jew now looked at him with anger as well as contempt. "You think I go there to live? Certainly not. I go to close my branch office, then I come away double-quick. The Hungarians are terrible people – they are ravening beasts. Now it is very dangerous in Cluj."

"Dangerous?" Yakimov was startled.

"What do you think?" the Jew scoffed at him: "You think the Rumanians hand over like gentlemen. Naturally, it is dangerous. There are shootings in the streets. The shops are boarded up. No one has food . . ."

"Do you mean the restaurants are closed?"

The Jew laughed. He slapped his bag and said: "Here I bring my meat and bread."

Noting Yakimov's glum expression, he spoke with relish of raping, pillage, slaughter and starvation. The Rumanians had introduced land reform. Under the Hungarians the peasants would have to give up their small plots.

"So," said the Jew, "they are running wild in the streets. Already people have been killed and the doctors are packing their hospitals and leaving. They will attend no one. It is a terrible time. Did you not ask why the train came so late from Bucharest? It was because there was so much rioting. They feared the train would be wrecked."

"Dear me!" said Yakimov to whom it was now clear that Galpin had chosen the safer part.

"You go perhaps on business?"

"No, I am a journalist."

"And you do not know how are things in Cluj?" The Jew laughed and looked pityingly at Yakimov, while outside a gloomy twilight fell on a landscape in which there was no sign of life. Dinner was served, the worst Yakimov had ever eaten. He grudged the cost of it, especially as he was left with barely enough to pay for a night's lodging.

In the grimy ceiling of the car a few weak bulbs appeared. The landscape faded away, and now there was nothing to look at but the weary faces of other passengers.

About midnight they began rousing themselves, hoping for the journey's end. No coffee had been served since dinner. The kitchen had closed down, yet the train dragged on for another two hours.

When they reached Cluj, Yakimov rose to bid his companion goodbye, but the Jew, having collected his possessions some time before, was already up and fighting his way off the train. Most of the other dining-car passengers were doing the same thing, so that in a few minutes Yakimov found himself alone. The platform, when he reached it, was dark and empty of officials or porters. The offices were shut and padlocked. A soldier with a rifle at the station entrance re-roused Yakimov's apprehensions.

Outside the station he saw the reason why the others had left in such a hurry. There were no taxis, but there had been half a dozen ancient *trăsurăs* which had been commandeered and were moving off. Those who had failed to snatch one had to walk. It was surprising how few people there were. The train must have emptied at stations along the line and Yakimov set out with only a handful of other persons towards the town. These dispersed in different directions, so that soon he knew from the silence that he was alone.

He had expected mobs and riots, but now he feared the road's emptiness. It was a long road hung down the centre with white globes of light that were reflected in the glossy tarmac. The pavements were dark. Anything might lurk in the hedges. He was relieved when he reached the first houses. Almost at once he found himself in the cathedral square which, Galpin had told him, was the centre of the town. The main hotel was here. Galpin had promised to telephone and book him a room. Seeing its vestibule lighted, he told himself thankfully that they had waited up for him.

When he entered and gave his name the young German clerk made a gesture of hopelessness. No one could have telephoned because the telephone equipment was being dismantled; not that a call would have made any difference. The hotel had been full for days. Every hotel in Cluj was full. Rumanians were coming here to settle up their Transylvanian affairs. Hungarians were crowding in to seize the business being relinquished by others. "Such is the take-over," said the young man. "There is not a bed to be found

in the whole town." Looking sorry for Yakimov, who looked
sorry for himself, he added: "At the station you could sleep on a
bench."

Yakimov had another idea. He asked the way to the house of
Count Freddi von Flügel. Seeming pleased that Yakimov had this
refuge, the young German came to the hotel entrance with him
and showed him a white eighteenth-century Hungarian house
that stood four-square not a hundred yards away.

Despite the heat of the night, all the shutters of the house were
closed. Its massive iron-studded door made it look like a fortress.
Yakimov hammered on this door for five minutes or more before
a grille opened and the porter inside, speaking German, ordered
him to be off and return, if he must return, in the morning. Yakimov, putting his hand in the grille to prevent its being closed on
him, said: "*Ich bin ein Freund des Gauleiters, ein sehr geschätzter
Freund. Er wird entzückt sein, mich zu begrüssen.*" He repeated these
statements several times, becoming tearful as he did so, and they
slowly took effect. The door was opened.

The porter motioned him to sit on a stone seat in a stone hall
that was as cold as a cellar. He sat there for twenty minutes.
Having come from the summer night, wearing his silk suit, he
began to shiver and sneeze. There was nothing to distract him but
some giant photographs of Hitler, Goring, Göebbels and Himm-
ler, which he contemplated with indifference. To him they were
nothing but the stock-in-trade of someone else's way of life. If
Freddi were "in with that lot", then all the better for both of them.

At last, at last, a figure appeared at the top of the stone staircase. Yakimov jumped up crying: "Freddi."

The Count, doubtful, frowning, descended slowly, then,
recognising Yakimov, he threw open his arms and sailed down
with rapid steps, his yellow brocade dressing-gown floating out
about him. "It is possible?" he asked. "Yaki, *mein Lieber!*"

Tears of relief filled Yakimov's eyes. He tottered forward and
fell into Freddi's arms. "Dear boy" – he spoke on a sob – "so many
bridges gone under the water since we last met!" He held to his
old friend fervently, breathing in the strong smell of gardenia that
came from his person. "Fredi," he murmured, "Fredi!"

The emotional moment of reunion past, von Flügel stepped
back and contemplated Yakimov with misgiving. "But is this
wise, *mein Lieber*? We are now, you know, in opposite camps."

Yakimov, with a gesture, swept such considerations aside.

"Desperate situation, dear boy. Just arrived from Bucharest to find the hotels full. Not a bed to be got in Cluj. Couldn't sleep in the street, y'know."

"Certainly not," von Flügel agreed: "I am only hoping for your sake you were not followed here. Have you eaten?"

"Not a bite, dear boy. Not a morsel all day. Poor old Yaki's famished and dropping on his poor old feet."

The Count led the way upstairs and, opening a door, snapped on switch after switch. Chandeliers of venetian glass sprang into light throughout an immense room.

"What do you think of my lounge?" He spoke the word as though it had an exotic chic. Yakimov, not much interested in such things, looked round at the purple and yellow room with its vast gilded chimney-piece flanked by life-size plaster negroes naked except for the chiffon loin-cloths playfully placed about their immense pudenda.

"Delightful!" Yakimov limped to a sofa and sank down among the cushions. "Crippled," he said: "Crippled with fatigue."

"I designed it all myself."

"And hungry as a hunter," Yakimov reminded him.

As his host moved about, admiring and touching his own possessions, Yakimov, impatient for a drink, looked at Freddi more critically. How changed he was! His hair, that had once fallen like silk into his eyes, was now cut *en brosse*. His features, never distinctive, were lost in wastes of mauve-pink flesh – and he had grown a shocking little moustache that stood out like a yellow scab on his upper lip. His famous blue eyes were no longer blue: they were pink. Yet Freddi had been recognisable at once from his movements, that were, as they always had been, curiously fluid.

Meeting Yakimov's eye, von Flügel giggled. Yakimov recognised the giggle, too. That and the features were all that remained of the golden boy of 1931.

"How well you are looking!" said Yakimov.

"You, too, *mein Lieber*. Not a day older."

Well satisfied, Yakimov unlaced his shoes saying: "They're killing me." He shook them off, then, looking down at his feet, saw his socks were tattered and dark with sweat, and shuffled his shoes on again. "Trifle peckish," he said when Freddi had made no move.

Freddi tugged an embroidered bell-pull. While they waited,

Yakimov's roving eye noted a tray of bottles. "How about a little drinkie?" he said.

"So remiss of me!" Von Flügel poured out a large brandy. Yakimov took it as his due. Freddi had done very well out of old Dollie when her fortunes were high and his were low.

"And what brings you to Cluj?" von Flügel asked.

"Ah!" said Yakimov, his attention on his glass.

"I suppose I should not ask?"

Yakimov's smile confirmed this supposition.

There was a sharp rap on the door. Von Flügel sat up and straightened his shoulders before commanding: "*Herein.*"

A young man marched in, uniformed, muscular, conveying, without any hint of expression, a virulent annoyance. Yakimov did not like his face, but von Flügel leapt up, fluid and giggling once more, and saying: "Axel, *mein Schatz!*" went close to the young man and talked at him in a persuasive whisper until something was agreed. When Axel slammed his way out, von Flügel explained: "The poor boy's a little put out. We brought him from his bed. The cook is a local man. He goes home after dinner and I am then dependent on the boys."

When Axel returned, he brought a plate of sandwiches, which he put down with the abruptness of the unwilling and went off slamming the door again.

Yakimov, deliciously infused with brandy, settled down to the sandwiches, which were rough but contained some sizeable chunks of turkey. He silenced Freddi's apologies, saying: "Poor Yaki's used to living rough."

When he had eaten, the Count, who had been watching him with a waggish expression, went over to a corner that was cut off by a Recamier couch. "I have some amusing curiosities I really must show you," he said.

Yakimov lifted himself wearily out of the cushions. Von Flügel, having drawn aside the couch, beckoned his friend into the corner and handed him a magnifying glass. On either wall hung a Persian miniature. Yakimov examined them, tittering and saying: "Dear boy! Dear boy!" but he had no interest in that sort of thing and hoped he was not in for a night of it.

"Over here, over here," said von Flügel, leading him across the room to a tall cabinet set with shallow drawers. "You must see my Japanese prints."

"Oh, dear!" said Yakimov, taking the prints handed to him: "One must sit down to enjoy such things."

He tried to return to the sofa, but von Flügel held to him, pulling him here and there between the purple and yellow armchairs, and opening Chinese lacquer cabinets to display his collection of what he called "delectable *objets*".

As the effect of the brandy wore off, Yakimov became not only bored but cross. He had forgotten that Freddi was such a silly.

"Being in an official position," said von Flügel, "discretion is forced upon me, but one day I hope to have all my things out and displayed about the lounge."

"Lounge!" Yakimov said: "Where did you pick up that awful house agent's jargon?"

"Am I being vulgar?" asked von Flügel, too excited to care. "I *must* show you my Mexican pottery."

When Yakimov had been shown everything, von Flügel seemed to imagine he was the one who had earned a reward. He said in a tone of humorous complaint: "You still haven't told me what you are doing in Cluj."

Yakimov, sinking into his seat, said: "First I must have a drink, dear boy." His glass full, he sipped at it in better humour. "If I told you I was a war correspondent," he said, "you wouldn't believe me."

Freddi looked surprised. "A war correspondent! In which zone?"

"Why, in Bucharest, dear boy."

"But Rumania is not at war."

Yakimov thought this a quibble. "Anyway," he said, "I was a newspaper man."

"Indeed!" Von Flügel smiled encouragement.

Sitting with hands folded in his lap, he looked, thought Yakimov, like a benign old auntie, and his heart warmed to his friend. He giggled: "You and Dollie used to think that Yaki wasn't too bright. Well, I reported that Calinescu business for an important paper."

Von Flügel lifted a hand in astonished admiration. "And you come here to report the return of the Hungarians to their territory?"

Yakimov smiled. Delighted by the impression he was making, he felt a need to improve on it. He said: "I might as well tell you, this assignment is just a cover. My real reason for being here is . . . Well, it's pretty hush-hush."

Von Flügel watched him intently and, when he did not add to this revelation, said: "You are evidently a person of consequence these days. But tell me, *mein Lieber*, what exactly do you *do*?"

Not knowing the answer to this question, Yakimov backed down an old retreat route: "Not at liberty to say, dear boy."

"May I hazard a guess?" von Flügel archly inquired. "Then I would say you are attached to the British Legation."

Yakimov raised his eyes in astonishment at the accuracy of von Flügel's guess. "Between ourselves," he said, "speaking as one old friend to another, I'm on the *inside*. I know a thing or two. As a matter of fact, there's very little I don't know."

Von Flügel nodded slowly. "You work, no doubt, with this Mr. Leverett?"

"Old Foxy!" Yakimov immediately regretted his exclamation, which was, he realised, a betrayal of his ignorance. Von Flügel smiled and said nothing. Yakimov, discomforted by a sense of lost advantage, stared into his empty glass for some moments before it occurred to him that he had in his possession the means of re-establishing interest in himself. He drew from his hip pocket the plan he had found in Guy's desk. "Got something here," he said. "Give you an idea . . . not supposed to flash it about, but between old friends . . ."

He handed the paper to Freddi, who took it smiling, looked at it and ceased to smile. He stared at it on both sides, then held it up to the light. "Where did you get this?" he asked.

Disturbed by the change in Freddi's tone, Yakimov put out his hand for the paper. "Not at liberty to say."

"I'd like to keep this."

"Can't let you do that, dear boy. Not mine really. Have to give it back . . .'

"To whom?"

This question was put abruptly, in a hectoring tone that pained and bewildered Yakimov. If he had forgotten Freddi could be a silly, he had never known that Freddi could be a beast. He said with hurt dignity: "This is all very hush-hush, dear boy. 'Fraid I can't tell you anything more. Really must have the paper back."

Von Flügel rose. Without answering Yakimov, he crossed over to one of his cabinets, put the plan into it and locked the door.

Uncertain whether or not this was a joke, Yakimov protested: "But you can't, dear boy. I must have it back."

"You may get it before you leave." Von Flügel put the key into his pocket. "Meanwhile, we shall find out if it is genuine."

"Of course it's genuine."

"We shall see."

During this exchange von Flügel's manner had been stern and unamused, now it changed again. Advancing on Yakimov, he clasped his hands under his chin and his gait became a caricature of himself. Yakimov, watching him, was embarrassed by behaviour that he could only describe as odd. His embarrassment changed to fear when von Flügel, reaching him, stood over him with the malign stare of an old crocodile.

"Whatever is the matter, dear boy?" Yakimov tremulously asked.

"What is this game? You take me for a simpleton, perhaps?"

"However could you think that?"

"Does one enter a lion's den and say: 'Eat me. I am a juicy steak'?"

Von Flügel's whole attitude expressed menace, but to Yakimov it seemed such a deplorable performance that he imagined at any moment the whole thing would collapse into laughter. Instead von Flügel went on with increasing grimness: "Does one come to a Nazi official and say: 'I am an enemy agent. Here is my sabotage plan. Hand me, please, to the Gestapo.'"

"Really, dear boy, the *Gestapo!*"

"Yes, the *Gestapo!*" Von Flügel savagely imitated Yakimov's outraged tone. "What else do I do with a British spy."

Yakimov, for the first time, felt genuine alarm. There seemed to be nothing left of his old friend Freddi. What he saw beside him was indeed a Nazi official who might hand him over to the Gestapo. At the thought he almost collapsed with fear. "Dear boy!" he pleaded on a sob.

Freddi, a stranger and a dangerous stranger, had become the interrogator. "What little trick do you come here to play? What do you call it? The double bluff? We can soon discover. I have in this house a number of strong young men with fists."

"Oh, Freddi," Yakimov whimpered, "don't be unkind. It was only a joke between friends."

"That plan wasn't a joke."

"I told you it didn't belong to me. I pinched it. Just to amuse you, dear boy."

"You said you belonged to British Intelligence."

"No, dear boy, not in so many words. Can you see poor Yaki as a secret agent? *I ask you!*" Crouching in the sofa corner, watching with the perception of terror, Yakimov saw uncertainty on von Flügel's face, but not conviction. If he, von Flügel, could change into a Nazi official, then what might Yakimov not become in these strange times? Gradually von Flügel's face softened with contempt. He sat down. Speaking in the tone of one who will brook no further nonsense, he asked: "Where did you get that plan?"

Yakimov in his relief was not only willing to answer, but to answer more than he was asked. He was, he explained, a lodger in the flat of Guy Pringle, an Englishman who lectured at the University. He had found the plan in the flat and had borrowed it, just for fun. "Meant no harm," he said: "Didn't really know what it was, but I had m'suspicions. Queer comings and goings in that flat, I must say . . ." As he went on for some time about his suspicions and the "queer types" whom the Pringles entertained, he reminded himself of how he had worked to make Guy's production, but when it was over Guy had abandoned him. He said: "If you ask me, Pringle's a Bolshie."

Von Flügel nodded calmly and asked: "What sort of 'queer types'?"

"There's that fellow David Boyd. Now *he* works with Leverett and no one knows what he does. And there's a very strange chap hangs around the kitchen. He pretends he's related to the servant but he speaks English like a gent. The Pringles have kept him under cover. He was in a blue funk when I walked in on him."

Von Flügel set his teeth on his lower lip and appeared to reflect on this. He asked at last: "What are you doing in the apartment of such people?"

"Went there in all innocence, dear boy. Thought them very nice at first."

Von Flügel nodded and spoke portentously: "Charm is the stock-in-trade of such persons. It is intended to put you off your guard."

Yakimov nodded. He had, indeed, been put off his guard – and who better able to do that than Guy Pringle? He began to feel justified in giving the game away to Freddi. Freddi was a friend, a dear old friend, and Yaki had done no more than warn him. "When I saw that plan, I felt I ought to show it to you," and Yakimov ran happily on about the suspicious character of everyone he had seen there, the suspicious nature of everything that had ever occurred.

Von Flügel, still distant and severe, listened without much comment, but at the end he said: "One thing I would say to you: remove yourself from that flat at the earliest date. More, I would say remove yourself from Bucharest. I say it for your own good."

Yakimov nodded meekly. He had no wish to do anything else. He felt, now that he had re-established himself in Freddi's favour he might settle in here very comfortably. He lay back and closed his eyes. Exhausted, physically and emotionally, he felt himself sifting like a feather down through the softness of the earth. He heard von Flügel say: "Come. I will show you to your room," but had no time to reply before he was lost in sleep

The next morning confirmed his belief that life with Freddi would comply with his needs. After he had taken his bath, he and Freddi, in dressing-gowns, lay in long chairs to take breakfast on the balcony. The coffee was pre-war coffee, the food was excellent. Freddi was his old charming self. There were, unfortunately, a number of those horrid young men about, but Axel was the only one whom Freddi treated indulgently. With the others he was the stern commandant of *das Braune Haus*.

His memory of the previous night left him with an uneasy sense that he had been a trifle unfair to poor old Guy, but lying in his valetudinarian languor he could not worry unduly. After all, Guy *had* been unfair to him.

Breakfast over, the two men remained in the early sunlight, looking down at an ancient Citroën piled with furniture and bedding, that was being dragged to the station by a mule. All the petrol, Freddi explained, had been plundered by the outgoing Rumanians, who now refused to send in fresh supplies. "A hopeless people!" said Freddi. In a side-street a queue of people could be seen outside a shuttered bakery. From somewhere in the distance came a sound of shooting. Yakimov made movements as though he were thinking of getting up. "I should dress," he said. "I'm supposed to be getting the tempo of the town."

"So you really are a journalist?" said Freddi.

"In a manner of speaking. Not an aristocrat's occupation, I'm afraid."

"This is not an aristocrat's war."

Yakimov struggled to a sitting position.

"Is this activity really necessary?" Freddi asked. "The streets are unsafe. I would not recommend that you wander about. Such news as there is we can get from the boys." He rang a bell and a young man entered at once. "Ah, here is Filip. Filip, whàt is the news?"

Filip recited the latest incidents. A man resembling the Hungarian Consul had been set upon by Rumanian peasants and been left unconscious with an eye kicked out. Some people who had queued all day before a grocery store, finding the shop empty and the grocer gone to Braşov, had set fire to the shop, and the family living above had been burnt to death. There had been trouble at the hospital where Hungarian doctors had accused Rumanian doctors of removing equipment which had originally been Hungarian. One doctor, pushed over a balcony, had broken his neck.

As this recital of disorders went on, Yakimov nervously twitched his toes and murmured: "Dear me!"

"Don't be alarmed," said von Flügel: "These are the little inconveniences of change. No food, no petrol, no telephone, no public transport. The cafés are closed. Soon the lights will go out, the water will be cut off, the gas will cease to come through the pipes – but here all is well. We are well stocked with food and drink. There is a great range in the kitchen that burns wood. There is a well in the courtyard. We could withstand a seige." He glanced at Yakimov. "Perhaps you would care to make some notes."

"I forgot m'little notebook."

Von Flügel ordered Filip to bring pen and paper. When these were in Yakimov's hands, von Flügel explained how necessary it was to take Transylvania out of the control of the feckless, incompetent Rumanians and hand it over to the shrewd, hardworking Hungarians. At the end of an hour Yakimov had written, in his uneven hand, at the top of the sheet of paper: "The Takeover – A Good Thing."

This done, von Flügel said: "Surely it is not too early for an aperitif?"

Yakimov fervently agreed it was not.

His future still unsettled, he now mentioned the tiresome fact that he was supposed to be returning to Bucharest on the Orient Express that very night. "Not to tell a lie, dear boy," he added confidingly, "I don't really want to go back there. The food is atrocious and there's always some sort of rumpus going on. You advised me to leave Rumania, so I've decided I'd like to stay here."

"Here? In Cluj?" Von Flügel stared at him. "It's out of the question. When the Rumanians withdraw, this will be virtually Axis territory."

Yakimov smiled persuasively. "You could take care of old Yaki."

For a moment von Flügel looked aghast at this suggestion, then he said in a decided tone: "I could do nothing of the sort. As a member of the old régime I have to go very carefully myself. I could not possibly protect an enemy alien." He turned with a stern expression but, seeing Yakimov's gloomy face, relaxed. "No, no, *mein Lieber*," he said more kindly, "you cannot stay here. Return as you have arranged to Bucharest tonight. I will send Axel to obtain for you a *wagon-lit*. As soon as you arrive, put your affairs in order and take yourself to safety without delay."

"But where can I go?" Yakimov asked, near tears.

"That, I fear, you must decide for yourself. Europe is finished for you, of course. North Africa will go next. Perhaps to India. It will be some time before we get there."

For the rest of the day, Yakimov ate and drank with a mourning sense of farewell to the might-have-been. Towards evening, von Flügel, indicating that his friend must prepare for departure, said that Axel would give him sandwiches for the journey. Von Flügel himself had been invited that evening to a dinner given in his honour by the Hungarian community, so could not see Yakimov to the station.

"One thing, *mein Lieber*," he said as Yakimov got sadly to his feet: "you know the carpet-shop opposite Mavrodaphne's? When I was last in Bucharest, I saw there a very fine Oltenian rug. Thinking it a little expensive, I unwisely delayed its purchase, now I wish I had taken it. I wonder, would you buy it for me and have it delivered to the German Embassy?"

"Why, certainly, dear boy."

"You cannot mistake it: a black rug with a pattern of cherries and roses. Mention my name and they will produce it. It was about twenty-five thousand. Should I give you the money now?"

"It would be as well, dear boy."

Von Flügel opened a drawer that was filled with decks of new five-thousand-*lei* notes. He carefully peeled off five of these and held them just out of Yakimov's reach. He said: "I had better take your address in Bucharest, just in case . . ."

Yakimov gave it readily and the notes were handed over. "By the way," he said, "you still have that plan I showed you last night."

"I'll post it to you tomorrow. Now don't forget the rug. A *black* rug with cherries and roses, a delightful piece. And don't linger in Bucharest. I can tell you, in strictest confidence, Rumania's next on the list."

The friends parted amicably, Yakimov with regrets, von Flügel with a slightly off-hand urbanity. In a hurry to dress, he told the chauffeur to drive Yakimov to the station and return without delay.

As the car crossed the square in the evening light, the black wing of a plane, bearing the words '*România Mare*' dipped over the cathedral spire. Crowds of peasants were gathering at the street corners, running in groups this way and that, ready to make a stand but lacking leadership. They shouted at the sight of von Flügel's Mercedes and shook their fists.

The chauffeur, a Saxon, laughed at these gestures. He told Yakimov that the peasants had believed that Maniu was arriving to incite a revolt against the Vienna award. A deputation had waited all day at the station, then learnt that Maniu was at his house outside Cluj, having come by road. They rushed to see him and found him packing up his belongings. Saying he could do nothing, he advised them to return peacefully to their houses and accept the situation.

"So they are disappointed," said the chauffeur complacently, "And Domnul Maniu no doubt is sad."

"No doubt he is," said Yakimov, who was sad himself.

The long road to the station was crowded with townspeople and peasants making their way to the trains. They swarmed in front of the car with their belongings on carts and barrows, ignoring the hooting of the Mercedes that had slowed to a crawl.

"Hah, these Rumanians!" said the chauffeur with contempt. "In 1918 they drove out the Hungarians with much brutality, now they fear revenge."

The Orient Express, on which Yakimov had his sleeper, was due in soon after eight o'clock. The chauffeur congratulated Yakimov on being in good time, handed him his bag and left him to push his way in through the crowd that heaved and struggled about the station entrance.

When he at last reached the platform, he could scarcely get on to it. It was piled with furniture, among which the peasants were making themselves at home. Several had set up spirit-stoves on tables and commodes, and were cooking maize or beans. Others had gone to sleep among rolls of carpet. Most of them looked as though they had been there for hours. There was a constant traffic over gilt chairs and sofas, the valued possessions of displaced officials. Now that the train was due, dramatic scenes were taking place. Hungarian girls had married Rumanians and, as the couples waited to depart, parents were lamenting as though at a death. Yakimov stepped over two women who, howling into each other's faces, were lying in an embrace at the very edge of the line. He made his way through the *melée* until it began to thin at the platform's end, and there he waited.

Time passed. The express did not come. After an hour or more, he tried to inquire when it was expected, but whichever language he spoke seemed to be the wrong one. His Rumanian was answered with "*Beszélj magyarul*," and his Hungarian with "*Vorbeşte româneşte*," and his German with silence. Wandering about, he came on the Jew whose acquaintance he had made in the dining car, and learnt that the train was signalled two hours late. It might arrive about ten o'clock. At this Yakimov took himself back to the end of the platform where he found a vacant arm-chair, an imitation Louis XIV piece, not comfortable but better than nothing, and ate his sandwiches.

Darkness fell. Two or three lights came on, leaving shadowy areas lit only by the blue flames of the spirit stoves. Suddenly, amazingly, a train came in – a local train of the poorest class. A fierce energy at once swept through the peasants. Gathering up their possessions, they flung themselves at the doors only to find they were locked. Without pause they set to smashing the windows. Once inside, the men hauled up their women, children and baggage with roars that threatened death to any official who should restrain them. The air was filled with screams of anger and fear and the cracking of flimsy woodwork.

Yakimov watched in dismay. He knew this could not be the express but he suffered acute trepidation, realising what would happen when the express did come in.

The local train filled up in a minute, then the peasants began clambering to the carriage roofs, pulling their families after them. The uproar drowned the warning whistle. The train moved off with women and children hanging by arms and legs, unable to make the muscular effort to mount farther. Their shrieks rose even above the clamour of those left behind, who ran down the line, howling despair and threats until brought to a stop by rifle-fire from a bridge. When the train had gone, there were plaints and groans, but no one, it seemed, was seriously hurt, and every-one climbed back to the platform and settled down to wait again.

A clock struck in the distance. It was eleven. Yakimov stood up, certain the express would be coming at any moment, but half an hour later he sat down again, growing more apprehensive with the passing of time. A second local train came in and was charged like the last one. While it stood at the platform, another train arrived and stopped out of sight on the next line. People began shouting to one another that this was the express.

Yakimov, trembling in painful anxiety, waited for the local train to draw out, but it did not draw out, then came a cry that the express was leaving. People ran in either direction alongside the train that blocked the way and Yakimov ran with the rest. Stumbling over slag-heaps and rails, he rounded the hot, fire-breathing engine of the local train and reached the express. Its engine had been shunted off: the carriages remained. He found the *wagon-lit* and climbed up, but the door was locked. He thumped on the glass, shouting "*Lassen Sie mich herein*" to people standing in the corridor. They watched him, but no one moved. Suddenly the *wagon-lit* began to move. Clinging to the door-handle, his suit-case between his legs, Yakimov was swept into darkness. Then the *wagon-lit* stopped with a jerk that almost threw him off the steps. They were out in the bare and windy countryside. Knowing if he climbed down he would be lost, he hung sobbing with fear on the step while the carriage started back, as though galvanised by an electric shock. He was thankful to see the station again. The *wagon-lit* stopped: he climbed down between the two trains. At once the local train drew out. The foot-plate grazed him; the engine, at the back, passed him in a shower of sparks, and he screamed in panic. The express had reassembled itself. He ran to the rear where he could see the light of an open door. He reached it, threw his bag in and climbed after it. He was in terror lest someone should prevent him from entering, but there was no one to prevent him. This was the back way into the dining-car. He looked into the kitchen. The cook, a little gollywog of a man, was cutting up meat. Stunned and humbled, like one who has come into peace out of a raging storm, Yakimov stood and smiled on him. The meat looked dark, stringy and tough, but the cook was working at it with the absorption of an artist. Gently, affectionately, Yakimov asked if he might pass through. The man waved him on without a glance.

The blinds were pulled down inside the car. There were a number of vacant seats. The diners, again all men, sat talking, indifferent to the shrieks outside. When he was safely seated, Yakimov pulled aside his blind and glanced out at the crowds running helplessly up and down the line. Someone spoke to a waiter, who explained that the train was locked, inviolate, because the morning express had been besieged by peasants who had not had the money to pay the fare. They had refused to get off and had to be carried to Brasov. That must not happen again.

Someone on the line, seeing Yakimov looking out, thumped the window and cried piteously to be allowed in. He felt now as disassociated as the other diners. Anyway what could *he* do?

There were more shots and cries and a heavy pelting of feet. Faces seemed to press against the glass and stay there a moment, like wet leaves, before disappearing. Then the train began to move. People ran beside it, gesticulating, their mouths opening and shutting, but there was no hope for them. Something – a stone, probably – struck the window beside Yakimov. He let the blind drop and gave his order to the waiter. When he had eaten, he rose to find his berth and found that the door into the rest of the train was locked. He appealed to the waiter, but no one was empowered to open it. At last, weary of argument, he returned to his seat, put his head down on the table and slept.

The return journey took even longer than the outgoing one. The express had been due into Bucharest next morning. It actually reached the capital as darkness fell. Yakimov had had to spend the whole time in the dining-car, again taking meal after meal, paid for with Freddi's money.

At Bucharest station, there were no porters. No one collected tickets. The place was deserted except for the newly arrived passengers who remained at the entrance, whispering together, reluctant to emerge. Yakimov looked out. The street, usually swarming at this hour and adazzle with flares, was deserted, but he could see nothing to fear. The worst of it was there were no taxis or *trăsurăs*. Another long walk! He hung around awhile, hoping someone would explain their apprehensions, but no one

spoke to him and nothing happened. He decided to set out. H
went alone.

The stalls of the Calea Grivitei were shut and abandoned. The
pavements were empty. Occasionally he saw figures in doorways,
but they slid back out of sight before he reached them. The town
was unnaturally silent. He had never before seen the streets so
empty.

At last, at the junction of the Calea Victoriei, he came on a
group of military police with revolvers at the ready. One of them
ordered Yakimov to stop. He dropped his bag in alarm and put
up his hands. An officer came forward and sternly asked what he
was doing out of doors. The question frightened him; he realised
that his fellow-passengers had known something he had not
known. He started to explain in German – the safest language
these days – how he had arrived on the Orient Express and was
walking home. What was wrong? What had happened? He received no reply to his questions but was ordered to produce his
permis de séjour. He handed it over with his passport. Both were
taken under a lamp-post and examined and discussed, while a
soldier kept him covered. The discussion went on for a long time.
At intervals one or other of the men turned to stare at him, so he
feared he would be arrested or shot out of hand. In the end his
papers were restored to him. The officer saluted. Yakimov might
proceed, but must make a detour to avoid crossing the main
square.

Obediently he went down a side-street into the Boulevard
Breteanu and, adding about half a mile to his walk, reached the
Pringles' block, still very agitated. The hall was in darkness. The
porter had been conscripted some time before and not replaced.
As Yakimov made his way up in the lift, he was suddenly convinced that the invasion had begun. The city not only seemed
empty, it was empty. People had fled. He would find the Pringles
had gone with the rest.

At the thought he might find himself deserted in a German-
occupied country, he almost collapsed. To think he could have
stayed on the express and been carried right away to safety! His
self-pity was acute.

He was shaking so he could scarcely get his key into the lock.
The flat, when he entered it, was in darkness, but there were
voices inside. Reassured at once, he switched on the sitting-room
light.

"Put that light off, you damned fool," someone whispered from the balcony.

He switched the light off, but the moment's illumination had shown him Harriet standing against the jamb of the balcony door and Guy and David Boyd lying on the balcony floor, peering out through the stonework of the balustrade. It was David who had spoken.

Yakimov tiptoed in. "Whatever is going on, dear boy?" he asked.

In reply, David said: "Shut up. Do you want them to take a pot at us?"

Yakimov crouched against the doorway opposite Harriet, and looked out into the square. At first he could see nothing. The square, like the streets, was deserted, the lights shining on cobbles and stretches of tarmac bare of everything but the marks of tyres. The palace was in darkness.

After a long interval of silence, Yakimov whispered to Harriet: "Dear girl, do tell Yaki what is happening!"

She said: "The army has been called out. They're expecting an attack on the palace. If you look over there" – she pointed to the entrance to the Calea Victoriei – "you can see the tip of a machine-gun. There are soldiers all over the place."

Peering out, he began to see a movement of shadows among shadow. The first shop in the Calea Victoriei was visible and from its doorway heads were stretched. There were other movements among the scaffolding and half-demolished buildings in the square. These movements were all made cautiously, in silence. He heard a distant sound of singing.

"Who is going to attack the palace?"

Yakimov spoke piteously, feeling that no one wanted to tell him anything.

"We don't know," Harriet answered. "We think it must be the Iron Guard, but there've only been the usual rumours and confusion."

"It couldn't be the revolution, could it?"

"It could be anything. There was a lot of shouting for the King to abdicate, then the police went round clearing the streets and the military came out. David came in and said there was this rumour of an attack on the palace. That's all we know."

"The King won't abdicate, will he?"

Overhearing this question, David snuffled gleefully. "You wait and see," he said.

Yakimov picked up his bag and went into his bedroom. He sank down on to his bed, weary yet unable to contemplate rest. His consternation came not only from Hadjimoscos' predictions of anarchy and the guillotine, but from the fact that the word "revolution" had always fluttered him. Revolution had destroyed his family fortunes and sent his poor old dad into exile. He had grown up with his father's stories of the downfall of the Russian monarchy and the appalling end of the Russian royal family. Yakimov imagined that in a short time now, perhaps in an hour or two, the workers would abandon trains, planes and ships. The military would requisition petrol. They would all be stuck.

Freddi had warned him not to linger in Bucharest and Freddi had said that Rumania was next on the list.

Everyone had always said that the Germans could not afford trouble here. A rising would be the signal for an immediate German occupation. It occurred to Yakimov that in casting suspicion on Guy – rather meanly, he realised, but he had no time for compunction now – he could have brought trouble on himself, for here he was, one of a discredited household, and he might not get time to prove he had not been implicated.

His thoughts went to the Orient Express which he had just left, and which always stood at least an hour in the Bucharest station. Why not hurry back to it? He had walked safely here, and could as safely return. And, for once, with Freddi's money on him, he was "well heeled".

Saying: "Now or never, dear boy," he jumped up and began pulling out the oddments of clothing that were left in the drawers. He stuffed his bag full.

He did everything quietly. He felt a need to keep his departure secret, not from any fear of being detained, but from a nervous sense of shame that, having given old Guy away, he was now himself doing a bolt. Were he to try and explain his going, he might somehow betray his betrayal.

His window opened on to the balcony. As he crept about, he could hear David Boyd whisper: "Here they come. Now we'll see something." There was a noise outside. He moved across to the window and looked into the square. A line of soldiers stood blocking each end of the road which ran from it. Their rifles were poised to fire.

The noise was growing. Evidently a mob of some sort was making for the palace. Yakimov could only hope that the fracas here would draw attention from the side-streets by which he would reach the station.

Before he left he took down his sable-lined greatcoat which hung behind his door. With coat, suitcase and what was left of Freddi's twenty-five "thou", he tiptoed from the flat. Down in the street he heard the rifles fire, and he ran towards the Boulevard Breteanu.

He reached the station unaccosted and unharmed. The Orient Express, ignorant of the events that Yakimov had left behind, was still awaiting the passengers that, strangely, did not arrive. Having acquired Yakimov, it seemed content, and almost immediately set out for Bulgaria. At the frontier there was a slight altercation because he had no Rumanian exit visas, but a thousand *lei* put that right.

He obtained a berth in the almost empty sleeping-car and next morning awoke to the safety of Instanbul.

PART THREE

The Revolution

15

DURING THE FIRST DAYS OF SEPTEMBER the murmur of the crowded square had become for Harriet as familiar as the murmur of traffic. Shortly after Yakimov had set out for Cluj, it suddenly became a hubbub, there were new shouts of "*Abdica*" and a sound of breaking glass. Here, she thought, was uprising at last. When she went out to look, the crowd was in a ferment and the police were getting their hoses ready for action. The threat was enough. The uproar died down, but people did not disperse. This time they were not to be moved. If they might not speak, they could remain, a reproach to the despoilers within the palace.

Harriet remembered, when they took the flat, she had said to Guy: "We are at the centre of things." Now it seemed they were at the centre of trouble.

A little later, when the office workers had been added to the mob, there was a sudden burst of cheering. Guy had just come in and he joined Harriet on the balcony. With her long sight she could see a man in army uniform standing, hand raised, on the palace steps. Guy could see nothing of this but heard the crowd yelling in a frenzy of jubilation.

"Can it be the King?" said Harriet. "Has he done something to please them at last?"

Guy thought it unlikely. Despina came running into the room, waving her arms and shouting that something wonderful had happened. Antonescu had been brought a third time from prison and a third time offered the premiership – on his own terms. He had accepted, and at once demanded the resignation of Urdureanu.

Now, cried Despina, striking her fist into her palm, the country would be set right.

That, apparently, was everyone's opinion. Antonescu was being treated as a hero. His car could scarcely get out of the palace gate for the press of admirers. When it disappeared into the Boulevard Elisabeta, everyone began to move off as though there were nothing left to wait for.

By early evening, the resignation of Urdureanu was announced. Guy and Harriet, going out to meet David, felt a change in the air. The sense of mutinous anger had gone and near-elation had taken its place. And this, they felt, was merely a beginning. As Despina had said, the country would now be set right. One man, parting from a friend shouted: "*En nu abdic*," raising laughter among all who heard him. The friend answered that Antonescu would make him change his mind.

David had invited the Pringles to eat with him and was waiting for them in the English Bar. He suggested they go to Cina's on the square. They could seldom afford this restaurant, but the evening was a special one.

"Anything may happen," he said, "And if it does, we shall have a ring-side seat."

The day had been very hot and the evening was as warm as mid-summer. The garden tables were all taken by people who seemed to be awaiting an event.

"Would it be the abdication?" Guy asked.

David sniggered and said: "It seems to be expected."

They were given a table by the hedge. Sitting in wicker chairs beneath the ancient lime trees, they watched the passers-by strolling in an amiable way about the square. Two or three dozen people, the remnants of the morning crowd, stood round the statue of Carol I. Suddenly everyone was on the alert. People began running towards the palace. The diners in the garden became excited and began shifting about in their seats and demanding information from the waiters. When the waiters could tell them nothing, they complained as though the news were being unjustly withheld from them. Several people called for the head waiter, an old man who knew everyone. Entering the garden he held up a hand and said in gentle, smiling reproof: "A decree, merely a decree," then quietly gave details to the waiters who went round from table to table repeating them.

The decree had cancelled the royal dictatorship, leaving the King with nothing but the right to wear decorations and present them to others. When required to sign it, he had raged like a madman and accused Antonescu of high treason, but he had been forced to sign in the end.

"Alas, the poor old Great and Good!" said David. "He's become a mere figurehead. And now what will the General do? He can't rule alone. He'll have to call on the Iron Guard or the army, and I imagine he knows the army too well to trust it."

Guy said: "You think we're in for an Iron Guard dictatorship?"

David shrugged: "I can't see any alternative."

So their position, Harriet thought, was more precarious than ever.

As the foliage clotted above their heads, strings of coloured lamps were lit among the branches. Within the palace, where the King had been stripped of everything but his decorations, appeared the galaxies of the chandeliers. Above the palace, a single star, embedded in the cerulean satin on the sky, shone with great brilliance. The roofs were lustrous with the last radiance from the west.

Suddenly, in the middle of the garden, the orchestra stand sprang alight and the musicians, in white blouses and velvet knee breeches, filed between the tables, bowing to right and left. They climbed into the stand: there was a howl from the violin, a pause and then a frenzy of music was released upon the diners.

Harriet thought of the last time they had eaten here. It had been mid-winter and, sitting beside the double window, their table had been lit by the sheen from the garden which, fleeced with snow, had looked small and intimate. Two broken-down cane chairs were outside on the terrace, their seats cushioned with snow. Snow picked out the delicate traceries of the chair backs and limned every curve and indentation of the roofing of trees. Beneath the trees, caged in the complex of branches, was the snow-capped orchestra-stand, a piece of chinoiserie, lacquered in gold and yellow. Who, seeing it now, hung with lights and leaves and flowers, could think that in a little while it would be left forlorn.

Last autumn Inchcape had told Harriet that an enemy never invaded in the winter. He had said: "The snow will come soon and here we shall be, tucked away safe and sound."

She felt a nostalgia for the snow which recalled for her some enchantment of childhood, a security she had known before her childhood changed. But the times had changed. Last autumn the Germans had been two frontiers away. This autumn, when the snow blocked the passes, it would enclose a host of Germans and the whole of the Iron Guard.

The Pringles awoke next morning to quiet. The Guardists had already taken up their position by the palace-rail but they stood there alone. The other inhabitants of the city were content to leave matters to Antonescu.

Despina, coming in with the breakfast things, talked excitedly about this champion who had risen to right everyone's wrongs. He had been the only one who dared oppose the King and he had suffered for his opposition. Now he had triumphed. He was the ruler. As for the King – she made a gesture as though she would jerk her hand off her wrist. The King was "nobody".

Whether the King was nobody or not, Harriet thought, he had been the ally and protector of the English community. She was not sorry that he was still on the throne.

Neither was Guy. If he felt no enthusiasm for the King, he felt less for Antonescu who had, from necessity, been set up as a symbol of honest strength in the midst of perfidy and confusion. People saw him as a solution simply because there was no solution. They might have cause to regret their illusion.

The day passed without incident. To most people it seemed the situation had been resolved so they were astonished when the police appeared in force that evening and ordered everyone off the streets.

The Pringles, on their way to the English Bar, found themselves encompassed in the square. They hurried to reach the hotel before they could be turned back, but the revolving door was locked. No one could leave or enter. They ran to the glass door of the hair-dressing shop: that, too, was bolted. The windows began to fill with the faces of guests inside. Harriet saw Clarence looking out at them and waved to him. Could he not obtain their admission? He shook his head in bewildered helplessness.

Galpin, Screwby and other journalists were peering out of a side window. A porter thrust his way in front of them and pulled down a blind.

The emptied square looked vast, the cobbles reflecting the rosy gleams of the sunset. In the hotel, the palace, Cina's and the other buildings, all blinds had been pulled down, their pallid surfaces imposing a sabbatical void upon the evening.

A police officer, seeing the Pringles, the only civilians now at large, told them to go home. Guy asked the reason for this police action and was told that martial law had been declared.

"Why?" Guy asked. "What is happening?"

The officer shrugged and looked blank, then unable to keep his knowledge to himself, he said an attack was about to be made on the palace.

"By whom?"

The officer did not know.

As the Pringles passed out through the cordon, troops were arriving in lorries. A tank, painted sky-blue, had stationed itself outside the hotel. Machine-guns were being set up wherever there was cover. In the street outside the entrance to the Pringles' block a military van with a loudspeaker was demanding not only that everyone stay indoors, but that the blinds be drawn and balconies vacated. Anyone found in the street after half-past six would be in danger of arrest.

Entering the flat some fifteen minutes after leaving it, the Pringles were delighted to find that David had arrived during their absence and was peering out through the balcony door.

"What is happening?" Harriet asked.

"A *coup*, I imagine," said David. "Organised by the general. He's divested the King but Lupescu and Urdureanu are still in the palace biding their time. In fact, people who know are laughing at the decree. The King will simply wait until he can seize power again. So we have this attack on the palace. A put-up job, but it may work."

"It's a revolution?"

"A sort of revolution. If we get down out of sight we'll be able to see everything."

There was no sound from the square. Traffic had stopped. Darkness fell and still nothing happened. The two men lay peering through the stone tracery while Harriet pressed against the door-jamb. There was no sign of life below. Everyone, police as well as military, was concealed in shadow. The horseman on his giant horse sat in solitude. About him the lights were reflected on a world of polished ebony.

The silence of the waiting town had no undertones. It was as complete as the silence of the country.

At last Harriet, cramped and bored, went out to the kitchen. The servants were all on the roof awaiting events. Harriet made sandwiches and took them into the room. The three sat cross-legged to picnic on the balcony floor. When Harriet returned to her position by the door-jamb, she said: "I can hear singing." The song was no more than a pulse in the air. As they listened,

Yakimov arrived. The singing grew louder. With it came the sound of marching. The marchers were coming from the centre of the town. The singing stopped, cut short by an order, and there was a sound of shouting instead. The shouts grew nearer. An order was given in the square. The shadows came suddenly to life.

"Now," said David, "we should see something."

Soldiers with rifles at the ready were running out of the darkness to range themselves across the junctions of the Calea Victoriei and the Boulevard Elisabeta.

The noise of approaching feet and voices came like a rush of water, and soon it was possible to pick out individual threats to the King, Lupescu and Urdureanu. There was a repeated call of death to the King.

The marchers were now very near. Another order was given in the square. The soldiers ranged across the Boulevard Elisabeta raised their rifles. The marchers came on. An officer bawled again. The soldiers fired into the air. The report brought the uproar to an immediate stop. There was a moment of silence, then the scuffle of retreat – but, retreating, the marchers raised their voices in a song of defiance. It was "*Capitanul*".

The soldiers remained in position, but there were no more orders. "*Capitanul*" became again a pulse on the air, then faded out of hearing.

Guy and David rose to their feet. Guy said: "Let's have a drink."

Harriet asked: "That was a poor sort of revolution?"

"It was enough," said David. "Antonescu can now say: 'You're in mortal danger. I cannot protect you. You must go.'" Guy poured out the *ţuică* and David held up his glass: "Farewell to the King. He'll be gone before morning."

Later the story went round that that night Carol wrote on his dinner menu: "*Auf Wiedersehen*", resigned to going but certain his country must in the end recall so sharp-witted a King.

16

THE FOLLOWING MORNING Harriet could hear the babble in the square before she was out of bed. The city was celebrating.

During breakfast, Despina darted in and out of the room with stories shouted up to her by the other servants. The King, she said, had refused to sign the abdication order until 4 a.m., and then only after a squabble about the pension he would receive. He had been driven at once to Constanza in a German diplomatic car and put on board his yacht. Lupescu and Urdureanu had gone with him, but the palace was not empty. There was a new King, Michael; young, handsome and good, he would rule benignly, like an English king.

Meanwhile, people were pouring into the square from every side street, many of them peasants who had come from the country, the men in white frieze, the women brilliant as oriental birds in the dresses they wore only on feast days and holidays. It was clear that no one would work today. Harriet said to Guy: "Surely you need not go to the University?" but he thought he ought to put in an appearance, and took himself off as usual.

Harriet was still at the table when she heard "*Capitanul*" being sung beneath the balcony. She ran out, her coffee-cup in her hand, and gazed down on the ranks of green-clad men who were marching round the church below her. They cut through their audience, straight across the square to the palace, where the guards, who the night before had fired over their heads, now raised arms in the fascist salute.

As they lined up in their hundreds before the palace, the crowd surged about them, kissing their hands and slapping their backs.

The jubilation so stimulated the air that she felt jubilant herself. Yet what was there to rejoice about? The new régime might mean a fresh start, but the lost provinces were still lost. The country must still obey the demands of its voracious ally.

Harriet was recalled by shouts of "*Cornița*". Despina had been out and now, aglow with all the sensations, congratulations and fantasies of the market-place, stood in the room with one hand behind her back. As Harriet entered, she whipped out her hand with a flourish and presented a roast of meat.

It was Friday, a meatless day. "Special for the abdication," she said: "and it is not veal, it is beef." They had not eaten beef since early spring. "Now the King is gone," she cried, "there will be no more meatless days. We shall eat roast beef for every meal," and she said that when a peasant, recognising her as Hungarian, had refused to serve her, she had shouted: "*Sitie kiansinlai blogi*," and overthrown his basket of tomatoes. The bystanders were in such a state of revelry that they treated the incident as a joke.

"Is no one sorry the King has gone?" Harriet asked.

Despina shrieked with laughter at the idea. "No one, no one. A robber, a cheat, a lecher – such was the King! Away with him!" She made a rude gesture of dismissal and described how Carol and Lupescu, about to leave the palace with boxes of jewels and bags of gold, had been seized by Horia Sima and flown to Berlin where the Führer waited to repay old scores. "*O să-le taie gâtul*," she said, sweeping a finger across her own throat.

"Is this true?" Harriet unbelievingly asked.

True? Of course it was true. Everyone was talking about it.

An uproar from the square sent Harriet hurrying out with Despina at her heels. The young King was standing on the main balcony of the palace – a tall young man in army uniform, his ministers behind him. As he lifted a hand in greeting, the crowd howled its enthusiasm. For the first time, Harriet saw men and small boys clambering over the statue of Carol the Great. Soldiers, making way for the cars that were trying to reach the palace, shook hands on all sides with excited members of the crowd.

When the new King retired, those near the palace railing, made bold by the good-fellowship of the times, ventured inside. Soon, people were strolling in and out of the gates and round the small ornamental lawns as freely as in a public park.

Despina gasped in astonishment. Never, never, she said, had such a thing been done before.

Harriet felt she must go out and see these wonders at closer range, but as she was about to leave the flat, there was a ring at the door. Bella had called.

Harriet had heard nothing from her since their chance meeting in the Calea Victoriei. Now, her arms full of flowers, she threw herself on Harriet with more animation than she had ever shown before. Handing her a bunch of roses as though the occasion were one of rejoicing for them both, she said: "Oh, the excitement. It's wonderful. Wonderful," then seeing that Harriet was holding bag and gloves, she shouted: "But you can't go out. You might be attacked. Carol was pro-British, so the English are terribly unpopular. It'll pass of, of course – but, just at the moment, you're safer indoors."

"You weren't attacked."

"Oh, I'm different. I have Rumanian papers and I speak German. My German is so good the shopkeepers fall over themselves to serve me."

Harriet took her out to the balcony where she settled into a deck-chair, saying: "Why go out when you've got a front row seat?"

Her skin apricot, her hair bleached by the sun, Bella was looking extremely handsome and seemed almost intoxicated by the night's happenings. "How wonderful to have a strong man in power!" she said. "Everyone is saying that Rumania will regain all her territory."

"What makes them think that?"

"Because Antonescu is a real dictator. He knows how to deal with Hitler and Musso. He's one of them. I don't mind betting, within three months, this country will be on its feet again."

"What about the Iron Guard? They could cause a lot of trouble."

"Not them." Bella hooted at the thought of them. "The general will stand no nonsense from that rabble. Their leaders are all dead. People are saying they're like potatoes: the best of them are underground."

Bella's confidence was such she almost conveyed to Harriet her belief that there was nothing to fear: their world would settle down again. She felt cheered by Bella's visit that brought back to her the pleasures of their companionship. In this city a woman could go nowhere alone but two women, chaperoning each other, were free to do what they liked. She said:

"When this is all over, let us start going again to Mavrodaphne's."

"Yes, let's," Bella heartily agreed. She looked up eagerly as Despina, who had run out to a cake-shop, set down a tray of coffee and cream cakes. "How much do you pay that girl?" she asked when Despina had gone.

"A thousand a week."

"Merciful heavens! That's as much as a schoomaster gets. You spoil them. I've told you before. It makes things difficult for the rest of us."

A fresh burst of cheering greeted Michael's reappearance on the balcony.

"He's a nice boy," said Bella, "but not as colourful as his father. It's a pity about Carol, really. They say that when Antonescu shouted at him: 'You must abdicate,' he burst into tears and said: 'But I haven't done so badly.' It made me feel quite sorry for him."

"He had a gift for bursting into tears at the right moment," Harriet said.

Bella seemed to resent this. She said: "He was very virile."

"David Boyd says all these stories about his virility were put out by the palace."

"David Boyd!" said Bella with contempt. "A lot he knows about it." To restore Bella's good humour Harriet appealed to her for information: "What do you think has happened to Carol?"

"Nobody knows for sure," Bella nodded towards the palace. "He may still be over there," she said.

The Guardists, in full throat, appeared out of the Calea Victoriei.

"There's that bloody song again," said Bella. "But, you wait and see! The general will make mincemeat of that lot once he's established."

The Guardists, a small contingent, were leading a long procession of priests and nuns. Bella explained that it was St. Michael's Day – not only the name-day of the new king but the day of Michael Codreanu, the Iron Guard saint. This coincidence must have impressed the crowds, for they watched in a respectful silence until suddenly there was renewed uproar. A man was leaving the palace on foot. Bella started up.

"Good heavens," she said, "that's Antonescu himself. People are going mad. I must go down and see the fun."

As Harriet made to rise, Bella put a hand on her shoulder. "No, you stay here," she commanded. "I'll keep in touch. I'll ring up every day and give you the news."

As soon as she saw the lift descend with Bella in it, Harriet ran down by the stairs. Because of Bella's fears for her Harriet avoided the square, taking the first turning into the Boulevard Elisabeta. She had imagined the shops would be shut, but except for the sense of heightened activity life went on as usual. The peasants had brought in their produce on barrows. The restaurants were open. In the café gardens people sat beneath striped umbrellas drinking morning coffee.

In the Calea Victoriei, however, the new force was manifesting itself. Young men and women, pushing their way boisterously through the crowds, were handing out Guardist leaflets. A group of girls, flushed, rather wild in their appearance, and still rather bashful of their own importance, were going from shop to shop distributing posters. As fast as they were delivered, the posters appeared in the windows, portraying a romantically handsome young man, long-haired, large-eyed, dark as a gipsy, beneath which were the words: CORNELIU ZELEA CODREANU – PREZENT. This was an idealised image of the captain who was ever present among his followers.

Soon the face of Carol's enemy, who had been, until a few weeks before, a despised traitor, was exhibited everywhere as national hero, martyr and saint.

When Harriet entered the University, she knew at once that the building was empty, or almost empty. The porter had probably taken the day off. She went down the corridor. The lecture-room door stood open. No one had pulled down the blinds. Midday poured hot and heavy on to the vacant seats.

She found Guy in his office. He was sitting over some exercise-books, apparently intent, but jerked his head round when she entered. Hoping for a student, he looked surprised to see her. He said: "They've all taken a holiday."

"Why didn't you come home?"

"There were three classes this morning. Someone might have turned up for one of them."

"The Iron Guard is out in force today."

"I heard them. You weren't anxious about me, were you?" He took her hand affectionately. "No need to worry. The Guardists won't cause trouble at the moment. They don't want to spoil their chance of coming to power."

"Well, you needn't stay here any longer. Let's walk across the park."

He stood up, then thought to look at his watch. "The last hour has only just begun," he said. "I must allow a bit more time. Someone might turn up."

"They won't. They dare not risk it."

But Guy would not give up hope. He strolled round the room,

humming to himself, and Harriet, suffering for him, said: "I'll go out and wait on the terrace."

He remained inside some ten minutes longer. When he appeared he said in a jaunty way: "Come along, then. Let's go to the park."

The heat swelling in the air, pressed like an eiderdown on the senses, but there was no lull in the excitement. The gipsies were cock-a-hoop among their flower baskets, shrieking about them as though the day were a triumph for their race.

The park was full of peasants. As usual most of them were grouped in wonder, gaping at the *tapis vert*. Its grass was still trimmed and watered, but the swagged surround was losing its shape. The general neglect was evident. The hedges were unclipped, weeds and grass grew in the beds. The cana lilies and gladioli fell unstaked across the paths. The dahlias, that last year had been a firework display, were lost in a jungle of dead flowers and foliage.

The Pringles took the path that dropped down to the lake café. Peasants were sitting in the shade of the chestnuts, but stiffly, arms round knees, self-conscious here in the city, exuding, for all the festivity of their dress, a mute sense of endurance. In the past there had always been half a dozen men here selling sesame cakes and Turkish delight, but sweetmeats were rare and expensive now, and only one man remained. He held a tray of peanuts.

Guy and Harriet crossed the bridge to the café and sat where they usually sat, by the rail. Guy had brought a batch of exercise-books with him and while they waited for the wine he had ordered, he brought out his fountain-pen and set to work on them. Harriet had been given a copy of the Guardist news-sheet *Capitanul*. She now made her way through the leading article which was a laudation of General Antonescu. The general, called as a witness at the trial of Codreanu, had been asked if he considered Codreanu to be a traitor. He had crossed the court-room, seized hold of Codreanu's hand and said: "Would General Antonescu give his hand to a traitor?" As a result of this act, the Guardists claimed him for their own.

She put the pamphlet aside and watched Guy at work. She felt no inclination now to protest or interrupt. She was beginning to suspect that while Inchcape ignored truth, Guy merely pretended to ignore it. Perhaps it was for her sake he would not admit the hopelessness of their situation here. Anyway, she realised that while they remained he must make a show of having a job to do. He must believe that he was needed.

She looked away across the hazy, dirty water. Sitting here, a year before, they had thought of the war as a compact area of conflict about three hundred miles distant.

Rumania then had been sleek and prosperous, a land of plenty. Even this café, one of the cheapest, had given plates of olives, cheese and gherkins when one bought a glass of wine. Now those things were scarce. She seemed to remember the water, beneath its haze of heat, as translucent as crystal. Now it smelt of weed. The crusted surf round the café held captive floating bottles, orange-peel, match boxes and paper bags. As for the café itself, it reflected in its greyish weathered timbers, its crippled chairs, its dirty table papers, the decay of the whole country.

She sighed, feeling in the gummy September heat all the tedium of the year repeating itself. Guy, thinking she was bored, said: "Nearly finished," but she was not bored. Becoming conditioned to Guy's preoccupation, she was learning the resort of her own reflections. With him, in any case, talk was too general for intimacy. He despised the metaphysical and the personal. He did not gossip. She was beginning to believe that what he had lacked was a fundamental interest in the individual – a belief that would astonish him were she to accuse him. But she did not accuse him. Once she had believed that finding him, she had found everything: now she was not so sure. But here they were, wrecked together on the edge of Europe as on an island and she was learning to keep her thoughts to herself.

When he put down his pen, Guy picked up the news-sheet and pointed out the name of the editor. It was Corneliu Zelea Codreanu. Then followed the names of the editorial board.

"All dead," said Guy. "At every meeting these names are called out first and someone answers '*Present*'. No wonder the Iron Guard is called 'the legion of ghosts'."

"Still," said Harriet, "they have a sort of idealism . . ."

"Yes, indeed," Guy laughed, rising to his feet. "If they come to power, the same crimes will be committed, but only for the best possible reasons."

They crossed the bridge over the lake and walked through open parkland to the rear gate where stood the statue of a disgraced politician. Ever since Harriet had been in Bucharest, the head of the politician had been hidden in a linen bag. Today the bag had been removed. The politician – a short, stout man with head thrown back, one foot advanced, one hand extended in a Dantonesque gesture, was revealed as snub-nosed, his features clustered together like a bunch of radishes. No name was engraved upon the pediment.

Just outside the gate stood the mansion block where the Druckers had lived. The family had occupied the whole of the top floor. In those days the curtains in the great out-curving corner window had been of plum-coloured velvet, now they were of pink brocade. All the Drucker possessions, including, no doubt, the plum-coloured curtains had been forfeit to the crown.

Carol had got the trial over in good time and sold the Drucker oil holdings to Germany. Nobody cared. The whole affair had passed into oblivion.

Seeing her glance up at the top floor flat, Guy said: "I have been thinking about Sasha. And I've talked over the problem with David. The only answer, it seems to me, is: when we go, we must take him with us."

"How can we do that? They would never let him out of the country."

"Of course he would have to have a passport in another name, but these things can be arranged. Clarence had a whole department at work forging papers for the Poles. He must know someone who would help."

"Darling, you're wonderful!" she said, delighted by this suggestion, "I didn't believe you would give the matter a thought." She caught his arm, filled with all her old admiration for him and said: "Will you speak to Clarence?"

"Better if you speak to him. He'll do anything for you."

She was not sure of that. She felt some misgivings, but the very simplicity of the solution seemed to have extinguished the problem. It was as though a lock that would not open had fallen off in her hand.

Outside, the rejoicings, in which they had no part, were still going on. Listening to them, she felt that here she and Guy had no part in life. They existed off dangers peculiar to their small community. Even the problem of Sasha – which had been, like the secret cache of an alcoholic, something to which to resort in desperate times – was gone. What purpose was left to them? She felt a longing for England where the danger might be greater, but was shared by all.

David called in and the three sat on the balcony. There was a great deal of calling for the King. Plaudits greeted every arrival at the palace. Someone in the crowd was letting off fireworks. Guardist vans were relaying a radio speech in which Horia Sima described the *coup d'état* as yet another New Dawn.

"Dear me!" said David. "We seem to be getting a new dawn every day. But that," he snuffled, "is, after all, in the nature of things."

A rocket went up: a very small one that petered out on a level with the balcony. David snuffled again. "Do you realise," he said, "that in less than two months, Rumania has lost forty thousand square miles of territory? And with it, six million of her population? The drop in national income will be in the region of five hundred million sterling. Not a self-evident cause for rejoicing, would you say?"

Behind the palace the sky was aflame. Soon drifts of cloud, fine as smoke, dampened the autumnal fire and lights came on in the royal apartments. The sunset grew bleary. The bugle sounded from the palace yard. Harriet felt comforted by its familiarity. Kings came and went, and the nations fell, but men and horses must have rest.

17

NEXT MORNING THE GAIETY was gone and only a few peasants wandered about the square.

Bella, as she had promised, rang Harriet and described how the previous night the Guardists, grown drunk on the day's adulation, had marched through the ghetto area shouting threats to the Jews.

"We don't want all that again," she said.

This surprised Harriet who had never discovered in Bella much concern for the Jews. Bella explained that she was worried on her own behalf. In this country of dark-haired Latins, the Jews, contrary as ever, were notably blond or red-haired. As a result, Bella had always been suspect. So apparently, was Guy, the more so as he was reputed to favour his Jewish students.

Bella said: "It's no good telling people that in England it's the other way round. They don't want to believe you. They hate the thought of Jews having dark hair. It's different, of course, with educated Rumanians: the sort we mix with. They've travelled and seen for themselves. But these Guardists are riff-raff. They know nothing. They're ignorant as dirt."

"What about Antonescu? Isn't he red-haired?"

"Yes, he's got Tartar blood, but they all know who he is. No one's likely to make a mistake about him. It's different for me. Last time they caused trouble, I never went out alone. You'd better be careful."

"But I am dark," said Harriet.

"Well, you'd better keep Guy indoors."

Before Bella rang off, Harriet suggested they might meet for coffee somewhere. Bella said: "Not today. Not just yet. Better let things settle a bit." She was willing to visit Harriet, but it was another thing to be seen in her company.

Harriet, when she went out shopping, sensed misgiving in the streets. The meat shops were empty. All the stocks for the coming week had been sold to mark yesterday's rejoicings – and now the rejoicings were over. When would there be more meat? Who could tell? What were people to eat this week-end? No one knew. People were asking what had, in fact, happened? They had ex-changed one dictator for another: the known for an unknown who might bring the Iron Guard in his wake.

As though to enhance the anti-climax, Sunday was declared a Day of Atonement. Bucharest must atone for its slaughter of Codreanu and his comrades; for its pro-British past; and its frivolity. The church bells tolled from dawn till late at night. Cinemas, cafés, restaurants, even the English Bar, were closed. Every Rumanian, wherever he might be, was required to kneel down at eleven in the morning and pray to the Guardist martyrs for forgiveness. Processions of black-clad priests, heads bowed, trailed around all day in the glutinous heat.

The gloom was enlivened for the Pringles by a telephone call from Galpin. He wanted Yakimov. Yakimov was not in his room.

"Where's he got to?" Galpin angrily demanded.

Harriet did not know. For the first time, it occurred to her that she had seen nothing of him since Thursday evening. "Wasn't he in the bar yesterday?" she asked.

"No. Look here!" Galpin's tone was severely accusing. "He's got five thousand of mine. *And* I paid his fare to Cluj."

"He won't get far on five thousand."

"He'd better not try," Galpin said and his receiver was violently replaced.

Harriet went to ask Despina when she had last seen Yakimov. Despina, having been on the roof when he returned from Cluj, had seen nothing of him since the morning of his departure. She said his bed had not been slept in.

Harriet, puzzled, began to wonder whether indeed Yakimov had returned; or whether his brief appearance in the shadowy room had been but a conjuration of the evening's drama.

When she spoke to Guy he said confidently: "Yaki wouldn't go without telling us."

"Then where is he?"

Before Guy had found an answer to this question, Galpin came thumping on the door of the flat. He pushed his way in, apparently imagining the Pringles were hiding Yakimov. "He's had my money," shouted Galpin, "and I want my news."

In Yakimov's room, Galpin threw open the cupboards and pulled open the drawers so Harriet saw that, apart from some scraps of cast-off clothing, all Yakimov's possessions had gone.

Even his sable-lined greatcoat was missing from its hook. "He wouldn't take that if he were coming back," she said.

"The bastard!" Galpin shouted. "He's vamoosed. If I ever see him again, I'll scrag him."

When Galpin had gone, Guy said consolingly: "He'll be back."

"Well, he won't be back here," said Harriet with decision. "I want this room for Sasha."

Guy, torn between the claims of his two protégés, looked disconcerted.

Harriet said: "It is much safer for all of us to have Sasha inside the flat."

Guy agreed. Suddenly enthusiastic, throwing all doubts aside, he said: "But of course the boy must have the room. He can't spend the winter on the roof. What does he do all day? I haven't had time to see him lately. Is he still studying?"

"He reads and draws, but he's lazy. Down here you can keep an eye on him and he can have the wireless. He's fond of music."

Guy nodded. "He used to play the saxophone. We must do something for him. I wish we could borrow a gramophone." Suddenly beset by the urgency of Sasha's case, he said: "Let's bring him down straightaway," and sped off as he spoke. When he came back with Sasha, he was more elated by the move than the boy himself.

Despina had tidied the room. "It's super," Sasha said, then added as he sat down on the edge of the bed: "Jolly nice to have a real bed," but Harriet felt he scarcely cared where he was as long as someone stood between him and the discomforting world outside.

As he was arranging papers and pencils on the bedside table, she noticed he had brought down among his other things, his military uniform.

She said: "Did you have any sort of papers? I mean, a passport or *permis de sejour*?"

"I have this." He searched the uniform jacket and produced the *carte d'identité* issued to conscripts.

She saw it contained what she wanted, Sasha's photograph and said "This is evidence against you. I had better destroy it." She took it to the kitchen where she unpeeled the photograph and put it into her handbag. The card she tore into fragments and burnt in an ash-tray.

That evening Sasha sat down to supper with them. While they ate, they listened to the news, or what served for news these days. It consisted, on this occasion, of an indictment of Carol, who was described as the Pandora's Box from which all Rumania's evils had sprung. But, listeners were reminded, Hope had been imprisoned at the bottom of the box, and Hope, in the shape of General Antonescu, was in the studio. He would address the country.

Antonescu came at once to the microphone. Speaking in simple biblical language, he promised that once the country had expiated its sins, it would be restored to greatness. No one need fear. The new régime would bring neither bloodshed nor recriminations. For every useful member of Society, regardless of race or creed, there would be an ordered and protected life.

"Do you think we can count on that?" Harriet asked.

"Why not?" said Guy. "We haven't lost the war yet; and we may not lose it. The British are known to have great powers of survival. Antonescu doesn't want to antagonise us, and while our Legation is here, we're a recognised community."

Harriet asked Sasha what his family had thought of Antonescu. Sasha shook his head vaguely, apparently never having heard of him. "Despina says he's quite decent," he said.

Sasha had watched the revolution from the roof. What had he made of it all? He certainly had not been disturbed. It probably never entered his head that events could jeopardise his protected position. As for the fate of Rumania, why should that mean anything to him? Although he had been born here, he was no more emotionally involved with the place than were the Pringles themselves. Reflecting on his English schoolboy slang that at once placed and displaced him, she thought wherever he was, he would belong nowhere.

Guy's students, reassured by the general's speech, turned up in force at the University on Monday morning, but Sunday's gloom still hung in the air. Cinemas and theatres were to remain shut for the rest of the week. Although they had been ordered to return to work, thousands of people still kept half-hearted holiday, wandering the streets as though waiting for a sign that their disorganised world would become normal once again.

Bella had telephoned Harriet that morning, excited because she had been right in suspecting that Carol had not left immediately after his abdication. He had, in fact, remained in the palace another twenty-four hours, then gone by rail, taking a train-load of valuables.

"And all the El Grecos," Bella said, scandalised.

"But weren't they bought by his father?"

"Yes, with public money. Of course, Lupescu and Urdureanu went with him. One of the waiters on the train is putting it round that the three of them squabbled all the way, blaming each other for what had happened. At the frontier, the Iron Guard machine-gunned them and they had to lie on the floor. Just think of it!" said Bella, giggling as she thought of it herself.

Harriet expressed some concern that the ex-King and his followers should have been all day in the palace listening to the rejoicings over their downfall.

"Oh," said Bella, "don't you fret your fat over that lot. They'll live in luxury with the cash they've salted away. Nikko says it was a mistake, letting them go. They should have been arrested and tried and forced to disgorge. The Iron Guard needs some diversion. There's no knowing what they'll get up to now."

Bella seemed less confident that the Iron Guard could be kept from power. "After all," she said, "who else is there? Maniu's pro-British and Bratianu's anti-German. I can't see Hitler standing for either of them. And," she glumly added, "we've got these wretched refugees pouring into the town, filling up the hotels and cafés, and putting up prices again."

"What will happen to them?"

"God knows," said Bella.

The trains had stopped for two days when the news of the revolution reached Transylvania and most of the refugees were only now reaching the city. Those that filled the hotels and cafés were the fortunate few. The majority, the dispossessed peasants, had had to shelter beneath the trees of the park and up the Chaussée. Arriving during an interregnum, they received less consideration than the Poles had done. No one was empowered to deal with them. They spent their days standing dumbly before any large building where power might reside. Imagining that justice must eventually be brought out to them, they were prepared to wait days and weeks: and they probably would have to wait, for the Cabinet had not yet been appointed. The *prefectura* and ministries were empty of important people. The senior civil servants were spending their days with the processions of penitents that followed the priests and nuns about the streets.

Harriet, when she went out, took a *traşura* up the Chaussée as far as the fountain that marked the edge of the town. She was on her way to visit Clarence who lived in a new block on an unfinished boulevard. Never having been there before, she had difficulty in finding it. She might have telephoned him and arranged to meet him in the English Bar, but felt an unexpected call would be more likely to impress him with the urgency of her request.

When Harriet asked for Domnul Lawson his cook, a grimy woman with a sly manner, pointed, grinning, at the balcony as though to say: "He's there, where he always is." Harriet found him lying on a long chair, a copy of the *Bukarester Tageblatt* on the floor beside him, He wore a heavy white sweater across the chest of which was embroidered the word "Leander". His eyes were shut. He did not open them until she said: "Hello, Clarence," then he started up, confused by the sight of her, and was immediately on the defensive. In a complaining tone, he explained: "I'm supposed to rest. The mornings are getting chilly. With my weak chest, I have to be careful."

The balcony was in the shade, overlooking open fields from which came a hint of breeze. Swallowing back a derisive comment, Harriet mildly said: "I'm sorry if I disturbed you."

He gave her a suspicious glance. Seeing she was serious, he said: "I suppose you've heard? The blitz on London has begun."

She had not heard the news that morning. Looking down at the German paper, she asked: "What does it say?"

"According to this rag the whole city's aflame. They say the fire service could not cope. They claim tremendous damage done, thousands of casualties and so on. Probably a lot of lies – but who knows?"

"If we get back, there may be nothing to get back to."

He shrugged and dragged himself out of his chair. "How about a drink?"

While he went into the room and called to the servant for glasses, Harriet remained on the balcony, shocked by what she had heard. On the other side of the road there was a cornfield. The corn, a second or third crop, not more than a foot high, was still grey-green. Its freckling of poppies gave the vista a look of spring, but the mountains were visible in the distance – a sign that the summer haze was lifting and autumn had begun. There was even a glint of snow on the highest peak.

Clarence called her. She went into the room and looked about at the dark, carved furniture, the painted plates and the cloths and cushions embroidered in blue and red cross-stitch.

"Peasant stuff," said Clarence: "I bought it from the previous owner for a few thousand. I got the cook as well. She sleeps with her husband and three children in the kitchen. Not an ideal arrangement but if I'd got rid of them, they'd have nowhere to sleep at all."

"Do peasants have furniture as good as this?"

"Some do, but even the most prosperous have a miserable diet."

He handed her a glass of *ţuică*. She looked about her thinking that in this small room, which was exposed and overlighted like a birdcage on a wall, she would suffer from both claustrophobia and agoraphobia. Clarence, however, seemed content.

He said: "The flat suits me. I live, eat and sleep in one room, but I don't mind. I like to have all my needs within reach. But I'm getting rid of it. I haven't told anyone yet: I'm leaving."

"Leaving Rumania?"

"Yep."

"Oh!" Harriet, who on the long drive up the Chaussée had thought of Clarence gratefully as one who stood with them in peril, now felt a drop in spirits. She said: "You think it's time to go? That something is going to happen here?"

"I'm not worrying about that. It's simply that I've nothing to do here."

"What about your job at the Propaganda Bureau?"

"You know as well as I do, the Bureau is a farce."

"When will you go?"

"Oh, no hurry."

That was a relief, anyway. She asked: "And where will you go?"

"Egypt, perhaps. Brenda cabled me last week."

Brenda, Clarence's fiancée, was in England. When Harriet first saw her photograph, she had said: "A nice, good face," but Clarence showed no enthusiasm. He said now: "She's joined some sort of women's naval service and is going to Alexandria. She wants me to meet her there and get married."

"Why not?"

"Why not, indeed?"

"You now have Sophie to think about, of course."

"To hell with Sophie. Would you condemn me to that? Brenda at least would respect me."

Harriet smiled. "For what?"

Satisfied that he had provoked her raillery, he lay back in his chair and sombrely echoed her: "For what?" He thrust out his lower lip then, after some moments, said: "The gall of frustration has poured for years into my system. I'll die of it in the end." He gave her a long, brooding look, intended to be darkly significant, so she had difficulty in not laughing outright.

She decided to ask his help before things deteriorated further. Changing her tone, appealing to his generosity, she said: "I've come to ask your help. Before you go, there's something you must do for us."

"Ah!" Clarence looked down into his glass. He did not move but his attitude had become wary. After a long pause, he asked: "What?"

"We have to try and get someone out of the country."

"Not Yakimov?"

"Yakimov's gone."

"Indeed? He never paid back that ten thousand he got from the Polish fund."

"He never paid back anything. We're worried about Sasha Drucker. If we have to go, what will happen to him?"

"You were a couple of fools to keep him in the first place."

"Well, we did keep him and now we have to look after him."

"Why? He's not a child. Surely he can look after himself? He belongs here: he must have friends . . ."

"He hasn't. Anyway, his friends would be Jews. They couldn't help him."

Her urgent advocacy made Clarence sit up, sobered and vexed. He said sharply: "I can imagine Guy busy-bodying himself about this fellow. But why are you involved?"

Harriet reflected on the complex of instincts that caused her to protect such dependent innocents as Sasha and the red kitten but did not suppose Clarence would be satisfied by any attempt to explain them. After some moments, she said: "We can't just abandon him here. You must see that. We thought, if we could get him a passport of some sort, he could come with us."

Clarence stared blankly at her.

"Guy says you had someone who forged passports for the Poles."

Seeing where this was leading, Clarence smiled to himself. "They were made by Poles for Poles." He shifted in his chair, throwing one leg over the arm, and explained with superior patience: "The whole set-up was organised inside the Polish army: the Rumanian government connived at it. In those days, Rumania was our ally and the Poles were escaping to join the allied forces in France. The Rumanians did quite well out of it. They were paid so much per escape. It ran into thousands. This fellow of yours is a different matter. He's a deserter from the army and all the frontier officials would be on the look-out for him."

"Is there anyone left of the people you had working for the Poles?"

Clarence made a movement suggesting that even if there were, he personally was taking no risks.

"You *might* help, Clarence. *Please*. If you could get him a passport and drive him over the frontier into Bulgaria . . ."

Clarence interrupted her with an angry laugh. "My dear child, do you realise what you're asking? If I were caught with this fellow in my car, I'd stand a fair chance of ending my days in a Rumanian prison."

She said with persuasive sweetness: "At least, get me the passport."

Clarence stared from the window, his expression sullen, his glass forgotten in his hand. He had once said to her: "If you treated me properly, you could get anything you wanted from me," but she had, of course, to reckon with Clarence's ideas of proper treatment. They changed with his moods. He now said coldly:

"You can be very charming when you want something."

"Well, I don't want something for myself. I want to help this poor boy."

"Why? What do you care about Sasha Drucker?" He turned on her a stare of black resentment that made clear to her the fact that he might do something for her but would do nothing for Sasha. He would do even less when it was she who pleaded for him. It would have been better had Guy made the appeal.

She stood up. "We've taken him in," she said. "We feel for him as for a child who has a right to the elements of a reasonable life. That's all."

Clarence got slowly to his feet. She waited, but he remained silent, embarrassed, but sustained by his obstinate jealousy.

She took out Sasha's photograph and put it on the table, making a last plea: "Will you think about it?"

In acute exasperation, he burst out: "Think about *what*? You're asking the impossible. I can do nothing."

She left the photograph, feeling it might speak for itself, and went, saying nothing more.

She walked the two miles back to the centre of the town. For most of the way she felt empty with disappointment, then her old anxiety began seeping back again. What had seemed so simple a solution of the problem had proved no solution at all. When, after luncheon, she had Guy to herself, she told him of Clarence's refusal to obtain the passport. Giving an explanation not too painful to her own vanity, she said: "You might suppose he was jealous of the boy."

Guy laughed. "He probably is. He has always been very devoted to me, investing me with the qualities he lacks himself."

"You mean, he's probably jealous of your befriending Sasha?"

"What else?"

Leaving it at that, Harriet said: "Perhaps you're right. But what are we to do now?"

"We're not dependent on Clarence. God help us if we were. We'll try someone else."

"Who?"

"I don't know. I'll speak to David. Leave it to me and don't worry."

Towards the end of the week, the Pringles, about to enter the Athénée Palace, met Princess Teodorescu and Baron Steinfeld emerging. The baron was ordering a string of hotel servants who were carrying luggage out to his Mercedes. The princess stared furiously at the Pringles, making them feel that their appearance at that moment was the final outrage of an outrageous day. The baron, however, greeted them as though feeling some need to explain his departure. "We go to the mountains," he said. "We go late, we go in fear, but we escape the heat. If we stay, we melt away."

"*Hör doch auf*," said the princess, pushing him towards the car.

The Pringles, surprised not so much by this belated departure as the fluster attending it, mentioned it to Galpin when they went into the bar.

"They're escaping the heat, are they?" Galpin twisted his lips down in an ironical smile. "I bet they're not the only ones," and he went on to explain that the Guardists, having broken into

Lupescu's house, had that morning found a box of letters which incriminated some of the most famous names in the country.

"They've been pretending, the whole lot of them, that they've been Guardist all along. They now refer to Lupescu as 'the dirty Jewess', but she's got the laugh on them, all right. She left this box of letters, open, bang in the middle of her bedroom floor. They're from people like Teodorescu all addressing her as '*ma souveraine*' and 'your majesty' and saying they couldn't wait for the day when she would be crowned queen. It's damned funny, but the Iron Guard isn't amused. Humour isn't in fashion these days. I bet there'll be quite a few of the upper crust moving out of Bucharest to escape the heat."

The papers announced that the city's atonement would end on Sunday, the day Queen Helen, the Queen Mother, was returning from exile to reside with her son in Bucharest.

Sunday's pageantry began with the clatter of horses. The Queen's own regiment, out of favour since her departure, was galloping across the square in frogged uniforms and busbies, pennants flying, to meet her at the station. The whole city was in the streets to cheer them. Antonescu had promised new order, new hope, renewed greatness, and all, it was believed, would return with the wronged Queen who was the very symbol of the country's exiled morality. Here was the resolution for which everyone was waiting.

The noise brought Despina from the kitchen. She ran through the room to join Guy, Harriet and Sasha on the balcony, shrieking with delight at the hussars and the flags and the ferment of the square. Here was a new beginning indeed! But even while the dust of the horsemen still hung in the air, the sound of "*Capitanul*" could be heard swelling from the Calea Victoriei.

The Iron Guard had been silent during the week of atonement. There was a general belief that they were being discouraged while Antonescu was seeking some other agent to police his régime. Whether this was true or not, here they were and something in their bearing had changed. There had always been a touch of defiance about all their marching and singing in the past, but now it was exultant. When they finished "*Capitanul*", they started on the National Anthem, linking the tunes as though they had a peculiar warranty for both.

Harriet said: "I've never heard them sing that before."

The leading Guardists were cheered, automatically, accepted as part of the day's entertainment, but as the ranks passed stern-faced and contemptuous of the audience, the applause dwindled. People were uncertain what response was required of them, and gradually silence came down.

Guy said: "I don't like the look of this," and after a moment, he turned and went into the room.

The Guardists were still passing when a new interest revivified the crowds. The old Metropolitan, bejewelled like an Indian prince had appeared walking beneath a golden canopy. His followers, who had spent the week trailing round the streets as penitents, in black, were now exultant in cloth of gold. As this dazzling procession appeared in the square, the crowd surged towards it, leaving the Guardists to jackboot their way unheeded.

Sasha, excited by everything he saw, leaned out over the ledge while Despina clapped her hands, jumping up and down and crying: "*Frumosa, frumosa, frumosa.*"

Long after they had circled the square, the priests could be seen, agleam in the sunlight, climbing the rising road to the cathedral. A sound of gunfire announced the Queen's arrival. At once all the bells of the city rang out and cheers, relayed from the station, were redoubled by cheers from the crowd below. The clangour and chorus of bells cheering drowned the Guardists who lifted their heads, bawling in an effort to be heard.

Harriet looked into the room to say: "The Queen is coming," and Guy, who had been talking on the telephone, put down the receiver. "I've just rung the Legation," he said. "The Iron Guard is in power."

"You mean the whole of the Cabinet is now Guardist?"

"Yes, except for one or two military men and experts. Guardists have been appointed to all the important ministries."

"What will happen now?"

"Chaos, I imagine."

She took advantage of his disturbed expression to say: "You must close the summer school."

He was about to speak when the cheers started up in the square again and they returned to the balcony to see the hussars escorting the Queen and her son, who were in a gilded coach covered with roses. The coach passed through the square, then went on its way to the cathedral. There was sudden silence, then came the sibilant murmur of the mass relayed through the loudspeakers and as though a wind had passed over it, the crowd sank to its knees. Harriet could see the women pulling out handkerchiefs and weeping in an excess of emotion.

From somewhere in the remote distance there still came on the air the monotonous throb of "*Capitanul*".

Hotel Splendide Suleiman Bay,
Istanbul.

Dear Boy [wrote Yakimov]:

Is the old girl sold? If so, get Dobbie to remit cash through bag. Your Yaki is in low water. Food here poorish. Kebabs and so on. The English Colony a funny lot. When I tell them I'm a refugee from the oil fields, no one seems to believe me.

Don't delay
With the *lei*,
Your poor old needy Yaki.

Crossing to the corner of the Boulevard Brateanu, Harriet saw the Hispano still in the window, looking immovable, like a museum exhibit. She went in to inquire whether anyone was showing interest in the car. The salesman glumly shook his head.

Each of the showroom windows displayed a portrait of Codreanu. The same portrait stared out from the windows opposite, the empty windows of Dragomir's, the largest grocery shop in Europe. Queues waited for such food as there was.

The windows rattled as across the square, at sixty miles an hour, a fleet of Iron Guard motor-cyclists sped on their way to the Boulevard Carol where the richest men in Rumania lay under house arrest, awaiting the results of Horia Sima's enquiry into the origins of all private fortunes. Nothing might be moved from their houses. An armed guard stood at every gate.

Suicides were occurring daily. One of the first was of the Youth Movement leader, decorated last June by Hitler. Unable to account for a missing twelve million *lei*, he had shot himself. The police had gone on strike. Their work, they said, was too dangerous. Those who were in power one day, were in prison the next; those who had been in prison, were now in power. The Guardists had taken over and patrolled the streets with revolvers in their holsters.

As the motor-cyclists roared past, the salesman raised one eyebrow and one shoulder. Who these days would buy such a symbol of private wealth as this Hispano?

Bella, when she telephoned that morning, had said: "These Guardist police are worse than no police at all. All they do is go round the offices collecting for party funds. And not only the Jewish offices, either. They don't care whose money they take. They call it cleaning up public life, but even if you find a burglar in your house, you can't get a Guardist to come and arrest him. I hope you're staying indoors. Things'll settle down, of course, but, if I were you, I wouldn't go out yet awhile."

Had Harriet taken Bella's advice she would, like Carol's financiers and Chief of Police and Chief of Secret Police, have been a prisoner in her own home. As it was, made restless by insecurity, she wandered about the streets and went each day to meet Guy as he left his classes. She imagined he would be less liable to attack if he were with a woman.

Stories were were going round that thousands of people had been arrested and thousands executed.

People caught leaving the country were sometimes arrested, sometimes merely stripped of their valuable possessions and allowed to proceed.

"That Ionescu's gone," said Bella. "Him that used to be Minister of Information. He overbalanced trying to face all ways at once. He became a Guardist but he knew he was for it. His children were carrying little fur muffs. Muffs! – at this time of the year, I ask you! Naturally they roused suspicion. The customs men tore them to pieces and found them stuffed with jewellery and gold. I always thought him too clever by half."

Another who went was Ionescu's mistress, the singer Florica. She reached Trieste and then turned round and came back again. She was reported as having said: "I thought of my country and knew that at such a time I could not leave it."

But, as Bella pointed out, she was a gipsy and no true Rumanian, so her behaviour was, as one might expect, peculiar.

Harriet, as she walked about in the sticky autumnal heat, saw no open signs of persecution, not even of the Dambôviţa Jews. What she did see, daily, were processions of Cabinet ministers, civil servants, officers of the armed services, priests, nuns and schoolchildren following the most impressive funerals. For the Guardist leaders were busy disinterring their Martyrs. Raised in batches to which were given heroic names like the Decemvirii and would hold out, with a dramatic gesture, her empty basket. "In the market today, no sugar, no coffee, no meat, no fish, no eggs. Nothing, nothing."

Watching the processions, the daily pageantry amid utter confusion, it seemed to Harriet that the whole country had succumbed, without any sort of resistance, to a lunatic autocracy.

She said to Guy: "Everyone in Bucharest is trailing round after these Guardist turn-outs. Why is there no opposition to it all?"

"There's no chance of any *active* opposition," he said. "The only people with the moral fibre to oppose anything are in prison. The Communists – but not only the Communists: the Liberal Democrats, everyone and anyone likely to show a spark of revolt: they're all in prison."

"What about Maniu?"

"What can he do? Anyway, from what I've seen of him, I should not think he's much more than a showpiece: Rumania's 'Good Man'. He was the leader of the Transylvanian peasants, and Transylvania is lost. You must realise that this new dictatorship is much tougher than the old. There are not only prisons now, there are concentration camps: and there are these young men trained at Dachau, all waiting for a chance to beat someone up. Yet," Guy added, "there is opposition of a sort. A typical Rumanian opposition. Satire. It's the most difficult sort to repress." He told her how in the Doi Trandifiri, the meeting place of intellectuals, there was proof that the liberal sanity of the past survived. Deathly fearful though people were, there they were still able to laugh. They had nicknamed the Iron Guard "*le régime des pompes funèbres*" and a great many funny stories went round about Horia Sima and his visions. Sima was in conflict with Codreanu's father who declared that his son's spirit disapproved of the present leader and had appointed his father as his vicar-on-earth. The old man had to be put under house-arrest and, knowing he was in danger of assassination, he said he preferred to stay indoors as fewer accidents happened there.

"There's opposition, too," said Guy, "from a much more influential source – the German minister. He's tired of all this marching and singing '*Capitanul*'. He wants the country back at work. Several big industrial firms have had to close down because the directors are in prison and the workers are all in the Iron Guard. The financial situation is chaotic. Carol banked all the national wealth abroad in his own name. Now it's frozen. On top the Nicardorii, the bodies were paraded in giant coffins all over the city and reburied with ceremonies that must be attended by any who hoped to maintain any sort of position in public life.

Down in the Chicken Market Harriet found a memorial service being held over the spot where Calinescu's murderers had lain. The trembling old peasant who sold her a cabbage said that among the mourners were "the greatest men in the world".

Who were they? she asked and was told: "Hitler, Mussolini, Count Ciano and the Emperor of Japan."

After the ceremony the site was roped off and spread each day with fresh flowers, to the inconvenience of the market traffic.

"The great day, of course," said Bella, "will be when they dig up His Nibs at Fort Jilawa. They'll wait till November, the anniversary of his death. Then, Nikko says, trouble will really begin."

The papers announced that the demand for admission to the Iron Guard was so great, the list had to be closed.

Among those who appeared in Guardist uniform was the Pringles' landlord, who was also their next-door neighbour. In the past, when he had met Harriet on the landing, he had greeted her courteously: now, in his green shirt and breeches, his moustache sternly waxed, he stared over her head and she began to fear him. He might have – almost certainly did have – a key to their flat. She remembered the mysterious disappearance of the oil-well plan. He had been one of her suspects. If he came in while they were out, he would almost certainly discover Sasha.

Once or twice, when she left the flat, she saw a man dodge out of sight on the lower flight. She spoke of this to Guy, who thought it would be some agent of the landlord. Embarrassed at having English tenants, he might be seeking an excuse to break their agreement.

She said to Despina: "Keep the front door bolted. If the landlord wants to come in, do not let him."

"No, no, *corniţa*," Despina assured her, appearing to understand the whole situation. "If anyone comes, I do like this . . ." She opened the sitting-room door a crack and put her nose to it. "If it is the landlord – pouf! I do like this." She slammed the door shut. "He is a bad man," she added in explanation. "He beats his cook."

There were now four meatless days in a week, but even on the other days meat was hard to find. Despina would be away for two or three hours queueing at market stalls and often, on returning, brow and one shoulder. Who these days would buy such a symbol of private wealth as this Hispano?

Bella, when she telephoned that morning, had said: "These Guardist police are worse than no police at all. All they do is go round the offices collecting for party funds. And not only the Jewish offices, either. They don't care whose money they take. They call it cleaning up public life, but even if you find a burglar in your house, you can't get a Guardist to come and arrest him. I hope you're staying indoors. Things'll settle down, of course, but, if I were you, I wouldn't go out yet awhile."

Had Harriet taken Bella's advice she would, like Carol's financiers and Chief of Police and Chief of Secret Police, have been a prisoner in her own home. As it was, made restless by insecurity, she wandered about the streets and went each day to meet Guy as he left his classes. She imagined he would be less liable to attack if he were with a woman.

Stories were were going round that thousands of people had been arrested and thousands executed.

People caught leaving the country were sometimes arrested, sometimes merely stripped of their valuable possessions and allowed to proceed.

"That Ionescu's gone," said Bella. "Him that used to be Minister of Information. He overbalanced trying to face all ways at once. He became a Guardist but he knew he was for it. His children were carrying little fur muffs. Muffs! – at this time of the year, I ask you! Naturally they roused suspicion. The customs men tore them to pieces and found them stuffed with jewellery and gold. I always thought him too clever by half."

Another who went was Ionescu's mistress, the singer Florica. She reached Trieste and then turned round and came back again. She was reported as having said: "I thought of my country and knew that at such a time I could not leave it."

But, as Bella pointed out, she was a gipsy and no true Rumanian, so her behaviour was, as one might expect, peculiar.

Harriet, as she walked about in the sticky autumnal heat, saw no open signs of persecution, not even of the Dambôviţa Jews. What she did see, daily, were processions of Cabinet ministers, civil servants, officers of the armed services, priests, nuns and schoolchildren following the most impressive funerals. For the Guardist leaders were busy disinterring their Martyrs. Raised in batches to which were given heroic names like the Decemvirii and

18

Hotel Splendide Suleiman Bay,
Istanbul.

Dear Boy [wrote Yakimov]:

Is the old girl sold? If so, get Dobbie to remit cash through bag. Your Yaki is in low water. Food here poorish. Kebabs and so on. The English Colony a funny lot. When I tell them I'm a refugee from the oil fields, no one seems to believe me.

> Don't delay
> With the *lei*,
>> Your poor old needy Yaki.

Crossing to the corner of the Boulevard Brateanu, Harriet saw the Hispano still in the window, looking immovable, like a museum exhibit. She went in to inquire whether anyone was showing interest in the car. The salesman glumly shook his head.

Each of the showroom windows displayed a portrait of Codreanu. The same portrait stared out from the windows opposite, the empty windows of Dragomir's, the largest grocery shop in Europe. Queues waited for such food as there was.

The windows rattled as across the square, at sixty miles an hour, a fleet of Iron Guard motor-cyclists sped on their way to the Boulevard Carol where the richest men in Rumania lay under house arrest, awaiting the results of Horia Sima's enquiry into the origins of all private fortunes. Nothing might be moved from their houses. An armed guard stood at every gate.

Suicides were occurring daily. One of the first was of the Youth Movement leader, decorated last June by Hitler. Unable to account for a missing twelve million *lei*, he had shot himself. The police had gone on strike. Their work, they said, was too dangerous. Those who were in power one day, were in prison the next; those who had been in prison, were now in power. The Guardists had taken over and patrolled the streets with revolvers in their holsters.

As the motor-cyclists roared past, the salesman raised one eye-of that, the Guardists want to start a full-scale persecution of the Jews."

"Wouldn't the Germans encourage that?"

"No. What do they care about Rumanian racial purity. This is merely a raw material zone. Fabricius said to Sima: 'Persecutions are all very well in Germany where there are ten efficient Germans to one efficient Jew, but here there isn't one efficient Rumanian to ten efficient Jews. If we do get law and order here, we'll probably have the Germans to thank for it.' "

19

Now that he saw him every day, Sasha had become for Guy a more evident responsibility. Finding that he could not borrow or hire a gramophone, Guy brought in a mouth-organ which Sasha accepted with more excitement than he had shown over the room. "But this is spiffing," he said, gazing delightedly at the mouth-organ. "Really spiffing," and he took it at once to his room.

He kept the room tidy and made his own bed. He had pinned his drawings to the walls. The books he had borrowed from the sitting-room stood in a row on the bedside table. His possessions – a brush and comb, some pencils, paper and water-paints – were neatly set out before them. Whatever disorder might prevail in the outside world, he lived in order and was happy.

Sitting on the edge of the bed, he began to pick out a tune he had heard on the radio and which seemed to Harriet painfully applicable to their case:

"Run rabbit, run rabbit, run, run, run,
Don't give the farmer his fun, fun, fun . . ."

When they were alone Guy said to Harriet: "I've been speaking to David. He thinks Foxy Leverett might help us about Sasha."

"What could Foxy Leverett do?"

"Apparently he's an adept at smuggling people over frontiers. But the whole problem may be settled in a different way. Supposing, things being as they are, the Soviets decided to invade? They could get here before the Germans."

"You think the Russians would protect the son of a banker who worked for Germany and piled up a fortune in Switzerland?"

"No, but he'd be no worse off than anyone else. He could lose himself in a crowd."

Harriet was beginning to fear that the hope of losing himself in the crowd was the most they could offer Sasha.

Next morning, Bella, telephoning as was her habit, asked: "I

Although it was still early, Harriet walked to the University, needing to assure herself that the broadcast had not, so far, provoked trouble.

The door stood open. The porter, as usual, was nowhere to be seen. Anyone could enter. She felt furious with the man who, were he at his post, could at least give warning of attack.

She sat on the porter's bench and stared out through the peaked doorway at the glittering street. The gipsies, selling the only thing plentiful in Bucharest now, were in their usual high spirits. Their danger was as great as that of the Jews, but they knew nothing about it.

She could hear Guy's voice coming through an open door half-way down the passage. She could also hear, from somewhere distant in the street, the sound of "*Capitanul*". She had become so used to it, she would scarcely have noticed it had she not been listening for it. The Guardists were approaching the University. If any of them turned in here, she decided, she would rush to the door and shut and bolt it. She wondered if the Legation would let her have a revolver. She was becoming obsessed with the need to get Guy and Sasha through this situation unharmed. Sitting there, hypnotised by her own inactivity, she began to think of them as enclosed in a protective emanation that came of her will to save them.

She wondered how many students were in the room with Guy. She had always been somewhat irritated by the students and their claim on him. He imagined his energy was inexhaustible, but she felt that given the opportunity, they would drain him dry: and now it was for their sake that he was here at risk.

She rose and made her way silently down the passage to the lecture room. "*Capitanul*" was still wavering about in the distance. Not a great many were singing. She imagined a small posse out on some sinister mission.

The door of Guy's classroom had been propped open to create a draught.

Harriet, pressing against the wall, could see unseen through the opening. There were three students – two girls and a youth, sitting together in the front desk, their faces raised in strained attention.

Harriet moved to see Guy. Her foot slipped on the linoleum, making no more noise than a mouse. At once a frisson went through the room. The three heads turned. Guy's voice slowed.

He did not pause, but he glanced at the door. Harriet remained motionless, scarcely breathing. The lecture went on.

She tiptoed back to the bench and sat down again, satisfied, having discovered that beneath his apparent unconcern he was as alert as she was to the dangers about them.

20

THAT DAY, A FRIDAY, was the last on which the summer school opened. The following afternoon, Inchcape called on Guy to tell him that the new Minister of Information had ordered the school and the British Propaganda Bureau to close immediately.

He said: "Had to agree about the school – no choice, no choice at all! – but the Bureau is part of the Legation. I've just been to see H.E. I said: 'While the Legation remains here, we've a right to our Bureau.' I must say the old boy was pleasant enough. Indeed, he was pathetic. He seems dazed by the way things are shaping. 'All right, Inchcape,' he said. 'All right. If you want to keep your little shop open I'll see what can be done, but the school must close.' "

"Why?" Guy asked.

Inchcape shrugged. "The Minister said if the closure were not effected as from today, we would all be ordered out. No reprieve."

Guy was not satisfied. He said: "If they've relented about the Bureau, they're just as likely to relent about the school."

"No. Something's going on here. There's a rumour that a German Military Mission is on its way. The Guardist minister was adamant. They feel – not unnaturally, I suppose – that a British school is an anomaly in their midst." Inchcape's tone was rather smug but held a hint of defiance, so it occurred to Harriet that he had probably bartered the school for the Bureau: "Let me keep one open and you can close the other." Whatever the sacrifice, Inchcape must maintain an official position.

For her part, however, she was only too thankful to see the school end. She said: "So there's nothing to keep us here. We could take a holiday. We could go to Greece."

Guy, looking gloomy, said without enthusiasm: "We might get to Predeal, but no farther. I have to prepare for the new term . . ."

"But if the English Department is closed . . ."

"Nothing has been said about the Department closing," said Inchcape. "All they demanded, was the closure of the summer school."

"But surely they must mean the English Department, too. Yesterday, Guy had only three students. You can't open a department without students."

"Oh, they'll be swarming back when the term starts. They'll feel there's safety in numbers. We'll weather another winter here."

Making no attempt to argue on a point that would soon settle itself, Harriet said: "When can we go to Predeal?"

Before Guy could reply, Inchcape broke in: "Not next week. Our distinguished visitor arrives next week. This is an opportunity to make arrangements. I shall meet him at Baneasa, of course, but I'll expect my staff to be in attendance. Then we'll have to give a party; a reception. We can do nothing about that until we know the day of his arrival."

"What is the date of the Cantecuzino Lecture?" Harriet asked.

Inchcape looked at Guy saying: "It's held every other year. You must have been here for the last one?"

"1938. The beginning of October. My first term here. The Cantecuzino was the inaugural lecture of the term."

"So it was," Inchcape nodded, clicked his tongue reflectively while staring at his feet, then suddenly jerked upright. "Anyway, the old buffer's reached Cairo. He may get stuck there and he may not. We must be prepared."

Early on Wednesday morning, Despina woke Guy to say Inchcape wanted him on the telephone. Inchcape shouted accusingly: "That old nitwit's coming today. You'll just have to rouse yourself and get to the airport. I can't make it."

"When is he due?"

"That's the trouble. He sent a last-minute cable saying merely: 'Wednesday a.m.' It might mean hanging round there half the day. I've got this damned reception to organise. Pauli will deliver invitations. We must have a princess or two." The imminence of the real Pinkrose seemed to have disrupted Inchcape. In the extremity of his exacerbation he became confiding: "To tell the truth, I never thought he'd get here. I thought he'd hang around in Cairo for weeks. He must have got the organisation to charter a plane. Shocking to think of such a waste of funds. And," he added, putting the question as though Guy were to blame for the contingency, "where are we going to hold this lecture, I'd like to know? Last time, we took the reception rooms over the Café Napoleon, but all that's been pulled down. The University hall is nothing like large enough. Every possible place in the town has been turned over to the Iron Guard for divisional headquarters. I suppose we could get one of the public rooms at the Athénée Palace! The acoustics are poor, but does it matter? Pinkrose is no great shakes as a lecturer. Well, get into your duds and get down there. Take Harriet. Make a bit of a show. The self-important old so-and-so will expect it."

On their way to the airport, the Pringles were to confirm a booking for Pinkrose at the Athénée Palace.

The sky that morning was filmed with cloud, an indication of the season's change. There was a breeze. For the first time since spring, it was possible to believe that the Siberian cold would return and the country, under snow, lost all colour and became like a photographic negative.

Harriet said: "Do you really think we'll spend another winter here?"

Making no pretence at optimism now, Guy shook his head. "It's impossible to say."

On Monday, with no more warning than was given by a day or two of rumours, the precursors of the German Military Mission had driven into Bucharest. They were followed on Tuesday by a German Trade Delegation. The whole parking area outside the Athénée Palace became filled with German cars and military lorries, each bearing the swastika on a red pennant. The arrivals were young officers sent to prepare the way for the senior members of the Mission.

The story was that Fabricius had demanded demobilisation in Rumania. "Send your men back into the fields," he said. "What Germany needs is food." Antonescu, aghast, replied that he had been dreaming of the day when his country would "fight shoulder to shoulder with its great ally". He finally agreed that Germany should take over the reorganisation both of Rumania's army and economy.

Guy said, as they passed through the swing-doors: "Perhaps this is an alternative to complete occupation. It may mean they will leave us alone."

At that hour of the morning, the vestibule was empty. The booking had been tentatively made by Inchcape for an indefinite day of this week and now the hotel was full of Germans. Guy went to the desk, half expecting to be refused, but the hotel maintained its traditions. It had always been favoured by the British and did not forget past favours. Guy was courteously received. A room was available for Professor Lord Pinkrose.

The airfield lay on the southern fringe of the city. The opalescent sky cast a pallor over the grass plain that stretched some forty miles to the Danube. The wind blowing off the Balkans was like a wind from the sea.

There was nothing on the field but a customs-shed. The Pringles sat on the bench before it, waiting. Since the school had been closed, Guy had been low-spirited and restless, missing employment and having nothing to take its place. He had been told he must not use the University library or any other part of the building without permission. He sometimes went to the Propaganda Bureau to read Inchcape's books and cogitate on subjects for the new term. He now took from his pockets a novel by Conrad and two books of poems by de la Mare, while Harriet read Lawrence's *The Rainbow*.

They had waited less than an hour when one of the small grey planes of the Rumanian air-line arrived from Sofia. Harriet put down her book to watch the passengers alight. Behind the usual collection of businessmen in grey suits, carrying new toffee-coloured brief-cases, came a small male figure, much wrapped up, wearing a heavy greatcoat. He descended slowly, collar up, shoulders hunched, hands in pockets, glancing cautiously about from under the brim of a trilby hat.

"Could that be Pinkrose?" she asked.

Guy adjusted his glasses and peered across the field. "Surely he wouldn't come on the ordinary plane?"

The businessmen, knowing their way about, had made straight for the customs-shed leaving the last passenger wandering, alone, on the field. Guy rose and crossed over to him. They returned together. Guy was explaining how Inchcape, busy arranging a reception in Pinkrose's honour, had been unable to come to the airfield.

Pinkrose accepted this apology with a brief nod, grunting slightly, apparently leaving further comment until more was revealed to him.

He was a rounded man, narrow-shouldered and broad-hipped, thickening down from the crown of his hat to the edge of his greatcoat. His nose, blunt and greyish, poked out between collar and hat-brim. His eyes, grey as rain-water, moved about, alert and suspicious, like the eyes of a chameleon. They paused a second on Harriet, then swivelled away to flicker over the book in her hand, the bench on which she sat, the shed behind her, the ground, the porters near-by.

Introduced to her, he made a noise behind his scarf, holding his face aside as though it would be indelicate to gaze directly at her.

The porters were carrying his baggage: several suitcases and a canvas bag weighty with books. When these were loaded on to a taxi-cab, Pinkrose drew a hand from a pocket. He was wearing a dark knitted glove, in the centre of which was a threepenny piece. He then brought out the other hand, also gloved, holding a sixpence. He looked from one to the other, uncertain which coin was appropriate. Guy settled the problem by giving each porter a hundred *lei*.

As they drove back to the centre of the town, Pinkrose sat forward on his seat, his short blunt nose turning from side to side as he watched the wooden shacks of the suburbs, and the pitted, dusty road. At the sight of the first concrete blocks, he lost interest and relaxed.

Guy began questioning him about conditions in England.

"Quite intolerable," he said, his voice – which Harriet heard for the first time – thin and distinct. He did not glance at Guy and, having pronounced on England, he was silent for some moments then suddenly said: "I was thankful to get away."

Harriet would have liked to ask about his journey but she found his aura inhibiting. It seemed to her that any question concerning his immediate person would be taken as an impertinence. Guy may have felt the same for they drove in silence until they were about to enter the square. At this point the taxi was paused by an immense Iron Guard procession which was coming from the direction of the palace.

The sight astounded Pinkrose. He shuffled forward again, staring about, not only at the marching men but at the passers-by as though expecting everyone to share his surprise. That morning no one was giving the Guardists a glance. Their processions were becoming not only a commonplace but a bore. The air, however, resounded with cheers relayed over loudspeakers fixed around the square.

Pinkrose caught his breath as the Guardists were followed by an anti-aircraft gun and two tanks, all painted with swastikas and carrying Nazi pennants.

"What *is* this?" he burst out.

Guy explained that it was an Iron Guard procession. "I think," he said, "they're celebrating the new ten-year pact between Germany and Rumania."

"Good gracious me! I thought Rumania was a neutral country."

"So it is, in theory."

The procession past, the taxi crossed the square with Pinkrose jerking his head from side to side in anticipation of further shocks. And a shock awaited all three of them. As they stepped on to the pavement a gigantic flag unrolled above their heads: a Nazi flag of scarlet, white and black. Pinkrose stared at it, his lizard mouth agape.

The Athénée Palace had, on past occasions, put out a Union Jack or a Rumanian flag of no unusual size. That morning a new gilded flag-pole had been fixed on the roof and the swastika that hung from it fell three storeys to touch the main portico.

Pinkrose demanded: "What's this building?"

"The chief hotel," said Guy.

They entered. The hall and vestibule, that earlier had been empty, were now crowded with all the morning idlers who usually filled the cafés. Little tables were being placed everywhere to accommodate them. Drawn there by hope of seeing the German officers, they tried to hid their excitement beneath a show of animated interest in each other. There were a great many women who, dressed to impress, whispered together, tense and watchful.

Hadjimoscos, Horvatz and Cici Palu, usually in the bar at this time, were seated in a row on the sofa opposite the main staircase. Like everyone else, they were drinking coffee and eating elaborate cakes made of soya flour and artificial cream.

The hotel servants, harassed by the rush of visitors, ignored Pinkrose's arrival. Unable to find anyone to bring in the luggage, Guy carried it through the swing-doors himself. Saying: "I must go and ring Inchcape," he left Harriet with Pinkrose who, still muffled up, hands in pockets, gazed about him, baffled by the atmosphere of nervous expectation in which he found himself.

Every head was turned towards the staircase. Half a dozen officers had appeared, all handsome, all elegant, one wearing an eyeglass, and were descending with constrained dignity, apparently oblivious of their audience.

Some of the women took up the attitudes of graceful indifference, but most gazed spellbound at these desirable young men who were the more piquantly desirable because they had so recently been the enemy. When the Germans passed out of sight, the women fell together in ecstatic appreciation, their eyes agleam, their sensuality heightened by the proximity of these conquerors of the world.

Pinkrose's grey cheeks became yellowish. Newly arrived from a country at war, he was so unnerved by this first sight of the opponent, that he looked directly at Harriet to ask: "They were, if I am not mistaken, Germans?"

Harriet explained their presence: "There are a great many Germans in Bucharest. You'll soon become used to them."

Guy, returning at an agitated trot, said he had been unable to telephone as the telephone boxes were all occupied by journalists sending out some story to their contacts in Switzerland. "I don't know what it is," he said: "probably something to do with the Military Mission. We'll have to wait, so let us go inside."

Pinkrose and Harriet followed him through to the vestibule. As they passed the row of telephone boxes, Galpin darted from one of them and began to push past them, unseeing, intent in his pursuit of news. Guy caught his arm, introduced him to Pinkrose, whose appearance seemed to surprise him, then asked: "Has anything happened?"

"My God, haven't you heard?" Galpin's eyes protruded at them. "Foxy Leverett was picked up dead this morning. He was lying on the pavement, not a hundred yards from the Legation. It looked as though he had fallen from a window, but the nearest house was empty; in fact, shuttered. The owner is under arrest. My hunch is, he was tossed out of a car. Anyway, however he'd got there, he'd taken a terrible beating. Dobson says he only recognised him by the red moustache."

"Who found him?"

"Labourers. Soon after daybreak. And that's not all. One of the key men in Ploesti has disappeared. Chap called McGinty. That's just come through. It's obvious the bastards are not going to be satisfied with acting as hold-up men round the Jewish offices. They want blood." He glanced aside and catching Pinkrose's intent stare, he suddenly asked: "How did this little bloke get into Bucharest?"

In a tone that invited respect, Guy said: "Professor Lord Pinkrose has come to deliver the Cantecuzino Lecture."

"The what?"

Guy explained that the lecture, given in English every other year, was part of his organisation's cultural propaganda.

Galpin threw back his head and gave a crow of laughter. "Gawd'strewth!" he said and continued on his way out of the hotel.

Pinkrose turned stiffly, looking at Guy as though explanation, if not apology, were due, but Guy was too disturbed to give either. He conducted the professor to a sofa and asked him if he would like a brandy.

Pinkrose fretfully shook his head. "I never drink spirits, but it's a long time since I had breakfast. I'd like a sandwich."

Guy ordered him sandwiches and coffee, then returned to the telephone booths. At the hint of change in the weather, the central heating had been switched on. The room was stifling and Pinkrose, after sitting fully clad for some moments, began to unbundle himself. He unwound a scarf or two, then took off his hat revealing a bald brow, high, grey and wrinkled, surrounded by a fringe of dog-brown hair. This incongruous colour caught Harriet's eye and she had to do her best to look elsewhere.

After a while the greatcoat, too, came off. In a tightly-fitting suit of dark grey herring-bone stuff, old fashioned in cut, a winged collar and narrow knitted tie, Pinkrose sat surrounded by his outdoor wear. He gave Harriet one or two rapid trial glances before he brought himself to address her again, then he asked: "What was that man saying about someone being found dead?"

"The dead man was an attaché at the Legation. We think he had something to do with the secret service."

"Ah!" Pinkrose nodded knowingly. "I believe those fellows often come to a bad end." He was sufficiently reassured to set about his sandwiches when they arrived.

Harriet, watching him, felt no reassurance at all. What had happened to Foxy, could happen to Guy – or, indeed, to any of them. And Foxy had been a likeable acquaintance. Not only that, he was the one who was "adept at smuggling people over frontiers", the one who might have helped them with Sasha. To whom could they turn now? She could not imagine that Dobson would be much practical help, and they barely knew the senior men at the Legation.

A tut from Pinkrose recalled her to her immediate responsibility. He was looking inside his sandwich. With an expression of hurt fastidiousness, he set it aside, saying: "*Not* very nice," and took a sip of coffee. He grimaced as though it were cascara. "Perhaps, after all," he said, "I will have a small sherry."

Overhearing this as he returned, much recovered, Guy said in a ocular way: "How about *ţuică*, our fiery national spirit?"

Pinkrose twitched an irritated shoulder. "No no, certainly not. But I don't mind a sherry, if it's at all decent."

Unperturbed, Guy ordered the sherry, then sat down on Pinkrose's greatcoat, saying: "Professor Inchcape is on his way."

Moving the coat with flustered movements, acutely annoyed, Pinkrose said: "Ah!" in a tone that implied it was about time.

Guy asked him what would be the subject of his proposed lecture. Grudgingly, his head turned away, still rearranging his coat about him. Pinkrose thought he might survey the poets from Chaucer to Tennyson. Guy said: "An admirable idea," and Pinkrose raised his brows. It was becoming clear to Harriet that Guy's spontaneous friendliness towards the professor was rousing nothing but suspicious annoyance.

She was at first surprised, then she began to feel indignant – not so much with Pinkrose as with Guy, chatting enthusiastically about Pinkrose's not overbold project. She did not know whether to condemn his impercipience or to justify his innocence: and what she called innocence might, in fact, be no more than an unwillingness to admit anyone could feel animosity towards him. As he talked, Pinkrose watched him with distaste.

Looking afresh at Guy, Harriet noted that his hair was untidy, he had wine stains on his tie, his breakfast egg had dripped on to his lapel and his glasses, broken at the bridge, had been mended with adhesive tape.

She had become so used to his appearance, she had not thought to clean him up before they left.

She was thankful when Inchcape arrived to share the burden of Pinkrose's company. Catching Harriet's eye, Inchcape smiled as though he had a joke up his sleeve – not a pleasant joke – then said to Pinkrose: "So there you are!"

Pinkrose started up, a tinge of colour coming into his cheeks and affable with relief at the sight of his friend, said: "Yes, indeed! Here I am!" Smiling for the first time since his arrival, he looked like an ancient schoolboy. "And what a journey!" he added.

"We must hear all about it." Inchcape spoke as though Pinkrose were, indeed, a schoolboy and he, as ever, the headmaster. "But first I must have a drink." He turned to Guy, eyeing him as though the joke, whatever it was, was shared between them, and asked: "What have you got there? *Tuică?* All right, I'll have a *țuică*, too." He sat down opposite Pinkrose, frowning at him with ironic humour, and asked: "Well, how *did* you get here?"

Inchcape's manner towards this old friend, who, on his invitation had just travelled some five thousand miles, seemed to Harriet outrageous, but Pinkrose appeared to accept it. Smiling as though suddenly set at ease, he explained that he had been granted a priority flight to Malta.

"How did you manage that?" asked Inchcape.

With the glance of one who regards diplomacy as a form of conspiracy, he said: "A friend in high places. Then, believe it or not, I had to travel as a *bomb*. In the bottom of the aeroplane, you know. The pilot said to me: 'Better say your prayers. If we crash, you're a gonner.'"

"What is a 'gonner'?" Inchcape asked.

Pinkrose tittered, not taking the question seriously. "In Cairo," he said, "I met with difficulties. No one knew anything about me. I had to take the matter up with the ambassador and even then, for some reason, they would only take me as far as Athens. There, however, I discovered, to my relief, that there was a regular service to Bucharest, so here I am!"

Inchcape nodded. "So I see!" he drily said.

Although Pinkrose recounted his experiences with something near levity, it was clear that only his own determination had brought him here. He went on, rather fretfully: "England is so uncomfortable these days. And so tedious. People talk of nothing but this wretched invasion – rather overdue, I may say. We hear about it even at the high table. And life in general! So many new rules and regulations and petty restrictions! The black-out; the queueing! You, my dear Inchcape, were wise to take yourself off when you did. I cannot tell you how life has deteriorated. It couldn't be worse under the Nazis; anyway, for people like us. After all, Göring would have no quarrel with me. I've always been a good family man."

"Ah!" said Inchcape drily. "Then you won't be distressed if I tell you we may soon be under Nazi rule here."

Pinkrose tittered again. Inchcape swallowed down his *țuică* and, his patience exhausted, said: "Let's go and eat."

Pinkrose jumped up happily. As he gathered his coat, hat and scarves, he said: "I am looking forward, I can tell you, to some good eating. Travelled friends tell me that Rumanian food is among the best in Europe."

"Their information is out of date," said Inchcape.

Pinkrose chuckled. "You always were a cod."

The dining room was empty when they entered. Three large tables in the window alcove were reserved for the officers of the *Reichswehr*. Despite the fact that there were other tables unreserved, Inchcape was seized upon as he entered and guided to an obscure corner position which he accepted with an amused shrug. Passing the menu card to Pinkrose, he said: "It's a meatless day. The steaks and roasts listed are like the paper money here, they're not backed by hard currency. But you can have any one of the three dishes at the bottom. I recommend fish pilaff?"

It was some moments before Pinkrose could be persuaded that this was not an enormous joke. "But what about caviare?" he pleaded. "Isn't that a Rumanian product?"

"It all goes to Germany."

Pinkrose's face fell. "To think," he said, "I was the envy of my colleagues . . ."

"Tonight," Inchcape told him consolingly, "you'll meet all the wit and beauty of Bucharest. I have invited several princesses noted for their hospitality. In their houses, I assure you, there are no such things as meatless days. They'll do you proud. Meanwhile, have a fish pilaff!" He looked from Guy to Harriet, grinning in appreciation of Pinkrose's discomfort, then began to discuss the mysterious death of Foxy Leverett.

"These young attachés ask for trouble," he said. "They throw their weight around, imagining they're protected against all comers. But no one's protected against a knife in the back. I'm told that Leverett was drunk at the Amalfi the other night, and he kept the table in a roar with an imitation of Horia Sima. Doesn't do, you know! One has to respect the existing régime, whatever it may happen to be. And you have to learn to live with it."

Harriet asked: "You think we can learn to live with the Iron Guard?"

"Why not? It's all a matter of personality. If you can adjust yourself, you can live with anyone or anything. It's the people who can't adjust themselves who get into trouble."

Pinkrose nodded vehemently. "I do agree. *And*, you know, once things have settled down, the world's much the same whoever's running it."

Inchcape's mood of raillery had passed. He looked at his friend with understanding. "The important thing," he said, "is to survive."

As he spoke the German officers entered. With the aplomb of conquerors they crossed the dining-room floor and seated themselves at the reserved tables.

Neither Inchcape nor Pinkrose made any comment. Apparently they had already adjusted themselves to cohabitation with the enemy.

The meal over, Inchcape suggested that Pinkrose might care to rest before the reception. "Which will be quite a 'do'," he said. "Tomorrow night I fear I'm committed to a long-standing engagement. I'm dining with a young friend who wants to tell me his troubles but," he smiled quizzically at Pinkrose, "I imagine you can entertain yourself."

Guy said: "Perhaps Professor Pinkrose would have supper with us? We could go afterwards to the Brahms concert at the Opera House."

"Splendid idea!" Inchcape said without reference to Pinkrose.

Pinkrose looked displeased but Guy, in his eagerness, noticed nothing. Jumping to his feet, he said he would go at once to book seats and Harriet watched with an infuriated compassion as, speeding off, he tripped on the edge of the dining-room carpet.

Inchcape had ordered Guy to escort Pinkrose to his flat that evening, saying: "And for goodness' sake, come early and go early. I can't stand these junkets when they drag on."

As a result the Pringles arrived too early at the Athénée Palace and had to wait twenty minutes until Pinkrose was ready. He came down the stairs in an ancient dinner-suit, too short at the wrists and ankles, its single button strained on a thread across his middle.

"I must say," he said, becoming almost jovial in anticipation, "I am looking forward to meeting these beautiful and cultivated ladies who are said to entertain so lavishly."

Guy said: "I'll introduce you to the mothers of some of my students. Doamna Blum, for instance, and Doamna Teitelbaum. They're highly cultivated and would be delighted to meet you ..."

"No, no," Pinkrose interrupted impatiently, "I do not mean *that* sort of person. Everyone's been telling me I must meet the famous Princess Teodorescu."

Guy, rather tartly explained that that particular princess was no longer in Bucharest. "But princesses are two a penny here. It's only a courtesy title, anyway; it means nothing. You'll probably meet half a dozen tonight."

The sky over the square was rayed with lemon and silver but the colours were smudged and the wind blowing cool, damp and smoky from the park, had a smell of autumn.

It seemed to Harriet that recently a forlorn atmosphere had come down on the city, resulting, she believed, not only from the seasonal move indoors – the evening promenade which usually went on into October was now almost dwindled to nothing – but from fear. The Jews, of course, were afraid to go out, but these days it was not only the Jews who felt, like the old Codreanu, that they would be safer indoors.

She was relieved to reach Inchcape's sitting-room where the lamps were lit in their golden shades. Inchcape had not appeared yet. Clarence, the first arrival, sat alone.

Harriet had seen nothing of him since her visit to his flat. He had gone into some sort of retreat. Guy had telephoned him several times to suggest their meeting, but Clarence had always excused himself saying he was unwell. Harriet had imagined him lying all day on his balcony, gazing out over open country, brooding on his own inadequacy, but now he looked well enough. He showed, however, no desire to talk.

When introduced to Pinkrose, he rose reluctantly and mumbled something. Pinkrose mumbled back. Neither being designed to induce loquacity in the other, they drew apart as soon as they decently could and made no attempt to speak to each other again.

Inchcape entered in high spirits. Pauli, following, held an uncorked champagne bottle, its label of origin hidden under a napkin. While this was being dispensed, Inchcape, smiling to himself, brought out his latest acquisition: a purple velvet heart supporting three china arum lilies under a glass dome. "Amusing, isn't it?" he said. "I bought it at the Lipscani market."

Pinkrose bent over it, smiling thinly, and agreed: "It has a certain macabre charm."

Watching the faces of the two elderly men, Harriet suddenly saw them similar and bound in understanding.

Inchcape promised Pinkrose: "I will take you down to the Dâmbovita. You'll be delighted by the odds and ends one can pick up there. Ikons, for instance. In my bedroom, I have quite a collection of ikons."

Time was passing. The other guests were slow in coming. The front-door bell rang at last, but the newcomers were only Dobson and David Boyd.

Dobson, usually a vivacious guest, was greatly subdued by the death of Foxy Leverett, who had been his friend. He apologised that his stay must be brief: he had only come to make the acquaintance of Lord Pinkrose.

"I left the Legation in a pretty fair flap," he said. "McGinty was found this afternoon, here in Bucharest: in a lane behind the law courts. He's in poor shape."

"You mean he's been ill-treated?" Inchcape asked.

"He's been tortured. At least, he'd been strung up by his wrists and beaten. His back was in a shocking state. I must say, H.E. has been simply tremendous about all this. He went straight to the Minister of the Interior and demanded a full enquiry into Foxy's death and this business of McGinty. He said he would not rest until the culprits were brought to justice. It was just like the great days of Palmerston and Stratford-Canning. And the Minister of the Interior wept. He's supposed to be a Guardist, but he said: 'You English are a great people. We have always loved you. Some of us believe that even now you may win the war. But what can we do? There are too many of the young men. We can't control them.' "

"But why did they pick on McGinty? What had he done?"

"Nothing. But his name was on a list . . ." Dobson paused, sipped at his drink, then, having said so much, realised he had to say more. He added: "Before the war, Britain, France and Rumania compiled a list of engineers who could be relied on to destroy the oil-wells should the Germans occupy Rumania. This list was handed to Germany by the Vichy government. Voluntarily, I may say. The men who've been kidnapped were on it."

Clarence asked sharply: "Do you mean McGinty isn't the only one?"

Dobson looked about him, flustered. "Look here," he said. "Keep all this under your hat. There's no point in starting a panic here. These men were all specialists. They knew the risk they ran. They could have left when the others went: they chose to stay."

"How many have been kidnapped?" Clarence insisted.

"Four, including McGinty. The Iron Guard imagine there's some plot to blow up the wells. They're a pack of clumsy fools. They want information. They think they can get it by beating these chaps up."

"What about the other three?" Guy asked.

"No news yet." Dobson put down his glass then, turning to Pinkrose with his official smile, made a little speech welcoming him on behalf of Sir Montagu who was "tied to his desk". "I'm afraid it's a difficult time," said Dobson smiling.

Pinkrose agreed in a surprised tone: "Things do seem a little unsettled . . ."

"A little, a little. But H.E. thinks we should hang on here as long as we can. Show them we're not defeated yet."

"I heartily agree," said Inchcape.

When Dobson had gone, David and Guy went out to talk on the terrace. Inchcape, who now seemed more resigned to Pinkrose's arrival, began asking him, pleasantly enough, about their acquaintances at Cambridge. Harriet stood around awhile, waiting to see if Clarence would speak to her. When he remained aloof, she went out to the terrace where she could hear David snuffling in delight. He was saying: "Recent events have shocked poor old Sir Montagu to the core. He was heard to say (of course, I only have Dobson's word for it): 'So young David Boyd was right. Things have come unstuck in just the way he predicted.' " David was staring modestly at his feet. He sniffed his amusement, then said with his usual tolerance: "Sporting of the old boy to admit it, don't you think? But the fact is, he still thinks that somehow or other the situation can be salvaged."

Guy said: "It could be salvaged even now – by a Russian occupation. Not that Sir Montagu would welcome that."

"No, indeed! But I'm afraid there's little hope of it. The Russians don't feel too secure. They're not likely to enlarge a frontier they may have to defend."

In the pause that followed, Harriet took the opportunity to speak of Sasha Drucker: "Now that Foxy is dead, what can we do?"

"I wouldn't worry," David said in his usual unperturbed tone. "When a Legation goes, there are always a number of committed aliens packed on to the diplomatic train. It's taken for granted. No questions asked."

"You think you could take Sasha? That would be wonderful.

But supposing we have to go before the Legation goes: what could we do with him?"

Guy took her arm. "Let's face these problems when we come to them," he said and led her back into the room.

A gloom overhung the party. No other guests had arrived. Inchcape was becoming bored and Clarence remained silent, retired into a chair. When the doorbell rang, Pinkrose watched hopefully but the new arrival was not a beautiful, hospitable princess. It was Woolley. His face was lugubrious and his conversation did nothing to lighten the atmosphere. Like Inchcape, he was inclined to blame Foxy for getting himself killed, but the ill-treatment of McGinty he took as a warning of the fate that might overhang them all. He made no mention of the other engineers who were still missing, but said:

"I don't like the smell of things. I don't like it at all. People are getting out, and I don't blame them. The Rettisons have gone. Been here three generations. Now they've moved to the Levant. It's bad for business, all this shunting and shifting. You don't know where you are from one day to the next." He brooded awhile, his long, sallow, pendulous head hanging over his glass, then he looked up and sighted his old enemy, Harriet. "My lady wife's taken herself off, as is only right and proper. His Excellency wants the ladies out of the way. He said to me only yesterday: 'If I have to evacuate the English Colony, I'm only taking young men of military age.' "

Harriet's response was sharp and quick: "If Sir Montagu thinks he can take my husband and leave me behind, he still has a lot to learn."

Woolley gave her a long, sour, threatening look. "We'll see," he said.

"Yes, we will see," Harriet vigorously agreed.

There was a silence, protracted until Pinkrose suddenly threw out his hands with the gesture of a man tried beyond all endurance. "What *is* all this, Inchcape? Evacuating the British Colony! Taking young men of military age! What *is* going on here?"

Inchcape replied in reasonable tones: "As you noted yourself, my dear fellow, things are a little unsettled. After all, there's been a revolution. You must have heard of it."

"I heard something. *The Times* mentioned that King Carol had been deposed. That's always happening in Balkan countries. No one, at any time, suggested there was any danger."

"No one suggested there was any danger!" Inchchape parted his lips and looked about him. He asked the room: "What were the London officials thinking about? Are they so wrapped up in the piddling chit-chat of administration that they are totally unaware of conditions in Eastern Europe?"

His voice rose, indignant on Pinkrose's behalf but Pinkrose was not to be diverted. "You should have warned me, Inchchape. I take this badly. I take this very badly."

"Dear me!" Inchcape, his manner changing again, now began to ridicule his friend: "Aren't we in danger everywhere these days? Weren't you in danger in England? Very *real* danger, I may say. Aren't they likely to be invaded any day? Here we have only a war of nerves. Personally, I think things will right themselves. The young King and his mother are very popular. They went out yesterday and bought cakes at Capsa's. Yes, actually went out on foot, just like our own royal family! There can't be much wrong in a country where that happens."

Pinkrose looked somewhat appeased. "Nevertheless," he said, "I was misinformed. When you wrote in the spring, you described magnificent food, a feudal atmosphere, an ancient aristocracy, opulent parties, every comfort – a return, in short, to the good old days. And what do I find, after travelling all this way mostly in a bomb-bay? No meat on the menu. And what, may I ask, has happened to the wit and beauty of Bucharest? Your reception seems sadly ill-attended?"

Inchcape opened his mouth to reply, then paused. Harriet observed him with interest, never having seen him at a loss before. He answered at last: "The English are out of favour at the moment. I believe there's a reception at the Athéneé Palace for the German officers. I fear our Rumanian guests have all gone to entertain our enemies."

"Ah!" said Pinkrose. Mollified by the humility of Inchcape's confession, he said nothing more.

Woolley, who had stood apart from this exchange, sunk into his own disgruntlement, said suddenly: "I must be off," and slapping down his glass, he went without another word.

Clarence tittered. He had been drinking steadily and the effect of it was now evident. "I hear," he said, "that since his wife's departure, Woolley's found a little Rumanian friend." Holding out his glass at arm's length, he shouted: "Hey, Pauli, a refill."

Pauli crossed to him, grinning. English drunkenness being a stock joke in Bucharest.

Pinkrose, who had also been drinking, took Inchcape aside and whispered to him.

"This way," said Inchcape briskly. He led Pinkrose from the room and a moment later, darting back alone, he addressed Guy, Harriet and Clarence with an exploding air of conspiracy: "Look here! Things being as they are, we'll never get the old buffer an audience. The thing is, to prepare him. You'll have to give a hand. Begin intimating that this is neither the time nor the place for a public lecture in English. Suggest he might be molested. Get him scared so he'll tell me he doesn't want to lecture. Understand? But do it tactfully . . ." Inchcape came to an abrupt pause as he heard steps returning. Pinkrose entered.

"Well, now," Inchcape said pleasantly, "plans for our future delectation. What about this week-end? I'm afraid I'm off to Sinai: I booked my room weeks ago. I have to have a day off before the weather breaks. But I'm sure our young friends here . . . !" He smiled invitingly on Guy, Harriet and Clarence. "What are you all up to?"

Guy responded as was expected of him. "We are going to Predeal," he said. "Perhaps Professor Pinkrose would care to come with us . . ." He glanced at Harriet for her co-operation.

She said firmly: "I am quite sure Professor Pinkrose would rather go to Sinai with Professor Inchcape."

Frowning and stirring his foot on the carpet, Inchcape said: "Why not? Why not?"

Clarence, lolling so low in his chair that his buttocks were over the edge, drawled: "I'm going away, too."

Everyone looked at him. "Right away," he said. "You hear that, Inch, you old ostrich? I'm going right away, away from your bloody organisation. Away from what you call your sphere of influence. To warmer, more colourful climes. And you can't do a thing about it!"

Inchcape paused, realising he was being told something. He said: "What did you say?" Clarence repeated most of what he had said.

Inchcape exploded: "You're leaving us? At a time like this! And without warning!"

Clarence shuffled lower, holding his glass on a level with his nose. "Not without warning," he said. "I told you weeks ago that

I was sick of hanging around here doing nothing. I only stayed to please you. You have to have your little court. You must keep up the pretence that you've a position and a staff. But I've had enough. I've wired Cairo. I'm off as soon as I get my orders."

Inchcape, who had been staring severely at Clarence, now swung round and explained to Pinkrose: "Lawson was seconded to us by the British Council. If he is determined to go, we can't do anything about it. But it's a serious loss. One cannot get replacement these days."

Pinkrose nodded his sympathy and also stared severely at Clarence who was saying: "I'm no loss. Now if you were to go, Inch-boy, it would be different. British prestige would never stand the shock."

Ignoring this, Inchcape went on talking to Pinkrose: "My feeling is, that whatever the danger, a man should not desert his post."

Clarence gave a laugh. "You're in no danger. And your post is just a joke."

At this, Inchcape swung round in a rage. "At least, I'm sticking to it. As for danger, I'd remind you that I attended Calinescu's funeral."

"The whole of Bucharest attended Calinescu's funeral."

Pinkrose, upright, alert, his cheeks aglow, glanced keenly from one to other of the contestants. For the first time since his arrival he looked as though he were enjoying himself.

Guy went over to the pianoforte on which Inchcape's Chinese chess-set was arranged. Standing there, moving the pieces about, he appeared preoccupied but his face was sad and creased like the face of a Basanji dog, and as Clarence roused himself to press advantage, he said: "That's enough, Clarence."

"You're right, of course." Clarence stretched his arm and caught at Guy's hand. While Pinkrose goggled at this conduct Clarence said: "You're always right. You're the only one of us who can justify his existence here. The summer school may not be much, but at least it's a challenge . . . "

Guy drew his hand away. "The summer school was closed down last week."

Collapsing back into his chair, Clarence sighed deeply. "What the hell does it matter, anyway?" he mumbled.

The door opened and Pauli entered bearing two large dishes, one of rice and the other of some sort of stew. He filled plates and handed them round with lavish smiles. A local wine was served.

As they were eating, David remarked that he, too, would be away next-week-end. He was going to the Delta.

"Ha, the Delta!" said Clarence with a malign knowingness. "He says he's going to the Delta."

Pinkrose looked at Clarence in bewilderment. No one spoke until the meal ended and Inchcape rose to indicate the party was over. The gesture was not necessary. His guests were already preparing to go.

21

HARRIET NEXT EVENING was a discomfited hostess. The bones of Pinkrose's egotism remained visible despite his veil of sociability. She felt he intended they should remain visible. They represented protest. He was a guest, but an unwilling guest. He was making the barest of concessions to good manners.

That had been one of the mornings in which there was nothing in the market. "Nothing but cabbage," Despina said.

Harriet had gone to Dragomir's where there was food for those who could pay for it. The favoured customers there were no longer Rumanian males but German females: the wives of the attachés employed in vast numbers at the two big German diplomatic establishments. Strongly built and determined, living on so favourable a rate of exchange that they went shopping with bundles of thousand-*lei* notes in their hands, these women were formidable rivals whom Harriet would face only when desperate. She obtained two scrawny little chickens. She then tried to find a bottle of sherry, but sherry had disappeared from the shops. She ended up with an imitation madeira.

When offered this, Pinkrose eyed the bottle for some moments, one brow raised, before he said: "Perhaps I will try a half-glass." He sipped at it and finding it better than he had expected, expressed satisfaction by moving his bottom about on his seat. He allowed his glass to be refilled and said: "I cannot think why Professor Inchcape has put me into that hotel."

Harriet was surprised. "The Athénée Palace used to be practically an English hotel," she said. "We see it as a refuge, and the English journalists who live there almost never leave it."

"It's teeming with Germans," Pinkrose complained.

"The other hotel, the Minerva, is much worse. It's full of German diplomats. The officers of the Military Mission are only at the Athénée Palace because the Minerva had no room for them."

"Indeed!" Having made this attempt at conversation, Pinkrose retired into silence but his eyes were taking in every detail of his surroundings. Seeing them turn from the shabby upholstery to the shabby rugs, Harriet said: "We took this flat furnished. Things have received a lot of wear from different tenants."

As she spoke, he dropped his glance and his cheeks grew pink. Startled out of ill-humour, he said, pleasantly enough: "I take it the books are yours?"

She explained that the books, mostly second-hand, had been collected by Guy and brought to Rumania in sacks. He nodded his interest. Although he did not look at Harriet, he kept his attention pointedly in her direction and when Guy broke in on the talk, he looked aside in a discouraging way.

Guy had several volumes of poems by poets he had known when a student. He began taking these down to show Pinkrose signatures and inscriptions, but Pinkrose was not impressed. "These young men have a lot to learn," he said.

Guy leapt at once to the defence of the poets of his generation and while he talked, he refilled Pinkrose's glass. Too preoccupied and short-sighted to see when it was full, he went on pouring until the madeira ran from the table and dripped on to Pinkrose who tutted in exasperation. Full of apologies, Guy began to rub Pinkrose's trousers and Pinkrose, tutting again, moved his legs away.

Harriet called in Despina who, liking nothing better than to get into the room when visitors were present, spent so long mopping up round Pinkrose's feet that he said on a high note of irritation: "If we do not sup soon, we shall be late for the concert."

Supper, which he ate resignedly, was a hurried meal.

As they entered the main door of the Opera House, the Pringles were surprised by the opulence of the persons entering with them. Everyone was in evening dress, the men wearing orders, the women *décolleté* and lavishly bejewelled. Harriet began to feel something was wrong. This was not a usual Rumanian audience. The people were too large, too important-looking and they were all talking German. The vestibule was banked with flowers.

Pinkrose let out his breath in appreciation of so much splendour. "These days," he said, "we see nothing like *this* at home."

Harriet noticed that everyone who glanced once at the English party, glanced a second time in apparent disbelief. She said to Guy: "Do you think we're improperly dressed?" He ridiculed the idea and it did seem that it was they themselves, not their clothing, that gave rise to astonishment.

While they made their way to their seats, there were whisperings and a turning of heads, brought to a stop at last by the entry of the orchestra. When the musicians reached their places, they remained standing and the leader looked at the main box which jutted out at stage level. The audience, losing interest in the Pringles, also watched the box.

Harriet said to Pinkrose: "I think the King is coming," Pinkrose gave a gratified shuffle in his seat.

The door opened at the back of the box and a glimmer of shirt-front could be seen. The audience began to applaud. There entered a train of people comporting themselves with the studied graciousness of royalty, led by a large man who came to the rail and stood there. The Pringles recognised the heavy, sombre, unmistakable figure of Dr. Fabricius. The applause became clamorous. A woman in cloth of gold, his wife perhaps, made queenly movements with one hand. Fabricius bowed.

"Surely that's not the young King?" said Pinkrose.

Guy told him it was the German minister. Pinkrose's mouth fell open in disappointment but he nodded, prepared now to accept anything.

While the Legation party was entering, the box opposite had been filled by officers of the Military Mission who were escorting several resplendent women. Harriet, unable to keep from smiling, whispered to Pinkrose: "There are some of the princesses you hoped to meet."

The conductor raised his baton. The audience rose. Expecting the Rumanian national anthem, the Pringles and Pinkrose did the same. Some moments passed before the Pringles realised they were standing for *Deutschland uber Alles*. When he did so, Guy plumped back into his seat and Harriet, more slowly, followed. Pinkrose, looking embarrassed by their behaviour, remained at attention. The anthem finished, there was a pause: then came the *Horst Wessel*.

Perplexed, Guy began, for the first time, to examine his programme. He looked across at Harriet and hissed: "Gieseking."

She realised what had happened. Guy, eager and short-sighted, had bought the tickets without consulting the boards outside the theatre. This was a German propaganda concert.

When Pinkrose sat down, Harriet began to explain the mistake, but he had guessed it for himself and silenced her with a movement. "As we are here," he said "let us enjoy the music."

The pianist had taken his seat and Beethoven's Fifth Pianoforte Concerto began.

Harriet, thankful for Pinkrose's attitude, felt as he did, but Guy was looking wretchedly unhappy. He sat through the first movement with folded arms and sunken chin, and as soon as it ended, he stood up.

Pinkrose stared at him in acute irritation. He whispered: "It's no good. I'm going."

Harriet, who had been entranced by the performance, said: "Do stay," but he pushed past her. She felt she must go with him and as she rose, Pinkrose said in alarm: "I don't want to be left here alone."

The pianist sat motionless, waiting for the interruption to end. As much amused as annoyed, the audience watched while the three English interlopers got out as quickly as they could.

In the vestibule, Guy, his face damp with sweat, apologised for having led them into the predicament and for having led them out of it. He explained: "I couldn't stand it. I kept thinking of the concentration camps."

Too angry to speak, Pinkrose turned and strutted out of the Opera House. The Pringles went after him but he managed to keep just ahead of them all the way back to the hotel.

As he was halted by the revolving door, Guy tried to apologise again but Pinkrose held up his hand. He had suffered enough. He wanted to hear no more.

PART FOUR

The Raid

22

THE TRAIN RISING INTO THE MOUNTAINS CARRIED, trapped within it, the heavy air of the city. During the week the heat had renewed itself. Bucharest was suffering the last dragging days of summer.

At Ploesti, where there was a long stop, life was at a standstill. Syrupy sunlight poured over the denuded earth and gleamed on the metal of refineries and storage bins. Oil-trains stood in the sidings, each tank bearing the name of its destination: Frankfurt, Stuttgart, Dresden, München, Hamburg, Berlin.

Inside the carriage where the Pringles sat there was no sound but an occasional grunt and the buzz of captive flies. The dark-blue plush smelt of carbon and was sticky to the touch. Granules of carbon lay among the dust on the window ledges. The other occupants of the carriage were army officers, all sprawling lax and sleepy with boredom, on their way to the frontier to guard a country that had lost almost everything it possessed.

Guy, with a rucksack of books between his knees, sat in full sunlight, pushing up his glasses as they slipped down the sweat on his nose. He was planning a course of studies.

The English journalists who had flown in to cover the abdication were still in Bucharest, detained by one outrage after another. In all, eight oil engineers had been kidnapped by the Iron Guardists. One of them had been found dead ("of a heart attack", said the newspapers) in a Ploesti back street. The rest survived, the worse for ill-treatment.

That morning the old minister who had thought it better to be united under the Russians had also been picked up dead in the Snagov woods, his hair and beard torn out and stuffed into his mouth. He had lately become a fanatical Guardist, but that had not saved him.

Galpin never left the Athénée Palace. With the aspect of a prophet who sees his worst predictions fulfilled, he said to anyone who entered the bar: "It's simply a case of 'Whose turn next?' "

They were all, it seemed to Harriet, awaiting a final collapse that might extinguish them. All, that was, except Guy. With the new term approaching, he was absorbed in preparation for it. He managed to be as busy as he had ever been, while Harriet spent more and more time with Sasha. Like people in a waiting-room, they sat on the balcony exchanging nonsense rhymes, playing paper games, telling ridiculous jokes, and giggling together as helplessly as children. There was no time to put one's mind to more serious pursuits. She knew they were on the verge of confusion, but Sasha appeared to believe their life could go on, uneventful and carefree, for ever.

She had been longing to get away from the capital, but now their week-end was come her apprehensions were heightened. Anything might happen while they were away. And what of Sasha, left in Despina's care? It had been during their last trip to Predeal that the kitten had fallen to its death. Despina, sympathising with her fears, had promised to open the door to no one. Sasha, however, had been no more concerned by her departure than the kitten had been.

He said: "We have a villa at Sinai," speaking as though it stood there empty, awaiting the family's return. "I know Predeal. Sarah went to school there. Hannah would not go – she would not leave my father."

Harriet remembered the little girl. "I could see she adored your father," she said.

Sasha nodded. "She cried all night when he married again."

"Did you mind?"

"We all minded, but Hannah most. We did not want another mother."

"You loved him very much, didn't you?"

"We all loved him." Sasha still identified his feeling with those of his family. He did not acknowledge the separation. He added: "*She* wanted to take him from us. She was beastly. Wicked."

Harriet laughed. "When I was a child I used to think my aunt was a wicked stepmother, but now I realise she was just rather stupid. She said anything that came into her head. She probably forgot it the next moment and thought I did, too."

After a long delay, the train moved out of Ploesti into foothills that were straddled by the old wooden derricks of pioneering days.

Beyond this area were alpine meadows, but soon the rocks broke
through and the landscape changed into the grey shale and pines
of the lower Transylvanian Alps.

When they left the stale and stifling carriage, the Pringles were
startled by the glassy outside air. Scentless in its purity, it was as
cold as ether on the skin. They wanted to start walking at once,
but first they had to report their arrival to the police. The police
officer, unshaven and grimy, reeking of garlic, pushed aside a
collection of dirty coffee-cups and stamped their permits with
extreme slowness, Free to stay in Predeal for no longer than a
week, they carried their luggage through the long main street to
the hotel.

The village, with its grey highland look, was in shadow, but the
peaks above were still looped in the reddish light of the evening
sun. Minute glaciers, like veins of marble, made their way down
the grey rock-surfaces. Snow lay already on the upper ledges. At
this height the autumn was fairly advanced. Patches of beech were
golden-tawny, thrown like lion-skins among the black fur of the
pines.

Predeal was both a winter and a summer resort, so out of date
that the village hall announced an English film.

Harriet was slightly unnerved by the extraordinary quiet of the
place. She felt they had been mad to leave the capital at such a
time. If there were an invasion, they would receive no warning
here. But Guy stretched his arms, throwing off the year's worries
in a moment. As he breathed the light and tonic air, he said:
"This is like flying out of a fog."

Their bedroom was small and bare with a stove that was lit at
evening and fed with pine-logs. They were met by a scent of wood-
smoke, delicate and sweet, that comforted Harriet. She began to
look forward to her holiday. As soon as they had dropped their
bags they went out to walk in the blue, chill air. The sky
changed to turquoise. The shops lit up. The village street hung on
the mountainside like a chain of light. They found the village
bright enough during the day, but a wintry gloom came down after
the shops shut. There was no entertainment but the cinema where
the film broke down a dozen times during a showing, each break
being numbered on the screen and described as an "interval". In
their little ski-ing hotel there was nothing to do. Guy set out his
books of verse and novels by Conrad, preparing to spend the holiday in work.

On their first morning, as he chose an armful of books to take to the public gardens, Harriet said: 'But can't we go for a walk?''

"Later," Guy promised. "Let me break the back of this first." She, he suggested, might visit the famous *confiserie*, the far-seeing owner of which had laid in vast stocks of sugar in early summer. Now people came from all the large cities to eat his cakes.

Harriet was surprised to discover how greedy this fact made her feel.

Guy took a seat in the small ornamental garden where the grass, damply green in the mild, misty sunlight, was scattered over with russet leaves. There was nothing to see here but some beds of small, brick-coloured dahlias. Harriet wandered off through a neighbouring market where the ground was heaped with apples, tomatoes and black grapes. Some of the notorious Laetzi gipsies stood about – wild, bearded, long-haired men who eyed her as though they were cannibals.

The *confiserie* was crowded. The inside tables were all taken and the counter was tightly packed about with people who had to hold their plates above their heads. Outside there were chairs vacant near the rail. Harriet soon discovered why. The beggars were at her elbow even as she sat down. There were three children, their bones hung with scraps like greasers' rags. One, with a withered leg, hopped with his hand on the shoulder of a smaller boy. The third, a girl, had lost the sight of an eye. Perhaps she had been born that way, for the eyeball remained in its socket, blankly white, like a filling of lard. The children were urged forward – not that they needed much urging – by two teen-age girls who now and then stopped their whine of "*Foame*" to titter as though this persecution of the foreign woman were too funny for words.

Harriet handed out her small change, but it was not enough to buy release. The children went on jigging and whining beside her. While waiting to be served, she watched a small green and gold beetle crawling towards a hole in the rail beside her. If it went to the right, they would get away. It went to the left and it suddenly seemed to her that their danger had become acute. Her appetite had gone. She ordered coffee. While she waited she stared out at the road and watched a peasant leading a horse and cart out of a lane opposite. The horse, its bones straining against its hide, stumbled when it reached the main road cobbles. At once the peasant flung back his whip and lashed the creature about the eyes. The blows were given with savage deliberation as though the man wanted no more than an excuse to vent a chronic rage.

She leapt to her feet with a cry, too appalled to care for the surprise of her neighbours. By the time she reached the pavement, the assault was over. Horse and peasant had turned the corner and were away down the road. She knew, if she pursued them, her Rumanian was not good enough to make her protest effective. Anyway, it would be ignored.

She gave up all thought of cakes or coffee and hurried back to the public garden. When she reached Guy, she could scarcely speak. Surprised by her agitation he said: "Whatever is the matter?"

She sat down, exhausted, and gulped back her tears. Seeing the peasant vividly, his brutish face absorbed and horribly gratified by the outlet for his violence, she said: "I can't bear this place. The peasants are loathsome. I hate them." She spoke in a convulsion of feeling, trembling as she said: "All over this country animals are suffering – and we can do nothing about it." Feeling the world too much for her, she pressed her face against Guy's shoulder.

He put his arm round her to calm her. "The peasants are brutes because they are treated like brutes. They suffer themselves. Their behaviour comes of desperation."

"It's no excuse."

"Perhaps not, but it's an explanation. One must try to understand."

"Why should one try to understand cruelty and stupidity?"

"Because even those things can be understood: and if understood, they can be cured."

He squeezed her hand, but she did not respond. He talked to distract her, but she remained withdrawn as though violated and unable to throw off the shock.

After a while he picked up his books again. "Why don't you take a proper holiday?" he said. "We're quite well off at the present rate. Wouldn't you like to take the boat to Athens?"

Her expression lightened a little. "You mean you would come with me?"

"You know I can't. Inchcape doesn't want me to leave the country. And I have to prepare for the new term. But that's no reason why you shouldn't go."

She shook her head. "When we go, we go together."

After tea, Guy felt he had done enough for the day and was

willing to take a walk. When they reached the forest, he looked in through the aisles of pines, all intent and silent as though each tree held its breath, and refused to enter. He said that within living memory it had been a haunt of bears. "Let's keep to the road. It's safer." The road carried them above the trees into the bare rock fields where the cold was keen. The sky was mottled with a little cloud and here and there a chill hung on the air like powdered glass. At first Harriet thought it was ash blown from a bonfire, then she found it was melting on her skin. She said with wonder: "It is snow." When they reached the first white pool of snow, she pressed her hand on it, leaving the intaglio of her palm and fingers. Much lighter and surer on her feet than Guy, excited by the rarefied air, she climbed at great speed until she was alone amid the silence of the topmost slopes. She heard Guy shout and, looking back, saw him standing a long way below, like an unhappy bear, defeated by the shifting rubble of the path. She sped down into his arms.

They returned to the hotel, which stood by a dimpled meadow that was covered with small flowers. Some cows had been driven on to the grass during their absence and Guy paused, unwilling to cross among them. He saw all the animals as potential enemies. He distrusted the Bucharest cab-horses and had even been frightened of Harriet's red kitten. She took his hand and led him towards the nearest cow, which lifted its head to stare at them but did not cease to chew. Watching its mouth slipping loosely from side to side, Guy said: "These beasts are probably dangerous."

Harriet laughed. "I love them," she said.

"What, these frightful creatures?"

"Not only these. All animals."

"How could you love something so totally different from yourself."

"Why not? I don't simply love myself. I think I love them because they are different. They are innocent. They are hunted, harried, slaughtered by human beings who imagine they have a God-given right to destroy whenever it's in their interest to destroy."

Guy nodded. "You want to protect them. I can understand that. But why this extraordinary love for them? It doesn't seem reasonable to me."

She did not try to explain it. Guy, she knew, believed that man's

compassion for his own kind was the only true compassion to be
found in this cold universe. She longed for proof of a more disinterested compassion; a supreme justice that would avenge all
these tormented and helpless innocents. Trembling with her own
excess of feeling, she stretched out her hand to the cow, but at the
threat of her approach it moved warily backwards.

After supper, Guy lay on the bed propped with pillows and
gave himself up again to his books. Harriet, drowsy from the
mountain air, lay in the crook of his arm, happy in his warmth
and contact. He paused in his reading to say: "You do not see
much of Bella these days. Or Clarence either. You have made so
few friends in Bucharest! Don't you feel the need of people?"

She said: "Not when I have you – which isn't often."

"You've quite enough of me. If you had more, you'd be bored."

She glanced up at him, realised he believed this and smiled in
denial, but he was not looking at her. She closed her eyes and slept.

When they came down to breakfast on Sunday and found
Dobson sitting at one of the tables, Guy gave a great cry of "Why,
hello." He would, Harriet knew, have been equally delighted had
the newcomer been almost anyone known to them: and it might
have been someone worse than Dobson who seemed charmed by
the sight of them. He had driven up late the previous night "for
a breath of air", and would have only one day in Predeal. He
suggested that after breakfast they should go for a walk together.

Harriet left it to Guy to make his excuses, but the invitation
was too much for him. It was not only that he was a little flattered
by it: he could not refuse the diversion of fresh company.

As they left the hotel, Dobson suggested they should visit a
Russian church a couple of miles away, saying: "We might hear
something interesting. I was enormously fortunate last time I
went there. They were singing the *Cantakion* for the Dead."

Dobson spoke on a note of such breathless anticipation that
Guy paused only a moment before saying: "All right." At the
same time he looked at Harriet as though she might save him, but
she, a little piqued, said she would like nothing better.

They went behind the village, climbing steeply among small
châlets and villas. The path was dusty, slippery with flints and
overhung by old chestnut trees, their leaves ochred and reddened,
forming parasols of colour that set the shade aglow. The ground
beneath them was stained with trodden nuts and leaves. In one

garden stood a giant rowan, weighted and bronzed with berries. Many of the villas were shuttered, their gardens overgrown as though they had been unvisited all summer.

The path dwindled, the houses were left behind, and they came out on to a plateau that stretched away into remote upland hills. They walked silently on the grass that was short, greyish and set with harebells and wild scabious.

Dobson talked easily and pleasantly. Harriet found his presence in Predeal reassuring. It was true that as a diplomat, especially protected, he had less to worry about than they had, but it was unlikely he would leave Bucharest if danger were imminent. Harriet, nearly two days away from the tensions of the capital, was beginning to feel like a patient propped up for the first time after an operation; Guy asked if anything had happened since they left Bucharest.

"Well," said Dobson, "Friday, as you probably know, was the anniversary of the death of Calinescu. The Guardists spent the day marching about."

They were in sight of a hollow from which the golden domes of the Russian church rose among trees.

Abruptly changing from the subject of the slaughtered Calinescu, Dobson said: "This convent was started by a Russian princess, an abbess who came here after the revolution with a following of nuns. Queen Marie gave them the land. They collected a crowd of refugees; a lot of them are still living. Some dark tales of intrigue and murder are told about this community. What a novel they would make!"

The Pringles had known Dobson as an agreeable man who treated them and their orders to leave the country with a vague serenity. Now that he felt more was expected of him, they were experiencing the active charm of his attention and they found it delightful.

Watching him as he walked before her with his plump, incurved back, his softly drooping shoulders, his rounded backside rising and falling with each tripping step, Harriet wondered why she had once decided he would not be easy to know. Who would be easier? And here, it occurred to her, was opportunity to intercede for Sasha! Yet, she hesitated – she scarcely knew why.

She had felt an instinctive trust of Foxy Leverett. Reckless and casual though he had been, he seemed a natural liberal. Dobson,

for all his geniality, was something apart. Supposing the diplomatic code required him to betray the boy? Feeling no certainty
he would not do it, she kept silent and was fearful Guy might
speak. Guy, however, made no mention of Sasha and probably
did not give the boy a thought.

They were descending into the hollow where the atmosphere
was humid and warm and the tall feathery grasses were still soaked
with dew. Dobson led them into the shade of a vast apple orchard
where there was no sound but a ziss of wasps and the creak of
boughs bending beneath their weight of fruit. They walked
through a compost of rotted fruit.

Beyond the orchard was a flat field and a river running level
with flat banks. The church stood amid silver birch trees, the
leaves of which were yellow as satinwood. To Harriet it seemed
that not only the church, but the river reflecting the light among
birch trees, and the trees massed around the buildings in a mist of
reddish gold, all had a look of Russia. The place was not unfriendly, but it was strange. "A distant land," she thought, though
distant from what she could not have said. In this country, where-
ever they were, they were far from home.

They crossed the bridge and took the path to the convent. The
church and main buildings, of stone, were surrounded by dismal
wooden hutments, the living-quarters of the lay community. Four
women in black, heads tightly bound up in black handkerchiefs,
were approaching the church along a path, each keeping her
distance from the others. As the first of them, a very thin, old lady,
stared with interest at the visitors, her dark, wrinkled, toothless
face, eaten into by suffering, took an expression ingratiating and
cunning. She gave a half-bob at them before turning into the
church.

Guy came to a stop, frowning his discomfort, but Dobson went
on without glancing round and entered through the heavy,
wooden doors.

Harriet said: "Come on, darling, let us look inside," and led
him after Dobson. She received, however, no more than a glimpse
of the candle-lit interior where a priest, hands raised, was making
gestures over two nuns who lay on the ground before him like
little, black-clad, fallen dolls. Guy gave a gasp, then bolted, letting
the door crash behind him. The old women of the congregation
started round, the priest looked up, even the nuns stirred.

Much shocked, Harriet hurried out after him. Before she could remonstrate, he turned on her: "How could you go into that vile place where that mumbo-jumbo was going on?"

A few minutes later, Dobson came out, sauntering, his face bland, giving the impression that nothing could surprise him – but he had less to say on the way home.

Harriet walked in complete silence, knowing that Guy might, by his action, have antagonised the whole powerful world of the Legation. Guy, too, was silent, probably in reaction from the scene that had so revolted him inside the church.

They returned through a shabby area of untidy, uneven grass where flimsy châlets declared themselves to be *pensions* and private sanatoria. The road crossed a stream of clear, shallow water that purled over rusted cans and old mattresses. Harriet paused to look down and Dobson, perhaps conscious of her discomfort, leaned beside her on the parapet and said: "If you were some great lady of the eighteenth century, Lady Hester Stanhope for instance, you would be standing on the boundary line between the Austrian and Turkish empires," and as Harriet grew slightly pink at this analogy, Dobson smiled in reassuring admiration.

He joined them at their table for luncheon and tea. After tea he invited them to drive with him to Sinai.

When he brought his car out of the hotel garage, it proved to be Foxy Leverett's De Dion-Bouton. Claret-coloured, picked out in gold, with a small, square bonnet, its large body opened out like a tulip to display claret-coloured upholstery of close-buttoned leather. The brass headlamps and large tuba-like horn were beautifully polished. Dobson eyed the car with a smile of satisfaction. "I think she'll get there," he said. "She's in spanking shape."

On the road to Sinai, he was as talkative as ever. Pointing across the plateau towards some bald, ashen hills, he said: "Did you ever see such mean hills? They look as though they had something to hide, don't they? They've a bad reputation among the peasants here. I remember when Foxy and I came here to ski last winter, we thought we'd try out those hills. When we told our cook, Ileana, where we were going, she flopped down on her knees and gave an absolute howl: 'No, no, domnuli, no one ever goes there. They're bad lands.' Foxy said: 'Get up and stop being an ass.' All the time she was cutting our sandwiches, she was snivelling away. She kissed our hands as though certain she'd never see us again.

"Anyway, we drove over there and had a long climb up – they're higher than they look. The snow was magnificent. When we got to the top, Foxy said: 'It's ridiculous to say no one ever comes here. Look at all these dogs' footprints.' Then it struck us. We strapped on our skis and got down that hillside faster than we'd ever got down anything in our lives before. When we arrived back Ileana had all the cooks in the neighbourhood holding a wake for us. They screamed their heads off when they saw us. They thought we were ghosts." Dobson had been increasing speed as he talked and he now pointed with pride to the indicator. "Doing forty," he said. The car trembled with the effort.

The conversation now was all about Foxy: Foxy killing bear in the Western Carpathians, Foxy shooting duck at the Delta, Foxy taking "a record bag of ptarmigan".

Harriet burst out: "I hate all this shooting."

"So do I," Dobson cheerfully agreed, "but it's nice to keep a bit of bird in the larder. Something to peck at when you come in late."

They passed a cart-load of peasants who pointed at the De Dion, the men bawling with laughter, the women giggling behind their hands.

Laughing with them, Dobson said: "How Foxy would have loved that," and he continued a threnody on his friend – sportsman, playboy and Legation jester: "The best fellow in the world! We shared a flat in the Boulevard Carol." He went on to tell how Foxy practised revolver-shooting, using a Louis XIV clock as a target. One night he shot at the ceiling and sent a bullet into the bed of the landlord, who said: "Anyone else but you, Domnul Leverett, and I would have told him: 'This is too much.' "

The road was lined with garden restaurants. It was all very urban, but as soon as the car turned off the main road they came into a wild region of stone peaks where the rock was patched over with alpine moss and there was no vegetation but a few dwarf juniper bushes. In every hollow among the hills a small lake lay dark and motionless.

Dobson stopped the car and they went for a walk over the cinderous ground between the rocks. There was a little grass round the lakes where a few lean cows grazed. Pointing to one of them, Guy said: "Harriet says she loves these creatures."

Dobson gave his easy laugh. "She's probably quite willing to eat them," he said, and Harriet stared at her feet, conscious of her human predicament. Putting an arm round her shoulder, Guy rallied her: "Come on, tell us, why do you love them?"

Irritated that he questionned her in front of Dobson, she said defiantly: "Because they are innocent."

"And we are guilty?"

She shrugged. "Aren't we? We're human animals that maintain ourselves at the cost of our humanity."

He squeezed her shoulder. "Guilt is a disease of the mind," he said. "It's been imposed on us by those in power. The thing they want is to divide human nature against itself. That permits the minority to dominate the majority."

Dobson smiled blandly, apparently detached from the Pringles' conversation, but Harriet, certain he was listening intently, did not encourage Guy to say anything more on this subject.

They drove into Sinai as evening fell. Dobson said: "We'll snatch a bite before trying our luck," taking it for granted that the Pringles anticipated with as much pleasure as he an evening of losing money at the casino.

The casino attempted a grandeur that was thwarted by Balkan apathy and the harshness of the overhanging crags. A chill had entered the air after dark. The yellowish bulbs that lit the casino gardens, touching rocks and trees and the wavering fronds of the pampas grass, could not dispel the gloom of the failing year. The paths glistened with damp.

The large entrance hall was deserted. Such life as there was about the place had taken itself to the main salon where only one table was in use. Lit by low-hung, green-shaded globes, the gamblers sat, absorbed and silent, in the penumbra around the table.

Dobson found a seat. Guy stood behind him, watching the play, while Harriet tiptoed to the end of the table, where she paused and looked down its length at the faces intent upon the turning wheel. She thought: "What a collection of oddities!" seeing them as though they grew like distorted mushroom growths from their chairs. One man, whose shoulders were abnormally wide but who rose barely eighteen inches above the table, had a vast, formless face, like a milk jelly, glistening with ill-health. Beside him was an ancient, skeletal female, her mouth agape and askew, as though she had died without succour. One male head was abnormally large like a case of giantism. Here and there were faces, not aged and yet not young, having the immaterial look of arrested decay.

It seemed to Harriet that in this room without windows, artificially lit both by day and by night, these people, with their pallor of indoor life, existed in a self-contained world, beyond consciousness of war, change of government or threat of invasion, indeed unaware there was an outer world, like insects in a gall. They would scarcely know if the Day of Judgment were upon them. For them life's prodigiousness was diminished down to a little ball spinning in a wooden bowl.

The ball fell into a groove. A stir, almost a sigh, touched the players. It fell upon a stillness so complete she could almost feel, as they must, that did conflict exist anywhere at all, it was too remote to matter.

The croupier's rake came into the light, pushing the chips about. No one smiled, or showed concern or pleasure, but as one player, in placing his stake, accidentally touched that of another, there broke out between them a quarrel, brief but vicious, like a quarrel between the insane.

The ball was spun again. Harriet took a step forward to watch and at once the man seated before her glanced round, his face distorted with irritation at her nearness. She tiptoed on.

When she reached the other side of the table, she looked across at Dobson and realised Guy was no longer there. He had found someone to talk to in the dim, empty regions beyond the table. When she reached him, she found his companions were Inchcape and Pinkrose. He was talking with his usual animation, but in an undertone, while Inchcape, hands in pockets, head bent, listened, tilting backwards and forwards on his heels. Pinkrose stood a step apart, watching Guy with an expression that told Harriet the Gieseking concert would not be forgotten in a hurry. Inchcape looked up.

"Hah! So there you are!" Inchcape said as she approached. "Let's go and get a drink." Walking ahead, he glanced back for Harriet and as she caught up with him, said: "Have you enjoyed your break?"

"Very much. And you?"

"Don't speak of it." He dropped his voice. "I never could abide that old so-and-so."

"Then why did you invite him to Rumania?"

"Who else would have come at a time like this? How does he strike you?"

"Well . . ." Harriet evaded the question by asking: "Why, I wonder, is he so suspicious of poor Guy?"

"Him!" Inchcape snorted in amused contempt. "He'd be suspicious of the Lamb of God."

In the bar, that was large, bleak, bare and empty except for the barman, Inchcape told them he had lost chips to the value of five thousand *lei*. "That was my limit," he said. "As for Pinkrose here! Tight-fisted old curmudgeon, I couldn't get him to risk a *leu*." He turned on Pinkrose. "You're a tight-fisted old curmudgeon, eh?" He gave Pinkrose's shoulder a push. "Eh?" he insisted, staring at him with quizzical disgust as though he were a wife of whom he was more than half ashamed.

Pinkrose, sitting with his legs tightly together, his feet side by side, his little waxen hands folded on his stomach, smiled vaguely, apparently taking Inchcape's chaff as a form of admiration, which perhaps it was.

The bar was cold. The windows had been opened during the day and were still open, admitting shafts of damp, icy air. Pinkrose began to twitch. He pulled his scarfs about him, looking miserable, but before he could say anything the waiter came to them.

"I know," said Inchcape indulgently. "We'll have hot *ţuică*. We'll celebrate the coming winter. I like to hibernate. I shall devote the next six months to Henry James."

The *ţuică* was served in small teapots. Heated with sugar and peppercorns, the spirit lost its rawness and gave the impression of being much milder than it was. Pinkrose drew back, frowning, as a pot was put before him, and said: "No, really, I think not."

"Oh, drink it up," Inchcape said, with such exasperation Pinkrose poured a little into his cup and sipped at it.

"Umm!" he said, and after a moment admitted: "Pleasantly warming."

Dobson came to look for them and, as he sat down, Guy asked him: "What luck?"

"None," he cheerfully told them. "But, then, one doesn't expect to win. One plays for the fun of it. Dear me!" He stretched out his legs and rubbed a silk handkerchief over his baldness. "How one longs for the normal life! I'm not as young as I was, but I'd

be overjoyed if I could close my eyes and open them to find myself enjoying a debs' dance at the Dorchester or Claridge's!" He
smiled round, never doubting but that the others would take
equal pleasure in such a transportation. "As it is" – he folded his
handkerchief carefully and put it away – "tomorrow back to the
plough." Turning to Pinkrose, he pleasantly asked: "Are you
staying long?"

Pinkrose flinched as though the question were inexcusably
personal. "I really cannot say," he said.

Inchcape said: "Oh, he'll soon be taking himself off." He leered
at Pinkrose, repeating as though his friend were deaf: "I was just
saying, you'll soon be taking yourself off."

"My goodness gracious! I've only just arrived," said Pinkrose.
"A special passage had to be arranged for me; and I imagine the
same will be done for my return."

"Who do you think's going to arrange it?" Inchcape asked.

Ignoring this question, Pinkrose went on: "And what about my
lecture, I'd like to know? Isn't it time you fixed a date?"

"We'll have to abandon the lecture."

"Abandon the lecture? Are you serious, Inchcape? I plan to range
over the development of our poetry from Chaucer to Tennyson.
Central Office was of the opinion it would have considerable
influence on Rumanian policy."

Inchcape laughed through his teeth. "My dear fellow, if Chaucer
came here it would have no influence on Rumanian policy. If
Byron came, if Oscar Wilde himself came, he could not get an
audience for a public lecture on English literature."

"Are you suggesting I should return home without a word? A
pretty fool I'd look! What would my colleagues say?"

"Tell them you left it too late. You should have come six months
ago."

"I was not invited six months ago." Pinkrose's lips quivered. For
a moment he looked as though he might burst into tears, then he
suddenly smiled. "But you are, as they say, 'having me on'. My leg
is being pulled, isn't it?" He glanced about in an inquiry that no
one attempted to answer.

Harriet had her own inquiry: "If no one will come to the
Cantecuzene Lecture, who is going to turn up to hear Guy?"

"That's different. Students are young, loyal, uncommitted, eager
to learn . . . But it's the look of the thing that matters. We must
open."

"Is Guy expected to run the Department alone?"

"Well, if the students turn up in force, I might take a seminar for him."

There was a long silence. Harriet felt she could have said more, but the drink, warm and sweet, had begun to release her from care. If this were not the best of all possible worlds, what did it matter? Perhaps the best was yet still to come.

Dobson yawned and said he was taking a short holiday in Sofia. "I want to hear some opera," he said.

Guy turned to Harriet. "Why don't you go with him?" he suggested.

Harriet's fugitive happiness was gone. For some moments she was too embarrassed to speak, then she protested: "Darling, you are extraordinary! What makes you suppose that Dobbie would want me to go with him to Sofia?"

Dobson sat up to assure her: "I should be delighted."

"Of course he would," said Guy, who had never doubted it. He looked at Dobson and explained: "The situation here is becoming too much for her."

"I should never have thought it." Dobson smiled as though Guy were being slightly ridiculous. "As indeed he is," Harriet thought. She felt particularly annoyed that after she had, as she imagined, demolished the question of her going, it should be brought up again.

Pinkrose had finished his pot of *ţuică* and his eyelids were drooping. He nodded forward, then, rousing himself with a start, said: "I shall return to the hotel. I like an early night."

"Yes." Inchcape rose, saying briskly: "To bed. In this barbarous corner of Europe, where else is there to go?"

Outside, a wintry wind blew among the trees. Dobson, finding that Inchcape and Pinkrose were also returning to Bucharest next morning, offered them a lift. Inchcape was inclined to accept, but when Pinkrose saw the De Dion he shook his head decisively. "Oh, no! Dear me, *no*! I never could travel in an open car."

"Oh, get on, you old stick-in-the-mud!" Inchcape, irritated beyond endurance, gave Pinkrose a push that sent him teetering down the road towards the main hotel.

The drive back to Predeal was very cold. Harriet was depressed, feeling that in some ways Guy was intolerable. When they reached their room, conscious of her withdrawal, he put his arm round her and said: "Don't worry. We shall be all right."

"I'm not worrying," she replied coldly.

"You aren't sorry you came to Rumania with me?"

She shook her head, but moved out of his hold.

"Are you sorry you married me?"

He evidently needed reassurance, for when she said: "Sometimes I am," he looked very grieved. He asked: "Do you feel you needed a different sort of person?"

"Perhaps."

"Who? Clarence?"

"Good heavens, no. No, no one I have met. Perhaps no one I shall ever meet."

He asked despondently: "You mean you no longer love me?"

"I don't mean that, but I'm not sure you want to be loved very much. You want room for a lot of other people and things."

"But I have to work," he expostulated. "I have to see people, to move around. You move around, too . . ."

"Yes, there's plenty of give and take. You are quite willing for me to spend any amount of time with other people: Clarence, for instance, or Sasha. It gives you freedom and you know there's no risk. You're too good to lose."

He stared at her, hurt, looking as though this were all too much for him and she realised they were arguing on different levels. He was being practical, she emotional. She wanted to accuse him of selfishness, to point out that his desire to embrace the outside world was an infidelity and a self-indulgence, but she realised he would never understand what she meant.

"You've never mentioned before that you are discontented."

"No?" She laughed. "Truth is a luxury. We can only afford it now and then."

He laughed, too, his dejection gone in a moment. Humming to himself, happily and tunelessly, he prepared for bed.

Dobson had left before the Pringles appeared for breakfast. The cold of the previous night had presaged a change in the weather. The sky was indigo with cloud. White mist unrolled like cotton-wool down between the mountain peaks. Everything outside looked bleak and wet.

The hotel was desolating in this gloom. The central heating had been turned on that morning, but so far it had done no more than fill the air with the reek of oil and rust. In the main room the bare wooden chairs and bamboo tables were damp to the touch. A smell of dust came from the bulrushes that stood about in pots.

A drizzle began to fall. No one in Bucharest thought of rain and the Pringles had not come prepared for it. Saying: "You won't want to go for a walk today," Guy settled down to his books.

Harriet wished they had gone back with Dobson. Although she thought of their return as something like a plunge into a boiling cauldron, she looked forward to the warmth and entertainment of the capital. Besides, she was anxious about Sasha.

Watching Guy contentedly preparing a course for which there might be no students, Harriet wondered where for him reality began and ended. He could be misled by the plausible, deceived by the self-deceiving, impressed by the second-rate: all in the name of charity, of course. But was such charity truly charitable?

At one time she had been indignant when others were critical of him. Now, she realised, she was criticising him herself. Even more surprising, she could feel bored in his company.

And yet, watching him as he sat there, unsuspecting of criticism or boredom, an open-handed man of infinite good nature, her heart was touched. Reflecting on the process of involvement and disenchantment which was marriage, she thought that one entered it unsuspecting and, unsuspecting, found one was trapped in it.

23

BUCHAREST, WHEN THEY REACHED IT, was also wet and no longer warm. The streets were dismal. The block of flats, designed to reflect sunlight, were blotched and livid in the grey air. This was one of the days – like the day of Calinescu's funeral – that broke like a threat into the fading glow of summer.

As soon as they entered the flat, they heard the sound of Sasha playing "We're Gonna Hang Out the Washing on the Siegfried Line". Harriet realising they were back among all their old unresolved anxieties, was not only relieved but annoyed by the mouth-organ. It seemed a symbol of Sasha's unquestioning acceptance of their protection. She went in, intending to chide him for wasting time, but he looked up with so much pleasure at her return, her annoyance was forgotten.

Dear Boy [wrote Yakimov from the Pension de Seraglio],

They think I am a spy or something and they're trying to run me out on a rail. Where next? I ask myself. I'm told Bucharest is full of Nazis spending *lei* like *apa*. If one of them makes an offer for the Hispano, seize it.

Don't forget your poor old desperate Yaki.

The telephone rang. Clarence said, urgently, that he was glad they were back, for he wanted to come and see them. "Yes, do come," said Harriet, thankful to be diverted from the cheerless anticlimax of return.

Clarence, entering the flat, was clearly the bringer of important news. He frowned at the ceiling and as soon as he had accepted a drink said abruptly: "I've come to say good-bye."

Guy said, startled: "You're going so soon?"

"I'm taking the night train. I'm going on to Ankara."

Both Pringles were disconcerted by this news: Guy the more so for, whatever he might care to think, it was evident their circle was disintegrating.

Harriet said: "Why to Ankara?"

"I've to report to the British Council representative. There's some talk of an appointment in Srinagar."

"How wonderful! You almost went to Kashmir once."

"This time, perhaps, I'll get there. But I'm just as likely to end in Egypt."

"Where you would meet up with Brenda?"

Clarence did not reply but, smirking slightly, he stretched himself out in his chair and said: "Poor old Brenda! Whatever did she see in me?"

"She may have thought you needed her."

Clarence shrugged and drawled: "Who knows what I need?"

He seemed aware that he was inviting Harriet's ridicule and to be, for some reason, forearmed against it. Because of this, Harriet said cautiously: "Well, if you go to Kashmir, I envy you."

Lifting his eyelids slowly, Clarence gave her a long look, then glancing down again, said in remote, measured tones: "Sophie is coming with me."

Harriet was startled into saying: "Good heavens!" and Clarence smiled his satisfaction.

"Why, this is splendid!" cried Guy and, leaping up, he refilled the glasses for a toast. "You're getting married, of course?"

Clarence, his smile fading, shrugged again. "I suppose so. It's what she wants," and he gave Harriet a quick glance full of reproach. She thought: "He is doing this to punish himself," but Guy was full of congratulations and encouragement.

"This is the best possible thing for Sophie," he said. "She's not a bad sort of girl. Living here alone, an orphan, half-Jewish, belonging to neither community, she has never had a chance. It will make all the difference to her to get away. You'll see. She'll make a splendid wife."

Harriet had her doubts and so, it would seem, had Clarence. He did not respond to Guy's enthusiasm and, after Guy had further extolled Sophie's virtues, Clarence gloomily mumbled: "I've always wanted to help someone. Perhaps I can help her."

"You could do the world for her," Guy confidently assured him.

Clarence turned his head towards Harriet, his expression yearning and miserable as though even now she might relent and save him. But, of course, she would not. No, not she. He turned away brusquely, finished off his drink, sat upright and said: "One thing I must do before I go: I must return these shirts to the Polish store."

"You mean the shirts you gave to Guy?"

"You know I didn't give them. They weren't mine to give. I lent them. Now they must go back."

"But the store is closed. You sold all that stuff to the Rumanian army."

"The sale's still being negotiated. It takes time for these deals to go through. I'm leaving the matter in the hands of an agent. I've given an inventory and everything must be accounted for. There were some vests, too, and a Balaclava helmet."

"That ridiculous helmet!" Harriet's indignation collapsed into mirth.

As though the demand were the most reasonable in the world, Guy said: "Of course we must return the things." He looked to Harriet as the only one likely to know where they were.

Without further ado, she went into the bedroom and began searching the drawers. The vests were at the laundry. Guy had long ago lost the Balaclava helmet. She returned to the room carrying three shirts.

"All that's left," she said.

Looking grimly justified, Clarence rose to take them, but Harriet did not give them to him. Instead, she strode out to the balcony and threw them over the balustrade. "If you want them," she said, "go down and get them."

He hurried to the balcony and stared down to where the shirts were settling on the wet, grey cobbles below.

"Well, *really!*" Scandalised, he watched while several beggars converged upon the booty. The shirts were snapped up in a moment.

Clarence looked to Guy for support.

"Darling, you shouldn't have done that!" Guy said with no real belief in his power to remonstrate with Harriet.

Taking no notice of either of them, she waved encouragement to the beggars as they stared up.

Looking deeply hurt, Clarence returned to the room and threw himself back into his chair. He dug his hands into his pockets. "How could you?" He gloomed for some moments, then said: "Just when I'd brought you what you asked me for." He drew a small book from his pocket.

Alight with amusement at her own action, Harriet snatched

the book from his hand and leafed it over. She came on the photograph of Sasha.

"A passport?"

"Yes, for your young friend Drucker."

"Clarence!" Harriet threw out her arms to him and he smiled as one who deserved no less.

Standing up rather sheepishly, he explained: "It's an Hungarian passport – in the name of Gabor. Most foreigners are known to the *prefectura*, but there are so many Hungarians here, they can't keep track of them. We've put in visas for Turkey, Bulgaria and Greece. All he'll need when the time comes is an exit visa."

Realising the passport was both a parting gift and a token of truce, Harriet ran to Clarence and embraced him with a warmth to which he immediately responded. He held her overlong, saying: "You will not forget me?"

"Never, never," she cried, refusing to be serious.

Guy said: "We'll miss you."

"Soon there will be no one left," said Harriet.

Clarence picked up his scarf, preparing to depart.

"But this isn't the end," Guy said, unwilling to see him go. "We'll be at the station to see you off."

"No. I hate farewells from trains. I'd rather say good-bye now." Clarence spoke with decision and Harriet felt he did not wish them to see him possessed by Sophie. Nor, she thought, did she wish to see it.

"What's happening to your flat?" she asked.

"A new tenant comes in next week: a German consular official. I'm glad to say he's keeping on Ergie, my cook, and her family. I don't know where they'd go if they were thrown out, poor things!"

They went to the landing with him.

"We'll meet again," said Guy.

"If you have to leave here, why not come to Kashmir? We'd find a job for you." Clarence wrung Guy's hand, then caught at Harriet and pecked her nervously. She realised he was not very sober and his eyes were moist. Not waiting for the arrival of the lift, he swung away from them and ran at a furious speed down the stairs.

24

THE WEATHER WAS SLOW IN REGAINING ITSELF. The sky remained broken, twilight fell early and the air was brisk.

The new term would start early in October. Guy had heard nothing of the reopening of his department, but he was preparing for it and a day or two after Clarence left he decided to pay a visit to the University.

The visit was to be a sort of reconnoitre. He might bump into the dean or one of the professors, or he might find his students hanging about the common-room as they used to do. Anyway, there would surely be someone there who would have something to tell him.

Harriet was doubtful about this essay into forbidden territory, but Guy refused to be dissuaded. He saw the University staff as friends. He had always been popular and privileged there and was sure he would be welcome. The visit would conclude all uncertainties. When she realised he was determined to go, she said she would walk with him as far as the building and then wait for him in the Cişmigiu. When he left her at the park gate she took the main path, intending to wait at the café.

There were very few people about. A haze, silvering the sky, gave a ghostly softness to the light. The distant elevations were washes of pearly transparency.

The flower-beds now had almost nothing to show except the lank stalks of withered plants. Dahlias and chrysanthemums fell, bedraggled, across the paths. On the long and almost leafless stems of the rose-bushes there were a few roses, small and colourless, too hard pressed to look like any particular sort of rose.

The dovecots seemed to be empty. From somewhere in the distance came, dismally, the sqawks of the white peacocks.

Leaves were falling, littering the grass and sticking in wads to the damp asphalt of the paths, but beside the lake the trees were still thickly feathered, hanging over the water, drop-winged, like gorged and sleepy birds of prey.

Harriet found the café closed. She walked round to the bridge from which she could look on to the pier and see the chairs and tables stacked under tarpaulins and roped down against the coming of the winter wind. She was suddenly saddened by the sense of change in which she felt they had no part. When the café reopened, where would they be?

The lake water was pewter-dark, shirred here and there by currents of silver, and broken by the trails of the mallard ducks. Behind her the waterfall gushed bleak as a burst pipe.

Hearing a step, she turned and came face to face with Bella's husband, Nikko. He looked nonplussed by this meeting, but when she said: "Why, Nikko! How nice to see you! When did you get back?" he cried: "Harry-ott!" stumbling forward in delight that his English friends were still, in spite of all, his friends. His black eyes shone and his teeth flashed from beneath his black moustache.

"We thought on our return you would have left," he said, "but now I find you here and am so glad."

"Yes, and Guy even believes the English Department will re-open. What do you think?"

"Who can say?"

Seeing he evaded the question, Harriet changed the subject, asking: "How is Bella?"

"Very well. Our holiday has restored her. But the summer was trying for her. Usually we are all the time in the mountains. My poor Bella! She suffers that I am away so much. I get little leave, then I am recalled and she weeps. Each month it becomes more difficult. Our great ally" – he made a grimace – "demands that officers are always on the alert. For what, I ask you? But you – which way do you walk?"

Finding he was crossing the park to the rear gate, she said she would pass the time by walking with him.

They crossed the bridge together. As they went, a blur of white came into the sky where the sun hung behind the haze. The lake turned to silver. The still and humid air cut off the sound of traffic so they seemed to be moving into areas of cushioned silence.

Beyond the bridge there was a walk of lime trees, brilliantly yellow in the grey air, beneath which two German officers sauntered, in trench-coats with skirts swinging, the heels of their jackboots clicking on the paths. They gave an impression of acute boredom.

Nikko, not in uniform, eyed them, cautiously silent until he and

Harriet were well past, then he said in an undertone: "They have not yet won the war. I can tell you, Harry-ott, we are sick of the demands of the Germans. They will devour us. People are remembering the English, so honest, so dignified, so generous, and they say: 'Perhaps even now the Allies will win.' And, I say: 'Why not?' September is at an end, yet there has been no invasion. What has happened, we ask, to this talked-of invasion? The Germans put it off. They make excuses. Do not quote me, but we know already it is too late. They *cannot* invade."

Harriet turned on him in hopeful surprise. "Why not?"

"Why not?" Nikko gave her a look of astonishment. "Surely you must know why not? Already the fogs cloak your shores. The Germans cannot find their way."

"Oh!" Harriet gave a laugh of disappointment. "I'm afraid we can't rely on the fogs."

Nikko knew better. "Then why do they not invade?" he asked. After a moment, he added: "They are a strange people. I remember last time when they came here, I was a little boy. We had a German officer billeted in our home. He was not so bad, you know. It was a time of great fear, and we did for him what we could. When they retreated, taking everything they could carry, this man, leaving us, gave to my mother a great parcel – this size; very big. He said: 'This is a gift. I give you because you have been so kind.' After he was gone, she opened it and inside there was a bed-quilt. We all looked at it, thinking how nice, but my mother said: 'I have seen before such a bed-quilt. I have *already* one like this,' and she went up to the cupboard to look. What do you think? He had given to my mother her own bed-quilt! Have you ever known such a strange people?"

As Harriet laughed, Nikko said: "I have loved England; I was long ambitious to work in England. I would be interested, I need say, only in a top-hole job, for I have top-hole qualifications. I read *Punch* and *The Times* – not now, of course, for they do not arrive, but my subscription is paid. And, as you observe, my English is unerring. But the war nipped me in the bud."

Harriet laughed again. "It nipped us all in the bud," she said.

Nikko, having recalled his enthusiasm for England, now said with conviction: "I think the English Department will open again. Why not? It will open because they love Guy. He is a great man."

"Do you think so? Well, perhaps he is, in some ways . . ."

"A great man!" Nikko insisted, permitting no reservations.

"And why? Because he is himself. Many Englishmen came here to be important people – the sahibs, as they called it. They would show these foreigners how to run the world. But not Guy. He came as one of us – a chum, you might say, a human being. Only the other day as we came into Bucharest, I said to Bella: 'How I wish I had known better Guy Pringle. Now he will be gone, and I shall never know him.' "

Harriet smiled at the pattern of approval, never disclosed before and said nothing.

Sensing her doubt in his serenity, Nikko said: "Before you came, you understand, I had not much opportunity. Guy and Bella did not see eye to eye. She invited him to a cocktail, he did not turn up. She said: 'That young man is not an advertisement for England. They should not have let him come here. He is badly dressed, he cultivates Jews, he is not careful what he says. The important English do not approve him.' All this perhaps was true, yet I approved him. I said: 'Invite him again. He is always so busy . . .' "

"Much too busy," commented Harriet.

"But she would not invite him again, not until you came. You she approved."

"Oh," said Harriet, uncertain how to take this.

"But I admired Guy," Nikko went on, not feeling the subject was yet exhausted. "I admired him because he spoke to one and all and dressed so badly. He wore that old overcoat. Do you remember that old overcoat? What Englishman here would be seen dead in such a coat? No, no, they must impress us. But it is not necessary, you know. We are impressed already by the English qualities. We know here that to be English is to be honest. You do things to your own disadvantage because you know them to be right. That is remarkable, I can tell you. So we love you."

"I'm not so sure of that," said Harriet, feeling the need to introduce some sobriety into this conversation. "I often feel the Rumanians are suspicious of us, and resentful."

"A little, perhaps." Conceding the point, Nikko hurried past it: We envy you. You are a great, rich nation. We think you despise us, but we love you nevertheless. See!" He paused at a railed area of uncut grasses among which some flowers ran riot. "This is the English garden."

Harriet looked in astonishment. She had sometimes wondered

about this patch that she would not have described as a garden of any kind.

"Yes," Nikko assured her. "It is a genuine English wilderness. So you see," he nodded as though proving his point, "we have an English Bar and an English garden."

"Yes," said Harriet. They had now reached the gate and she paused before saying she must turn back.

Nikko took her hand. "Good-bye, Harry-ott. Let us, this winter, meet more often. Persuade Guy to come and have dinner with us."

She promised she would. Nikko looked pleased, as though a whole future of friendship lay ahead, but Harriet felt in their parting a note of farewell.

When she returned to the lakeside she saw Guy walking rapidly, down between the chrysanthemum beds, his expression troubled, his appearance more dishevelled than usual. When she called to him, he glanced towards her but did not smile.

"What is the matter?" she asked.

"I must see Inchcape. Will you come with me?"

As they walked together back to the main road, he described to her how, entering the University building, he had found all the doors of his department locked. Even his own study door had been locked against him. He had noticed the porter, with whom he had been a favourite, sliding out of sight as he entered. Guy, determined to speak to him, had tracked him down to the boiler-room in the basement. The old man, stammering in his embarrassment, asked: What could a poor peasant do?

"These are wicked days, *domnule*! Bad men possess our country and our friends are severed from us."

"He said that?" Harriet asked in admiration.

"Something like that," said Guy. "He said he had no keys for my rooms. They had all been taken away by the Foreign Minister."

"Have you much stuff in your office?"

"Some of my books. A lot of Inchcape's. My overcoat."

"Oh, well!" said Harriet, feeling things might have been worse.

Guy sighed, apparently stunned by a rebuff that did not surprise her in any way.

"Do you think Inchcape can do anything?" she asked.

"I don't know."

She could scarcely keep up with him as he made his way to the Propaganda Bureau. She had no wish for the department to reopen, but, remembering how, on the day of the abdication, she had found Guy waiting for the students who did not come, she felt an acute pity for him. Whatever he chose to do – and it was, after all, done from a sense of responsibility and a need to be occupied – he must be her first concern.

When they reached the main road, they became aware that something had occurred. A crowd stood opposite the English Propaganda Bureau, gazing across at it. The pavement outside it was empty of people: those who approached it, swerved away from it as though it held contagion. The trespass of the bystanders on to the road had caused a traffic hold-up. The result was an hysterical din of motor-horns.

Guy and Harriet were conscious of being watched as they crossed the road to the Bureau. The pavement when they reached it was a litter of splintered wood, glass and scraps of torn cardboard. The Bureau window had been shattered; its faded display wrecked. The model of the Dunkirk beach-head seemed to have been attacked, savagely, with hammer blows. The "Britain Beautiful" posters had been ripped down and screwed into balls. Everywhere lay remnants of the photographs of ships and soldiers.

Despite the disorder there was no sign of police or any official keeper of law and order.

Guy said: "Wait here. I'll look inside," but Harriet kept at his heels. The door stood ajar. Inchcape was alone in the downstairs office. He was sitting in the typist's chair, pressing a folded handkerchief to the corner of his mouth. He greeted the Pringles with a wry smile.

"It's all right," he said; "they barely touched me."

As he spoke, blood welled out of the corner of his mouth and trickled down his chin. Blood and serum from a wound under his hair was trickling down into his left ear. His natural pallor had taken on a greenish tinge.

"For heaven's sake," said Guy. "We must get a doctor . . ." He went to the telephone, but Inchcape detained him with a gesture.

"Believe me, it's nothing."

There was a sound of car-doors banging outside, then Galpin entered with Screwby and three other journalists from the English Bar. Galpin crossed to Inchcape, observed him keenly, flicked open a notebook, then asked: "What happened? What did they do to you?"

Inchcape regarded him with distaste. "An accidental knock or two. They came in merely to sabotage the work of the place. The attack was all over in a matter of minutes." He turned pointedly to Guy and in a changed tone said, smiling: "I rang your flat first. When I couldn't get you, I rang Dobson. He's on his way."

Galpin gave his attention to the condition of the office. "They've done a proper job." He looked at his companions and said: "My stringer here says there were these hooligans knocking the old boy about, smashing the windows, destroying things – all in broad daylight, in a crowded street. And not a soul lifted a finger. They just scurried past. Just look at them now." He flicked a hand at the audience across the road. "Piss-scared." He turned on Inchcape again and as though speaking to someone of limited intelligence he explained: "We'll want a statement. Tell us in your own words: when it happened, how it happened and who you imagine the assailants were."

Inchcape turned his head slowly and stared directly at Galpin. "I am waiting for Mr. Dobson," he explained in a style that echoed Galpin's own. "Any statement I have to make will be made when he arrives."

Disconcerted, Galpin took a step backwards, bumping into Screwby who was moving forward to say, in fulsome tones: "I must say, sir, I admire your pluck."

Inchcape's only acknowledgement of this tribute was a twist of the lips that caused him to wince. Blood welled out again.

Galpin, piqued, muttered to the others: "Well, I only hope someone's sent for a doctor. Things could be worse than they look."

"No doctor has been sent for, nor do I want one," Inchcape said and, glancing aside at Harriet, he added: "Heaven keep me out of the hands of Rumanian doctors."

Dobson arrived. Looking about him, he said: "Oh dear!" Flustered and at a loss, he stood pulling off his gloves, then suddenly became businesslike. "The fellows who did this," he asked, "were they in uniform?"

"No."

"Ah, an unofficial attack. When we protest, no one will know anything. If we persist, we may get an apology, but that will be the end of it. The authorities are powerless, of course."

Galpin said: "We're all powerless." He was showing signs of impatience. "What about that statement?" he asked.

Everyone waited. Inchcape, the centre of attention, was wiping his mouth again. After some moments, he smiled his old ironical smile and began: "I was in my office upstairs, innocently reading Miss Austen, when I heard a fracas down here. Half a dozen young men had burst in and started smashing the place up. I heard my secretary screaming. When I got down, she'd made a bolt for it – no doubt wisely: she had, in any case, begun to doubt the justice of the Allied cause."

Inchcape paused to smile to himself, apparently recalling the whole occurrence with philosophical amusement. "When I appeared," he went on, "one fellow slammed the door closed and locked it. There were seven or eight of them. Two or three gave their attention to me, the rest were absorbed in their destructive frenzy. I was hit on the head by a framed portrait of our respected Prime Minister . . ."

"Deliberately?" Galpin demanded.

"I don't know. The blow knocked me backwards into this chair. When I tried to rise, someone gripped my shoulders and held me down. One of them – the leader, I suppose – then saw fit to question me."

"What questions were you asked?" said Dobson.

"Oh, the usual. They wanted to know who was head of the British Secret Service here. I said: 'Sir Montagu.' That flummoxed them." Inchcape laughed at the recollection, but Dobson, frowning like an unhappy baby, burst out: "Really, there was no need to bring H.E. into it."

"You know they can't touch him. And if they tried, he's well protected."

Dobson seemed about to speak, then shut his mouth, silenced by the change that was coming over Inchcape's appearance. Bruises like leaden shadows were beginning to show on his brow and cheeks. His handkerchief was dark with blood. Guy offered him another, but he shook his head. "I'm all right," he said.

Galpin interrupted accusingly: "They must have knocked you about?"

Inchcape, clearly under greater strain than he would admit, caught his breath and answered with sardonic brevity: "A little perhaps."

Though he could not admit he had suffered the indignity of attack, the journalists were not deceived. One said: "I can't imagine a few accidental taps got you into this condition."

"Are you suggesting that I am lying?" Inchcape sharply asked.

"All right." Galpin snapped a band round his note-book and put it away. Buttoning his jacket, he looked round at his fellows with the air of one who has got all he wants here and has other calls on his time. "We'd better get back," he said.

They began moving off. Guy, saying he would take Inchcape home, went out to the street to find a cab. Galpin, on the pavement outside, was saying: "It's my opinion he's brought this on himself."

"In what way?" Guy asked.

He jerked a thumb at the Bureau. "He insisted, against advice, on keeping open. But there was more to it than that. I bet the lads who did this job *knew him*. Knew him too well, I mean. That's why he's keeping his mouth shut. He's always been a mean old bastard. If you ask me, the lads had something on him."

"What rubbish!" Guy said in disgust. "It was obviously a Guardist outrage."

Galpin snorted. He got into his car and as a parting shot, called out: "One has to pay for one's pleasures, you know."

Inchcape made his way to the cab with an unconvincing show of vigour. Getting into it, he stumbled and Guy had to hold him up.

At the sight of his master, Pauli gave a cry of distress and waved his arms in the air. Inchcape pushed him away with affectionate impatience, saying: "Go and make a good strong pot of tea for all of us."

While they drank it, Inchcape talked gleefully about his quick-wittedness in naming Sir Montagu as head of the Secret Service. "You should have seen their faces. They knew the old charmer was out of their reach. And having got their answer, they couldn't think of anything else to ask me."

Before the Pringles left, Inchcape said to them: "For heaven's sake, don't breathe a word of this to Pinkrose. He'd get into a panic. So promise me, not one word."

The Pringles promised.

25

NEXT MORNING, Pauli telephoned Guy to say he was worried about his master's condition. The previous evening, Inchcape, though insisting that he was perfectly well, had been unable to sleep until he had taken veronal. That morning he looked much worse and all life had gone from him. He was, in Pauli's opinion, very sick; and he was asking for Guy.

When this call came, Harriet was in the bathroom. Guy shouted to her that he would be back for luncheon and left the flat before she could ask where he was going. When she went out to the balcony, she could see him making his way rapidly across the square.

He was, in fact, unusually disturbed, and not only by his fears for Inchcape. The previous evening, in need of a drink, he had gone to the English Bar where Galpin had claimed to have "inside information" to the effect that the military mission was soon to be followed by the Gestapo. The Germans had already installed a Gauleiter, who was becoming the talk of town. He was said to be paralysed from the waist down. Though he lay in bed all day, seeing no one but his agents, he knew everything about everybody. Galpin said: "The whole German colony's piss-scared of this bastard. Even Fabricius. The Rumanians, too. They say that a deputation of Rumanian statesmen called on Fabricius last night to beg the Führer to send in an army of occupation. He said that Germany doesn't plan to occupy Rumania just yet. That's all my eye. Everything points to the fact that it's any day now."

Harriet, who had been playing a paper game with Sasha, had not accompanied Guy to the bar. When he returned, he did not tell her what he had heard there.

Unnerved by her outburst at Predeal, he had, for the first time, begun to fear for her. He had always thought of her as a pattern of courage, someone tougher than himself about whom he need not worry. Now he was beginning to realise that she had audacity without stamina. His means of living with a situation was to put its dangers behind him. Her method was to keep them in view so they might not come on her unawares. She lived in a state of preparedness that brought undue stress. He told himself he must protect her against her own temperament. He would save her from shock, even the perhaps not very great shock of seeing Inchcape in a state of collapse.

But there was more behind Guy's discomposure than that. He was suffering from shock himself. Both Inchcape and he had been named on the German radio. Both were the natural prey not only of the Iron Guard but of the Gestapo, rumoured to be on its way here.

Convinced that a testing-time was at hand, he tried to tell himself that he now knew exactly what would happen. He would be attacked without warning and struck about the face and head by thugs. He realised that in thus attempting to steady an inner nerve with certainty, he was simply imitating Harriet. And where did it bring one? To the verge of a breakdown. He could only hope that when his time came, pride would prop him up as it had propped up Inchcape. The trouble was, he had a peculiar horror of physical violence and could not foresee what his reaction would be. Even Harriet, half his size, could frighten him when she lost her temper. He flinched or cried out in the instant of being hurt. Afterwards, he would pull himself together, but that first instant stayed with him, a self-betrayal.

Whatever happened, he must save himself from Harriet's observing eye.

Pauli, opening the door for him, lifted a hand in mute dismay at what he would find. He said nothing but hurried into Inchcape's bedroom. He had feared Inchcape would be prostrate and was relieved to see him sitting up in bed, but the relief was gone as soon as Inchcape turned his head.

Noting Guy's change of expression, he said: "They haven't improved my beauty, have they?"

"It could be worse."

"How much worse?" Inchcape winced as he attempted an appearance of jocularity. Both his eyes were blackened, one of them hidden by the swollen lids. A purple bruise, spreading from under his hair, covered one side of his face. His lips protruded, and his other features, naturally pallid and fine, were so distorted that he looked, against the whiteness of the bed-linen, like a grotesque native mask.

Guy had carried for years in his mind the memory of Simon's bleeding, stupefied face – but Simon had been the victim of amateurs. Brutality had progressed since then.

Guy said: "Apart from the bruises, are you hurt at all?"

"Back aches a bit. Have a drink." Inchcape reached out towards a bottle of brandy on the table beside him, then, as though some prop had been withdrawn, he fell back among the pillows and gave a groan. He looked at Guy, gasped and said: "Don't stand there, staring. Sit down, for God's sake." He attempted his old impatience, but it was a shadow of itself.

"Let me get you a drink." Guy poured out the brandy before he sat down.

The bedroom was small, lit by a single small window that was overhung by plane leaves. On the walls were ikons so dark that to Guy they represented nothing. He wondered if it were the pervading gloom that made Inchcape look so ill.

Inchcape sipped his brandy and after a moment started to talk: "I rang H.E. this morning. I told him I was not to be coerced by these louts. I was determined to reopen the Bureau, but apparently the Bureau's been officially closed by the Rumanian authorities. Still, I'm not standing for it. I shall fight." He dug his elbows into the pillows and made another irritable effort to sit up but failed again.

Inchcape was an elderly man but one who had maintained vitality and youthfulness: now some inner power had gone from him. His neck, rising from his pyjama jacket, looked wretchedly scraggy. His whole physique seemed to have aged and weakened overnight. He said: "Dobson rang a while ago, was very pleasant, as usual. He advised me to take myself off to Turkey. I said I wouldn't dream of it. They're not going to scare me so easily."

Guy nodded his understanding. Yet with the English Department and the Bureau closed, would it not be better for Inchcape to go? He had imagined that the presence of the Legation guaranteed their safety. Well, he could no longer have any illusions about that. His work had come to nothing. He had been abused. Nothing remained but his determination to stay as long as Sir Montagu stayed.

"Still," said Guy, "there's no reason why you should not take a few weeks' leave after this."

Inchcape's one visible eye glinted at him and Guy's spirits gave a jerk. So defiance was now a sham! Inchcape wanted only to be persuaded – though, unpersuaded, his pride would probably keep him here. Suddenly Guy saw that Harriet and he might get away together unharmed; for if Inchcape went he could scarcely demand that they must stay.

"After all," said Guy, "Dobson is off to Sofia."

"That's true. Though I can't say that I approve it. And I'm told the old charmer himself recently chartered a plane and flew to Corfu. Spent a week there. A nice thing, I must say, at a time like this."

"Oh, I don't know." Guy, in fear of rousing Inchcape's obstinate opposition, found himself lapsing into clichés: "Quite a good thing to get away from a situation – enables you to get it into focus."

Latching on to Guy's extenuating tone, Inchcape permitted himself a measure of agreement. "Of course, there's more to these trips than meets the eye. There's no knowing whom Sir M. met when down there, or what was discussed. I've often thought myself I could pay a call on our agent in Beirut. I could put him wise about a few things. He's still in direct telephonic communication with London office, you know. And they should be made to realise how things are changing here. The rise in the cost of living, for instance! We can't go on indefinitely on pre-war salaries."

Guy had not heard before of this agent, but was prepared to believe in him. The organisation supplied men to the American University in Beirut. He said: "There's probably an air-service between Istanbul and Beirut."

Inchcape opened his mouth, but did not speak. There was a pause, then he nodded. It seemed to Guy that the trip was practically agreed upon. He was about to suggest that while Inchcape went to Beirut, he and Harriet could visit Athens, when he noticed Inchcape's hand trembling on the white satin counterpane. He felt stricken. Telling himself that he was harrying this aged and lonely man out of the one place in the world where he had importance, he put his hand on Inchcape's and pressed it.

At this touch, Inchcape's lips shook: a tear trickled out between his swollen lids. "We can't give in, Guy," he said. "We can't run away. We must be represented."

"We aren't running away," Guy assured him. "You are merely taking the leave that is due to you. I shall be here to represent you."

"That's true." As though he knew he had committed himself to defeat, Inchcape let his head fall back and sobbed without restraint.

Awed by this collapse of a man who had until now appeared to be inflexible, Guy realised he had always taken Inchcape at his face value, accepting him as his chief, to be obeyed and honoured. He had never doubted that much of Inchcape's temerity was based on self-deception, but it appalled him to see this temerity collapse at the moment reality broke through. But perhaps it was the indignity that had destroyed Inchcape. The whole place must seem to him contaminated by this assualt on him. No wonder he wanted to get away.

For a while Guy sat silent, at a loss before Inchcape's weeping, then, realising that initiative had now passed to him, he said: "And another thing: London office must be told that we face a final break-up here. It's only a matter of time. We should be instructed where we're to go, what we're to do when we get there. We don't want to become refugees without employment."

Inchcape nodded again. Finding a handkerchief, he dabbed gently at his eyes and nostrils. "You're quite right," he said. "It's not only advisable I should go, it's imperative. And there's no time to waste."

"None. You should go as soon as you feel equal to the journey."

"Oh, I'm all right." Inchcape gave something between a laugh and a gulp. He made another effort and this time managed to sit upright. "I'm not crippled. The sooner I get away, the sooner I'll be back. I won't take much: change of underwear, a few books, just a grip and a brief-case. I like to travel light. If there's no plane to Beirut, there should be a train of some sort. An execrable journey, I imagine, but interesting. If nothing important crops up, I might get the Orient Express on Sunday night."

"Do you think you will be well enough?"

"Nothing wrong with me. Just a few bruises." And now that matters were settled, Inchcape did seem much recovered. He threw back the coverlet, put his legs out of bed and began, in a feeble way, to feel for his slippers. Not finding them, he gave up and lowered himself back to the pillows, but he shot Guy a keen look. "You've not said a word to Pinkrose?"

"No, I haven't seen him since it happened."

"Good. He's not likely to hear in the ordinary way. He takes a pride in keeping himself to himself. When he rang up last night,

Pauli told him I was in bed with a temperature. That'll keep the old cheeser at bay. He won't risk catching anything."

"Don't you think we should let him know you're going?"

"No, definitely not. He'd get into a proper tizzy. He'd have a heart attack. Or worse, he'd insist on coming with me. I couldn't stand it." Inchcape fixed Guy, his expression piteous: "I'm not fit for it."

Guy wondered what they were to do with Pinkrose after Inchcape's departure, but, afraid to raise any problem that might impede it, he said: "Very well."

"Don't tell anyone," Inchcape said. "I'll be back before they even know I've left the country."

It was clear to Guy, as he returned home, that in sending for him Inchcape had merely sent for a persuader. Guy could not flatter himself that he had done much, but he felt pride, even a mild exultation, that by making the right gesture he had persuaded the poor old chap to take himself to safety. The resolute, he saw, were weaker than they seemed.

It occurred to him that Harriet, tackled in some such oblique manner, might be just as easily overthrown. Not that the conditions were exactly similar. Inchcape had collapsed at a first blow from reality. Harriet had never let reality out of her sight. When she said she would not leave, she saw as clearly as Guy did the dangers of staying – probably more clearly. Still, he was not discouraged. He had his own obstinacy. Once assured in his purpose, he could be as wily as the next man.

There were two weaknesses through which she might be assailed: himself and Sasha. Supposing he persuaded her to go to Athens on his behalf! Better, perhaps, persuade her to make the journey as friend and protector to Sasha.

He had long recognised her attachment to the boy without resenting it. He was glad that each could enjoy the companionship of the other. And he had no illusions about himself. He was overgregarious, busy, disinclined to suffer constraint. Were he to accuse her of neglecting him, she had more than enough fuel for counter-accusation. If she felt the need for a friend and companion, better an innocent relationship than one that might prove less innocent. And something had to be done about Sasha. Even if he were not in danger, his life as he lived it now was hopelessly unprofitable. He had never been a brilliant pupil, but he had been a willing one. Now, in captivity, he had become idle and would not put his mind to the tasks which Guy set for him. He did not even want to read. The most he would do was play games with Harriet or cover with childish drawings the large sheets of cheap cartridge paper which she bought for him. Sometimes, at his most active, he amused himself by helping Despina in the kitchen, but that amounted chiefly to gossiping and giggling.

When Harriet had shown him the faked passport, he had looked at it blankly. When she explained: "This means you can leave Rumania," his only reaction had been dismay: "But I don't have to go, do I?"

"Not now, of course. But if we go – and we may have to – you can come with us."

Sasha's expression had revealed his fear of change, or of any sort of move even made in their company. He wanted to spend the rest of his life like a pet in a cage.

When Guy reached the sitting room he found Sasha and Despina putting the knives and forks on the table. The two were laughing together at something.

Despina, who was familiar with Harriet and motherly with Sasha, kept up the Eastern tradition that the man of the house was a minor despot. At the sight of Guy, she took herself off.

Sasha said: "Despina is so funny. She was imitating the cook from downstairs who sneaks into our kitchen and pinches our sugar. If anyone catches her at it, she whines: 'Please, please, I came only to borrow the carving knife!' "

Guy smiled, but thought that Sasha, though he spoke like a schoolboy, was, in fact, a young man. At his age many Rumanian men were married. The only hope for the boy was to be forced into an independent existence. If he and Harriet travelled together, he must be made to see himself not as the protected but the protector.

As soon as he had Harriet alone, Guy told her of Inchcape's collapse. "He's going on Sunday to Beirut."

She jerked up her head, her face brilliant with excitement. "He's going for good?"

"In theory, no: but I doubt whether he'll come back."

"So there's really nothing to keep us here, either. We can go. We can go to Athens, and Sasha can come with us. We can all go together."

Guy had to break in on her frantic delight: "No, I can't go. Not yet. I've had to promise Inchcape that I would stay. He wouldn't go otherwise. He felt he had to be represented here. And then there's Pinkrose. But look" – he seized her hands as her face dropped – "look," he coaxed her, "do something for me."

"What?"

"Go to Sofia with Dobson."

She pulled her hands from him, vexed, saying: "No, I wouldn't go to Sofia, anyway. The only place I want to go to is Greece, but I'm not going without you."

"All right, better still, go to Athens. Take Sasha with you. And I can join you there. *Listen,* darling. Be sensible. There are two reasons why you should go. I think Sasha should be got out of here in good time. If he travels on the plane with you and Dobson, he'll have your protection. They probably won't even question why he's going. He'll be treated as a privileged passenger. If there should be trouble, we can rely on Dobson to exert his influence."

"What makes you think that?"

"I do think it. I'm sure Dobson will look after you both. He'll be like a mother to you."

Neither agreeing nor disagreeing, she asked in a noncommittal tone: "And the other reason?"

"If I go to Turkey, I'll probably be sent to the Middle East. I hate those hot, sandy countries. I want to go to Greece, just as you do, and if you're there already I have the excuse of joining you."

Before she turned her face aside, he could see the idea of a mission was working on her. She bit her lip in doubt.

"And," he said, "if things settle down here, you can come back."

But she was still resistant. "This uncertainty could drag on for months. We simply haven't the money . . "

He interrupted, urging her: "Go for a few weeks, anyway. See the head of the organisation in Athens. Tell him I want to work there. You know you can do it. If he likes you, he'll want to employ me: so when I leave here, there'll be somewhere for me to go."

It all seemed odd to Harriet, like a conversation outside reality, yet it was breaking down her resistance. Bewildered, half persuaded, she said: "If I want to come back here, they may not let me in. People are being expelled all the time."

"If you get a return visa before you go, they must let you back."

Reluctant, even at this point, to give way, she kept the argument dragging on, but in the end she found she had agreed to get a return visa. Having secured this, she could take Sasha to Athens and return alone if Guy did not join her there.

Despite something like near-intoxication from the prospect of escape, Harriet resented the fact that Guy had persuaded her to go.

Men like Woolley saw women as a "drag" in times of danger. Mrs. Woolley had been sent to England at the outbreak of war and had recently been sent somewhere else. Harriet, of a different generation, saw herself as an equal and a comrade. She was not to be packed off like that – and, yet, against her will, she had let herself be talked into going

For Guy the day was one of modest triumph. In sending ahead Harriet, Sasha and that old self-deceiver Inchcape, he was not only safeguarding them, but clearing the decks for action in a war he had chosen to wage, the war against despotism. He believed the ultimate engagement was at hand. He could now face it alone.

26

HARRIET WOULD MAKE NO PREPARATIONS for her journey. She would not even mention their plans to Sasha. She would do nothing until she had obtained the visa that was an earnest of her return. She got a bleak and sparkless satisfaction when it seemed she probably would not obtain it at all.

She had had to queue for the exit visa, but it was given without question. For the return visa, she was directed to a compartment which contained no clerk. No one was waiting before it. She stood for some time, then inquired and was told the clerk was not in the building. He might reappear at five o'clock.

In the late afternoon she returned to the *prefectura*, but the compartment was still unattended. She demanded to see the official in charge. When he eventually came, he took her passport away and left her waiting twenty minutes before he brought it back. She could be granted a return visa only if she supplied a letter of recommendation from her Legation.

She set out for the Legation, disheartened by fatigue and in-decision, and heard from a side-street the barrel-organ that played the old Rumanian tune, the name of which no one could tell her. Haunting and mysteriously simple, it reminded her of the day she had gone for a sleigh-ride up the Chaussée with Guy and Clarence. She thought of the shop-lights gilding the snow and felt an acute nostalgia for winter. She told herself she would not go. She could not leave Guy. She did not even want to leave Bucharest.

She wandered on and, crossing the square, saw Bella walking towards the Athénée Palace. The two women came face to face under the Nazi flag.

It had been a day of mild autumnal sunlight and Bella was in a new woollen suit with mink skins strung from elbow to elbow. This was their first sight of each other since her return to Bucharest. Seeing Harriet, she called out: "I was going to ring you! What do you think I got on the black market today? Just over six thousand to the pound. *And* it's rising. My dear, we're rich! I've been buying everything I could lay my hands on. After all, you never know, do you? I've just ordered a new coat – Persian lamb, of course. I picked out my own skins. *Tiny* little things! I wrote my name on the back of each so there'd be no hanky-panky. I'm getting half a dozen new suits for Nikko – best English tweed. The thing to do is to buy up what's left. *And* shoes – a dozen pairs each. Why not, I ask you? We've money to burn." Elated by her rise in fortune, she looked up and smiled at the flag and the clear pale sky beyond it. "I love this time of the year," she said. "So delicious after the fug of summer. It makes one feel so *alive*." She seemed aglitter with life, almost dancing in her new green lizard-skin shoes. Not finding Harriet very responsive, she looked at her more closely and thought to ask: "But how are you and Guy? What do you think of things?"

Harriet glanced up at the swastika. "Doesn't that disturb you?"

Bella looked up again and gave an uncertain laugh. "Does it?" she asked. "I don't know. In a way, it makes me feel safe. It's nice to be protected, even by Germans. And, you know," she gazed seriously at Harriet, a rather petulant gleam in her eyes, "Rumania has been very unfairly treated. The Allies guaranteed her, then did nothing. *Nothing*. There was that plot to blow up the oil-wells, and there've always been those outside interests controlling Ploesti. Foreign engineers everywhere. No wonder we've been in an awkward position. You can't blame the Rumanians for wanting the foreigners to go."

"When they go, what will the Rumanians do?"

"Get in German experts, I suppose."

"So there will still be outside interests controlling Ploesti! Or don't Germans count as outsiders any more?"

Bella, looking sulky, tilted up her chin as though sniffing out injury. She made a movement, seemed about to go, but, held by some memory of their earlier friendship, gave Harriet a look at once annoyed and compassionate. "But what about you? Aren't you nervous, being here? I mean, it's different for little me. I've a Rumanian passport." Suddenly the thought of something restored her humour. She gave a laugh: "People think I'm a German, you know. I can get anything I want."

Harriet, fearing to enhance Bella's isolation here, had not mentioned her possible departure, but now she realised that Bella's high spirits were not a result of hysteria. She had found a means of managing her situation: she was shuffling off her own identify and taking on an aspect of the enemy.

Harriet said: "Guy wants me to go to Athens for a few weeks, but I'm having difficulty in getting a return visa."

Hooting with laughter, Bella gripped Harriet's arm. "My dear, you can get one in the twinkling of an eye. It's just a matter of going about it the right way. Put a thousand-*lei* note inside your passport. But why get a return visa? If you've any sense you'll stay there once you get there."

"I have to come back. Guy isn't supposed to leave without orders."

"Oh, I'll keep an eye on him. I'll see he doesn't get into mischief."

Bella was enjoying herself. Here she was, secure and snug, while others must take themselves into exile. She could advise from a position of vantage. "You might like me to look after some of your things," she said. "Those nice Hungarian plates, for instance. I wouldn't mind giving them a home."

"If we finally go, you can take what you like."

"Well, I must be on my way." Bella gathered her minks about her. "I've got several fittings this evening. I want to buy gloves. Look, give me a ring and tell me how you manage about the visa. I'll call and see you before you go." She hurried away with a happy "Cheerio!" and Harriet returned to the *prefectura* where she again asked to see the official in charge. When he came upon the thousand-*lei* note in her passport, he whipped it out so quickly Harriet scarcely saw it go. He stamped in the return visa.

"Doamna is intrepid," he said in English. "These times, the British who go do not wish to come back." Smirking, he handed her the passport with a little bow.

Harriet wondered how Sasha would accept the news of their going. He accepted it impassively. After all, she thought, he merely lived as his family had lived for generations: in seclusion, dreading flight, but prepared for it.

"What about Guy?" he asked.

"He'll come when he can."

She and Guy had planned to support Sasha until he could find work. He surprised her now by his immediate appraisal of what his position would be abroad. He pointed out that, once he was beyond Rumanian jurisdiction, he could draw on the fortune banked in his name in Switzerland

"I shall be very rich," he said. "If you need money, I can give it to you."

"You would have to establish your identity."

"Surely my relations would do that?"

Harriet smiled and agreed, but wondered where his relations might be.

As nothing important cropped up, Inchcape's departure was fixed for Sunday. He had only four days in which to make his arrangements, but he made them wholeheartedly. He decided to give up his flat.

On his return, he explained to Guy, he would go to a *pension*. "No good shutting one's eyes to the fact," he said. "Sooner or later, we'll have to take ourselves off, probably at a moment's notice. Better be prepared for it. Besides, one's safer in a *pension* than living on one's own."

When the Pringles called for him on Sunday evening, Pauli, opening the door, blinked at them with red-rimmed eyes. He led them through the hall filled with packing-cases and in the disordered sitting-room, where all the gold-shaded lights were lit, began to lament his quandary.

The great wish of his life, he said, was to follow the professor wherever he might go. Alas, Pauli had a wife and three children. He had been prepared to leave them but the professor, the most clement of masters, had insisted that Pauli's duty was here.

Pauli made no pretence of believing that Inchcape would return. There was too much evidence against the possibility. At the thought of their eternal separation, Pauli's eyes overflowed, his shoulders shook. He pulled out a ball of wet handkerchief and scrubbed at his face while Guy patted his shoulder, saying: "When the war is over, we shall all meet again."

"*Dupa răsboiul*," Pauli repeated and, as though for the first time struck by the thought that the war might end, he brightened at once. Nodding, blowing his nose, saying again and again "*Dupa răsboiul*," he hurried off to tell Inchcape that they had arrived.

Harriet said: "*Dupa răsboiul!*" thinking of the war that divided them like a sea from progress and profit in the world. The total effort of their lives might go down in the crossing of it. "And afterwards," she said, "what will be left? We may no longer be young, or even ambitious. And it may never end. We may never have a home."

Wandering about among the packing-cases, she paused at the tables and examined Inchcape's bowl of artificial fruit. There was a fig made of malachite, a purple plum, a flame-coloured persimmon. She held a pear to the light and, seeing the spangling within, said: "Do you think, if I asked him, he would give me these?"

"Of course he wouldn't." Guy was shocked at the idea and, hearing Inchcape's footsteps, he added warningly: "Put them down."

Inchcape's bruises were changing to green and violet. He looked scarcely better than he had done on the morning after the attack, but he had regained all his own sardonic swagger. He crossed over to a Chinese cabinet and took out three bottles, in each of which a little liquid remained.

"Might as well finish this," he said. "What'll you have? Brandy, gin, ţuică?"

He had put on his overcoat and Pauli could be heard heaping up luggage in the hall, but Inchcape seemed in no hurry to go. Having poured out the drinks, he went round adjusting the shades of the lights and observing their effect. One of the ivory chessmen had toppled over. He restored it. Glancing about with satisfaction at his possessions, he said: "Pauli will pack everything beautifully. He'll put the stuff into store and keep an eye on it for me." He showed no great regret at leaving his possessions, but he was not a poor man. He could replace them.

Pauli came in to say he had found a taxi and taken the luggage down. When they left the room, he was standing by the open front door, sniffing, At the sight of Pauli's grief, Inchcape's jaunty air failed and his face grew strained. He put his hands on Pauli's shoulders, seemed about to speak but moments passed before he said: "Goodbye, dear Pauli."

This was too much for Pauli, who collapsed to his knees with an agonised cry and, seizing Inchcape's hand, kissed it wildly.

Inchcape smiled again. He began edging towards the door, but Pauli shuffled after him, keeping a hold on him until they were in the outer passage. With a quick but gentle movement, Inchcape disengaged himself and sped down the stairs. Guy and Harriet followed, pursued by Pauli's heart-broken sobs.

On the long journey through the dark back-streets to the station, the three sat silent. Inchcape's head dropped, his face was sombre: then, suddenly, he looked up to say: "You haven't breathed a word to Pinkrose?"

They had not, though seeing Pinkrose sitting alone in the hotel they had felt guilty towards him. Had he approached them with any show of friendship, they would have had difficulty in maintaining the deception, but he avoided them, keeping "himself to himself".

"It would be intolerable to find the old buffer on the train," said Inchcape. He glanced at Guy. "Tomorrow, you can tell him I've been called away on urgent business. Don't tell him where I've gone. Say I'll be back, but if he wants to go himself encourage him. There's nothing he can do here. If he went to Athens, he might get a Greek boat to Alexandria."

"Where would he go from there?" Guy asked.

Inchcape chuckled. "Heaven knows. Let him organise his own return. He put plenty of pep into getting here." He smiled, reflecting on his friend, then said in a tone of the profoundest denigation: "He's not a peer, of course. Scottish title, I believe, though he's not got any sign of Scottish blood. A title like that's mere flim-flam. I wouldn't use it myself. And he inherited very little money. Even as a young man he was a queer fish. He simply came to Cambridge and never left it. It gave him all he ever wanted." Inchcape laughed to himself. "He loves to tell that old story of the don who was granted an interview with Napoleon. 'No doubt a remarkable fellow,' said the don afterwards, 'but anyone can see he's not a Cambridge man.' "

For some time after this Inchcape sat quietly shaking with amusement, perhaps at the anecdote, or perhaps at Pinkrose, but more likely, Harriet thought, at getting away and leaving Pinkrose here to fend for himself.

Three porters had to be employed to carry Inchcape's baggage to the train. Seeing Harriet watching the procession of suitcases, he explained: "I'm taking my summer clothing and a few valuables to leave in a safe place. One doesn't want to lose every stitch one's got."

The express stood in the station, but little activity surrounded it. Most of the carriages were empty. No one travelled for pleasure these days. The few passengers who stood about on the platform were lost in the echoing gloom. One group comprised the young English engineers from the telephone company. Guy, when he stopped to speak to them, learnt that they had been ordered, a few hours before, to quit the country. When they appealed to the Legation, they were advised to accept dismissal and go.

Inchcape, his sleeper secured, his luggage stowed away, stood at a corridor window. He smiled down on Guy and Harriet who, standing on the platform, uncertain whether they were expected to go or stay, could only say: "Well, have a good rest and enjoy yourself," then, after a pause: "Look after yourself."

"I'll put our case pretty forcibly when I get there," said Inchcape. "We demand a rise in pay and the right to abandon ship when we think it advisable, eh?"

There was a long pause. The atmosphere was dispirited. Perhaps it seemed to Inchcape there was something forlorn in the appearance of the two young people in front of him, for he said in a tone of self-justification: "You'll be all right. You're young."

"Does that make a difference?" Harriet asked.

"All the difference in the world. Before you're forty you never think of death: after forty you never think of anything else." He laughed, but as he gazed at them in the dingy light he seemed to Harriet pitiably aged and ill. "Besides," he said, "you'd be worse off in England."

Harriet said: "I'd rather be bombed with my own people than cut off here."

Inchcape gave a laugh. "You *think* you would."

Conversation lapsed again and Inchcape, glancing back through an open door which revealed his made-up berth, said: "Look, no point in hanging about. Dear knows when this train will take itself out. Everything's to pot these days. I feel a bit under the weather, so I'll say good-bye and get my head down." He reached out of the window and gave one hand to Harriet, the other to Guy, smiling his old sardonic smile while a single tear trickled down his discoloured, battered face: "Good-bye, good-bye. I'll be back before you have time to miss me." He pulled his hands free and, turning abruptly, entered the sleeper and shut the door.

Harriet put her hand into Guy's. As they wandered off through the cavernous dark of the station with its smells of carbon and steam, its desolating atmosphere of farewells, Harriet reflected that she herself would be gone in a day or two and Guy would be left alone.

27

RESTLESS IN UNEMPLOYMENT though he was, Guy was in no hurry to explain things to Pinkrose. He had intended to go to the Athénée Palace on Monday morning but delayed so long that luncheon was on the table and he decided to wait until evening.

As they were about to eat, the telephone rang. It was Dobson to say that Pinkrose had appeared at the Legation in a state of great alarm. That morning Galpin had seized on him in the hotel hall and insisted on telling him about the attack on Inchcape. He had gone at once to Inchcape's flat where he had been told by Pauli that his friend had left Rumania. In panic he had sped to the Legation and demanded that a plane be chartered immediately to fly him home.

"By the way," Dobson interrupted himself, "is that right? *Has* Inchcape taken himself off?"

"Yes."

"Why all this secrecy?" Dobson's tone was light, almost humorous, but there was an edge on it. Not waiting for an answer he talked rapidly on: "Well, my dear fellow, the noble lord is now your pigeon. He was over an hour here, wasting everyone's time, making ridiculous claims to special passages, etcetera. We just haven't time to cope. H.E. told him to fly to Persia or India, but he says he has no money. I suggested he might go to Athens, where he'd be out of the way of trouble and probably meet kindred spirits. Anyway, we've got him his exit visa. He's free to go whenever he likes. Meanwhile, be a good chap, keep him out of our way. Try and persuade him that, contrary to his belief, the entire Guardist movement is not, repeat *not*, directing its activities against his person." Dobson ended on a laugh, but rang off abruptly.

Guy sat down at the table, saying: "I'll go immediately after luncheon."

After luncheon he sat on. Knowing how acutely painful the coming interview would be for him, Harriet made no attempt to harry him. She was leaving next day and went into the bedroom to sort out the clothing she would take. After some minutes he followed her in, his face despondent, and said: "Perhaps you'd come with me. The fact you are still here might reassure him."

"All right, but I must first speak to Sasha."

She had bought Sasha a small cheap case to hold such clothing as Guy had given him. He wanted to take some of his drawings and, as these would have to be placed flat at the bottom of Harriet's portmanteau, she went to his room to tell him to sort them out. She found him curled like a kitten on the bed.

She had complained about the constant noise of the mouth-organ and now, his hands wrapped about it, he was playing almost without sound.

His possessions were neatly arranged on the table. The drawings were ready for her too pack.

She said: "What is that ridiculous tune you're playing?"

He took his lips from the mouth-organ to say: " 'Hey, Hey, Hey, Ionesculi'. Despina sings it."

She said, trying to speak sternly: "You know, when you get to Athens you'll have to start some serious study."

He smiled at her over the instrument, then put it back to his lips.

Though it was siesta-time when Guy and Harriet reached the hotel, the hall and vestibule were crowded. Again, as on the day of the arrival of the military mission, the hotel servants could not accommodate a half of those who had come in to drink their after-luncheon coffee.

Galpin, standing in the hall sourly surveying this assembly, told the Pringles that a rumour had gone round that a high-ranking German officer called Speidel was arriving that afternoon. "He's still young and handsome, so they say. Look as those bloody women! Like a lot of randy she-cats. And there's that bitch back again, on heat, as usual."

Princess Teodorescu had entered the hotel. She had returned to Bucharest relying, like the others of her class, on German influence to protect her against the Iron Guard. It was said it had already found a lover among the young German officers, several of whom stood round her while she talked furiously, twitching her shoulders and making frenzied gestures at them. She was wearing a new leopard-skin coat. Was there any more repellent sight, Harriet wondered, than a silly, self-centred, greedy woman clad in the skin of a beast so much more splendid than herself?

Hadjimoscos was of this party. Slipping about on his kid shoes, his plump little body looking soft, as though stuffed with sawdust, he moved from one officer to another, talking earnestly, lifting his flat, pale Tartar face in rapture, occasionally placing his little white padded hand on a German sleeve. They were joined by a stout, flat-footed man who walked like a peregrine: a noted German financier brought here to advise on Rumania's disintegrating economy.

"But" – Galpin turned slowly and nodded towards the desk – "you've seen nothing yet. Look who's over there." The Pringles followed the direction of his gaze and saw that the scene was being closely watched by two keen, dog-faced fellows in the black uniform of the Gestapo.

"When did they arrive?" Guy blandly asked.

"No one knows. But they're not the only ones. There's dozens of them. You've heard about Wanda?"

"No," said the Pringles, feeling they should proceed to Pinkrose but willing enough to be detained.

"Ah!" Galpin jerked up his long, morose, dishonest face with an intimation of tragedy. "They've chucked her out, the bastards."

So that was another face gone from the English circle.

Pinkrose, when Guy knocked on his door, cried: "*Entrez, entrez*," in a high, agitated voice.

They found him on his knees, stuffing his clothing into his bag. He was wearing a flowered cotton kimono of a sort worn in Japan, by tea-shop girls. He jerked his head round and, seeing the Pringles, seemed startled by their temerity, but he had nothing to say. He returned to his packing.

Guy attempted an explanation of Inchcape's departure. "He hopes to be back very shortly," he said.

Pinkrose appeared not to listen. Scrambling to his feet, he stripped off the kimono and pushed it in with the rest. He was wearing shirt, trousers and several woollen cardigans. He hastily got into his jacket, saying: "I'm catching the boat-train to Constanza." He went round, collecting the last of his possessions, keeping at a distance from the Pringles as though afraid they might seek to retard him. As he moved he said, breathlessly: "I take this badly, Pringle. I take it very badly. I shall not forget it. Inchcape has not heard the last of this, not by any means. His man *lied* to me. He repeatedly told me that Inchcape was ill in bed; and all the time he was plotting to slip away to safety – abandoning me, an invited guest, in a strange town where I was liable to be attacked by ruffians. Unforgiveable. I travelled several thousand miles to deliver an important lecture and . . ."

While he recounted again the details of his journey, emphasising its dangers and discomforts, he was ramming a great many small bottles and boxes into a portable medicine-chest.

"And you, Pringle," he said, giving Guy a malevolent glance, "*you* were a party to all this. I saw you in the hotel more than once. You did not choose to let me know what was going on. I had to learn from a stranger."

As Guy, listening with an air of miserable guilt, made no attempt to defend himself, Harriet broke in on Pinkrose to say: "Professor Inchcape did not want you to be alarmed. He gave definite orders that you must not be told anything until after he had gone."

Pinkrose, winding his scarves about his neck, drew his breath through his teeth, but made no other comment. A small threatening smile hung round his lips. After some moments he said: "The whole matter will be fully reported to head office. The board can judge. Meanwhile, I am forced to pay my own fare to Greece. I shall expect to be reimbursed; and I can only hope the Athens office will accord me the courtesy and consideration that has been so sadly lacking here."

The boat-train to Constanza left at half-past three. Pinkrose had barely time to catch it. That and the fact the Black Sea could be rough at this time of the year caused Guy to find his tongue. He said: "Why not wait until tomorrow? My wife is going to Athens by plane. Dobson is also going . . ."

"No, no," Pinkrose broke in impatiently, "I am looking forward to the sea journey. It will do me good." He picked up his greatcoat. As Guy stepped forward to hold it for him, he swung away with a look that suggested Guy's good-natured helpfulness was simply another indication of his duplicity.

A porter entered to collect the luggage. Pinkrose had ordered a taxicab, which now awaited him.

Harriet said: "Good-bye." Pinkrose shot her a glance, apparently not holding her culpable, and made a movement towards her which, given time, might have turned into a handshake – but he could not wait. Without a word to Guy he was gone.

The Pringles felt a sense of trespass at finding themselves alone in the room. Harriet put her arms round Guy's waist. "Darling, how can I go tomorrow and leave you here?"

"You're going to get me a job," he reminded her.

Her despondency lifted somewhat as, turning the bend in the stairs, they saw David down in the hall. He had gone "to the Delta" – whatever that might mean – when they went to Predeal and this was his first reappearance. There had been at the back of Harriet's mind a suspicion that he might not reappear at all. His covert trips at this time could too easily lead to disaster. Or he might, knowing the time was at hand here, have made his way over a frontier. But there he was, looking comfortable and confident as ever, and Harriet felt warmed by the sight of him. As Guy delightedly hurried down to greet him, David's small mouth curled at one corner in amusement at his friend's exuberance. He was about to sign the register and said: "I found, when I returned this morning, that the Minerva had given me up for lost. A member of the master race was occupying my room. My baggage had been put into the cellar. Fortunately, when I reached here, a room was just being vacated."

"Pinkrose's room, I suppose," Guy said and he described the attack on Inchcape and what he called "the flight of the professors".

Snuffling to himself at the picture of Pinkrose in the Japanese dressing-gown, David said: "I know several chaps who'd've paid to see that. Pinkrose owns one of the most magnificent houses in Cambridge, but no one ever sees inside it. He's practically a recluse. The sad thing about all this is that Inchcape is probably his only real friend."

When he heard that Clarence had also gone, David smiled indulgently. "I *liked* old Clarence," he said and gave a laugh of surprise at his own admission. He added: "I don't think any of us will be here much longer," and the Pringles, knowing he could not tell them any more, asked no questions.

As they moved together through the hall, David caught his breath, seeing for the first time the black Gestapo figures. He raised an eyebrow at Guy, but neither made any comment. They left the hotel with a sense of nothing to do but await an end. They did not want to separate.

David had to look in at the Legation and asked the Pringles to go with him.

Standing at the kerb, waiting for a *trăsură* to stop at the hotel, they watched a fleet of Guardist motor-cyclists in new leather jackets and fur caps. They passed uproariously, stern-faced and purposeful, as though on their way to an execution or an interrogation of treachery, but after circling the square at top speed, scattering the pedestrians and driving cars into the kerb, they disappeared whence they had come.

"Not a useful occupation," Harriet said, "but it must be great fun."

Waiting in the *trăsură* while David reported his return, Harriet held tightly to Guy's hand. He said to comfort her: "You heard what David said? I may be leaving here sooner than we think."

"Um." Harriet feared he might stay just too long and never leave at all; but she had ceased to plead with him, knowing he felt bound to see things to their conclusion, whatever the conclusion might be.

When David rejoined them, he said: "I have to meet someone, but not yet. Shall we drive up the Chaussée?"

The sun was low in the sky. They had put down the *trăsură* hood and they felt in their faces the keen little breeze that would sharpen through the coming weeks into the wind that brought the snow. The Chaussée had already an air of winter. The trees, parched by the fires of summer, were completely bare. The garden restaurants had packed up. The cafés had taken in awnings and parasols: some had closed down altogether. October was here and life had retired indoors.

David said: "There's a belief going round that Germany has important plans for Rumania, that she'll regain her position in the scheme of things." As he sniffed and snuffled, Guy asked: "What do you think?"

"I think the Germans will devour this place, ruthlessly. They're demanding conscripts now. Not a word about it in the papers, of course, but I'm told the Rumanian peasants are being herded into cattle-trucks and sent to train in Germany. Poor fellows, they go willingly because their officers tell them they're going to fight for England. They say: 'Tell us about these English. How do they look in the face?' "

Harriet said: "Do they actually think the Germans are British?"

"They don't think. When the times comes, they'll be told: 'This is the enemy. Fight!' and they will fight and die."

They were now in open country and could see the Snagov woods like a plum-coloured haze in the distance. The Snagov lake reflected a brazen sky. Here and there a window flamed, but the fields, flat and empty, had a dejected air in the rich autumnal light.

David said: "I have to meet this fellow at the Golf Club."

"The Golf Club!"

David laughed. "It's by way of being a secret meeting. That's why the Golf Club was chosen."

"I've never seen the Club," Harriet said.

"Come and see it now. You may not get another chance."

The Club, that stood behind a zareba of evergreens, had been built in the twenties by prospering English business men. With remarkable artistry they had, in this climate of extremes, reproduced the dark brick, moss-patched lawns and dank paths of a late nineteenth-century English mansion. The front door stood open. The house appeared to be deserted. Guy, Harriet and David passed through to the sitting-room which, with two vast French windows opening on to the golf course, extended across the back of the house. It was filled with chairs covered in faded chintz. Small tables were stacked with tattered copies of English journals.

Outside the light was changing. The sun had sunk behind trees so the whole of the green was in shadow. A smell of cold, damp earth entered with the air through the open glass doors. From somewhere upstairs came the brr-brr of an unanswered telephone.

The Pringles did not ask whom David had come to meet, but he said: "I see no cause for secrecy. This fellow who's coming is the chairman of a new advisory committee set up in Cairo. He's been flown here full of zeal, no doubt imagining even at this late hour something can be done. So remote is diplomacy from reality, H.E. still doesn't know quite what went wrong, so he's detailed me to try and explain things." Two men had walked around the side of the house. "There they are, now," David said and went out to join them.

One man was Wheeler, a senior member of the Legation, whom the Pringles had met at parties; the other was a stranger, handsome, of middle height, in early middle age, wearing a dark greatcoat and bowler-hat and carrying a rolled umbrella.

Seeing David, who approached them confidently but with a certain deference, being so much their junior, the two men paused. When he joined them, they began pacing together, moving slowly fifty yards or so in one direction, then turning and moving back again. The grass, green after the first rain, luminous in the uncertain light, exuded a mist that obscured the distant bushes and drifted about the legs of the men as they strolled about.

Harriet remembered the period of the fall of France when she had sat day after day with other English people in the garden of the Athénée Palace which she had not entered since. Now, in another time of stress, she was in the Golf Club, which she had never visited before and would probably never visit again. She turned away from the window, saying: "What shall we do?" She felt that she and Guy were like people left in an empty world. Everything was theirs. They could do what they liked, but there was nothing to do. She began wandering about, picking up the magazines and putting them down again. At one end of the room there was a bar, shut-up and padlocked. On the walls were antlers, horns and many other second-hand trophies of the chase. There were also crossed spears and shields taken from some African tribe.

She said: "Is this what they imagined home was like?"

Guy picked up a putter which had been left in a corner and said: "Let's go outside."

They walked to the first green. Standing at an unobtrusive distance from the three in conference, Guy began to address an imaginary ball. Harriet had nothing to do but watch.

The air was full of the sissing of grasshoppers. The sun had set and twilight was beginning to sift down when the Pringles noticed the chairman, with David and Wheeler at his heels, making towards them, his expression amused. Not waiting to be introduced, he spoke to Guy with the easy affability of a man conditioned to importance; "I thought you were killing snakes."

Guy blushed slightly, laughing. "No, just killing time."

The chairman seemed delighted by this simple wit and glanced at Wheeler who, attempting to reflect the chairman's good humour, looked at Guy as though he had acquired new interest and said: "This is Guy Pringle. He was a lecturer at the University here," letting the past tense make its own comment.

"Ah!" the chairman said with a sympathetic nod.

Harriet was introduced. The chairman, whose name was Sir Brian Love, put his umbrella behind him and, leaning on it, raised his face, which was smooth, beautifully shaven and pink with good eating, and sniffed the damp and woody air of evening. "Very pleasant here," he said, imparting an atmosphere of well-being. Wheeler, a thin man, his thin mouth drooping between folded cheeks, waited, fidgeting with a car-key on a ring.

The three young people also waited, expecting dismissal, but Sir Brian seemed in no hurry to leave the Club. "Smells like England," he said. "Hot as hell in Cairo. No sign of autumn there. I doubt whether they *have* an autumn." He laughed and said to Wheeler: "Couldn't we all go somewhere and have a drink?"

Wheeler looked startled, then, worried by this suggestion, said: "There's really no time, Sir Brian. H.E. dines at seven, and as you're going back tonight . . ."

Sir Brian nodded, but still showed no inclination to move. He looked up at the dark Club windows. "Not much going on here," he said.

"Practically no members left," said Wheeler.

"Still, it's delightful after the Middle East."

"Were you in England recently, sir?" Guy asked.

"Less than a month ago. You'd find it much changed, I think. Changed for the better, I mean."

While Wheeler, with knotted brows, concentrated on the task of getting the car-key off the ring, Sir Brian talked in a leisurely way of a new sense of comradeship which he said was breaking down class-consciousness in England and drawing people together "Your secretary calls you 'Brian' and the liftman says: 'We're all in it together.' I like it. I like it very much." Once or twice, while talking, he gave a slightly mischievous side-glance at Wheeler, so the others warmed to him, feeling he was one of them and on their side against the established prejudices of the Legation.

Wheeler, not listening, gave a sigh. The key had come off the ring. He gazed at it, perplexed, then set himself the more difficult task of getting it on again.

"After the war we shall see a new world," Sir Brian said and smiled at the three young people, each of whom watched him with rapt, nostalgic gaze. "A classless world, I should like to think."

Harriet thought how odd it was to be standing in this melancholy light, listening to this important person who had flown in that afternoon and would fly out again that night – an unreal visitant to a situation that must seem unreal to him. Yet, real or not, the other men would be left to the risk of imprisonment, torture and death.

Sir Brian suddenly interrupted his talk about England to say:

"So it's all over here, eh? Geography defeated us. The dice were loaded against us. No one to blame. These things can't be helped."

His tone was conclusive: he stood upright, preparing to depart.

David moved forward. "In my opinion," he said, "this could have been helped."

"Indeed!" The chairman paused in surprise.

"We lost this country months ago through a damn-fool policy of supporting Carol at no matter what cost to the rest of the community. The better elements here refused to serve under such a rule. Maniu and the other liberals would have been with us, but we had no use for them. We kept a pack of scoundrels in power. No wonder the country was divided against itself."

"Ah!" Sir Brian was noncommittal: a just man, he was prepared to hear all sides. "And what are the facts, as you see them?"

Wheeler rubbed his brow in a despairing way.

Speaking authoritatively, all diffidence gone now, David said: "A united Rumania – a Rumania, that is, who'd won the loyalty of her minorities by treating them fairly – could have stood up to Hungarian demands. She might even have stood up to Russia. If she'd remained firm, Yugoslavia and Greece would have joined with her; perhaps Bulgaria, too. A Balkan *entente!* Not much perhaps, but not to be sneezed at. With the country solid, enjoying a reasonable internal policy, the Iron Guard could never have regained itself. It could never have risen to power in this way."

Sir Brian, hands together on his umbrella-handle as on a gun-butt, stood upright, head bowed at the neck in an attitude of mourning.

Wheeler cleared his throat, preparing to arrest this indictment, but David was not easily arrested. "And," he persisted, "there were the peasants – a formidable force, if we'd chosen to organise them. They could have been trained to revolt at any suggestion of German infiltration. And, I can tell you, the Germans don't want trouble on this front. They would not attempt to hold down an unwilling Rumania. As it is, the country has fallen to pieces, the Iron Guard is in power and the Germans have been invited to walk in at their convenience. In short, our policy has played straight into enemy hands."

Sir Brian jerked up his head. He briskly asked: "So it's now too late?"

"Too late," David agreed.

The chairman gave Wheeler a glance, no longer mischievous. He had asked for facts but clearly felt the facts were getting out of hand. Wheeler, too, was losing patience. "I really think . . ." he began.

"Dear me, yes." Sir Brian shot out his hand to David, to Guy to Harriet, concluding the discussion. "It's all been very interesting. Very interesting, indeed!" The charm was well sustained, but something had gone wrong with it. He led the way round the side of the house, the others followed. He was talking, affable again, but his affability was for Wheeler.

It was almost dark. There was no sign of light or life about the house, but the front door still stood open and through it Harriet glimpsed the white jacket of a servant whose keys clinked in his hand. He was waiting to lock up when they, the last of the British, had taken their departure.

While Wheeler opened his car-door, Sir Brian looked back at the three young people and lifted his umbrella-handle to his hat-brim before getting into the car. He did not smile. Wheeler said nothing at all but slammed the door furiously and made off. Watching the red tail-light draw away, Guy said: "We're all in it together, are we? The *bastard!*"

David remained indulgent. "The duplicity of office! And Wheeler is a prize ass. He once said to me: 'If diplomacy were as simple as it appears to the outsider, my dear Boyd, we'd never have wars at all.' "

In reaction from a sense of reprimand that touched on their youth, the three, on their way back to the town, laughed uproariously together while the wind blew coldly at them across the dark deserted *grăfinăs*. They were glad to reach the lighted streets.

As they turned into the square, Harriet looked across at the large, brilliant window on the corner of the Boulevard Breteanu and saw that it was empty. The Hispano, that for two months had stood there like a monument, stood there no longer. Guy ordered the *trăsură* to stop outside the show-room and went in to inquire. He learnt that the car had been bought by a German officer who had paid the full sixty thousand *lei* without question, the rate of the Reichsmark being such that the cost of the Hispano was less than the cost in Germany of a toy. The money was being sent to Mr. Dobson at the British Legation.

Where were they going to eat? David asked. Harriet wanted to

take her farewell dinner at Cina's or Capşa's. They decided to
drive to Capşa's.

The main restaurants were always refurbished when they
returned indoors for the winter months. There was about them all
a sense of a new season that held its own excitements. After the
vacancy of the streets, Capşa's interior, with its red plush and
gilt and vast crystal chandeliers, seemed dazzling to the three
entering, chilly, from the open *trăsură*.

Food now was not only meagre, it was often bad, as though
shortage had led to hoarding and hoarding to decay. But Capşa's,
much patronised by the German community, had kept a certain
standard. The better cuts of meat were, of course, put aside for
high-ranking Germans and their guests, but the open menu usually
offered chicken or rabbit, hare in season, and even caviare of a
sort. Later in the evening the place would be crowded, but now
there were a good many vacant tables.

Seated by the door, accompanied by two of the young officers
of the mission, were Princess Mimi and Princess Lulie. Their
faces went blank at the sight of the English. As the three advanced,
there was a small stir in the room. The head waiter intercepted
them with a look of surprised inquiry as though it were possible
they wanted something other than food.

Speaking Rumanian, David asked for a table. The head
waiter replied: "*Es tut mir leid. Wir haben keinen Platz.*"

David protested in English: "But half the tables are unoccupied."

The other, from past habit, replied in the same language: "All
are booked. In these times it is necessary to book."

David opened his mouth to argue, but Harriet said: "The food
here is deplorable, anyway. Let's go to Cina's." She turned with
the hauteur of the beset and, as she passed the princesses, she
caught the eye of one of the young Germans who were watching
her with sympathetic amusement.

"Well, to Cina's then," said David when they were on the pavement again.

"No," said Harriet, near tears. "We'll only be turned out again.
Let us go somewhere where we're not known."

They decided on the Polişinel, a restaurant dating back to boyar
days, once very fashionable, where Guy and David had often
eaten when Guy was a batchelor. They found another *trăsură* and
drove down to the Dâmboviţa.

The Polişinel, built when land was cheap and plentiful, surrounded a large garden site. They went to the main room which, lit by a few brownish bulbs, stretched away into acres of shadow. Only the proprietor was there, dining with his family. At the sight of the foreign visitors, he rose, delighted, and bawled importantly for the waiter. He probably thought they were Germans, but the English, thus welcomed and made to feel at home, forgot their earlier experience.

An old waiter fussed over them, placing them at a window table which overlooked the garden, then hurried to switch on more lights. He brought a large, dirty menu, hand-written in purple ink, and whispered: "*Friptură*, eh?" It was not a meatless day, but he spoke as though suggesting a forbidden pleasure and the three gratefully agreed to it.

The proprietor bawled again and in trailed a dilapidated gipsy orchestra which, seeing the quality of the company, struck up with spirit.

"Oh, Lord!" said David. "They think we're rich."

"We are by their standards," said Guy.

David pulled his chair round so his back was to the smiling players and did his best to talk above the din: "There's a story going round. Horia Sima and his boys went to the Holy Synod and demanded that Codreanu should be made a saint. The head of the Synod said: 'My son, it takes two hundred years to make a saint. When that time has elapsed, return and we will discuss it again.'"

Now that attention had been deflected from the foreigners and their wealth, David settled down happily forgetful of the music. The two men talked about Russia. Neither had visited this country to which they looked for the regeneration of the world, but the previous spring, when Soviet troops were rumoured to be massing for an invasion of Bessarabia, David had reached the Russian frontier. He had stood beside the Dniester and looked across to where there were a few cottages. The only sign of life was an old peasant woman working in her garden.

That he should tell them even as much as this of his travels in Rumania was a sign that their life here was over and his travels at an end.

"Was it possible to cross into Russia?" Harriet asked.

"No, there was no boat or bridge, no means of crossing." There was nothing but the water, grey with cold, and ruffled by the bitter wind: and beyond the water league upon league of snow-patched, yellow earth stretching into infinite distance.

Harriet told them about the Jewish frontier village which Sasha had described to her. She said: "Were all the Bessarabians as wretched as that?"

"Perhaps not," said David, "but they were wretched enough. The majority of them welcomed the Russians. The Rumanians have never learnt to rule by persuasion rather than force. They deserved to lose their minorities: not that their own people get much better treatment. The peasants have always been robbed. Why should they want to work when everything they make is taken from them? They've always been fleeced by the tax-collector or the money-lender, their own army or some other army. Now they feed the Germans. They've been kept in the position of serfs, yet, given the opportunity, I believe they would prove intelligent, creative and hard working. In my opinion, the best thing that could happen to this country is the thing they dread most – to be overrun by Russia and forced to adopt the Soviet social structure and economy."

Guy smiled at a prospect that seemed to him too good to be true. "Will that day ever come?"

"Perhaps sooner than you think. The Rumanians imagine that with German support they can get back Bessarabia. If they try, the result could be a Russian occupation of Rumania, and perhaps of the whole of Eastern Europe."

A flower-girl came round taking from her basket small bunches of marigolds and pom-pom dahlias which she placed on the tables, then stood at a respectful distance while the diners decided to buy or not. Guy gave her what she had asked – a small sum – but she looked surprised. She had done no more than mention a point from which the bargaining might begin.

Sniffing the bitter, pungent smell of the marigolds, Harriet looked out at the garden, which was pebbled and much cluttered with stone statues. There were several old trees that had reached up beyond the surrounding buildings and now, too tall for their strength, bent and soughed in the wind. On the opposite side of the garden were the once famous *salons particuliers*, all the windows lit. In some the curtains were drawn as though the rooms were in use. In others the curtains were looped back with heavy cords so it was possible to see gilt and white walls and chandeliers with broken bulbs and lustres missing. Through the nearest window

Harriet could see a table ready laid for two and a sofa covered in green satin – a pale, water-lily green, probably very grimy. The rooms had not changed in fifty years and some people said they had not been cleaned either. Harriet was touched to see, as everything broke up about them, this seedy grandeur still limping along.

Noticing that she was not listening to their talk, Guy said: "She does not attach much importance to passing events."

Harriet laughed. "You have only to let them pass and they lose their importance."

"You may pass with them, of course," David said with a wry, sombre smile.

The food was slow in arriving. They had been served with soup. Some twenty minutes passed before the waiter placed their knives and forks, then, at last, came the *friptură*.

"In its day," David said, "this restaurant served the best steaks in Europe."

"What have we got now, do you think?" Guy asked.

David sniggered. "Apparently some *trăsură* has lost its horse."

The men remembered the spring and early summer of the previous year, when they had often come to the Polişinel garden and talked of the war that overhung them all. Diners would still be arriving at midnight and would remain until the first cream of the dawn showed through the trees. While there was one customer left, the musicians would play a series of little tunes, maudlin, banal, pretty, but, in deference to the hour, they played more and more softly, often breaking off in the middle of a phrase and starting up with something else, or just plucking a note here and there, a token of music, patiently awaiting their reward.

"How shall we reward them now?" Guy asked. He took out a thousand-*lei* note.

Harriet and David looked askance at this extravagance, but he handed it over. "For the pleasures that are past," he said.

When they reached the Pringles' flat, it was little more than eleven o'clock and David agreed to come in for a final drink. The hall was in darkness. The porter had been conscripted long ago and never replaced. They found the lift out of order.

There seemed to Harriet something odd about the house – perhaps the lack of sound. Rumanians sat up late. Usually on the stairs voices and music could be heard until the early hours of the morning; now there were no voices and no music. The three walked up from one dark landing to another, hearing nothing but their own footsteps. On the eighth floor they saw a light falling obliquely from above.

Harriet said: "It comes from our flat. Our front door is open."

They stopped and listened. The silence was complete. After some moments Guy began moving soundlessly up the last flight of stairs with David behind him. Harriet paused, unnerved by the stillness and the sight of the front door lying wide open. No sound of life came from within. Cautiously she went up a step or two so she could see past the two men in the hall. The sitting-room door stood ajar. The lights were on within.

Hearing her step on the stair, Guy whispered: "Wait." He gave a push to the sitting-room door: it fell open. Nothing moved inside.

David said: "No need to ask what's happened here."

Guy came out to tell Harriet: "We've been raided."

"Sasha and Despina? Where can they be?"

"They must be hiding somewhere."

They went through the flat, walking among a litter of papers, books, clothing and broken glass. Drawers had been emptied out, beds stripped, books thrown from shelves, pictures smashed, carpets ripped from the floor. They realised this had been done not in a frenzy of destruction but in a systematic search. The breakages and the disorder were incidental. And for what had they been searching? For something that could be hidden in a drawer or under a mattress – so not for Sasha. But perhaps it was Sasha they had found.

Anyway, there was no sign of him. His room, like the rest of the flat, was in confusion.

Guy led the way into the kitchen where the door on to the fire-escape stood open. Here drawers had been emptied, canisters of tea, coffee and dried foods had been turned out in a heap on the floor.

Harriet looked into Despina's room. It was empty. Her possessions were gone.

They went out on to the fire-escape. The well at the back of the house, on to which the kitchens opened, was usually, even at this hour, in an uproar of squabbling and shouting. Tonight all the doors, except their own door, were shut. There were no lights. the kitchens appeared to be deserted.

Harriet went up the ladder to the roof. The doors to the servants' huts were closed. Harriet pulled open that which had been used by Sasha. There was nothing inside. She called: "Sasha! Despina!" No one answered.

They returned to Sasha's room. The bed-covers were on the floor and, as Harriet piled them back on to the bed, the mouth-organ fell from among them. She handed it to Guy as proof that he had been taken, and forcibly. Under the bed-covers was the forged passport, torn in half – derisively, it seemed.

Remembering her childhood pets whose deaths had broken her heart, she said: "They'll murder him, of course."

"No," Guy said. "Why should they! I'll go to the Legation in the morning. They'll make some inquiries. Don't worry. We won't let it rest."

Harriet shook her head, unable to speak. She knew there was nothing anyone could do. The Rumanian authorities had little enough power against the Iron Guard. The British Legation had none at all. In any case, Sasha was an army deserter. His arrest was legal, and he was without rights.

David said: "I don't think we should stay here. They're quite likely to come back."

He kept watch on the landing while Harriet rapidly packed her suitcase. Guy put some shirts and underwear into his rucksack then went into the sitting-room and began picking up his books. Some of them had been trampled on and were spine-broken with the marks of heels and footprints on the pages. Recognising the savagery against which he had declared himself, he told himself: "The beast has broken in." He was thankful that Harriet was going next day. After that anything might happen.

He managed to fit a couple of dozen books into the rucksack and put six more into his pockets. He picked up a last one and put it under his arm. It contained the sonnets of Shakespeare.

Before they left the flat, they shut the back door and switched off the lights. They had no time to right the disorder. They left it as they had found it. They reached the street with a sense of having made an escape.

"I felt pretty nervous in there." David said.

"God," said Guy, "I never felt so frightened in my life before."

Harriet remained silent until they were in the square, then she said: "I can't leave tomorrow. And now there's no reason why I should."

"Oh, you must go," said Guy. "You have to find me a job. If

you stayed, you couldn't do anything. And Dobson is expecting you at the airport."

David's room contained two beds. Suddenly exhausted from shock, Harriet threw herself on one of them and was asleep in a moment. The men, too alert to sleep, sat up most of the night, talking, drinking and playing chess.

28

WHEN SHE AWOKE NEXT MORNING and remembered what had occurred, Harriet was surprised that she felt nothing. She prepared for her departure, no longer caring whether she went or stayed.

David had been called to the Legation and said good-bye to Harriet in the vestibule. As she and Guy left the hotel, they saw Galpin packing luggage into his car. Guy asked him if he were leaving.

Galpin shook his head, but said: "Something's in the wind. It's my hunch the balloon's going up."

"You think it's a matter of days?"

"It's a matter of hours. Anyway, I'm prepared. I'll give you a lift if you like."

"Harriet's off to Athens this morning. I have to stay."

"Stay? What for? A bullet in the back of the neck?"

A rare and peculiar look of obstinacy came over Guy's face. "I've a job to do," he said.

"Well." Galpin moved away, twisting himself into his raincoat as he went. "One person taking no risks is yours truly." He hurried back to the hotel.

Dobson was already on the airfield when the Pringles arrived. The morning was chilly and he was wearing an overcoat with an astrakhan collar. Having been told that Harriet would be accompanied by one of Guy's students, he asked: "Where's your young friend?"

Guy told him what had happened. The student was Sasha Drucker – no point now in hiding that fact. Guy said he intended reporting the matter to the Legation and enlisting the help of Fitzsimon who had played Troilus in his production.

Dobson listened with an expression, sympathetic but quizzical, which seemed to ask: What did Guy hope for? If the British Legation could no longer protect its own nationals, what could it do for this descredited Jewish youth who had disappeared into chaos? He said: "All over Europe there are people like Sasha

Drucker . . ." He made a gesture of despair at the measureless
suffering which in their lifetime had become a commonplace.

Guy glanced at Harriet, saying: "I am sure Fitzsimon will do
what he can."

Harriet looked away. Believing he was done for, she wanted to
turn her back on everything to do with Sasha. She said: "I think
we should take our seats."

Guy, troubled by her lack of emotion, said: "Cable me when
you arrive."

"Of course." She gave her attention to the airport officials, one
of whom went off with her passport. She protested and was told
it would be returned to her on the plane.

When Guy put his arms round her to kiss her good-bye, her
main thought was to get the parting over. Dobson took her arm,
sweeping her through the last corroding moments by making light
of the journey before them. "I always enjoy this little hop over the
Balkans," he said.

The plane was about to leave when an official entered and,
saluting her, presented her with her passport. The doors were
closed, the plane slid off. As they rose, Harriet looked down and,
glimpsing the solitary figure of Guy, who was watching after her,
was stabbed by the thought: "I may never see him again."
Immediately she wanted to return and fling herself upon him.
Instead, she opened her passport and saw the word "*anulat*"
stamped across her re-entry visa. She said in dismay: "They've
cancelled my visa." Her indifference was shattered. Suddenly in
panic at the reality of her departure, she said: "But I must come
back. They can't keep me from my husband."

Dobson was reassuring: "You can get a visa in Athens. The
Rumanian consul is a charming old boy. He'll do anything for a
lady," and he went on to talk of the Danube, which had appeared
below, a broad ribbon with river-craft and strings of oil barges
black on its silver surface: "Did you know, there are maps dating
back to 400 B.C. which show the Danube rising in the Pyrenees?"

"But surely it doesn't rise in the Pyrenees?"

Dobson laughed, so delighted by her ignorance that she began
to feel at ease. She was grateful for his company. Before the war,
when she had travelled about alone, she had enjoyed her own
independence. Now she wanted to cling to Dobson as to a vestige
of her normal life with Guy. She buoyed herself with the thought
that she was on a mission. She had to find a job for Guy and a

refuge for them both. She began to think of Bella, who would be the only English woman in Bucharest when her English friends departed. She spoke of this to Dobson, who smiled without concern and said: "I told Bella the Legation would take her out if we have to go, but she showed no interest."

"You could not expect her to leave Nikko."

"Oh, we would take Nikko, too. They both speak several languages. We could make good use of them." Dobson gave a laugh in which there was a hint of annoyance. "The truth is, she thinks she'll be a jolly sight more comfortable where she is."

Across the frontier, there was nothing to be seen but a fleece of white cloud through which the hill-tips broke, dark blue, like islands. As the morning advanced, the cloud dissolved to reveal the sun-dried Balkan uplands. Several times the plane, caught in an air-pocket, dropped steeply and there came, detailed, into view, stones, crevices and alpine flowers.

Sofia appeared amid its hills, a small town, grey beneath a grey sky. It seemed to be the destination of most of the passengers. "I wish I were staying here," said Harriet.

Dobson smiled at her absurdity. "Athens is delightful," he said. "You'll meet the most charming people." Preparing to leave her, he saw no reason at all why she should not be happy to journey on alone.

When the plane landed, Harriet walked with Dobson across the airfield to the barrier. A chauffeur awaited him and as he handed over his luggage, Harriet glanced back and saw that her suitcase had been put out on the grass. Her plane was taxi-ing across the field.

She gave a cry and said: "They're going without me."

"Surely not," Dobson said, but the plane was already rising from the ground. He spoke to the Bulgarian chauffeur who went to the customs-shed and came back with the information that the Rumanian plane had announced it would go no farther. Passengers for Athens must proceed on the German Lufthansa.

"But why?" Harriet was alarmed, remembering that Galpin had said: "When trouble starts, the air-service is the first thing to stop." She asked: "What has happened?" but there was no one who could tell her.

Dobson said: "Probably some rumour has scared them. You know what the Rumanians are like."

Harriet said: "I can't go on the Lufthansa." She was genuinely afraid. A story going round Bucharest described how some British businessmen in Turkey travelling on the Lufthansa, contrary to protocol, had been taken not to Sofia but to Vienna, where they had been arrested and interned.

Dobson smiled at her fears. "For myself, I'd feel safer on the Lufthansa than on any Rumanian plane."

"But it's forbidden."

"Only in a general way. You won't be allowed past the barrier here: you can't return to Bucharest: so you have no choice but to travel in the transport available."

The large Lufthansa stood on the airfield with a German official at the steps. Harriet felt sick at the sight of it. Stricken by her own plight, she appealed to Dobson: "Please wait with me until I go."

He said: "I'm afraid I can't. The Minister's expecting me for luncheon."

Near tears, she pleaded: "It's only about twenty minutes."

"I'm sorry." Dobson made a murmur of regret. He had lost his lightness of manner and she felt something inflexible beneath the reverence with which he said: "I cannot keep the Minister waiting."

After Dobson had been driven away, Harriet sat for a while on the bench by the shed and gazed at the German plane. Passengers were beginning to board it and she knew there was no purpose in delay. As Dobson had pointed out, she could neither stay here nor return whence she had come. She knew now what it was like to be a stateless person without a home.

Five men were filing up the steps of the plane, all, it seemed to her, inimical. Immediately in front of her was a little old man pulling on a string a toy dog, a money-box of sorts. He glanced back at her with a smile and as she noted his straggle of grey-yellow hair, his snub pink face, his wet blue eyes, she thought he looked as sinister as the rest. However, when she reached the official at the step, he produced a British passport and his aspect changed for her. Looking over his shoulder, she read that he was a retired consul called Liversage, domiciled in Sofia, born in 1865. The Germans treated the two British nationals with frigid courtesy. Harriet was thankful for the presence of this old man and his toy dog.

As they entered the plane, he stepped aside to let her choose her seat, and when she sat down, sat down beside her. He took the toy dog on his knee and, patting its worn hide, explained: "I collect for hospitals. Have collected hundreds of pounds, y'know. Thousands in fact. Been collecting for over fifty years."

The journey no longer frightened her. She asked herself, was it likely they would divert the plane in order to capture one young English woman and a man of seventy-five?

As they flew over the mountains, Mr. Liversage talked continually, pausing only to receive the answer to some question he had asked. Where was she coming from? Where going? What was she doing in this part of the world?

"Is your husband a 'varsity man?" he asked. He spoke pleasantly, but the question was clearly important to him. Her answer would place her. She wondered, would a provincial university be described as a " 'varsity"? She decided to say: "Yes," and Mr. Liversage seemed content.

Near the Bulgarian frontier, the sky began to clear. Over Macedonia, the plane suddenly emerged into brilliance, coming almost immediately into sight of the Ægean that sifted its peacock blues and greens against the golden shore of Thrace. They passed, almost at eye-level, a mountain like an inverted bucket, but before she could comment on it Mr. Liversage had talked them past it. While she looked below, seeing the Sporades fringed purple with weed, lying in shallows of jade and turquoise, Mr. Liversage talked of his life in Sofia where he had "a nice little place, nice little garden: lived very happily". But he had been advised to leave. Bulgaria, too, was threatened by the war that crept east like a grey lava to overwhelm them all.

"So here we are!" he said, his old hand with its loose, liver-spotted skin, patting the dog's rump. "Going to Athens. Probably settle down there. Bit of a lark, eh?"

Perhaps it was. Harriet smiled for the first time since she had entered the ravaged flat the night before. The memory had begun to retreat as they flew out of the Balkan world, leaving behind all intimations of autumn, returning into summer. Everything below was parched to a golden-pink. The sun, pouring in through the windows, grew steadily fiercer as the day advanced.

Throughout the journey, which lasted until evening, Mr. Liversage held his dog on his knee. He had brought a packet of sandwiches, which he shared with Harriet. Sometimes, as he talked, his hands were tensed about the dog so his knuckles shone, but his manner, matter-of-fact and cheerful, suggested it was for him an everyday occurrence to be uprooted in this way and no cause for complaint. The plane flew due south, showing no inclination to turn from its course. Indeed, Harriet realised, they were already over Athens.

"We will meet again," said Mr. Liversage as they began to descend.

Seeing the marble façades and the surrounding hills luminous in the rose-violet light of evening, she was thankful to come to rest in so beautiful a place.

29

WHEN, AFTER LUNCHEON NEXT DAY, Harriet came upon Yakimov, she felt jolted.

She had been wandering about the unfamiliar streets in a transport of release from all she had left behind. The previous evening she had gone to the cinema where the news-film had shown not the inexorable might of the German panzer divisions, but a handful of British sappers planting a mine among scrubby bushes somewhere in North Africa. At the back of her mind was the determination to return to Bucharest, but meanwhile there was the solace of this new world where to be English was to be welcome.

Yakimov, perched like a grasshopper on an old-fashioned bicycle, interrupted a dream, reminding her of the past. He leapt from the machine at the sight of her and came running downhill crying: "Dear girl! But this is wonderful! What news of the Hispano?"

"It has been sold."

"*No!*" He fetched up breathlessly beside her and began excitedly mopping his face. "Just when your poor old Yaki was asking himself where he could get a bit of the ready! What did she fetch?"

"Sixty thousand."

"*Dear girl!*" His large, pale, shallow eyes seemed to brim their sockets in delight, so she had not the heart to tell him that his sixty thousand was now worth less than ten pounds.

He was wearing his tussore suit and his Indian yellow shirt. The dark patches beneath his arm-pits had become darker and now had an edging of salt crystals. A leather strap over his shoulder held a leather satchel filled with roneoed sheets. She asked what he was doing, bicycling in the heat of the early afternoon.

"Got to get these delivered," he said: "news-sheets put out by the Information Office. Important job. They roped me in as soon as I arrived. Probably heard I'd been a war correspondent. Couldn't refuse. Had to do m'bit. Well . . ." He prepared to remount, holding the bicycle away from him as though it were not only unmanageable but vicious. "May say, you've got out just in time."

She caught his arm. "Has something happened?"

"Well, there's this rumour of a German occupation."

"But Guy is still in Bucharest."

Yakimov, one foot on the upraised pedal, blinked at her, disconcerted, then said: "I wouldn't worry, dear girl. You know what these rumours are." He gained his seat and, trembling forward, attempted his baby wave. "We'll meet again," he said. "I'm always at Zonar's."

Harriet stood in the road, looking after him. It was some minutes before all her old disquiet immersed her and she wondered how, in this strange place, where even the alphabet was unknown to her, she was to discover what was happening. Her hotel was small, staid and cheap, a resort of English residents. Someone there might be able to tell her something.

In the resident's sitting-room, four women sat, each in her separate corner. The gaunt one drinking tea could only be English, Harriet decided and, usually diffident with strangers, she addressed her now without apology or excuse: "Can you tell me, please? Is there any news about Rumania?"

The woman looked startled, then reproving of Harriet's anxious informality. There was a pause before she replied: "As a matter of fact, we have just been listening to the news. The Germans have occupied Rumania."

Clearly it was a matter of no concern to these women. Feeling that she alone knew the reality behind this announcement, Harriet burst out: "My husband is there," and she remembered how she had thought she might never see him again.

The woman, to whom she had spoken, said: "He'll be put into a prison-camp. You'll have him back after the war. My husband is dead," and having administered this rough comfort, she poured herself another cup of tea.

Harriet went to the hall and asked the clerk to direct her to the British Legation. She made her way through the deserted streets in the afternoon dazzle of salt-white walls, and found that at that hour no one was in the Legation but a Maltese porter. She told him her story, saying: "There's no knowing what the Germans may do to my husband. He's on a list of people wanted by the Gestapo." She pressed her hands over her eyes and choked in anguish, feeling an appalled remorse that she had left him without reflecting on what she might be leaving him to.

The porter, kindly and willing to help, said: "Perhaps nothing has happened at all. You know how these stories get around. I'll tell you what I'll do, I'll telephone Bucharest. I'll get through to the Legation and ask for news. I'll ask particularly about your husband."

"How long will it take?"

"An hour, perhaps two hours. Have tea at a café. Go for a walk. And when you come back, I think there will be good news."

But when she returned there was no news. The porter had been unable to contact Bucharest. "They've brought down 'the blanket'," he said, keeping up a show of optimism, but she could feel his uncertainty. This isolating "blanket" was proof that something had happened or was about to happen inside the country. He promised to try again, and again she set out to wear away time by walking first in one direction, then in another.

As evening fell, she was back at the Legation. The porter could only shake his head. "Later," he said, "I try again."

Too tired to walk farther, Harriet sat on a bench in the chancellery hall and watched people come and go. The staff had returned and the porter had duties to which to attend. No one spoke to her and she was reluctant to speak to anyone. She could do no good by pestering busy officials. If there were news, the porter would bring it to her. Some time after dark, he came out of his room and looked at her. Embarrassed now because he could do nothing for her, he said: "Better go home. Come back in the morning. Perhaps tonight we can get through."

"Is someone here at night?"

"There is always someone here."

"Then I can come back later?"

"If you wish. You might try about eleven o'clock."

Forced into the street again, she longed to confide her misery and could think only of Yakimov. Suddenly, she saw him as a friend – an old friend. Unlike the women at the hotel, he knew Guy and would sympathise with her dismay.

She ran down the hill to the city's centre. In the main road she set out to search the cafés, not knowing one from the other. Earlier in the day, people had been sitting out on the pavements, but the evening had become chilly. The chairs were empty. She went into one café after another, hurrying round them, becoming almost frenzied in her search. By the time she came on Yakimov she was trembling in a distress that was near despair.

He rose, shocked by her appearance, and said: "Dear girl, whatever is the matter?"

She tried to speak, but, fearful of bursting into tears, she could only shake her head.

"Sit down," he said. "Have a drink."

Yakimov's companion was an elderly man, heavily built, whose white hair looked whiter in contrast with the plum-dark colour of his skin. To give her time, Yakimov said genially: "Meet Mustafa Bey. Mus, dear boy, this is Mrs. Pringle from Bucharest. She doesn't really approve of poor old Yaki." He smiled at her. "What will you drink? We're having brandy, but you can get anything here. Whisky, gin, *ouzo* – whatever you like. It's all on Mus."

She chose brandy and, as she drank, regained herself sufficiently to talk. "About the German occupation of Rumania," she said, "it must be true. They've brought down a "blanket". You know what that means."

Mustafa Bey nodded his sombre, heavy head. "It is true," he said.

Harriet caught her breath and said: "What will happen to Guy?"

"Guy's no fool," said Yakimov. "He can look after himself, y'know."

"Our flat was raided the night before I left." Harriet saw, as she spoke, a tremor touch Yakimov's face, and she thought of the oil-well plan. The tremor betrayed him. She knew who had taken the plan, but it scarcely mattered. She had much more to worry about.

Yakimov was saying: "The Legation'll look after the dear boy. They got all sorts out of France and Italy. Dobbie's fond of Guy, and Dobbie's a good chap. He'd never abandon a pal."

Harriet said: "Dobson's in Sofia."

"No? Dear me!" No doubt thinking of his sixty thousand *lei*, Yakimov said to Mustafa Bey: "I could do with another, dear boy."

Mustafa Bey lifted a large mauve hand and signed to the waiter. More brandy was brought.

Harriet, her agitation suspended, felt very tired. She watched the clock on the wall behind Yakimov while he talked of the pleasures of Athens. Food, he said, was plentiful.

"And there are a lot of our friends here: Toby Lush, for instance."

"Is Toby Lush here?"

"Yes. In a very influential position, I'm told. So's his friend Dubedat. And a Lord Pinkrose has just arrived from Bucharest. You'll feel quite at home here when you get settled."

Harriet nodded. She thought of Guy and thought of Sasha. She wondered if, without them, she would ever feel at home anywhere in the world again. She asked how long Yakimov had been in Athens.

"Just a week." Yakimov had regained the simple grandeur of manner with which he had first assailed Bucharest society, and seemed at home himself in his new haunt which had not yet found him out.

As the hand of the clock neared eleven, she could scarcely breathe; then, suddenly unable to bear more of it, she jumped up saying: "I must get back to the Legation."

Yakimov rose with her. "I'll come with you."

She was surprised. "Please don't bother," she said. "You've been very kind, but . . . "

"Of course I shall come, dear girl. Your poor old Yaki isn't as bad as you think. Not unchivalrous, y'know, not unchivalrous." His sable-lined coat had been hanging on the chair behind him. He now draped it round his shoulders, taking on an air of rakish elegance, and said to Mustafa Bey: "I shall be back quite soon."

Mustafa Bey nodded with a leaden solemnity.

"Delightful place," said Yakimov when they were in the street. "The nicest people. Mustafa is a dear old friend. Dollie and I stayed with him when he had a house in Smyrna. Used to be a millionaire or something. Now he's on his uppers, just like your poor old Yaki."

Reminiscing about happier days, he walked with her up the hill to the Legation villa. When they reached the door, she said: "Would you go in and ask?" somehow feeling that a shock might be less shocking transmuted through another person.

Yakimov trotted in as though to show by his willingness that there was nothing to fear. She leaned against a lamp-post. The street was empty and, except for the glimmer in the chancellery, there was no sign of life. She watched the door through which Yakimov had entered. He was scarcely in when he came out again, smiling like one who bears gifts. Her spirits leapt as he said gaily:

"Just as I thought, dear girl. Everything's all right. Bucharest is quiet. It's true an army of occupation is expected, but no sign of it yet. The Legation's staying put and they say British subjects won't be molested. My guess is, you'll have the dear boy with you in a brace of shakes."

Suddenly emptied of qualms, too tired to speak, she started to weep. She wept for Sasha, for her red kitten, for Guy alone on the airfield, for the abandoned flat, the damaged books left on the floor, for war and an infinity of suffering and the turmoil of the world.

Yakimov, saying nothing, led her gently down the hill. When she started sniffling and blowing her nose, he asked where she was staying.

At the door of the hotel, he said: "A good night's rest will make all the difference."

"You've been very kind to me," Harriet said. "I wish I could do something for you in return."

He laughed in modest amazement. "Why, dear girl, look what you have done! You took Yaki in. You gave him a home. Who could do more?"

"I'm afraid that was Guy's idea."

"But you fed me. You let me stay."

She felt ashamed that what she had done, she had done so unwillingly. She said: "I see you still have your wonderful coat."

He eagerly agreed, "Yes," and, turning the front hem, revealed by the light from the hotel door the shabby sable inside. "Did I ever tell you the Czar gave it to m'poor old dad?"

"I think you did tell me once."

He lifted her hand and put his lips to it. "If you need me, you'll always find me at Zonar's." Patting her hand before dropping it he said: "Good-night, dear girl."

"Good-night."

He waved before turning away. As he went, the fallen hem of his greatcoat trailed after him along the pavement.

The Balkan Trilogy

Olivia Manning

The Great Fortune

The Great Fortune, the first of three outstanding novels by Olivia Manning which have come to be known as The Balkan Trilogy, is set in a Bucharest throbbing with the tensions of the war, and introduces Harriet and Guy Pringle who have just embarked on married life. As they discover more about each other, the story of an ex-patriate Russian émigré unfolds, observed in minute detail.

'I have never been to Bucharest, but such is Miss Manning's power, that at the end of this book I felt as though I, too, had spent that particular year there' – Elizabeth Jane Howard

'Deserves to be a best seller not just because it is a balanced, subtle, witty and humane work of art, but because it is wonderfully entertaining as well . . .' – John Davenport in the *Observer*

Friends and Heroes

Friends and Heroes is the third volume of the Balkan Trilogy in which Harriet and Guy Pringle, now in Athens, struggle to save their marriage against a background of rumours, betrayals and political intrigues.

'So glittering is the overall parade . . . and so entertaining the surface that the trilogy remains excitingly vivid: it amuses, it diverts and it informs, and to do these things so elegantly is no small achievement' – Frederic Raphael in the *Sunday Times*

Not for sale in the U.S.A. or Canada